Praise for *The Fire Starters*

'One of the most exciting and original Northern Irish writers of her generation.'
SUNDAY TIMES

'Blew me away with its power, anger and wit.'
JOSEPH O'CONNOR

'Jan Carson seems to have invented a new Belfast in this gripping, surprising, exhilarating novel.'
RODDY DOYLE

'Captivating, intelligent and courageous.'
IRISH TIMES

'Gripping, affecting, surprising. I inhaled it.'
LISA MCINERNEY

'Spectacular. At once grittily real, wildly magical and insanely alluring.'
DONAL RYAN

'Shimmering with wit, simmering with an incandescent rage, shot through with a seam of wild magic . . . Jan Carson is on fire.'
LUCY CALDWELL

'Carson's playfulness delights again and again, even as she explores her city's darkest corners. Sound the siren: this novel truly burns bright.'
IRISH INDEPENDENT

The Raptures

Jan Carson

doubleday

TRANSWORLD PUBLISHERS
Penguin Random House, One Embassy Gardens,
8 Viaduct Gardens, London SW11 7BW
www.penguin.co.uk

Transworld is part of the Penguin Random House group of companies
whose addresses can be found at global.penguinrandomhouse.com

Penguin
Random House
UK

First published in Great Britain in 2022 by Doubleday
an imprint of Transworld Publishers

A CIP catalogue record for this book
is available from the British Library.

ISBNs 9780857525758 (hb)
9781781620472 (tpb)

Typeset in 11.25/14.5pt Adobe Garamond by Jouve (UK), Milton Keynes
Printed and bound in Great Britain by Clays Ltd, Elcograf S.p.A.

The authorized representative in the EEA is Penguin Random House Ireland,
Morrison Chambers, 32 Nassau Street, Dublin D02 YH68.

Penguin Random House is committed to a sustainable
future for our business, our readers and our planet. This book
is made from Forest Stewardship Council® certified paper.

For Alan. Proud to be your sister. Grateful to be your friend.

'This is a study of the people I uneasily call my own.'

Susan McKay, *Northern Protestants:
An Unsettled People*

*'So high you can't get over it,
So low you can't get under it,
So wide you can't get 'round it,
Oh, wonderful love!'*

Traditional, 'Jesus' Love Is Very Wonderful'

25 June – Hannah

Miss McKeown said it wasn't always going to be like this. Eventually, it would get better here. Matty raised his hand and asked if eventually was going to last much longer. Miss gave him one of her looks and never bothered answering. She probably thought he was being sarcastic.

Matty was only asking because he wanted to know. He's not smart enough to be sarcastic. Matty's still reading baby books though today's our last day of P7. It's not his fault. He's got no dad and his mum's rubbish. She never goes over his homework or checks his reading. Granny says Matty's been dragged up. Mum says it's not nice to talk like that. I'm to be kind like Jesus and share my crisps with him at break time; first pick of the bag, before I get down to the wee broken bits. Everybody else's mum must've said the same thing because we're all nice to Matty. We pretend not to notice the way he smells or the worn bits in his trousers. When we line up to pay for school dinner tickets, we let him go last, so he doesn't have to see us seeing him get his for free.

I'm not poor like Matty. I'm not stupid either. I'm the second smartest in our class. Only William's sharper than me. That's probably because he's a boy. God made girls from boys' leftover bits. It says so in the Bible: Genesis chapter 2. Last year, in Sunday school, I got a gift token for the Faith Mission bookshop because I could recite the first three chapters of Genesis off by heart. Word perfect. No hesitation. I didn't need to check the Bible once.

I'm pretty clever for a girl. Obviously, I'd never say this out loud. It'd sound like I was being prideful. Pride's one of the worst sins you can do. Only murder and adultery are worse. I'm not exactly sure what adultery is. I think it's when you act more grown-up than you actually are: drinking wine and playing cards or maybe giving your parents lip.

I should've looked it up in the dictionary when we were learning vocabulary. I probably won't get the chance now. I don't think you do vocabulary in big school. It's a pity. I really like words. There's a space at the back of my jotter for writing new ones next to their meanings. I've learnt so many, I'm almost out of room. *Sarcastic. Fantastic. Evangelical,* which is what we are, in my family. *Encyclopaedia. Environmental. Rhododendron. Rhododendron*'s the hardest word in the spelling book.

I don't need to ask Miss McKeown for a definition. I know that *eventually* means a really long time. Just saying it makes me tired. It's a word that feels like a waiting room. We've had the Troubles here for a really long time. I asked Granda Pete how long they've gone on for. 'How long's a piece of string?' he said. This is a thing adults say when they don't know the answer but still want to sound smart. I asked my dad the same question. He said it wasn't the sort of thing wee girls should be thinking about. According to Dad there's lots of things wee girls shouldn't think about. We don't talk about the Troubles in our house. The Bible says you shouldn't have anything to do with the World. Worldly things are politics, gambling and the pictures. I'm not that bothered about politics or gambling. I just wish we weren't against the cinema.

Last summer Caroline's birthday was in the big cinema over in town. She invited me. That was nice of her. Most of the ones in my class don't bother asking if I can go to their parties or come round to play. They know my parents won't allow me. Outside of school, we don't do anything that isn't church. I still asked Dad about going to Caroline's birthday. I told him the film was only a PG. 'It's about a big dog that's always knocking stuff over,' I said. 'There's no swearing in it or anything.' He said no. I knew he would. Every time I ask about the pictures, Dad says, 'Cinema starts with sin, you know.' I don't know what he's talking about. We drive past the State on the way to church and the sign's definitely spelt with a C.

I've never been to the pictures but we do have a television in our house. Cinema's pretty much the same as telly. It's just on a bigger screen. Every night, after dinner, Dad watches the news. I'd rather watch *EastEnders* like everybody else, but it's banned in our house because the people in it are always swearing and getting divorced. The news is better than nothing and, while Mum's redding up the dishes, I get Dad and Hannah time. When there's bad stuff reported – and there's never a night when nobody dies – Dad makes a clickety noise with his tongue. He shakes his head. 'Dear, dear,' he mutters and writes the details down in his notebook. *Car accident. Aughnacloy. 2 killed. Pipe bomb, Cross-maglen. 4 army injured. Incendiary device in C&As.* I never say anything. I click my tongue and make the same sad noise as Dad. News isn't for discussing. It's for praying about later on.

I can tell from watching the news that most folk are fed up with the Troubles. The people who get interviewed are always crying. Or looking angry. Or looking angry and also crying because more people have got themselves killed. People have had enough of it. *No more bombs*, they say. *No more shootings. No more army boys on the streets. We want something better for our weans. Them lot need to wise up and start talking to each other.* I'm not sure who's stopped talking to who. Ian Paisley's never done talking and Gerry Adams talked so much they've got somebody else in to do his voice. I suspect it's the ones in the balaclavas who need to talk. Maybe to each other. Or to the police.

I don't know why we have the Troubles here but I know it's us children who deserve something better. We're the future of Northern Ireland. We had a special assembly about it last month. A woman came down from Londonderry. Principal Taylor arranged for her to speak to the older ones. There'd have been no point in her talking to the juniors about serious stuff like the Troubles and peace. Until P4 you only do playing and colouring-in. The woman arrived in the afternoon. This meant we got out of maths, so everybody was in great form. The lady had a fella with her from the paper. He made us line up in the playground for a photo. Boys at the back. Girls at the front. Lief with the girls because he's wild tiny for a boy. We held a big banner in front of our legs so you could only see us from the middle up. It was yellow, with the words *the future of Northern Ireland* written on the front in shiny, black letters. Just before he clicked the camera the man made a face and stuck his tongue out. We're all cracking up in the photograph. Principal Taylor pinned it up on the noticeboard.

We don't usually have women taking assembly. It's nearly always ministers. Ministers are always men. They come in to do a wee Bible lesson and say a prayer. The best ones bring puppets or Flannelgraph. Sometimes we sing a couple of choruses; only if it's one of Mrs Getty's days with P5. She's the only teacher who knows how to play the piano and the singing sounds woeful without it. *Like cats in a tumble drier,* Kathleen says. The ministers are never from our church because our church isn't in Ballylack. It's in the town, five miles away. Pastor Bill wouldn't mind driving out. It's just that there's half a dozen other churches in the village and they get first dibs on visiting our school. Dad says it's OK to listen to other ministers. They're Protestants like us; just a different kind.

We're the evangelical charismatic sort which means we believe in getting saved and going to Hell, Jesus and also the Holy Spirit.

4

In our church the women wear hats. We use the Bible with the old-fashioned words but sing modern choruses off the overhead projector. We speak in tongues and do special praying with hands on. We don't believe in the cinema or chewing gum. (The chewing-gum thing might just be my parents because I've seen ones from the Youth Fellowship blowing bubble-gum bubbles round the back of the Minor Hall.) We're not the popular kind of Protestant. There aren't that many of us. In Ballylack there's only us and Granny and Mrs Nugent. In the town it's a bit better. There's enough to fill a medium-sized church. At Christmas and Easter it's pretty bunged. Granda Pete's not our sort of Protestant. I'm not sure what kind he actually is. Granda says Prods are like potatoes. There's five dozen different varieties. They're all much of a muchness when you peel them back.

The woman who came to our school was called Sinéad, which means she was probably a Roman Catholic. You can tell from their names and how they keep their gardens. Catholics are more through-other than us. After the assembly I heard her talking to Miss McKeown. '*Jesus*,' she said, 'I could murder a coffee.' I knew she definitely wasn't a Protestant then. Protestants don't take the Lord's name in vain. Sinéad had come to tell us we were the future of Northern Ireland. We needed to work together for peace. I already knew a bit about this.

Every year our school goes on a trip with the ones from Tully-barret Primary. Last year we all went to Belview Zoo. It was class. I liked the sea lions best. The year before we went to Tardree Forest. It's only two miles down the road. I didn't think this counted as a proper trip. The teachers made us walk round with the Catholics. We were meant to be on a scavenger hunt and also making friends with each other so the Troubles would end and we could get peace. We didn't know what to talk about. We couldn't pronounce their funny names. And Kathleen said their daddies were all in the IRA (they were the ones who blew up her mum). I still wanted to be nice to the Catholics. Jesus was nice to everyone. Even lepers, and if you had leprosy in them days it was really contagious. Bits of your face went black, then fell off. I wanted to be nice like Jesus was, but I didn't trust Catholics. They were different from us in lots of ways. When it was their turn to bring the packed lunch, their sandwiches were made with fake ham. The minging kind you get in a tin.

Once everybody was in for the special assembly and we were sitting *criss cross apple sauce* on the wooden floor, Sinéad told us she'd come to tell us about a writing competition. It would be running in *every single primary school in Northern Ireland.* 'Both Protestant and Catholic,' she said, as if we didn't know what *every single primary school* meant. Sinéad wanted us to imagine what our country would be like in the future, when we were adults in charge of everything. 'Imagine,' she said, 'what Bally-lack will be like in twenty years' time, or ten years' time, or even five. You'll all be sixteen then; almost grown up. What do you think will be different? How are you going to shape the future? Boys and girls, I don't mind telling you, I'm extremely hopeful about the years ahead. Your generation's going to change things. The future's your responsibility. By the time you're up and leaving school, we could have peace in our wee country.'

Principal Taylor clapped when she said this. All the teachers started clapping too. We copied them and clapped really hard. We didn't know why we were clapping but Principal Taylor always says he wants to see best manners when there's a visitor around. When everyone had run out of clap, Sinéad stuck the competition rules up on the overhead projector and went through them one by one. None of us really listened. We were only inter- ested in the bit where it listed the prizes. First prize was a computer for the winner and five computers for their school. There were book tokens for second and third and some smaller prizes for the runners-up. None of us heard anything except free computers.

It wasn't just us kids who lost the run of themselves. Miss McKeown tried to pretend the competition was just a bit of fun but you could tell she was already imagining where she'd put her new computers and all the projects we'd do on them. As soon as the special assembly was over, she herded us back to the classroom. There was still an hour and a half of maths left but she said we could forget about sums for one day. 'While Sinéad's important message is fresh in your minds,' she said, 'you should all start working on the competition.' She took a piece of pink chalk and wrote the title in big capital letters across the blackboard. IMAGINE THE FUTURE. She made us get into small groups and start brainstorming about what we thought Ballylack would be like when we grew up.

I was sitting at the top table. Me and William are always sitting at the top table. Lizzy was there too because she'd done well on her Friday test. Mim hadn't, but their mum kicks up a fuss when anyone tries to separate the Twins, so she was sitting next to her sister. I don't like speaking out loud in groups. I have lots of thoughts inside my head. I just never know if they're the right ones or which are OK to say out loud. There are three types of things I let myself say: things that are all right to say anytime, things – like stuff about church and Jesus – which I only talk to my parents about, and things I wouldn't want them hearing, like 'crap', which is a word I sometimes say, under my breath, when I'm by myself and feeling fed up. I usually volunteer to take notes. It means I don't have to speak. I wrote IMAGINE THE FUTURE across the top of my jotter page in bubble writing. Then I sat there quietly, scribbling down everything the other three said.

When it came to feedback time, all the groups had come up with roughly the same ideas. In the future we'd stay up late and set our own bedtimes. There'd be no homework or rules about what we could eat. Kids would be more important than adults. The adults would have to listen to us. School would only be three days a week and the summer would be six months long. Maths and geography wouldn't exist. There'd be way more PE, dancing and good music. Mim made me write down *Pop Music* and underline it, so Miss McKeown knew we weren't talking about classical.

Most of the things I wrote down were different from how I imagined the future myself. I wasn't brave enough to say what I actually wanted to see: more people getting saved, less divorces and no more bombs. These were things I already asked Jesus for, every night, in my bedtime prayers.

Once Miss McKeown had heard all our ideas she stood in front of the blackboard for ages, just staring at the competition rules. 'Right,' she said eventually. She let the word *right* leak out like it was both a word and also a sigh. 'You see, the thing is, I'm not sure they're after essays about not having homework in the future or being able to drink as much cream soda as you fancy. I think they're looking for something a bit more – *how should I put this?* – inspirational. Like about peace and getting along together. Do you know what I mean?'

We all looked at Miss McKeown like she was mad. We were eleven. Some of us were actually still ten. Half of us had never been out of Northern Ireland. Matty hadn't been any further than the zoo. We could only imagine with the heads we had, and our heads were full of what we knew: school and church and the odd bus run up the North Coast. When we thought about the future, we couldn't see past the end of Main Street. We couldn't imagine what we didn't know yet.

Miss McKeown could see our confusion. She came round to the front of her desk and sat on the edge, legs dangling. She always perched on her desk during Friday Treat, while she read aloud from Enid Blyton or the *Chronicles of Narnia*. Once, Lief said he'd seen right up her skirt and she had white pants on with wee pink flowers. Nobody believed him. Lief was always full of big talk.

'Look,' Miss McKeown said, and her voice was soft and a bit slippery, 'it's not always going to be like this. Eventually, it's going to get better here.' Matty interrupted then, but Miss was determined not to be distracted. 'Sinéad's right. You lot are the future. You've a chance to make something of this country; stop the fighting and the awful things we've done to each other. You're only young. Imagine all the things you could do. Have a good think and tell me what this place would be like if you were in charge.' She tapped her head just above her ear, then placed her hand on her chest just above her left boob. 'Use your heads, children, and don't forget to use your hearts too.' She looked like Mum looks when we sing 'Amazing Grace' in church; her eyes all swimmy, like she was about to gurn.

We loved Miss McKeown. All of us thought she was the best teacher ever. She was kind and funny, pretty too. Caroline said she looked like Cindy Crawford, who is a famous model I don't know. We didn't want to let Miss McKeown down. So, we said all the things she wanted to hear. We'd a fair idea what she was after. It was like coming back from a Tullybarret trip. Principal Taylor always made us write stupid essays about learning from people who are different from us. They got posted up to some place in Belfast where the politicians live. We shouted all the right words out. Miss McKeown smiled and wrote them up on the blackboard in pale blue chalk. Her writing got scribblier the more we said.

'Peaceful!' shouted William. 'When we're in charge, we'll make sure everybody gets along.'

'Happy,' said Kathleen. 'Things will be a lot more fun when we're grown-up.'

'Friendly,' added Ross. 'We'll make sure no one's lonely or gets left out.'

'Exciting,' said Lizzy. 'I think the future will be full of adventures.'

'Exciting,' said Mim. She always said what Lizzy said.

'Better,' I whispered. 'It'll just be better.'

I kept my voice small and quiet because I wasn't brave or very sure. I didn't want anyone to hear and laugh. Miss McKeown heard and smiled at me with her softest smile. She wrote my word up on the blackboard next to the others. Then, she looked straight at me and no one else. 'I hope you're right, Hannah Adger,' she said. 'I hope you lot make things much better. I believe you're more than capable.' For one wee minute I believed that she wasn't just talking about William or Lizzy. I felt like I could be capable too.

In the future I might be part of things, not left out like I usually am, always on the edge of things. Banned from the cinema. Not allowed to crimp my hair. Forbidden from learning about the dinosaurs because they weren't as old as our science books said they were. Left behind to do colouring-in every time something unsuitable comes up. Like going to the panto in town. Like singing The Beatles in the school choir. Like joining the rest of P7 for our end-of-term nature walk, across the fields to Millar's Gap, to hear about the Raggedy Tree and the fairies who lived in it. Dad wouldn't hear tell of me going. *Absolutely not.* He even phoned Principal Taylor to lodge a complaint. *You should be ashamed of yourself, encouraging children to dabble in the occult.* Miss McKeown ignored him. The rest of the class went on without me. I was mortified but not surprised. I'm nearly always left behind.

While they were gone, I drew Miss McKeown a picture of the Raggedy Tree. I'd no idea what a magic tree looked like, so I copied the front of Enid Blyton's *The Magic Faraway Tree.* I used tracing paper to do the outline, then filled it in. Miss McKeown said it was a work of art. She pinned it up on the noticeboard behind her desk so the Raggedy Tree was looking down on us all. 'Did I get it right?' I asked. 'Not exactly,' she said. 'It's a bit smaller in real life and there are wee bits of cloth tied all over it from where people made wishes in the olden days.' I asked Miss

McKeown if she'd made a wish on the Raggedy Tree. 'Maybe,' she said, and smiled in a sort of secret way, 'but wishes don't work if you can't keep them secret . . . Can you keep a secret, Hannah Adger?' I nodded, yes. 'I made a wish for you lot,' she said, running her eye quickly across the class. 'I wished that the future would be kind to you all, that you'd be happy and live big lives.' Miss McKeown could be quite sappy. She was always reading us poetry. Her eyes went runny for a moment, then she snapped back into herself and laughed. 'For goodness' sake don't be telling your dad I was wishing on the Raggedy Tree. I'm already in the bad books for taking this lot over there.' I did not tell anyone.

We all wrote our essays about the future and sent them off to the competition. None of us won a computer or even got placed. The boy who came first was on the news. He was from a Belfast school where the children wore blazers and funny caps. His name was Miles. He sounded like Mary Poppins would sound if she was a boy. Nobody talks like that round here. There's nobody called Miles in Ballylack. When I saw that boy on the telly I knew the future was not for us. Things don't change here. I couldn't imagine Ballylack any different from how it is now. I did not say this to my dad. I did not say it to anyone.

Then it was almost time for the holidays. My head got filled up thinking about caravans and barbecues, bike rides, paddling pools and Holiday Clubs. I forgot about not winning the competition. I wasn't really thinking about the future at all. When I did it was only near things I focused on: the end of the summer and big school in town. It was waiting to swallow me up. The actual, grown-up, different future felt very, very far away. I was eleven years old. I was young for eleven. People were always saying how young I was. My parents made all my decisions for me. I couldn't imagine this ever changing. I had no notion what the summer would bring.

The Summer Begins

IT'S THE LAST day of June in Ballylack. The summer holidays have just begun. At ten past ten – evening, not morning – the first child dies.

He draws his last rattling breath and reaches for his mother's hand. She's been sitting for hours in a hospital chair. She is stiff and cold and sleep-deprived but she would never, even for a second, leave her wee boy by himself. By the time she unfolds her arm to reach across the bed's metal railings and clasp his hand, he's already gone. She doesn't let go for almost an hour.

The boy's name was Ross; the McCormicks' youngest lad. He was known for being a sickly child. Prone to asthma and fevers. First to catch whatever's doing the rounds. It's not his first stint in the children's ward. Unlike his brother – the godlike Ryan – Ross was not the sporty type. Nor much to look at either. A chubby wee lad with protruding teeth. Everybody in Ballylack knew him to see. Some thought him feeble, which, though excusable in a girl, was not to be tolerated in a boy. Others blamed the mother. They said she had her second lad spoiled. *Babied until she had him ruined. How much of his sickness was in her head?* Still, if you asked the locals who hovered outside Thompson's shop, they wouldn't have said a bad word against him. Ross was Ballylack born and raised. They thought of him as one of their own.

During the last week of term a tiny lump, no bigger than a baked bean, had appeared in Ross's armpit. It was soft to the touch and lightly furred, like a wart but fleshier; the sort of thing which sprouts unbidden from the puckered jowls of elderly women. It grew quickly. Other bumps and lumps appeared in his neck. Mrs McCormick assumed it was glandular fever. She'd had it herself about Ross's age. Dr Simpson confirmed the diagnosis. Glandular fever had been doing the rounds of the big schools. Ross's brother must've brought it home on the bus.

Ross was exhausted and feverish. For three days he flopped between bed and the living-room sofa, where he watched cartoons and ate nothing but ice cream and Angel Delight. His throat was raw, his head pounding. His skin was clammy to the touch. Sometimes the fever left him feeling drunk in the head. He talked utter nonsense and didn't seem to know where he was. Still Dr Simpson said there was no need to be alarmed. *Lots of rest and plenty of fluids. The lad'll make a full recovery.* Mr McCormick asked Dr Simpson if he thought Ross would be up and about in ten days' time. He'd booked a fortnight in Lanzarote. They were leaving the night before the Twelfth. The deposit would be lost if they didn't show up. Dr Simpson couldn't or wouldn't give him an answer. *It's hard to tell with glandular fever. It's one of those illnesses that has to run its course.*

Ross didn't make anything of it. He deteriorated quickly. Suddenly the pain was no longer soft. It shrieked through his bones. It hurt every time he tried to move. He was transferred to the hospital, where they wired him up to a drip and began running tests. It became apparent that this wasn't glandular fever. None of the doctors knew what it was. They picked through Ross's medical notes. The child's had every illness under the sun and while this could be the mark of an over-anxious mother, it could also mean

13

there's something fundamentally wrong with him. On the fifth day Ross went downhill rapidly. It looked like they were losing him. His skin turned the sort of colour you don't come back from.

Ross didn't realize how ill he was. His parents chose to keep it from him. They didn't know how to say what they needed to say. *You're very poorly, son. Your organs are failing. It looks like you're probably going to die.* They avoided all talk of the future, focusing instead on getting Ross over each small hurdle. Blood tests. Drip changes. Trips to the toilet. The minister appeared on the ward. He prayed that Ross would soon recover but advised them to take each hour at a time.

His brother brought him football magazines and packets of Haribo he wasn't allowed to eat. Ryan felt guilty. Here he was, once again, the lucky one. He was better-looking and better at football and now, more likely to see September. He felt truly crap about this. And a small bit relieved that it wasn't him. The pair of them talked about television and computer games. The conversation was stilted; Ryan suspected that his brother was going to die. It was weird to be talking about normal things when Ross might not be there by the end of the week. Ryan wondered if there were things he should be saying. Like *I love you* or *I'm going to miss you*. He'd never talked like this to his brother before but he knows from the movies that people are meant to say all sorts of sappy shite when they know somebody's about to die.

Two days before he died Ross asked his mother for new football boots. Though she knew she was throwing good money after bad, and wept loudly at the till in Style 'n' Sport, she still bought him the most expensive kind: the sort that are one colour all over, like the cartoon idea of a shoe. She'll keep these shoes unopened in the box for several years and eventually bin them. She can't bear to think of Ross's boots sitting pretty on some other lad's foot.

Whatever was ruining him spread through his body, slowly at

first then with lightning ease. It ran through his veins and laid siege to his heart. *Chirrump, chirrump, chirrump* went his myocardium, losing speed with every contraction, until his blood grew thick as shop-bought custard and couldn't be coerced into further circulation. He died on the last day of June, his face a swollen balloon of itself, pale and bloated from the drugs. In death, he was an awful funny colour, both pallid and florid at the same time. The nurse reassured his mother they could fix this with make-up for the funeral. His mother wasn't listening.

Ross had only just turned eleven. He was still a child, though the thought of girls was already pressing. He'd sometimes go through the *Kays* catalogue for pictures of women in bras and pants. He'd yet to touch a girl himself, had yet to taste coffee or travel anywhere in an aeroplane. He'd been looking forward to Lanzarote. It would've been his first time in a foreign place.

Poor Ross. It's never easy going first.

There's been no talk of the boy's passing yet. It'll be midmorning before the news spreads. In the houses and farms of Ballylack, people are getting on with their everyday doing. They're feeding the cows and drinking tea, watching the telly and heading to bed. There's no expectation that tomorrow will be much different from today. '93 has been an unremarkable year. The summer's shaping up to be equally forgettable. It's neither hot nor particularly damp. It isn't a World Cup year or one for the Olympics. Major's in Downing Street. Clinton's in the White House. Folks aren't sure what to make of him. *Keep an eye on that one, he's got notions*, they like to say. There's talk of Clinton wading into the Troubles. Word is, he thinks he can sort it out. *Let the same fella have a run at it. Better than him have tried and failed.*

Down South, Ireland win the Eurovision for the umpteenth year in a row. 'In Your Eyes' is the song in question. You'd have a hard time dancing to it though it's got a catchy hook. Makes a change from the usual earnest shite. *Plonk. Plonk. Plonk* and

15

words about peace. *What are the young ones listening to?* Shaggy. Ace of Base. 2 Unlimited. 'Feel good' Euro hits. They don't sound half so 'feel good' pumping through the tinny speakers of the GAA clubs and community centres where Ulster's youth hang out. Dancing. Smoking. Drinking cheap vodka decanted into Fanta bottles. *No, no limits, we'll reach for the sky,* the youngsters sing. Fists pumping furiously to the beat. Black bomber jackets soaking up their sweat. They go buck mad every time 'No Limits' comes on. It's only a tune to them; not the call to arms it could be. No limits indeed. What a load of bollocks. These kids hail from Augher, Clogher and Cullybackey. Say it out loud. *Cull-Eee-Back-Eee.* You can practically hear the fences. They couldn't be more limited if they tried.

Elsewhere, in the Province, they're still at it; killing each other with bombs and guns. It is the twenty-third or -fourth summer of this nonsense. Depends on when you started keeping count. Most folks are fed up with the whole thing. They're adamant the killing must stop. There is war in Bosnia and Afghanistan. There's a brutal one winding up in Rwanda. You can't turn on your telly for seeing dead bodies piled everywhere. Blood pooling in the gutters. Women howling and getting on. The people here are sick of death. This isn't a Third World country. This is Britain. Or this is Ireland. Or both. Or neither. Or its own institution, peculiar as a maiden aunt. Either way, it's a civilized country. It's been a whole two years since McDonald's arrived. It should never have got to the state it's in.

Same old, same old. Twenty-odd years of everyday killings. Routine set in years ago. Everybody's just trying to get on with enjoying the summer. Those who can have booked their holidays over the Twelfth. *Best to get out before things kick off.* The ones with money are heading to the Continent. *Just to be sure of a bit of heat.* Everybody else is making the most of the weather. If it isn't raining, it's considered 'gorgeous out' and not to be wasted. Now's the time to get the good of a garden, if you're lucky enough to have access to one. The buzz of lawnmowers harmonizes above the hedges. Barbecues sizzle with sausage fat. Children kick footballs down by the swings. The insect hum of combine harvesters zithers and twitches on the breeze. This is the sound of an Ulster summer. This, and the distant rumble of Lambeg drums.

Ballylack's no different from any other one-street village, orbiting a market town. It has a pub, a shop and a primary school. The older kids bus into town, where the Grammar's decent but the High School's a glorified holding pen for kids on a fast track to pulling necks at the chicken factory or returning to work on their daddies' farms. There's half a dozen churches in the village and a sorry excuse for a housing estate – two dozen semis grouped round a scrubby strip of grass – a community centre, a doctor's surgery and a play park that's seen better days. The children congregate round the climbing frame, hanging from the monkey bars. Arm sockets burning. Upside down. Hooked by the ankles till the blood runs to their heads. They'll kick at the dirt and kick at the walls and kick a ball if a ball's forthcoming and lament the loss of the second swing, which came off in March and has yet to be replaced. There's no money for fixing swings. There's not much to do in Ballylack. The children here know nothing else.

School's out for eight long weeks. It falls to the mothers to keep their offspring occupied. When the rain holds off, it's not so bad. Here, in the country, a child can be turfed out at sunrise and left all day to their own devices. They always come home when the hunger kicks in. It's different when it rains and the northern summer's no stranger to rain. Then the mothers must do their best with children's programmes and colouring books. They'll scour the paper for Holiday Clubs which offer Bible teaching and Jaffa Cakes. Three blessed hours of daily respite.

You don't even have to pay the Born Agains. They'll take your weans for free and call themselves grateful. *More fool them*, the mothers think, and hope their children don't come home too full of pious talk. They're thankful for the offer all the same. They wouldn't look a gift horse in the mouth. Two months is an eternity when you've a rake of wee ones under your feet.

1993's like every other summer in Ballylack. Same old, same old till the problems with the children start. Ross McCormick is the first. They're that used to him being poorly his death is not a big surprise. Nonetheless, it's a tragedy. The general consensus is glandular fever with complications. Though the doctors have already ruled this out, the Ballylack rumour mill's still running with it and will no doubt continue to speculate until the autopsy report comes back from Belfast. The family are still waiting on it when they bury Ross three days after he's breathed his last.

Just a child, the old folks will say as they stand waiting for his funeral to start. *Such a waste*, as if Ross were an overlooked mandarin furring at the bottom of the fruit bowl. Because he was young, people will come to the funeral who didn't really know Ross that well. This is seen as a form of respect. It is also blatant nosiness. Rarely do they get a dead child in Ballylack, and when they do, it's always a baby. Baby funerals are usually closed.

They will bury Ross in his school uniform: grey flannel slacks, white shirt, striped tie and Clark's scuff-proof shoes, scuffed cloudy from months of lunchtime football. His mother will take charge of his dressing. She'll want him looking well despite his swollen head and his mottled skin. Ross doesn't own a suit. He's not had the chance to acquire one yet. Hence, the uniform and the perfectly knotted school tie. He'll look like a little man in the coffin. His hair, parted slickly to the left, as if he isn't dead at all, just waiting on the school photographer to coerce him into one last cheesy smile.

The First

IT'S FOUR IN the morning on 1 July when Hannah gets up to pee and finds Ross in the bathroom waiting for her.

At first, she doesn't notice him. It's dark. She hasn't turned on the light. She knows her way without looking. Most nights she makes the same faltering-footed journey from her bedroom to the toilet and back. She keeps her eyes closed as her bladder drains, then fumbles along the wall, feeling for the toilet roll. She finds nothing but a barren cardboard inner. Hannah knows this is the work of her dad.

It's Mum who keeps the house ticking over. Dad's blind to trivial things like empty toilet rolls and overflowing bins. *Too heavenly minded to be any earthly good*, is how Granda Pete puts it. Hannah's not supposed to listen to Granda on account of the fact he's backslidden. He says his pains keep him from church. Dad's sceptical. *The same pains aren't keeping him out of Henderson's.* He's asked Pastor Bill if he'd give Granda a pastoral visitation. Some conversations are easier had with strangers. Hannah's dad doesn't know how to ask his father if everything's OK, faith-wise.

Hannah opens her eyes and gives them a rub. She lets them grow accustomed to the fuggish dark. In the corner by the sink there's an unopened pack of toilet rolls. She leans forward and hooks it with her toe, drawing it slowly across the floor. As she reaches down to extricate a roll, she notices something in the bathtub. At first, it's not obvious what she's looking at. An ill-defined shape, Christmas-tree-sized. It hovers on the edge of her vision, like a thumbprint smudged against the milky hum of the bathroom tiles. *A towel*, she thinks, *or lots of towels, all piled up*.

Then it moves, just slightly, but enough to make her realize exactly what she's squinting at. In the space of a heartbeat, Hannah's wide awake.

'Ross?' she whispers. Half question. Half statement. Barely audible above the burbling sound of the bathroom's pipes.

He's perched awkwardly on the bathtub's edge. She can see he's older than the last time she saw him. Significantly older, like five or six years. She couldn't put a figure on it, but this new version of Ross is quite a bit taller and starting to look a lot like his dad. On his chin, there's the first shadowy hint of a beard. It's only ten days since she saw him, but Ross looks like a different person. An almost adult. A nearly man. Hannah can still tell it's him. It's the way he sits. He's been sitting this way since nursery school. Like somebody's knocked his stuffing out.

Afterwards, Hannah will wonder why she didn't scream. She's not used to finding people hidden around the house. Her parents don't go in for visitors. When they do, it's usually church folk round for a Bible study. These people arrive at pre-arranged times and rarely ever stay later than ten. It is an exceptionally well-ordered house. Hannah's family don't do noise or fuss. They certainly don't do boys in the bathtub at 4 a.m.

Still, Hannah has no physical reaction. She doesn't flinch. Or start. Or make any sudden noise. Later, she'll tell herself she was half asleep. Swept up in the end of a dream. The truth is she's completely present. She's just conditioned to keep her emotions in check. She knows how to take a loudish feeling and let it settle, so her words are always calm and restrained. The loudest thing in Hannah's head isn't panic or even fear. It's mortification; a creeping sense of prickly shame. Ross has seen her almost naked. *What must she look like squatting here, knickers puddling round her ankles? Is she making an odd expression?* She has no notion what her face does when she's peeing. A red, hot blush spreads across her cheeks. The shame of it. She's hot with shame. Hannah has been brought up to believe the fault is always with her.

One-handed, she tries to manhandle her pyjamas up and over her bottom, covering her private parts with the other hand. She forgets to wipe. Too late, she remembers and wonders if Ross will think her disgusting. She has a vague idea from animals that boys' parts are different. Maybe they don't have to wipe. Everything gets tangled around her knees: pyjamas, knickers, her own fingers fumbling to unpick reams of knotted elastic. She's sure he's had a good old eyeful. The blood is thumping in her ears. She flushes the toilet, lowers the lid and sits down. She should wash her hands. *It is disgusting not to wash your hands.* But she's not sure her legs will make it the three short steps from toilet to sink.

'Sorry,' says Hannah.

Who is she apologizing to? Ross? Her parents, who're sleeping soundly in the next room over? The Lord Jesus? Granted, he's probably not best pleased about the situation: the bathroom, the lateness, the two of them together, in the dark.

'I'm sorry,' she repeats, and waits for Ross to respond.

Ross opens his mouth. No words come out. He tries again. Silence. More silence. Then a gurgling sound. Hannah's reminded of a blank-eyed goldfish, gulping its way around a tank. Ross holds his palms aloft in a parody of frustration. He tries to smile. The smile begins slipping the instant it settles on his lips. Hannah's afraid he's going to cry. She's never seen a grown man cry. It's an experience she's keen to avoid. Best to tackle the problem head on. She makes her way over to Ross, half crawling, half sliding across the lino. She offers him a roll of toilet paper. Ross holds it in his hands, turning it round, looking for an entry point. Eventually he gives up and claws a wad from the middle. He uses it to wipe his eyes. He's properly gurning now.

'Are you OK?' Hannah whispers.

Ross makes a flat shape with his hand and wobbles it in front of his face. He's somewhere between all right and falling apart.

'What are you doing here?'

He shrugs.

'Did they let you out of the hospital? Are you feeling better? What's happened to you? You don't look like you used to look.'

Ross shrugs again. He doesn't know.

Hannah has a lot of questions. Ross won't talk. Or possibly can't. He just sits there, rocking backwards and forwards on the bathtub's edge. Every so often he makes a fresh attempt at speaking. Hannah watches the muscles constrict at the base of his throat. Nothing more than a strangled gulp ever makes it out of his mouth. Frustrated, he begins thrashing around, knocking shampoo bottles and shower gels off the bathtub's edge. He tugs at the plastic shower curtain and stamps his feet against the floor. It's strange to watch him tantrum like a toddler. It doesn't sit well with his new-old body. It is almost ludicrous. Hannah's not laughing. She's worrying about her parents. There's only a thin wall separating them from the bathroom. They're bound to be able to hear this racket. Any second now they'll come storming in.

'Ssshhhh,' she hisses, raising a finger to her lips. 'You'll wake my dad.'

Ross quits thrashing. His shoulders droop. His head slumps forward. He begins to sob hysterically. Hannah doesn't know how to comfort him. Maybe she should put her arms around him; hug him like Mum cuddles her. She's never touched a man before; well, nobody but Dad and Granda Pete. She wouldn't know how to go about it. *What part of Ross should she touch?* She doesn't want to give him any boyfriend ideas. She sits on her haunches and smiles up at him. She feels like that woman in the Bible, the one who wiped Jesus's feet with her tears and hair. There's a lot of women in the Bible. Mostly called Mary. Mary this or Mary that. This one's always intrigued her because she sounds a bit mad. Nobody gets her except Jesus. She reminds Hannah of herself.

Hannah has chats with the Jesus in her head. It's not really praying. It's more like talking to an imaginary friend. She lets all her *Thees* and *Thous* slip. She just calls him Jesus, which is not what you're meant to do in prayers. You're supposed to say *The Lord Jesus Christ* or *Dear Lord Jesus*. Just *Jesus* is disrespectful, like addressing an adult by their first name. Hannah does it anyway and talks to Jesus about things that aren't holy, like getting her ears pierced and not wanting to go round the Estate handing out Bible tracts with Mum. The Jesus in her head understands. He makes *uh, uh* noises to show he's listening. He sounds a bit like Granda Pete. *This, too, shall pass*, he tells her, in a gentle voice, not unlike the nice dentist Mum takes her to in town. *This, too, shall pass* is a favourite saying of Granda Pete's. It means don't get your knickers in a twist. Even the most horrible moments will eventually be over. Hannah doesn't think it's in the Bible. And if it isn't in the Bible real Jesus definitely wouldn't be saying it. She wonders who this Jesus is, the one who whispers in her ear. She can hear him now, mumbling away.

'This, too, shall pass,' she repeats, and pats Ross softly on the knee. A knee feels like an OK place to touch. She wouldn't want to chance a higher-up part. The patting seems to do the trick. Ross looks down at her and smiles. He nods his head. *Yes, yes, yes.* Hannah understands immediately. She has been a comfort here. Whatever's bothering Ross, he'll now know there is an end in sight. He stops crying and wipes the whole toilet roll across his face, mopping up the last of the tears.

Hannah says it again, once more for effect, 'This, too, shall pass,' and smiles. She pats Ross's knee a bit more and adds, 'I'm always here if you need a listening ear,' which is something Mum says on the telephone. Ross places his hand on her hand and pats back. It is nice to sit here, patting each other in the dark, but Hannah's very aware of her parents next door.

'Now,' she says, 'we better get you out of here before my dad appears.'

Ross nods. He rises from the bathtub and Hannah sees just how tall he's grown. They used to be about the same size. Now, he's towering over her. She wants to ask why this is, how he's managed to shoot up so quickly. Maybe something they've given him in hospital. There's no point asking when he clearly can't answer. Instead, she tiptoes him across the landing, down the stairs and along the hall. She turns the front door key quietly. When the door opens, Ross steps outside and hesitates on the welcome mat. Theirs says *Bethel* in swirly writing, because that's the name of their house. Ross smiles. Hannah smiles. Ross smiles some more. Hannah wants him to go away now. New Ross is beginning to freak her out. *How can she say this without sounding rude?* She tries to remember what her parents do when they're ushering people out the door.

'Well,' she says, 'thanks for dropping by. Don't be a stranger.'

It's such a Dad thing to say she can't help extending her hand at the same time. Her dad always says goodbye with a firm hand-shake and a blessing. He'd consider it rude not to, especially in the company of other believers. Ross takes her hand. He squeezes it firmly. His hand is cold. Not freezer cold. More like the first morning water out of the tap. Hannah doesn't like the feel of him.

'Goodnight, Ross,' she says, and tries to withdraw her hand.

Ross doesn't let go.

Hannah pulls.

Ross pulls back.

He's taller than her, and a lot stronger. He's pulling with all his might, his face contorted and pink with effort. Hannah's bare feet begin to lose traction on the hall carpet. She can feel herself slipping. She digs her heels in and leans back. There's a pain in her wrist where the skin is stretched. It's stinging like a Chinese burn. Ross is about to drag her outside when she remembers the door. She hooks it with her foot. She practically slams it in his face. The shock causes Ross to release his grip. Hannah's hand slides loose. She almost topples, but rights herself quickly. She shuts the door and locks it quickly. She's shaking now, the tremble running from her pulled arm all the way down to her bare feet.

She feels bad about slamming the door. Christians don't throw people out when they most need help. She remembers Corrie ten Boom, who had all those Jews concealed behind her wardrobe, and that one bold woman in the Bible who managed to hide the spies. She almost opens the door again. But she doesn't want Ross to come back in. He has his own home to go to. And his parents. They're better placed to help him with whatever's wrong.

She places an eye against the peephole. Ross is still standing on the welcome mat. He's sobbing now, hand extended towards the house. He looks like a little kid, reaching for a grown-up's hand. Hannah's sensible. She knows she can't do anything for him. This doesn't stop her feeling guilty. She presses her hand against the door so it's only inches from his fingers. 'Dear Lord Jesus,' she mouths silently, 'bless thy child Ross. Lead him by still waters, calm his sorrows, soothe his troubled brow. In thy precious name. Amen.' This is a proper prayer. Much more effective than talking to the Jesus in her head.

Having prayed, she feels a bit less guilty. Hannah tiptoes back up to bed. It takes a good hour to fall asleep. Her thoughts are running too fast for her head. She dreams she's following Ross around Ballylack. He's taking her on a guided tour. Every so often he glances over his shoulder just to make sure she's keeping up. Hannah asks him questions. So many questions. Ross resolutely ignores them all. Instead, he points out trees and lamp posts, benches and houses. They're all exactly where they should be. The second swing's still missing. The scaffolding's still up round the community centre where the roofers are taking the asbestos out. The phone box next to the doctor's still smells like pee. It still has *UVF* scrawled on it in red paint. Thompson's looks exactly the same. It's even got the lolly freezer pulled up outside, like earlier today when Hannah and Mum popped in for milk. When she looks through the glass, Hannah can see the ice pops and Twisters covered in freezer snow. She could slide back the lid and help herself. She doesn't bother. Something tells her these lollies won't taste like lollies should.

Because something's wrong with this Ballylack. It feels like a museum of itself. There are no people here aside from them. No birds or animals either. Things only move if they make them move. The only sounds are the sounds they make. It's quiet. So quiet. And Ballylack is never quiet. There are always people milling about. Talking and laughing. Walking their dogs. Dragging their children home from school. There are always cars and tractors lumbering slowly down Main Street, taking the speed bumps cautiously. Hannah wonders where the people have gone.

And the air is different from normal air. It presses up against her skin. It's thick and gluey. As if it isn't going anywhere. This is Ballylack and it's not Ballylack. Hannah's not sure where she is. She grabs Ross's wrist and forces him to turn around and look at her. 'What exactly is this place?' she asks. Ross shrugs, then sweeps his arm wide as if to say, *Look around you. It is what it is.* He goes stomping off in the direction of his parents' house.

Hannah perches on the kerb to gather her thoughts. She wraps her arms round her legs and tents her T-shirt over her knees. This is how she sits when she wants to feel small. And safe. And tight in herself. But she doesn't seem to fit together any more. Her legs are too long. Her belly's all blubbery and there are proper boobs sprouting from her chest. Her body won't bend to meet itself. She thinks, in this moment, of poor Alice, stretching and shrinking, drowning in tears. Miss McKeown read them *Alice in Wonderland* earlier this year, eking it out over six Friday Treats. Hannah's not Alice. She's still herself. She can see the scar on her shin from falling through Granda Pete's greenhouse when she was three. And she knows she's Hannah inside her head. But she's different here in this other place. She's less real. Or more real. Or maybe some in-between version of herself. It's like being underwater at the swimmers, cut off from real-world noise with all her thoughts sealed inside her head.

Hannah wakes at seven, earlier than usual. Something is scratching at her face. Thin, wispy branches. Soft and greasy slips of fabric. She's still got one foot in the other Ballylack, dreaming she's stood beneath the Raggedy Tree. She can feel its fingers reaching for her. She wakes suddenly, swiping branches from her face. Her hair is plastered across her forehead, stuck to her cheeks and in her mouth. She tries to remember what happened in the night. It's hard to differentiate between dream and real. She slips out from under the duvet to peer through her window. Ross is no longer standing in the drive. There are scuff marks in the gravel where he stood. They could've been made by Ross's trainers or next door's cat, who's always doing his business in their front yard.

At ten past seven the telephone rings. At half past Mum comes into Hannah's room. Dad follows behind her. They're holding mugs of tea. They perch on either side of her bed. Mum's obviously been crying. There are fresh red lines around her eyelids. Her nose is pinker than it usually is. She takes Hannah's hand in her own. It's warm and sticky. There's a damp Kleenex balled up in her palm.

'Hannah,' says Dad, 'we have some sad news. Mrs Nugent's just called to let us know poor Ross has died.'

'Ross McCormick,' says Mum, though there's no need for further clarification. Everyone knows he's been in the hospital these last few days.

'When?' asks Hannah.

'Yesterday evening,' says Dad.

'Oh,' says Hannah. She manages to stop herself from saying, *I already knew*. She's only just realized this herself.

'It's so sad when children die,' says Mum.

She wraps her arms around Hannah. It hurts to be held so hard. Hannah thinks about Ross, the way he locked on to her hand and wouldn't let go. She cries then, big, shuddering sobs, dampening the shoulders of Mum's dressing gown. Mum rubs her back. Dad goes downstairs for the tissue box.

The two of them say over and over again, 'It's so sad, Pet. It's so, so sad.' They don't say, *At least Ross is in Heaven*, because they aren't too sure if he was saved. Hannah isn't sad. Or at least, she's not *just* sad. There are far too many thoughts ricocheting round inside her head to be specific about what she feels. Sad and confused. A wee bit angry. Maybe something like afraid.

She turns to the Jesus in her head. She needs a bit of reassurance. Now's the time for *This, too, shall pass*. She'd like to know last night was a one-off; that Ross won't be popping up again, and that she's done the right thing by him. She's really not sure if she's helped or made the situation worse. Hannah looks at the WWJD bracelet on her right wrist, bought from the Faith Mission with her Sunday-school prize token. *What would Jesus actually do if a dead fella appeared in his bathroom in the middle of the night?* Jesus isn't saying much today. Just like Ross, he's lost his voice.

The Living Spit

ALAN GARDINER IS not a bad man. He does his best. He honestly tries. But he always seems to put his foot in it. Take this afternoon, for example. They're on their way back from that wee lad's funeral, the one who's in his son's class at school. His wife's in the front seat, Ben's in the back watching the clouds or daydreaming; Alan has no idea what daft nonsense goes on in his son's head. Nobody's talking when up pipes the boy. 'What was wrong with Ross? Why did he die?' Alan's savvy enough to hear a note of fear in Ben's voice. There's a question tucked in behind his question. *Could I get sick like Ross? Am I going to die too?*

Alan's wife opens her mouth; she's about to answer. She's always the one who deals with the boy. Alan glances across the gearstick and catches her eye. Her eyes are red and raw from crying. She's a mother first and foremost. The funeral's really taken it out of her. He nods at her, once, decisively, as if to say, *I've got this one.* He considers placing a reassuring hand on her thigh and, at the last minute, lacks resolution. He can't seem to lever his left hand off the steering wheel.

Alan turns his head slightly to address the situation in the back seat. He knows exactly what Ben wants to hear. *You'll be grand, son. Don't worry. You're not going to die.* This is not what

Alan says. There's a disconnect when it comes to Alan and his son. He's never been able to say the right thing. 'There was something wrong with Ross,' he says. 'Sure, he was always off school, always poorly. It's sad and all, but it's no big surprise that he died. You remember when Mopsy had them kittens last year, Ben, and the littlest one just didn't take? You knew it was never going to make anything of it. Runt of the litter, if you know what I mean. Well, sometimes that happens with people too. Ross was probably a bit like that . . .'

Alan's wife cuts him off mid-sentence. She gives him one of her withering looks. 'What your father is trying to say is there's absolutely no reason to worry, love. We understand you're sad and a bit worried but you're not going to die anytime soon. That poor boy Ross just wasn't well.'

'Are you sure, Mum?' says Ben.

His wife doesn't answer. She turns all the way round in her seat and squeezes Ben's knee. When she turns back Alan can see she's crying again. It makes him jealous. He's missed yet another moment with his son. When he pulls the car into the yard, he doesn't come in for a cup of tea and a chance to put things right with Ben. He mutters something about the beasts and goes stomping off across the fields. On days like this Alan feels as if there's no room left in his house for him. He'd be angry with them if he didn't know it was his own doing. Instead, he just feels sad. Also lonely. Dreadfully lonely. Alan doesn't know how to fix his family. He wonders what is wrong with him.

Alan Gardiner is not a bad man.

He pays his taxes. He occasionally gives to charity. He wouldn't go as far as saying he loves his wife – *love*'s not a word he has much time for – but he treats her well enough. He feeds and clothes her, keeps a roof above her head. She wants for nothing. Neither do the children. Alan Gardiner has a pair of them: Ben, who is almost twelve, and a wee late one, Lucy, who's only just at the toddling stage. When he uses their names, which is rarely, for Alan's a man of very few words, he calls Ben *Ben* and Lucy *Lou*, though these are not their given names. Their mother insisted upon other names: strange, foreign words Alan can't bring himself to say. Even seeing them written down is troubling. They remind him of how he's different from his own children; all the things they'll never share.

Their mother's from the Philippines. You'd know to look at them. You'd know they weren't really from here. They have incredibly sleek hair. Alan tries not to stand next to them in photographs. Up close the difference is pronounced. There's very little of him in them. Maybe a slight downward tug round the mouth. A particular way of frowning when perplexed. On the whole they look like some other fella's weans. That's hard for Alan to stomach. They're the living spit of their mum.

Alan got his wife from the old folks' home. She'd been his mother's carer. There were a few foreign girls working in the home: mostly Filipinos and one Indian. Some of them already spoke with a sing-song Antrim drawl, though they'd never be considered local. Locals wouldn't lower themselves to do the things they'd do for minimum wage.

Alan had been on the lookout for a wife. He'd an ad running in the *Newsletter*. *Wanted. A wife to help about the house and farm. No children. No existing medical conditions. Timewasters need not apply.* With hindsight he'd have been better placing it in the Lonely Hearts section, but this was significantly dearer. He'd paid two pounds fifty and was somewhat dismayed to find his future wife listed between a tow-bar and a holiday flat in Cushendall. Nobody responded. Maybe a photo might've helped, of the farm, rather than Alan. Alan Gardiner wasn't a good-looking man. After two weeks he'd cancelled the ad. There was no point throwing good money after bad.

Alan wasn't experienced with women. He was almost forty yet had never felt the need for one. But with his father dead and his mother doting, he was struggling to keep the farm afloat. The house had descended into a pig sty and he was starting to fade away. Tinned soup, toast and yoghurts weren't enough to keep a working man going. Anything more complex required cooking, and cooking had been his mother's domain. Maganda traipsed into Alan's life just in time. Any later and he'd've been nothing but skin and bones.

He'd walked into his mother's room one wet afternoon to find Maganda shovelling puréed vegetables into the old woman's mouth. Five foot nothing in sinless white gutties, she'd smiled up at him from a stool sat between his mother's knees, plastic spoon arrested mid-flight. 'Please to be meeting you, Mr Alan.' Alan knew straight away that this one would do rightly. A foreign girl would be much less hassle than trying to court a local lass.

It wasn't looks which drew him to Maganda, though she was pretty enough, and not as dark as some of the others. He also found her breasts appealing. They were very large for such a short woman and pressed tightly against her uniform as if trying to effect an escape. During the three short days of their courtship Alan frequently thought about Maganda's breasts. He imagined himself unzipping the front of her work uniform so the pair of them came popping out, like helium balloons suddenly released. He also entertained a very specific fantasy wherein she cooked him a fry wearing nothing but a pair of frilly black knickers. Alan's erotic yearnings never progressed beyond this. He wouldn't have known how to imagine a woman fully nude with a frying pan.

Alan did not appreciate the finer points of Maganda's charm. Her soft smile, like a birthday candle blooming weakly in the dreary corridors of the nursing home. The way she sang – barely audible songs in her mother tongue – as she went about toileting the old folk. Her beautiful eyes. Her beautiful, beautiful, dark brown eyes. It was the heft of her thighs and arms which appealed. Maganda might have been little but she was substantial and built for hard work. Alan needed a woman who wouldn't mind breaking a sweat. He understood the difference between a farmer's wife and an ordinary woman. Farmers' wives were cut from sterner cloth. His younger brother had married a silly woman from Armagh; the sort of caleeried bint who dyed her hair blonde and painted her nails. She was so feared of the beasts she wouldn't go near them. This same brother was now out a fortune, paying a young fella from the village to do all the things his wife should be doing for free. Alan often wondered if he should have a word with this brother, tell him to take his wife in hand. But this would've required too much talking. He held his tongue and resolved that if and when it came his turn to acquire a wife, he would not be duped into marrying a soft or silly woman.

Maganda wasn't soft. Or silly. She was practical and level-headed. Alan could tell this from the way she went about her daily tasks: changing beds and saline drips. There would be no need for romance with her. After their first meeting he waited a few days for propriety's sake, then bought her a bunch of cellophane-wrapped chrysanthemums from Thompson's. He told her she had good, strong teeth which – though something he might just as quickly have said about a heifer – was a compliment in his books. On the third day of their courtship he popped the question. He didn't go down on one knee or any such nonsense. He just waited till they were alone with his mother before he asked, 'After Ma dies, would you marry me? I've a big house and a farm. You'd want for nothing.' He'd put a tie on that morning. He wanted to make a decent impression.

At first Maganda hadn't said anything. She'd kept on brushing his mother's hair with a soft baby brush, the same silver-backed one Alan had used as a child. There was no noise in the room, save the gentle whoosh of old-lady hair scuffed this way and that. The blush of embarrassment crept up Alan's neck, engulfing his whole face in a furious heat. He was about to excuse himself and leave when Maganda placed the brush gently on the dresser and turned towards him.

'Yes,' she said. 'I will.'

'Grand,' he said, 'I'll get it sorted,' and shook her hand to formalize things.

Though he'd not known in this moment, and Maganda would never get round to telling him, there was nothing left for her in the Philippines. She'd no great interest in nursing either. Alan knew none of this but still understood this marriage would be a compromise. It was a sensible decision. Alan respected her for it. He buried his mother a fortnight later. Two weeks after the funeral they married in the Presbyterian Church. This was to be the last time Maganda heard her proper name spoken. *Do you, Alan Mervyn Gardiner, take Maganda Rosamie Mendoza to be your lawfully wedded wife?*

Once married she was called Megan, or nothing at all. The locals didn't seem to know what to do with her. Alan Gardiner wasn't the sort to set a precedent. She quit the nursing home immediately. Alan believed a woman's place was in the home, so Maganda spent most of her time in the house or knocking about the farm: cleaning, cooking and steeling herself for Saturday nights, when her husband would take his weekly bath and afterwards clamber on top of her, going at her like a rutting bull. It wasn't ideal. They rarely talked about anything except the general upkeep of the farm. But at least he didn't hit her. He put food on the table and kept her in clothes. He bought her a new frock for summer and another, slightly warmer one before Christmas. Alan Gardiner was not a bad man.

There was no romance in the marriage, but they managed rightly for two and a half years. Then the child arrived.

Parenting has not come easily to Alan Gardiner. He's not a

people person and, arguably, children are people too. He prefers cows to people, potatoes to cows, for there's no noise off a spud, no possibility of sudden movement or fuss. He's happy enough having Megan about the house. Over the years he's trained her well. She occupies the various rooms like a piece of furniture. You'd hardly even know she was there. She keeps the place neat and functional. Alan only has to lift his head and mutter, *Megan?*, pitching his voice towards whatever he's currently in need of – food or clean socks, a quick fumble at her ample breasts – and she'll understand and immediately oblige. He feels no need to spoil her, though he isn't purposely cruel. He's not even come close to hitting her.

It's different with Ben. Alan cannot seem to learn his son. Every time he looks at the boy a thing like knives slides between them. It's not just the colour of Ben which doesn't sit well, or the slightness of his build, the sleekit way he carries himself across a room. It's the way he is stuck – *fairly glued* – to his mother. The pair of them lean into each other, whispering in their own private language. This secret talk intrigues Alan. It sounds to him like butterflies speaking, all clicks and silken, fluttery swells. He'd never say this to Megan. It's too soft a sentiment; not the sort of thing a man should voice. Nor would he think of learning a word or two himself. *What would be the point? It's Ballylack they live in, not bloody Manila.* Still, every time he comes upon his wife and son chattering away, Alan knows he's on the outside, peering in.

The boy does not belong to him. Oh, Ben's grown from his seed, all right. Alan's certain sure of that. Megan wouldn't dare stray, and who exactly would she find to cheat with, out here in the arse end of nowhere? No, it's more the matter of ownership that's bothering Alan. Ownership's something he understands. There are a hundred head of cattle in the top field, all tagged and marked as his, twice as many sheep again, grazing in his other fields. He has pigs in the midden and three dozen hens flaffing about the yard. He owns all these creatures. They belong to him. He feeds them and breeds them. He values them for their use. Though he wouldn't know how to vocalize it, he feels similarly about his wife.

The boy is a different matter entirely. The boy is his mother's. For all the fences Alan's tried to place around him – rules and chores and raised-hand threats – he's never managed to get the run of him. He isn't a disobedient wee lad. He's simply disinterested. Alan's seen the same look in wilful cows. Ben will bolt the minute the opportunity arises. There's no loyalty there. No sense of belonging. There's little to be done with such a creature. A kind hand won't broker any sort of bond. A firm hand's only likely to turn him. Ben's not cut out for farming. Alan knows no other way of being. There's a chronic lack of understanding between the two of them.

At first Alan tries to force a connection. He buys his toddling son welly boots and tiny versions of the tools he uses. He takes him out around the fields, hoisted up on his shoulders for a better view. He points out things that might interest Ben. The wee birdies chittering in the trees. Hamish, the big bull he keeps for breeding. Spring lambs. *What child doesn't love a lamb?* Nothing catches. The space between them swells each year until they've nothing to say to each other. Nothing but the weather and what Mum's fixing for their tea.

Alan doesn't hate his son. He doesn't know him well enough to work up a decent spite. He is disappointed, though. Disappointed by Ben's long stick legs and the way he has of speaking gently, like posh women speak on the radio. He doesn't understand how Ben can't tell one cow from another when he's spent his whole life looking at them. All the boy wants to do is run. Up and down the lane. Across the fields in the special spiked shoes his mother got him for Christmas. Round and round the biggest barn when it's too cold to venture outside. Round and round in perfect loops until tiny lumps of straw and chicken shit clog the treads of his trainers and he has to stop and hoke them out. The only thing Ben's good at is running. Alan doesn't know what to do with him.

It's different with the wee girl, Lucy. She's still small and cute as a button. She raises her fat arms to him when he comes in from the yard. Alan can't keep from reaching back. There's a space in the crook of his arm which fits her exactly; a way she has of looking at him like she knows he's her dad. It's been there since the moment he clapped eyes on her, blood-red and furious from the birth. 'That one's going to be Daddy's girl,' the midwife insisted as she bundled the baby into his arms. Something in Alan Gardiner melted then. He remains baffled by the pull of Lucy. How easy it is to want her. How natural and strange. He's still the same cold wall with everyone else, but with his daughter, Alan is gentle. He finds it easy to lean in.

Alan can sense this split in himself. It bothers him. He knows it's unfair to favour one child over the other. It's a weakness on his part; to know a thing is wrong and not be able to overrule the instinct, like kicking the pup when he's in a foul mood. It would help if Ben was more like Lucy. Once, just once, he'd like the boy to look up at him with something like respect. Love would do. But respect's more important in Alan's eyes. Even some interest would be a start. If Ben were to ask which heifers were close to calving or whether they'll be starting into the silage soon. The smallest gesture could be built upon. But the boy's not forthcoming and Alan doesn't know how to make the first move. He can't see anything of himself in his son.

Alan Gardiner isn't a bad man. He is proud and thran, but he isn't cruel. He loves his daughter more than his son. The guilt of this goes all the way down to his pale white bones. He sometimes thinks they'd get along better if it was only the three of them. It's an ugly thought. He's aware of that. At night, in bed, while Megan sleeps, Alan returns to this thought like a snuffling pig. He imagines Ben gone. The air in the farmhouse lighter without him. Things like they were in the early days, possibly even happier, on account of wee Lucy. It's a comfort to imagine his son away. It is a comfort and a dreadful shame. Alan knows he must never speak of it. He might pray it out if he ever prayed. But he's only religious in the formal sense. Christmas and Easter. Weddings and funerals. He fears God, though he's not sure he believes in him. Oh, but the fear's real enough, and the shame and the guilt. Alan Gardiner's weighed down with it.

Prayer and Fasting

THE ADGERS' CHURCH is in town. It takes about twenty-five minutes to drive there. The journey used to be shorter when it was just Hannah and her parents. Now, since Granda Pete's stopped going, they have to pick Granny up en route.

While Dad turns the car, Hannah runs in to get Granny. Granny's never ready to go. Hannah would be disappointed if she was. Waiting for her to find her good handbag or fill her offering envelope means time alone with Granda Pete. Hannah dotes on her granda. The feeling's mutual. It helps that she's his only grandwean. She was born so long into his son's marriage he'd started wondering if there'd be any children at all. Then they'd almost lost her when she finally arrived. Granda Pete can't bear to think about those long, hard days, peering at that tiny pink creature through the glass sides of her incubator. Hoping. Praying. Driving himself near silly with worry. Then, the great miracle of bringing her home.

Her parents have chosen not to tell Hannah what a miracle she actually is. It's yet another one of their daft religious beliefs. *What harm could it do, letting Hannah know how precious she is?* Her dad says he doesn't want the child feeling like she's some special case. It could make her prideful. She might start thinking she's better than other children. What a load of rubbish, thinks Granda Pete. He's never done telling Hannah she's the most precious wee girl in the world. Aye, a rake of grandbabbies would've been great – ideally a boy to talk football with – but this has never diminished Pete's affection for Hannah. She's his wee princess. She has been since the second he saw her. 'She's got your eyes,' he'd told his wife. This was only said to please her. Looking at baby Hannah was like looking at his mother reincarnated. *God love the child.* His mother had been awful homely-looking, but you'd have known from her face that she was kind.

Granda Pete always has something for Hannah on Sunday mornings: a bar of Caramac or a bag of Maltesers. 'That's to get you through the sermon,' he says with a wink. 'A shot of whiskey would serve you better, but you'd never get it past your da.' This morning he's sitting on the stairs holding out a packet of Chewitts. He tucks the sweeties into her cardigan pocket and slips a pound coin in with them. 'Your grandmother's just getting her hat on,' he says. 'Wait till you see the size of it. Your da'll have to open his sunroof to fit it in.' Hannah giggles. Granda's always making fun of Granny. Granny sets herself up for it.

Hannah allows Granda to lift her on to his knee. It makes her feel safe when he babies her. The soft itch of his stubble grating up against her cheek. His arms belted round her middle. She snuggles into his dressing gown, takes a big breath of his smell and holds it in her nose. It's a smoky kind of scent, woody and familiar, like burnt paper. Mum says it's cigarettes. Granda insists he doesn't smoke.

'Well, Hannah Banana,' he says, tickling her ribs so she squirms around inside her stiff Sunday frock, 'how are you this fine morning? Not having too much fun on the Sabbath, I hope.'

'I'm fine,' she says.

'Just fine? Not great, or marvellous, or stupendously brilliant?'

'Just fine, Granda. My belly's a bit sore.'

He stops jiggling her then. He takes her by the shoulders and turns her towards him. His face isn't laughing any more. He's looking at her intently, his big, bushy eyebrows drawn up in a V. She knows he's probably heard about Ross. Everyone in Ballylack's heard by now. It's put the grown-ups on edge. Mum's told her it's nothing to worry about. Ross has never been well. She's sticking to the line about glandular fever but this hasn't stopped her asking four times if Hannah's feeling OK. If she'd like to stay home today. Dad's not quite so sympathetic. Hannah would have to be literally dying before he'd let her skip church. Every Sunday morning she gets a stamp on her League of Church loyalty card. You can save them up like petrol stamps and get a book at the end of the year. Something holy from the Faith Mission about the Bible or missionaries. Hannah has six years' unbroken attendance. When Dad was a boy, he managed twelve.

'Any other pains?' asks Granda. 'Headaches? Dizziness? Do you have a temperature? Has anybody checked?'

Pete's doing his best not to panic, though Granny's furnished him with all the details of young Ross's death. The enormous goitre which formed on his neck; melon-sized, Granny's been told. The hallucinations. The seizures. The temperature of 104. If you want Granny's opinion – and Pete didn't – it sounded nothing like glandular fever to her. The phone hasn't stopped ringing all weekend. Dear only knows where they get their intel, but Granny's cronies are nothing if not well informed. For the most part Pete takes them with a pinch of salt. Daft auld women who've nothing better to do with their time than poke their noses into others' business. This weekend they're harder to dismiss.

'I don't want to fuss, Han, but you'd let me know if you were feeling poorly at all?'

'I'm fine, Granda,' says Hannah. 'My tummy's just a bit wobbly. It's probably hungry.'

'Hungry?'

'Aye, we're fasting.'

'What do you mean, fasting?'

'We were praying and fasting for Ross to get better. Dad said we should keep going. We're praying for his mum and dad now. There's other ones from church doing it too.'

'Jesus,' says Granda.

He's about to say something else when Dad toots the horn loudly, three times in a row. Granny comes flying down the stairs, sticking pins into her hat as she goes. 'Right, Peter, that's me off,' she says. 'Don't forget to put the spuds on at twelve.' She grabs Hannah by the wrist and has her out the door and down the drive before she can even hug him goodbye. She twists herself round to wave back at Granda.

'Don't worry,' she calls out. 'I'm grand.'

Granda Pete waves back. He makes his face into a smile. Hannah can tell he's only pretending. His eyes aren't crinkling up like spider's legs. He always gets spider eyes when he's happy. Hannah coined the phrase when she was wee.

Dad's not best pleased. He says they're running late now and what is it with women taking for ever to get themselves out the door. Hannah looks at her watch. They're not late at all. Dad likes to get there early. He's leadership, which means he has to give out the order of service and welcome people at the door. *Good morning. Nice to see you. You're very welcome.* Dad has three different greetings he rotates. When he's praying there's no variation. He always begins with the same set phrase. *Heavenly Father, we come humbly before Thee.* Pastor Bill also has his own way of starting a prayer. *Brethren, let us bow our heads.* They have different voices when they're praying. All men do. Hannah wonders if ladies also have praying voices. She'll probably never find out. Ladies aren't allowed to pray in church. They can't preach either. Though they are allowed to be in the choir and teach Sunday school.

Dad's praying voice is softer and slower; sort of syrupy. Pastor Bill's is thundering loud. Between sentences, Hannah can hear the moist click of his tongue dragging through spit.

Praying in front of everybody must make you sick with nerves. There's so many people listening, not to mention God. No wonder the men nearly always say the same thing. When Hannah's asked to pray at home, she uses the same words every time: 'As I Lay Me Down to Sleep' for bed, and Grace, if she has to bless the meal. 'The Lord's Prayer' covers everything else. She wouldn't dare pray out loud like she talks to the Jesus in her head. She'd get a skite from Mum for disrespect.

When they arrive at church, Dad removes his blazer from the hanger in the back seat and slips it on. He has two good suits for Sundays: a light one for summer and a darker winter one. When they return for the evening service, he'll swap his suit jacket for a V-neck jumper. The evening service is more casual. There's tea afterwards and choruses, which they sing out of *Mission Praise*. There's no such reprieve for Hannah or Mum. Church women wear a kind of uniform: skirts and blouses, long, ankle-grazing dresses, neat little cardigans with pearly buttons, patent-leather handbags and shoes in a matching shade. Hats. Hats. Hats. Hats as big as lampshades and hats which look like something's deflated on the wearer's head. Tall hats. Tiny hats, not much bigger than a hair bow. Flat hats. High hats. Straw hats. Bonnets. And the ever-present beret in a rainbow range of shades. There's not a bare-headed woman in the church. There's not a woman who would dare.

The church is almost empty. Granny sits at the side with her pal Eunice. They have very little in common except absent husbands and a fondness for Polo mints, which they suck surreptitiously throughout the service. Mum and Hannah sit in the second row from the back. Everyone sits in the same place each week. The three rows at the front are left empty for visitors and newcomers who've not yet decided where to pitch camp. No matter how early they arrive, Mrs Nugent's already installed in the back row. Meta Nugent's the only other person who comes to church from Bally-lack. Mum's offered to pick her up on their way. Mrs Nugent says that wouldn't be convenient. Granda Pete claims she comes the night before just to be sure she'll get her seat. *If you look closely, you can see she has pyjamas on under her dress.* Hannah knows she hasn't. She always sneaks a look anyway.

As soon as they've sat down and tucked their handbags beneath the seat, Mrs Nugent leans over. Hannah gets a waft of Parma Violets and old-lady pee. She remembers too late to breathe through her mouth. Granda Pete's taught her to do this when the farmers are spreading slurry. *It helps stop you choking on the stink.*

'Good morning, Mrs Adger,' the old woman says.

Mrs Nugent rarely speaks to Hannah, though sometimes she has a sweetie for her. Hannah prefers when she doesn't. It's usually a free-floating cinnamon lozenge, furry with pocket fluff. There are no sweeties this morning. Mrs Nugent's straight into the gossip. She wouldn't call it gossip. The Bible's very clear about tongues and keeping control of them. They don't do gossip in Hannah's church, although the Adgers' phone is never done ringing with news of this person's misfortune or the hard times somebody else is going through. *I'm not gossiping*, the caller will say. *I'm only telling you so you can pray.*

'That wee girl of the McCartneys is sickening now,' announces Mrs Nugent.

'Kathleen?' says Mum.

'Aye. The lassie whose mammy got blown up in the bread-van bomb. She's in your Hannah's class, is she not?'

'She is.'

'Well, they say she's got what the other lad had.'

'What?' says Hannah's mum.

44

'Aye, the dead one. What's-his-name McCormick. Robert? Roger?'

'Ross.'

'Aye, like I was saying. She's got the same thing. Temperature. Headaches. Completely exhausted.'

'That sounds like the flu to me. Or glandular fever.'

''S'not,' barks Mrs Nugent. 'It's some kind of infection that's going around. I wouldn't be surprised if the other lot's behind it. They'd like nothing better than to get at our weans.'

With her back turned, Hannah can't see the old lady's face. She has an image in her head of a turtle extending its wizened neck to snap and retreat.

'Rubbish,' says Mum. 'It'll just be the flu. There's a dose of it doing the rounds.'

'I'm just telling you what I heard from our Sally. She said they'd the on-call doctor out with Kathleen and he said it wasn't looking good at all.'

'Poor Mrs McCartney,' mutters Mum. 'You don't expect to be rearing your grandkids. She must be missing her daughter something shocking.'

'It's not just Kathleen. They say the Twins have it too.'

'Oh,' says Mum. Hannah can feel the pith leaking out of her, like she's been punctured and is slowly deflating across the pew. She reaches across Hannah's lap and takes her hand. She gives it a reassuring squeeze. Hannah squeezes back. 'Summer flu,' she mumbles under her breath.

'Well, it can't be a coincidence, can it? All them wee ones from the same class.'

'Hmmm,' says Mum.

'I'd be watching Muggins there closely if I was you.'

Mum starts like she's been poked in the ribs. She turns to look Mrs Nugent in the eye.

'I'd appreciate it if you didn't talk nonsense in front of my daughter.' Her voice is iron, but Hannah can feel the tremble running through her hand. The pinch of Mum's fingers squeezing too hard.

'Dear, dear, that's some temper you have on you, Sandra. I'll be praying for you, and your wee one.'

Mrs Nugent settles back into her seat. Two minutes later, she's leaning across the aisle, repeating the same message to Elsie McNeill. 'Did you hear, the wee McCartney girl's sick now too?'

Hannah keeps her lips buttoned. She reads the order of service and, to keep herself from crying, tries to find shorter words hidden inside the longer ones. She knows Mum is probably right. Ross has always been poorly. She won't let herself think about what she heard Granny whispering to Mum. 'They couldn't go for an open coffin, Sandra. The state of his face, it was such a mess.' Probably just an allergic reaction. Probably nothing to worry about. And the other girls? They probably just have the flu. Nothing at all to worry about. *But what if they don't? What if there's something else going on?* If Kathleen's really sick, and also the Twins, that's four people out of her class. There are only eleven of them altogether. Hannah does the maths. Four out of eleven is nearly half; far too many for coincidence. She wonders where the sickness will stop. *Before or after her?*

She thinks back to Ross's funeral. It's not hard to remember, it was only yesterday afternoon. Mum made her wear her school uniform. Everyone from her class was dressed the same. Everyone went to the funeral except Kathleen and the Twins, and Lief, whose parents did not agree with church. Hannah pictures them now. William. Matty. Caroline. Amy. Ben. Miss McKeown had been there too, wearing a black skirt and jacket, because that's what grown-ups wore to funerals. After the service, she'd waited for them at the back of the church. She'd hugged each one of her class in turn and asked if they were doing OK. Hannah could hear that she was struggling not to cry.

'Look,' she'd said, and fished a photo out of her handbag, 'I printed this out. I'm going to give it to Ross's mummy. Doesn't he look so happy?' She passed the photo around. Everybody said 'cool' and 'lovely' and 'that's really nice', even Ben, who hardly ever said anything. Hannah wished Miss McKeown had picked a different picture. Maybe one of Sports Day or the time they'd put on the Vikings play. She wasn't included in this photo. She scanned across her classmates' faces – all ten of them grouped in front of the Raggedy Tree, glad to be out of the classroom, grinning and giving each other bunny ears – and she couldn't help thinking they looked like a gang. They looked complete. She knew they wouldn't really miss her if she wasn't there.

This isn't a good thought to be dwelling on. Hannah's throat feels like she's wearing a too-tight scarf. She had this feeling before when she'd to read a poem at the Sunday-school social and everybody was staring at her. Mum thought it might've been asthma and took her to see Dr Simpson. He'd diagnosed anxiety. He taught Hannah how to imagine a calm space – like a beach or something – when she felt nervous. Dad wasn't keen on this technique. He said it sounded a bit New Agey. 'If you're feeling afraid, take your fears to the Lord Jesus. That's what prayer is for.'

Hannah tries to talk to Jesus now. *You'd think it'd be easy in an actual church.* All that comes out is *crap, crap, crap.* It's not what she should be saying to Jesus. It's certainly not praying. Still, she feels a little better now it's thundering round her head. *Crap, crap, crap. I don't want to get sick.* She concentrates on the breaths coming in and slowly out until her throat relaxes and her chest feels looser. *Stick close,* says the Jesus in her head, whispering into the silent part of her brain. She'd have preferred something reassuring, like, *You'll be grand.* But it's better than silence. It proves he's still there. Somewhere inside her. Holding on.

Church is the same as it always is. Prayer. Announcements. Bible reading. Hymn. Children's address and children's hymn, which is 'All Things Bright and Beautiful', because it's summer and summer's the only time it's ever bright or beautiful in Northern Ireland. In the summer they sing it most weeks, just to get the good of it. Then there's the offering and a much longer intercessory prayer. This one's different from the opening prayer, which is all about how great God is. The second prayer's a list of all the things people want from God. There are a lot of things on this list: an end to the Troubles, decent weather for the Sunday-school picnic, bodily healing for a whole rake of old folk suffering from a range of complaints, comfort for the recently bereaved and encouragement for the missionary couples they support in Africa.

When she was younger, and less theologically astute, Hannah used to picture God up in Heaven, taking notes on their intercessory prayer, making a To Do list for the angels to get working on. This morning it's mostly focused on the McCormicks. The pastor prays that they will receive comfort during this, their hour of need. He prays, a little more vaguely, for other children who are also poorly. He doesn't give any names or details. Hannah wonders what he knows. In the pew beside her, Mum whispers a barely audible *Amen* after every sentence, and an *Amen* so loud and resounding it makes Dad wince when Pastor Bill says, 'Protect our children from all evils and walk closely with them.' Hannah makes her eyes into half-open slits to glance at Mum. Her eyes are damp. She could be crying. She's been a bit weepy since the news about Ross. On the other hand, it might just be the general eye wetness – like condensation – which builds up during a really long prayer.

After he's finished praying the Pastor slips back into his speaking voice. 'A number of you have been fasting for the last few days. This morning, when I was praying, I felt the Lord say there were difficult times ahead. It's important not to lose sight of him in the midst of our troubles. I'm asking those of you who are able to join me in another day of prayer and fasting. We must petition the Lord for healing. For our children and our nation. *"Even now,"* declares the Lord, *"return to me with all your heart, with fasting, and weeping, mourning."* As we all know too well, the summer can be a difficult time in this part of the world. Brothers and sisters, we need to be on our knees constantly if we want to see peace in this place.' A general murmur of consent runs around the building. To her left and right, Hannah's parents nod along. 'Thank you all for your faithfulness,' says Pastor Bill. 'The Lord hears and answers in his own perfect time.'

Hannah hears almost nothing of the sermon. She's preoccupied, thinking about what's been said. Her thoughts are stuck in a frantic loop. *It's only the flu. It's only the flu. But what if it's not?* She can't stop thinking about Ross's face. In her head it's all pink and hammy, covered in pus and blisters like Granda Pete's hand the time he burnt it on the barbecue. Her whole body's pulsing with anxiety. She doesn't realize she's fidgeting until Dad places a cautionary hand on her thigh and gives her a *catch yourself on* look. She tries to pray for the others: Kathleen, Lizzy and Mim. Her prayers won't catch. She'll light on a name, start to ask Jesus to make them better, then find she's thinking about herself. There's a pain in her belly. It's probably just hunger. *Would you know yourself if you were really ill?*

She thinks about Ross. It's only a few days since he appeared. She wonders where he is now. *His body's in the graveyard behind the C of I, but where's the other part of him? The new-old Ross with the lonely eyes who couldn't tell her what was wrong. Is he still knocking about the village in some invisible way? Or has he moved on to another place?* Heaven, she hopes, for Hannah doesn't want anybody to go to Hell. Not even Gerry Adams, who's the wickedest person she knows. She hopes Ross is happier wherever he is. She's pretty sure he won't be coming back to see her. Nevertheless, she intends to keep using the downstairs loo for everything but baths.

Hannah sees things differently now. Last week there were two kinds of magic in her world: the *holy* magic God does with angels and miracles and the other *bad* magic which they sometimes pray against. Witches. Demons. Ghosts and Satanists who'd sacrifice children if they got the chance. Other people think this kind of stuff is made up, or harmless. In Hannah's church they know the Devil is real. They won't let their children dress up at Halloween for fear of giving Satan a foothold. They don't mess around with cures or fairy blessings or any of that sort of thing. Hannah's always understood and complied. No Halloween. No *Worst Witch* books. No reading the horoscopes at the back of Granda's paper. No Raggedy Tree. It doesn't matter how harmless it looked in Miss McKeown's photo. She wouldn't want to get close to it. She can't risk giving the Devil a foothold. Since Ross appeared, she's been a bit confused.

She assumes she's had an encounter with evil; an actual dead person came to see her. *She's not quite ready to call Ross a ghost.* Yet it hadn't felt wrong in the moment. It was just like talking to an ordinary person, albeit a very quiet one. And Jesus had been there. He'd given Hannah the words to say. This makes no sense – *no sense at all* – for God can't stand evil. The Bible's pretty clear on this. Maybe everything's more complicated than she thought. *What if Pastor Bill's not always right? Where does this leave her on all the other forbidden things?* Dinosaurs. Leprechauns. Paul Daniel's magic programme, which she's not allowed to watch but sometimes does, secretly with Granda, when Granny's not at home.

The roof is peeling off Hannah's brain. This morning the church feels very small. The men in their dark suits, glaring. The women in their funny hats. The old-fashioned hymns with old-fashioned words, so different from the music the ones in school like listening to. The praying and fasting. Especially the fasting. It seems daft to think you can get God's attention just by skipping your Coco Pops. Hannah knows Pastor Bill would have a pink fit if she said any of this to him. If she marched up after the service and said, *Here, some people don't go straight to Heaven after they die*, he'd only quote Bible verses at her. He'd only tell her she was wrong.

Mum's not in the mood for hanging around after church. 'Home,' she announces as soon as the Benediction's been pronounced. She makes a beeline for the door. The men are standing about the vestibule talking, as they usually do. This morning there's no mention of the weather or last night's football. They're all speculating about the sick children. 'It'll just be a virus,' says one old man.

'Aye,' says another. 'There's glandular fever doing the rounds.'

'And flu,' adds a third. 'They say the wee McCormick lad would've been grand if he'd not had all that other stuff wrong with him.'

There must be two dozen men congregated in the vestibule; several of them have weans themselves, or grandchildren about Hannah's age. They're all tripping over each other to convince themselves they've nothing to worry about. Mum puts her arm around Hannah's shoulder and steers her out to the car park so she won't hear. She's not quick enough. As Hannah's coming down the steps, she sees Mr McMillan take her dad aside. 'You keep a tight eye on your wee lassie, John. If she so much as sneezes, straight up to Casualty. Pastor Bill has had a word. We need to cover them weans in prayer.'

A Run in the Car

HANNAH'S STOMACH HEAVES the whole way home. She can't decide if it's hunger, anxiety or the wee windy roads. They're halfway to Granny's when she's struck with an urgent need to boke.

'Dad,' she says, 'can you stop the car? I'm going to be sick.'

'Now?' says Dad, exasperated.

'Right now.'

He brakes sharply and pulls on to the verge. Mum gets out and holds Hannah's hair back as she dry-heaves over the hedge. In the field beyond, a big Friesian cow watches her intently, its jaws circling round a mouthful of grass.

Granny winds her window down and shouts, 'Do you think it's the same thing them other weans have?'

'Not helpful, Mum,' snaps Hannah's dad. 'She's just hungry. She'll be grand when she gets some lunch in her.'

'I'm just saying, John. You can't be too careful.'

Dad puts one of his Country Gospel cassettes on and turns it up loud to mask whatever his mother was about to say. 'I've Got a Home in Gloryland' comes blasting out, startling a flock of sparrows. They rise as one, their tiny black bodies like punctuation marks floating across the field. Hannah watches them out of the corner of her eye. She's doubled over now, trying to coax yesterday's dinner up. Nothing emerges, but the act of retching seems to have shifted the gas around her guts. The nausea's gone. She unbends carefully.

'Better?' asks Mum, rubbing Hannah's back in slow circles.

'Uh huh.'

'Do you think you'll be OK in the car?'

'Probably.' She has no idea how she'll feel when they start moving again.

Mum insists upon getting the boke bucket out of the boot. 'Keep it on your lap,' she says, 'just to be on the safe side.' Hannah's prone to car sickness. Dad's keen to avoid losing another travel rug.

When she slides into the back seat, Kathleen's already there. She's squeezed into the space between Granny and her. Kathleen looks different: older, taller and less skinny. Her hair's a lighter shade of blonde. She's wearing very short denim shorts and a tight white vest. Her fingernails are painted neon pink. She hasn't got her seatbelt on. *Why would you bother if you're dead?*

Hannah's self-controlled, but she's not a wall. The realization hits her like a slap in the face. Before she can stop herself, she makes a little screechy sound.

Granny looks at her like she has two heads.

Mum turns around. 'What's that, pet?'

Hannah's got their full attention. Two sets of eyes are fastened on her. It's obvious they haven't noticed the apparition. It takes a second for this to register. She's the only one who can see Kathleen. And the only one who saw Ross. There must be a reason for this. She could well be hallucinating – *seeing things that just aren't there* – but she can feel Kathleen's bare thigh pressed up against hers. The clamminess is seeping through her skirt. *Could this be a miracle?* Maybe she's like Mary in the Bible – *the main Mary, Jesus's mum* – getting a special message from God. Sometimes

53

people in church get words from the Lord or even pictures, though she's never heard tell of anyone seeing the dead. That's probably more of a Catholic thing.

Should she tell her parents? They might think it the miracle to end all miracles. The church magazine might do an article on it. Or they could just as easily think it demonic, talking to ghosts. Hannah doesn't want to get labelled with that. Last year Gavin Kelso – who's in the Youth Fellowship – got possessed by a demon of lust. Pastor Bill brought him up to the front in morning service and the elders all laid hands on him. They'd managed to cast the demon out, though it made an awful racket as it left. Gavin had screamed a lot and wet himself. He'd hit Mr McMillan on the ear. Afterwards Pastor Bill said he was healed; *as good as new in the eyes of the Lord.* But even now people still look at Gavin funny and none of the church girls will go out with him, despite the fact he has his own car.

Hannah can't think of anything worse than being the centre of attention. If this is a miracle, people will surely talk about her. If it's something evil, they'll talk even more. Maybe, they won't believe her. They'll call her a liar – *a filthy wee liar* – and make her repent. Hannah weighs up the options in her head. It's probably best if she doesn't tell anyone what's going on. At least until she knows herself.

'Sorry,' she says, excusing her outburst. 'I thought I saw something out the window.'

'Never mind,' says Mum, 'just let us know if you start feeling bokey again.'

Hannah glances at Kathleen. She's about to launch into a rake of questions, but before she can get a single word out Kathleen's clamped her mouth shut. Her hand, pressed tightly against Hannah's lips, is just as cold as Ross's was. Her skin smells sweet and a little sickly, like nail varnish crossed with vanilla ice cream. She keeps Hannah's mouth sealed while she explains.

'Them lot can't hear me. I'll talk. You keep your mouth shut. They'll wonder what's going on if you start mumbling to yourself. Nod if you understand.'

Hannah nods gently. Kathleen releases her grip.

'Good,' she says. 'It's nice to see you, Hannah. I'd have preferred one of my real friends, but anything's better than nothing when you're stuck on your own with a big freak.'

Hannah pinches the soft flesh between her thumb and first finger. It helps to keep the tears from sneaking out. Dead Kathleen's no different from the Kathleen she's known for the last seven years. She's rude and mean and really pushy. Mum's always said it's not Kathleen's fault. She's not had a mummy to bring her up, only two old ones who've no real notion how to raise a child. Hannah looks past Kathleen to Granny. She's munching on another Polo. She never shares. Hannah wonders how she'd have turned out if Granny had brought her up. It can't be easy being Kathleen. She asks the Jesus in her head for a dose of extra patience. Jesus doesn't reply. Maybe she's left him back in church.

'I'm dead, so I am,' Kathleen announces. She waits for Hannah to react and, when she doesn't, motors on, 'It's not as bad as you'd think. I've never been that scared of dying myself. Sure, you really can't be, if you're from here. Because of the Troubles, I mean. Anybody could get killed at any time. You know my mum got blown up when I was wee?'

Hannah nods. She knows about Kathleen's mum. Everybody in Ballylack does. Kathleen's never done talking about it. She thinks having a blown-up mum makes her some kind of celebrity.

'I don't remember my ma at all, only the funeral and the baby coffin they put her in. Granny shouted at my dad, "For God's sake, Stephen, did you have to be so cheap?" and he was all, "What's left of her wouldn't have filled the toe end of a proper coffin." After the funeral he moved to Ayr. That's in Scotland, by the sea. Sometimes I wish he'd taken me with him. Anywhere'd be better than Ballylack. Anyway, like I was saying, I'm totally used to death.'

Kathleen's always loved the sound of her own voice. Miss McKeown used to pretend she didn't notice her raising her hand because once she started it was nearly impossible to get her to stop. Hannah tries to move her away from death and dying. She can't say anything, but she makes a hurry-up sign with her hand.

'Aye,' says Kathleen. 'It's pretty class being dead. Us kids are in charge now. There's no adults here. Nobody to stop us having fun. No rules. We can do whatever we want. And we're all grown-up. I don't really understand how it happened but I'm not complaining. All them ugly lumps have disappeared, thank God, and now I've got boobs and all.' She grabs a handful of breast in each hand and jiggles them in Hannah's face. 'Aren't they deadly? It's a pity there's nobody here to see them. Just Ross, and he's not up for anything.

'You should see him, Hannah. I think he's traumatized or something. That can happen if you have a big shock. He doesn't speak at all. Oh, he was glad enough to see me. Big hugs all round the day I arrived, and a bit of gurning too. You'd think he'd not seen another soul in months. But sure, you know your-self, he only died last week. Time's not the same down here. It feels like ages since I arrived. It's not just time. Everything's a wee bit off. I mean, this place looks exactly like Ballylack, but you'd know it's not. I wish we'd ended up somewhere cooler. Like Ibiza or Magaluf. Still, I'm for making the best of it.

'I'm starting a gang, so I am. It's a bit shite now because there's only the two of us. But the more people die, the better it'll get. We'll turn Ballylack upside down. We've been going through people's houses, nicking their best stuff for our den. It looks class already. Once it's fixed up, we'll have loads of parties and rake about. Ross is totally on board with it now. I had to have words with him. Sure, I couldn't take another second looking at that mopey face. "You're dead," I said. "Get over it. You can either spend eternity huffing or you can get pissed with me and have a bit of craic." Last thing I heard, the Twins weren't feeling the best. The doctors were muttering about them just before I died. They're worried it's a plague or something. I told Ross the Twins were right behind me and that seemed to cheer him up a bit. Maybe he's got a wee eye for Mim. Here, do you know what's going on, Hannah? What have they said about us dying? They can't still think it's a coincidence. Are they not going up the walls about the Twins?

'To be honest, I'm hoping it is a plague. The more ones that die, the more craic it'll be down here. Hopefully some fellas'll appear soon. I mean, Lief's weedy as got out, but he could be decent enough grown-up. He's got them cheekbones like Mark from Take That. And I suppose there might be older ones too. D'you know that fit lad who's always waiting on the bus in the morning: black hair, denim jacket, goes to the Grammar? I'm guessing you don't. Good girl like you doesn't look at boys. Well, here's hoping your man's caught whatever finished me. I wouldn't mind spending eternity cosied up with him. It's zero craic down here at the minute. But when more folk arrive it'll be class. We can basically do whatever we want. Well, anything except leave Ballylack . . . You are going to love it here.'

Hannah feels the tightness circling her throat again. It's hard to breathe. Kathleen's always been full of big talk. But what if there's some truth in it? Hannah really doesn't want to die. Not yet. Not now. Possibly never. She believes in eternal life. In a gold and shiny palace with angels. Not this strange in-between place she's been dreaming about. The thought of it makes her sick. Her lungs feel stuck together and dry. When she opens her mouth a rattly noise comes out like water rasping over pebbles. She tries to say something and begins to choke. Granny quits fumbling with her Polos and turns to look at her.

'Are you OK, Hannah?'

Hannah hasn't got enough breath to answer. Granny leans over into the front. 'Hannah's not well.'

'What?' says Dad, struggling to hear over the sound of Merle Haggard, who's in his garden, walking and talking with the Lord.

'Turn that down, John!' shouts Mum. 'Hannah's sick.' Even though they're moving, she unhooks her seatbelt and leans into the back seat, placing a hand on Hannah's knee. 'Breathe,' she says firmly. 'Follow me. Big, deep breath in through your nose. Hold it. Let it out through your mouth. Another big breath.'

Mum used to be a nurse before she had Hannah and Dad made her stay home. She's always calm in this kind of situation. She always knows what to do. Hannah keeps her eyes on Mum. She doesn't look at Granny, who's flaffing about in her handbag, searching for clean tissues. Or Dad, as he turns the stereo off and pulls over. She doesn't even look at Kathleen, who's leaning right into the side of her face, leering a little as she says, 'Jesus, Hannah, don't be having a panic attack. Everybody dies. It's not that bad.' Hannah keeps her eyes on Mum and, when the car comes to a standstill a few hundred yards from Millar's Gap, she lets Mum help her out to sit on the roadside, panting until her breath steadies and her lungs catch up.

'Do we need to go to casualty?' asks Dad.

Mum takes Hannah's pulse. She places a hand across her forehead, gauging her temperature. 'I don't think that's necessary. It's just a wee panic attack. She's grand now. Aren't you, Han?'

Hannah nods.

'Too much talk about sick children,' Mum mouths. 'Wee ears are always listening.'

'You're right,' says Dad. 'Let's change the subject.' He changes the subject straight away, sliding into the voice he keeps for joking around. 'Well, I don't know about you lot, but I'm starving. Let's get home before the potatoes are boiled to mush.'

When they get back into the car, Kathleen's gone, but the smell of her lingers, sugary and nauseous. Hannah rolls her window down and lets the cold air sweep her clean.

Granda Pete's waiting at the door when they pull in. He's changed out of his dressing gown into real clothes, though he's still got his slippers on. His face is stern. All the colour's drained out of him. When he hugs Hannah, he hugs her harder and longer than usual. She can feel his ribs pressing into hers.

'The roast's near ready,' he tells her. 'Away on in and get the table laid.'

Hannah goes into the kitchen. She doesn't get the cutlery out. She stands in the doorway earwigging on the adults.

'Meta Nugent's just off the phone,' Granda Pete whispers. 'The wee McCartney girl died this morning.'

Mum makes a noise like she's been punched in the stomach. The bottle of Shloer she's brought for lunch slips out of her hand and shatters on the hard wood floor. It's red grape, not white. The pool of it spreads into the living room, all over Granny's good cream carpet. It's bound to stain. For once, Granny doesn't give off. She hardly seems to have noticed it.

Names

THERE'S A LOT of talk around the village. Two children dead in less than a week. Two more sickening with something similar. It sounds like flu. It looks like flu. But perfectly healthy children don't normally die of summer flu.

Folks are quick to point out Ross McCormick was far from healthy. He was always pasty and out of breath. A hefty wee fella, like his da. He was already into adult-sized clothes. The other weans called him the Michelin Man, which was mean but not unjustified. Somebody's heard he had a blood condition. Or maybe something wrong with his lungs. Another one suggests leukaemia. A third says, 'Aye, and with leukaemia you've no resistance. The slightest wee sniffle could take you out.' There's absolutely no grounds for any of this. But wild speculation re-assures people when they tuck their own weans in at night.

As for Kathleen, she's easily dismissed. *That wee lassie of the McCartneys was wild as got out.* Everyone says so. Though every-one's heard it from somebody else. They spread rumours down the aisles at Thompson's. They telephone those stuck at home. There's a fair few people round the village unsurprised to hear Kathleen's dead. *Hmmmpphh,* they say, *I'll tell you what, there's more to that story than meets the eye.* This being village-speak for a cold and sobering sentiment: there's an element in Ballylack who firmly believe that some folks bring trouble upon themselves. Dear only knows what the child was into. Drugs or drinking. Sniffing glue. Somebody says she was running about with an older contingent. Seeing fellas from the town. God love the grandparents – they done their best – but they were never fit to look after Kathleen. *She led the pair of them a merry dance. A wilful child. Awful caleeried. Even at eleven you knew she'd turn out like her ma.*

The Twins are different. The Twins are lovely. Everybody loves the Twins. *Wee dotes. Wee darlings. The sweetest wee girls from the nicest family.* There's not a bad word said about them. If the Twins are sick, well, there might be something in it after all. Because nobody would suggest that the Twins, or their parents – *the equally lovely Liza and Cliff* – were culpable or even capable of harbouring any sort of issue at all. The Twins are perfect in every way. Doubly so. The Twins are perfection multiplied. When word gets out that they're in bed with dreadful headaches and achy, swollen joints, the same fatigue and roaring fever to which Ross and Kathleen have succumbed, the Ballylack grapevine cranks up a notch. People stop whispering behind closed doors. They drag their concerns out into the open. They phone the school, the doctor, the local police, whichever minister they sit under. They say the same thing over and over. *It's probably nothing, just a summer flu. But that's four children now and all of them in the same class at school.*

The police have more than enough to be getting on with. There's been rioting in Belfast and Bangor. More riots over in the Lurgan estates. Talk of talks has made everybody edgy and it's less than a week till the Twelfth. The police are anticipating trouble. There's always trouble at this time of the year. They haven't the manpower nor the interest to go chasing up hysterical phone calls. Just to reassure the mothers, they send two officers out to Ballylack. They'll visit the families of the P7 kids.

They aren't expecting to find anything. They've been given the 'summer flu' line and instructed to pass it on. Their presence is more of a PR stunt; any excuse to show the RUC's caring side. A nice young sergeant is dispatched from the barracks in town. He's accompanied by the area's only female constable. She doesn't complain, though she's not best pleased. There's a drug bust going down on the Doury Road. She'd been hoping to get in on it. But if there's children involved in an incident, it's par for the course, she'll always get sent.

Alan Gardiner isn't at home when they appear. He's away up to Belfast in the Land Rover. Maganda can't say when he'll be back or why he's left when all the other Ballylack parents are circling their children like anxious hens. She tells the police her husband's picking up a tractor part. 'For the Massey,' she adds, 'it's been playing up,' as if this detail will solidify the lie. Alan could be halfway to Limerick for all she knows. He's not a big talker at the best of times. Lately he's barely talking at all. He left this morning before the kids were up. 'I'm for Belfast,' he said, and didn't elaborate. Maganda asked if he wanted his breakfast first. He didn't even stop to answer, just lifted a soda farl from the cooling rack and slipped out the back door.

Alan's been like this since Ross's funeral, avoiding his wife and his son. The way he's skulking about the house reminds Maganda of her dad. When the drink began to leave his system, he'd start noticing the bruises on her mum. Then he'd go slouching round the front veranda like a creature who'd misplaced his spine. Her uncle was the very same, and half the fellas in their barrio. Maganda's known enough feckless men to recognize a guilty one. To his credit, Alan's never laid a finger on her. He's barely even raised his voice. His guilt is different from her father's. It is thicker, if anything. Thick and deep and hard to shift; the sort of guilt that needs to be exorcised. It's one thing to lay into your woman when you're paralytic with the drink, another thing entirely to admit you do not love your child. Yet this is what Alan Gardiner's carrying.

Maganda's been ignoring it for years. Trying to pretend that she doesn't see the way Alan is around Bayani. But since the children started sickening, it's been too obvious to ignore. Her husband's not acting like the other fathers, circling anxiously round their children. Alan can't bear to be in the same room with Bayani. He has no affection for the boy. Maganda's always known this, but knowing's one thing, acknowledging you know it is another. She wishes she'd never dragged it out of him.

The problem first became apparent when Liezel arrived. The way Alan looked at his baby daughter was day-and-night different to his son. Maganda knew this in her guts but she'd never have dared to bring it up. A question like that could turn a man. The wrong answer would come down like a guillotine, splitting her family severely in two. She'd been in Ulster long enough to understand there were some things better left unsaid. It didn't matter if the silence destroyed you. Speaking up could well make it worse. Maganda couldn't risk angering Alan. She hadn't anywhere else to go.

When the children started coming down with this dreadful disease – kids she knew from Bayani's class – people began to ring the farm. Neighbours. Ministers. Other parents. They wished to offer their concern. They wanted to know how Ben was keeping. And what the Gardiners were going to do. They didn't want to speak to Maganda, though it was always her who answered the phone. Such serious matters required a word with the man of the house. They'd pause when they heard her lilting voice, then ask if her *other half* was in. They might as well have asked if there were any adults home. She knew they were thinking it anyway. Maganda didn't make a fuss. She was polite. She never gave them any cheek but at the back of her mind she couldn't help thinking, what's the point in speaking to Alan? He can't even look his son in the eye. It's me who's dealing with Bayani's nightmares, me who reassures him he's not going to die and me who can't sleep for worrying that he might. It's me who actually parents the boy.

She'd cover the receiver with her hand and whisper, 'It's for you, Alan,' beckoning him towards the phone. Her husband would always shake his head and raise his hand, the same gesture he used when declining another pour of tea. *No, he wasn't in the mood to talk.* Back Maganda would go to the waiting caller. 'I'm sorry, my husband isn't available,' she'd say in her politest voice. This was much too formal for Ballylack, where most folks, faced with the same situation, would've offered a perfunctory, *He's out, so he is,* and hung up sharply to end the chat. Maganda had learnt her telephone manners from the marble-voiced receptionists on English TV.

In the days preceding Ross's funeral, Maganda had answered almost two dozen of these calls. Eventually she'd cracked. She was beside herself worrying about Bayani and, if the fear wasn't bad enough, she was also toilet-training Liezel, up to her elbows in piss and shit. When Principal Taylor called and asked to speak to Mr Gardiner, something inside Maganda snapped. She ignored her husband's silent protestations, passed him the receiver and walked away. The call couldn't have lasted more than a minute. She'd barely made it to the kitchen and filled the kettle when Alan came thundering in.

'I told you I didn't want to talk to anybody.'

'They're only calling because they care.' She might have added, *At least they want to speak to you,* but it didn't seem the time or place to begin a conversation she'd been rehearsing for the last thirteen years.

'They don't care about Ben. They're just nosy.'

'Of course they care, Alan. They're as worried about the kids as we are.'

Maganda looked at her husband then, really looked at his big red face looming across the kitchen table. She noticed the way his hands curled over the back of the chair, knuckles boning through his skin. This was not the cut of a worried father. The eyes were bone dry and the voice was steady, the lips were drawn up in a manner which did not obviously scream concern. Though she had no appetite for a confrontation, Maganda couldn't ignore the obvious any more.

'You *are* worried about the children, aren't you?' she asked. 'You're scared for Bayani too?'

Alan lifted the salt cellar off the table and started fidgeting with it. He had a shifty look off him, as if he was formulating a lie.

'Are you trying to say I'm a bad father, just because I'm not bawling and greeting like the rest of them? I'm a man, so I am. I'm not good with emotions. Doesn't mean I don't care.'

'You're all lovey dovey when it comes to Liezel. You've all the hugs and kisses for her.'

'That's different,' he said.

'How's it different?'

'She's only wee.'

'Bayani was a baby once too. I don't remember you doting on him.'

'Lucy's a girl,' he said. Maganda noticed how he wouldn't meet her eye. 'Sure, don't they always say wee girls are closer to their das?'

In this moment Maganda knew. And also admitted she'd always known. But even then, with that face on him, she would've forced herself to believe, if only Alan had professed to love their son. He couldn't. He didn't. Or rather he did, but it took him far too long to get to it. A dry silence crept across the kitchen table, forcing a confession out of him. 'Of course I'm bloody worried about Ben.' It came out all wrong. Angry.

Defensive. On a tide of spit. So Maganda was forced to confront the horrible truth. Her husband did not love her son. He wasn't worried as she was worried; *going up a wall*, as they said round here. Her mind went flipping ten years back through every day they'd been together: her, Bayani and his dad. She tried to remember a reassuring moment – father and son captured in mutual affection – and couldn't, and finally admitted that Alan had never cared for the boy at all. She did not take the matter further. She simply gave her husband a disgusted look, so he would know she knew how heartless he was, then she rose from the table to put the dinner on.

It's been thirty-six hours since the scene at the kitchen table. Alan and Maganda have been avoiding each other ever since. It is surprisingly easy to do. Alan is often down the fields or pottering around the various outhouses. Maganda puts his meals on the table. She keeps his clothes clean and the house neat. What little affection was previously present has dissipated like morning frost. She cannot stand the sight of her husband. She suspects that he feels similarly. The guilt looks like it's wearing him down. She is glad to see him suffering. Alan deserves to feel utterly awful. *What sort of man doesn't love his own child?*

Maganda isn't surprised to find two RUC officers at her door. Hannah's mum's been on the phone to let her know they're on their way. She isn't shocked or even nervous. What Maganda feels is mortified. No woman should have to face this kind of thing alone. Every other family's navigating the nightmare together. Once again, she feels like the loneliest woman in Ballylack. She's about to launch into excuses when she notices the male officer staring at her in a way she's come to recognize. He glances down at his notebook, flips a page, then looks up, clearly confused.

'Umm,' he says, 'we're looking for the parents of Ben Gardiner.'

Maganda doesn't know why she lowers her head. Even after all these years, she has not yet learnt how to stare them down. She notices she's still wearing her slippers. Everything would be that bit more bearable if she was wearing proper shoes.

'I'm Bayani's mum,' she says.

'Ben?'

'His name's Bayani. They just call him Ben in school.'

'Right,' says the officer, the penny finally dropping. 'So you're Mrs Gardiner?'

Maganda nods.

'And Mr Gardiner?'

'Up in Belfast,' she says, and mumbles the line about tractor parts. She ushers the officers over the threshold, into her house, which smells like piss and toddler shit. She should offer them a cup of tea. Tea is always the answer here. The lady officer's already excused herself and gone off to track the kettle down. Maganda doesn't know what she's meant to do now. She's alone in the good room with the staring policeman. She tucks her slippered feet under the coffee table self-consciously.

'I'm here about the sickness, Mrs Gardiner.'

'Call me Megan,' Maganda says.

It is better if he uses her made-up name. By better, Maganda means easier. By easier, she means easier for him. She knows a man like this with that thick, buttery accent will never get her real name right. She's used to this and other humiliations. She's learnt how to turn these moments around so no one feels awkward in her presence, no matter what foul nonsense they spout. Maganda's never been naive. She'd known exactly what she was getting into, taking up with a middle-aged bachelor, moving to a godforsaken farm. She's never expected to be anything but a rank outsider in a place like Ballylack.

She'd never expected, but she had let herself hope. And when the children started coming – Bayani first, then the two unnamed ones who'd slipped out early and, finally, wee Liezel – something had shifted deep inside. She'd no longer felt like a sticking point every time she ventured into the village. People still stared. They hadn't even been subtle about it. There was nobody foreign in Ballylack. Nobody but Maganda and the Leungs, who ran the Chinese takeaway. Because of this crucial service they were more accepted than she'd ever be. Maganda had grown accustomed to the locals' curiosity. For years now, they'd been staring at her and pretending they weren't. Every time she went into Thompson's for a pint of milk, she'd hear the dry whisper of their judgement come shushing out behind her. She'd tell herself it was unintentional. Ignorance rather than cruelty.

They called her Megan, like she was a child. All the other village wives got *Mrs This* or *Mrs That*. Maganda got a bastardized version of her Christian name. She could have said something, but she didn't. She always wanted to avoid a scene. She hadn't the gall to raise her strange, sing-song voice and say, *It's Mrs Gardiner, to you.* The truth was, Maganda had never felt like Mrs Gardiner. Here, in this lonely, raining place, she didn't feel like anybody at all. Sometimes, in the morning, when Alan was out seeing to the cows, she'd stand in front of the wardrobe mirror and try to see Megan Gardiner peering back at her. In these moments she'd feel like a Russian doll, all her other various selves tucked neatly away and forgotten. She'd reserve her largest sadness for the smallest and most deeply buried doll: the girl Maganda, with her dirty feet and waist-length hair. She'd recall the way she'd once read paperback novels on the front porch while her dad slept off his latest hangover. How she'd dreamt of the day she would leave Marikina. *More fool her*, she'd actually believed that this was a romantic thing to be wishing for.

Having Bayani had helped a bit. Maganda took the baby everywhere and used him as a kind of shield. There'd been strength in numbers. She was never as lonely when he toddled beside her, his small, sticky fingers curled around her own. The locals had seen her differently with a baby. They'd stopped to ask if he was teething yet; if she was getting any sleep. They'd leant into the buggy and wondered, audibly, if he took after her or his da. This had always made Maganda smile, for there was hardly anything of Alan in Bayani. He looked like another fella's child. Still, babies were babies, no matter what colour, and the people of Ballylack had a terrible fondness for weans. Though they couldn't get their tongues round his name, no matter how many times Maganda had sounded it out for them – *Bi-Ann-Ee* – wincing as they elongated the vowels and murdered the sweet lilt of it, they'd still chuffed the child's cheeks and given him *a penny for to buy sweets*. They'd stop her in the street to ask if *you and wee Ben* wanted to come to Mums and Tots.

For this and other kindnesses Maganda had been grateful at the time. The advent of Bayani was like a door opening into rooms she'd previously found shut. At first, she'd felt seen, then quickly realized the other women saw her only as Ben's mother. Without a child, without a husband, a woman like her could not exist in a place like Ballylack. Maganda has come to terms with this strange existence. At the end of the day, it was better to be someone's mother or somebody's wife than absolutely nothing at all.

When, at fourteen months, Bayani had toddled up behind her at the sink, wrapped his skinny arms around her thighs and called her *Mum*, Maganda had wept for almost an hour. *Mum* would be her name now. She knew she could wear it easily. She'd be *Mum* for the rest of her days. She'd made herself a cup of the milky tea she'd grown used to drinking and taken her small son on her knee, feeling the warm heft of him against her chest. She'd bounced him and dandled him and, with kisses and tickles, coerced a further four *Mum*s out of the boy. Quietly and without any kind of ceremony, Maganda had let all her other selves go.

And it's this Maganda who accepts the policewoman's mug of

greasy tea, who offers the strangers her home-made shortbread, the recipe lifted from the Dairy Council cookbook which has been her Bible since she became an Ulster farmwife. She listens intently to what they say. When the man says this is just a routine call, that they're not that worried so she shouldn't be either, she edges forward on the sofa until she's almost bent double. He tells her they're running tests on the bodies – *purposefully avoiding the word* autopsy, *for that kind of thing freaks women out* – but they'll probably not find anything. 'It'll just be the flu,' adds the lady officer, 'wait till you see, love. Those two poor children probably had underlying issues of some sort.' Maganda nods and begins to cry. She accepts a wad of tissues from the lady officer and dabs ineffectively at her eyes.

The man leans forward in his seat to touch her gently on the shoulder. 'And your son,' he says, glancing down to consult his notebook. He considers attempting a pronunciation and quickly dismisses the idea as daft. 'Ben . . . is he feeling OK? Any symptoms? Anything at all?'

'My Bayani is fine,' Maganda mumbles through her sniffles. 'He is out running. He loves to run. Sorry,' she says and, as she says it, wonders if she's apologizing for her tears or her perfectly healthy son.

'Well, that's good to hear, Mrs Gardiner. I wasn't expecting anything else. Like I said, we're quite confident this is just an unfortunate coincidence. The doctor's keeping an eye on the Twins. He thinks they just have a dose of summer flu.'

'And he's the expert,' adds the policewoman, smiling. 'He knows better than any of us.

'We should have the results back from Ross's and Kathleen's tests tomorrow. We're pretty certain their deaths weren't linked. It's so sad, but these things happen sometimes. Kids can have hidden conditions that don't get picked up.

'Please don't be worrying yourself, Mrs Gardiner. Keep a wee eye on that boy of yours. But if he's out running around the fields, it sounds like there's not much wrong with him.'

Maganda thanks them for their visit. She apologizes again for the state of the house. 'I'm potty-training my daughter,' she says. The lady police officer nods as if she understands. She's probably just trained to seem sympathetic. Maganda notes she doesn't have a wedding ring on.

As they leave, the sergeant calls over his shoulder, 'Thanks for the shortbread, Mrs Gardiner, and if you've any concerns at all, just pick up the phone and give us a shout.'

He smiles. She smiles. Everyone's smiling. There's nothing to worry about. Nothing at all.

Once they're gone, Maganda collapses on to the good-room sofa. She sits there, sobbing for half an hour, only pulling herself together when Bayani appears looking for his lunch. Maganda Gardiner's no different from the other mothers, weeping in living rooms across Ballylack. All the versions of herself have been reduced down to a single name. For this season, and perhaps for ever, she is absolutely, only, Mum. Mother to a precious boy. All of her, tied up in him. She glances over at the empty armchair where Alan sits at night, watching TV. *He might be slightly more absent this morning, but really, honestly, when has her husband ever been present?*

Maganda understands that from here on in, she'll have to be a father too.

After the Funeral

AFTER THE AUTOPSY Kathleen is brought to Gracey's Funeral Parlour. She'll spend the night here, before the funeral. Her grandparents can't bear the thought of her body in the house. Old Mr Gracey's looking after arrangements himself. He insists on it when there's children involved. Mr Gracey's been in the business for forty-six years. He knows when to speak and when to refrain; when to slip out of a sorrow-filled room, leaving the family to themselves. He doesn't enjoy children's funerals. *What decent undertaker does?* But he knows his presence is a reassurance. It's a comfort to find Harrison Gracey standing at the end of a hospital bed, or on your front step, hat in hand; to hear him say, with carefully lowered eyes, *Don't worry, I'll look after everything now.*

Mr Gracey remembers the child's mother. He'd laid her out too. By the time she got to him there was little left to put in the coffin: a heel and an ankle, an ear, some bones, the knuckle of a finger with the wedding band still attached. You'd have been hard-pressed to know if the bits belonged to a man or a woman. Mr Gracey knew, and handled each part with reverence. He's spent his whole working life in this place. He's seen other bodies blown to pieces; people shot, shredded and pounded to meat. He isn't squeamish. It's his job to maintain a stiff upper lip.

Children are different. He calls them *fallen sparrows,* for Mr Gracey's a man of the Word. He remembers every child by name.

He goes heavy on Kathleen's make-up. There's an odd, mottled quality to her skin and hundreds of tiny inflamed hives, as if she's been stung by a swarm of bees. He runs his finger lightly across her cheek. Even in death, a child's skin should be smooth. Kathleen's feels like woodchip wallpaper: a mix of scars and hard little pustules where the lumps have risen and failed to burst. He pins her last school photo up so he can get her face and hair right. She's not a pretty girl. There's always been a rodenty look off her. He could improve upon it. He doesn't. It's important that the body looks like itself. He fairly slathers the foundation on, though. And dusts her face in rosy blusher. Beneath the hives she's unnaturally pale.

They're ruling out natural causes now. The lad from the morgue who delivered the body said they'd found chemicals in her blood. They've been sent up to the lab in Belfast to compare with samples from the McCormick boy. 'Be careful, Mr G,' he'd said. 'They don't know what they're dealing with yet. It could be infectious. To be on the safe side, double glove.' Mr Gracey's the first person in Ballylack to know about the chemicals. He doesn't tell anyone. Not even his son. Mr Gracey's the soul of discretion. You have to be when you work with the dead. He takes a moment to pray over Kathleen's body. He always prays before he begins. This morning his prayers are a little more urgent. *God bless her folks and comfort them. Keep the rest of them wee ones out of here.*

When Kathleen's grandparents arrive to view the body, Mr Gracey doesn't say anything. He only speaks when he's spoken to. He shepherds the grandparents up to the coffin. *Softly, gently, with all due respect.* He notes the way they draw back sharply when they see what he's done.

'She's a funny colour,' says the granda. 'Is it fake tan you have on her?'

'I'm sorry,' says Mr Gracey. 'She was so pale. I was trying to put some life back into her cheeks.'

The grandmother reaches for his hand. 'She looks lovely, Harrison. You've done a beautiful job. Sure, I knew you would.'

Mr Gracey squeezes her hand when he thanks her. He tells the two of them to take as long as they need. All of a sudden, he feels awful tired. He might have a wee lie down in the back office. Children's funerals take it out of him.

The journalists have descended on Ballylack. They're only local hacks: freelancers jobbing for the *Telegraph* and junior anchors for the local news. That fella's here from Radio Ulster, the one with the shrill, distinctive voice. Two children dead in as many weeks is not enough to pique the interest of the Mainland press. It isn't nearly tragic enough. The Troubles have raised the benchmark for what's considered newsworthy. When six or seven lives can be lost in a bomb-blast second, it takes something truly horrendous to qualify as real tragedy. Nor can the children be entirely dismissed. A dead child's always a horrific thing. And if the rumours are to be believed, there's two more sickening and mysterious chemicals in the mix. *Now, that has the bones of a bigger deal.*

For the moment the journalists are watching and waiting, quietly speculating on what will happen next. They've been sent down from Belfast with strict instructions: dig around, use discernment, see if there's an actual story here. They go door to door like Jehovah's Witnesses, asking if anyone knew Kathleen or Ross. They make polite enquiries about the Twins. They're careful to pitch themselves concerned. They stand on strangers' doorsteps, eyes lowered demurely, notebooks in hand. They try to look like they actually care. Some of them do. They have kids of their own. They picture their children in bed at home, content and sleeping. For the briefest, unbearable moment, they let themselves imagine what the Ballylack parents are going through.

Others don't care. Oh, they say they do. They'll say anything to get their story. They'll invent their own weans for the empathy angle: *God bless wee Lyndsey and Donal, back at home.* They can feign concern like the best of them. They know to hold their tape recorders as if they are an afterthought. The police go lightly on the journalists. There's no need for heavy-handedness. Yet. They ask them to respect the mourners, to keep their distance at the church and cemetery. The older contingent set a precedent. They huddle in the car park, far away from Kathleen's grave. The younger lot, though keen for content and a nice clear photo, take their lead and hang back too. This isn't the Mainland. Journalists still have morals here.

They bury Kathleen in her school uniform. A neighbour goes into town to buy new shoes. Kathleen's grandmother can't face the shops, but she doesn't want her granddaughter buried in worn-out, end-of-term shoes. Some of her classmates come to the funeral. Despite the heat, they wear their uniforms too. It's intended as an act of solidarity. It only serves to mark them out. The six who've made it sit huddled up against their parents. They look like windblown ducklings. Everybody stares at them, wondering if their sickness has started yet. They stick close to the adults and keep their heads down. They don't know how to talk to each other here. They couldn't say why exactly, but the feeling falls somewhere between embarrassment and fear.

Hannah's no stranger to funerals. There's a lot of old people in their church. Because a funeral's a service, in a church, Mum makes her put a beret on. It looks rare with her school uniform. She's the only child wearing a hat. Everybody stares and whispers. *That wee girl's in Kathleen's class. You wouldn't know there was anything wrong to look at her.* Hannah thinks they're talking about her hat. She blushes walking into church, and blushes again as she leaves. She can almost hear Kathleen taking the piss. *Feel wick for you, Hannah Adger. It looks like something's died on your head.* She spends most of the service trying to control her own heat. Mum cries and keeps one arm hooked round Hannah's shoulder, like she's afraid she might up and leave. Hannah would love to, but there's a parent sandwiched on either side and nowhere to go if she did escape.

The Twins' dad has made it out. He looks like he hasn't slept in days. He's managed to get himself into a suit, though his wife clearly hasn't ironed it. Before the service begins, Hannah's dad leans over to ask how the Twins are doing.

'Not great,' says Cliff. 'But they're fighters. 'Specially Lizzy. Stubborn wouldn't be in it.'

He tries to smile and doesn't quite manage it.

'We're praying,' says Dad. 'Just let us know if there's anything you need. Anything at all.'

He grabs a handful of the other man's shoulder and squeezes it firmly. This is a thing men do when they're too upset to speak. The men in church are always shoulder-grabbing at funerals, and sometimes weddings too. Women don't do the shoulder thing. They talk instead. As soon as Dad touches him, Cliff begins to cry. He slides forward in the pew and makes a kind of wheezy noise. He shakes. Dad continues to hold on to him. Hannah wishes he'd let go. He looks like he's about to cry too. Men should be able to control themselves.

By the end of the service, a lot of folks are in a similar state. Afterwards, everyone lines up to offer their condolences to the family. Kathleen's father is over from Scotland. He has a girlfriend with him and a baby who gurns through the eulogy. There's more sympathy for the grandparents than the father. The loss belongs chiefly to them. As people file past repeating how sorry – how very, truly sorry – they are, the handshakes grow limper, the sentiments fainter. Every parent's preoccupied with the same bleak thought. *Dear God, don't let my kid be next.* Some of them have the sense to keep this thought to themselves. They carry it all the way home to their own kitchen tables. Then howl. Others – mostly mothers – cannot keep their panic in. They leak all over the vestibule. Outside, on the church steps, they hug furiously, clawing at each other for support. They sit sobbing in their cars while the car park empties around them. Out of respect they keep their windows up. There's no noise off them. No sound at all. Just the deeply unsettling image of pale, sad faces contorted behind glass. Like something you'd see on display at the Ulster Museum or in a tank up at Belview.

Mum sticks close to Hannah. Hannah sticks close to Dad. A rake of ones from her class are in the car park, standing around looking glum. Hannah spots William, Caroline, Amy, Ben and Matty, who's the only one not wearing school uniform. There's nothing new in this. Half the time Matty turns up for school in tracksuit bottoms because his mum's not done any laundry. Mum asks if she wants to go over and say hello. Dad says, 'Best not to,' and whispers over Hannah's head, 'We don't know how this thing's spread yet. I don't want her mixing with other children.' Hannah suspects this has very little to do with the sickness. Dad's always preferred her hanging out with nice churchy kids. The kind who won't lead her astray. She's to be a stranger and alien, set apart from the things of this world. Dad's drummed it into her so many times Hannah understands that she doesn't belong with the ones in her class.

Some days it's a privilege to be such a good witness. Other days it totally sucks. She thinks again of Miss McKeown's photo and how happy everyone looked, grouped around the Raggedy Tree. None of them were missing her. No one had even bothered to ask why she couldn't join in. Everybody already knew that she wasn't normal. *Hannah Adger's a weirdo. A stick in the mud. Her daddy won't let her do anything fun.* She glances across the car park again. She raises a hand and waves tentatively. Matty waves back. Matty's kind. Ben points to his head, then points to hers.

He mouths the words *Cool hat, Hannah*, rolling his eyes so she can tell he's taking the piss. Everyone laughs, even Matty. Hannah feels like she's going to cry. She slips a hand into Mum's pocket, looking for a clean tissue. Mum's brought a whole packet with her. She's been weepy since they left the house.

A few of the dads are gurning too. Some aren't just sad, they're also angry. Hannah can see the rage in the sharp, nervous way they carry themselves down the church steps, as if their shoes are full of stones. They congregate round the wayside pulpit. They want to know why this has happened, specifically why it's happening here, to their children. *Where will it end? How can they make it stop?* One father's spotted a rash on his daughter. Another has a son who's sniffling. They've heard a rumour that it starts with a rash. They've heard it starts with a runny nose. Or an upset tummy. Or a cough. Somebody's heard the McCormick boy swole up like a tinged cow before he died. They've heard too many conflicting reports. They're imagining all sorts when they look at their weans. Basically, they are terrified. They want someone or something to blame. Dad waits for a pause. Then he speaks. It would be remiss of him not to say something. *Giving a word in season* is what he calls it. Hannah wishes he wouldn't bother. She's embarrassed enough as it is.

'I know it's hard to accept,' he says, sliding into his church speaking voice. 'We might not have any answers this side of eternity. We have to trust that the Lord knows best.'

The Twins' dad lets out an enormous, body-shuddering sob. Ross's dad looks like he's going to deck Dad. Mum gives him a look which Hannah recognizes instantly. More often than not, she's the recipient. It means *Neither the time nor the place.* For once Dad seems to take the hint. No further Bible verses are forthcoming. For a moment nothing's said. The parents stand around in a loose huddle, silent, save for the occasional damp sniff and the gravelly crunch of a foot not accustomed to heels readjusting itself.

Ross's dad is first to break the silence. 'I don't want answers from your god, John. I don't believe he's even up there. If he is, tell me this, what sort of a bastard lets children die?'

Hannah is shocked. She's never heard a grown-up talk like this. She knows there are unbelievers out there. They live in housing estates and foreign countries and don't think twice about taking the Lord's name in vain. Sometimes, in church, they pray for them; only ever in the vaguest terms. Her Aunty Rachel's an unbeliever. Every morning they ask the Lord Jesus to get her saved. They're heartbroken for her and her backslidden husband, who she isn't really married to. Still, there's a limit to their concern. They never invite Aunty Rachel round to their house or go over to Antrim to visit her.

Hannah's never heard anyone this angry with God before. If this was the Bible, Mr McCormick would be struck down immediately. She looks round the parents, expecting someone – *her dad, for sure* – to make him apologize. No one does. They're hugging him and patting him gently on the back. They're encouraging him to keep talking. Some of them are even nodding along.

'Look,' continues Ross's dad, 'I'm not interested in the big questions right now. There's nothing anyone can say or do to bring my wee fella back. But you lot still have your kids. If we can get to the bottom of what's going on, maybe we can stop anyone else from going through what we're going through.'

A meeting is suggested. Sooner rather than later, for if anything happens to the Twins, they have an epidemic on their hands. The vicar offers the Minor Hall. He says he'll get the church ladies to make tea. Principal Taylor is co-opted into the conversation, and Dr Simpson. Someone asks if they should approach the RUC. It wouldn't hurt to keep them involved.

They're good for getting things sorted. Them and the boys in the balaclavas, but nobody wants to ask for their help. The last thing they need is the paramilitaries wading in. Or the politicians. Perish the thought. All talk. No action from that lot.

'A meeting sounds like a sensible idea. When should we have it?' asks Hannah's dad.

'Tonight,' says Ross's dad. 'Youse don't have any time to waste.'

The Meeting

L ESS THAN FIVE hours later, the grown-ups are back at the Church of Ireland. Principal Taylor sits centre stage, chairing proceedings. The vicar and a specialist from the hospital sit to his right. On his left is the local DUP councillor. He's wangled his way on to the panel, as is the way with the DUP. Next to him is a stranger, recommended by the RUC. Apparently, he's an expert in this kind of thing. He'd helped maintain order after the IRA took out a power plant on the border and, once again, during the floods. 'Obviously, the situation in Ballylack is very different,' says Principal Taylor, 'but Seán here is a safe pair of hands. He knows how to keep people calm in a crisis. You'd be well advised to listen to him.'

The stranger introduces himself. He says his name is Seán Donnelly. He's a crisis-management officer. A freelancer, he's worked for everyone from the Gardaí to the UN. He's only just back from a stint in Africa. His face is still leathery from the sun. Nobody needs told that Seán's from the South. That accent's speaking for itself. They wouldn't usually trust a Free Stater, but the families are desperate. They'll accept whatever help's offered, even if it speaks with a thick Ballymun accent. Once he's finished talking, there's a brief pause while they weigh him up. 'Folks,' Seán says, speaking confidently into the silence, 'I'm a dad myself. I can't begin to imagine what you're all going through. I'll do everything I can to help.' The room opens up a little. The tension lifts. A warm murmur of acceptance runs down the seated rows. Seán Donnelly senses it. Getting the locals on board is half the battle. He takes a deep breath and begins to explain what'll happen next.

He starts by bringing the locals up to speed. There have been two deaths and two further cases of children developing similar symptoms. He's not at liberty to name these children, though everyone present knows he's talking about the Twins. He is, however, able to tell them that all four children are from the same school class and that the same chemical substance has been found in their blood. A murmur of concern runs round the room and before Seán can say anything further about the steps they're taking to identify the source people begin shouting out questions. *Could it be something in the water at the school? Is it true the wee McClintock lad lost his sight before he died? Is it catching, whatever it is? They've heard it's catching. Should they be keeping their weans inside?*

Seán lets them talk for a couple of minutes. It's important to let people voice their anxiety. When the questions start petering out, he raises a single silencing hand. 'I understand you're all anxious, folks, but let's not panic before we have all the facts.' His eyes pan slowly across the room. They're all strangers to him. He wonders which faces are the significant ones. Who he's going to spend most time with.

The Minor Hall is absolutely bunged. Some folks have to stand at the back. Every child in Hannah's class is represented. Other parents – unsure whether their kids are at risk – have turned up too. It's the same crowd as earlier, though they've swapped their funeral blacks for tracksuit bottoms and trainers; whatever's comfortable and reasonably clean. During times like this, nobody's bothered about what they look like, nobody cleans or does laundry. They don't really think about eating either. Mr Leung's making a killing in the takeaway. Some families have been in for their third Chinese of the week. *I just can't face cooking at the minute*, they say. Mr Leung understands. He nods and gives them free prawn crackers. He wouldn't be here himself – sweating over the industrial-sized hob – if he didn't have to be.

Mrs Leung doesn't understand. She's never quite understood the way it is in Ballylack. 'Lazy bitch,' she mutters when Caroline's mum comes in to order her third *mixed meal for four* of the week, 'that lady need to cook good food for her girl: vegetable and soup to stop sickness.' She's refused to attend the meeting. There's nothing wrong with her Amy. Even if there was, she wouldn't trust the doctors to help. In this country people only get sicker when they go into hospital. Mrs Leung treats her girls' illnesses the old-fashioned way, with remedies learnt from her grandmother. And not a bit of harm it's done them. They're strong girls, never ill and quick at school. They're not flabby like the local children, nor pasty about the face. Mrs Leung's sure the local diet is responsible for the unpleasant look of the children. *Boiled potatoes. Mashed potatoes. Chips. Bloody potatoes with everything.* She tells Mr Leung she's not going to the meeting; somebody has to stay home and keep the shop open. Really, she just wants to avoid the other parents: the silly women her husband's always telling her to make an effort with.

All the families are represented. All the parents understand the seriousness of the occasion. They'll do whatever Seán Donnelly tells them to do; anything to protect their kids. When he announces that medical tests will begin in the morning, they all want their child to be first through the doors. Everyone except the Andersons. *Bloody hippies. The Andersons are a law unto themselves.* Meadow makes a point of standing up to say she doesn't trust modern medicine. She won't be subjecting Lief, or any of her other children, to these *so-called tests.*

'I don't want my babies pumped full of drugs,' she says. 'Rob and I only ever use natural remedies. We won't let you traumatize our children, poking and prodding them with needles because everyone's hysterical right now.'

The other parents collectively roll their eyes. They're well used to the Andersons objecting to everything. Somebody at the back of the hall shouts out, 'Wise up, Meadow!' Somebody else calls her a daft cow. Hearing this, Rob Anderson's face turns tomato red. He tugs at the sleeve of his wife's handknit jumper until she sits back down.

'We'll bring Lief in with the rest of them,' he mumbles, 'and the wee ones as well.'

For a minute, the rest of the parents see past his grimy dreadlocks, the beard and all those metal studs and hoops, to the wee lad who once kicked football in McAuley's back field. He might have turned a bit weird lately, but Rob Anderson's still a Ballylack boy at heart: sensible, level-headed, ready to take his place with the other villagers. He is just as concerned as the rest of them.

Everyone's taken the testing on board. When they hear Seán mention the word *antidote*, it feels like they've been tossed a life ring. They ask questions he can't answer. *How long will it take to develop a cure? Will there be any side effects?* Seán knows how to deal with their desperation. The trick to keeping people calm is to place the power back in their hands. 'I'll be honest with you, folks,' he says. 'I don't have any answers right now. But I do know the most important thing is to remain calm, keep your children calm and get them in for testing straight away. We need the whole community to pull together on this.'

The Debrief

HANNAH'S STAYING AT Granny and Granda's. The meeting's likely to run late so her parents have allowed her to sleep over. Mum's left a list of instructions for Granny. *Don't let her eat rubbish. No TV after seven. Bed by half eight.*

She might as well talk to the wall. Granny's already got plans for the evening. She's heading over to Myrtle Graham's. Myrtle's Church of Ireland but Granny hasn't let that get between them. They've been pals for almost seventy years, neither of them migrating more than a street or two from the houses they were born into. Once a week, they get together to drink tea and watch *Wish You Were Here* with Judith Chalmers. They're very taken with Judith Chalmers. She has a lovely way with her. Like an English Gloria Hunniford. They've been trying to copy her hairstyle for years, wasting vast amounts of hair lacquer in the process and never quite nailing the look. By the time they've watched *Wish You Were Here*, had a second cuppa and a good long chat about where they'd go if there was money for a run to the Continent, it'll be ten o'clock and Hannah will be fast asleep.

Granny doesn't tell Hannah's mum this. She knows her daughter-in-law thinks Granda Pete's a bad influence, so she just says, 'Absolutely, Sandra. She'll be in bed by eight and I'll make sure she does her prayers.' Granny's no stranger to the wee white lie. She wouldn't call it lying, though. It's just keeping everybody sweet.

Staying at Granda and Granny's is a rare treat. Mum and Dad don't go out that often. When they do, it's usually something at church which means they're back home at a decent hour. At Granny's Hannah gets a whole double bed to herself. It is longer than her both ways. She always has a Tunnock's teacake for supper and hot chocolate in her special Beatrix Potter mug. Though it makes Granny grumpy, Granda Pete lets her stay up late. They play Connect 4 and Scrabble. Granda always lets Hannah win. Tonight, when he comes tramping upstairs to read her bedtime story, he flips dismissively through the books Mum's packed. *Enid Blyton, boring! Narnia, boring! Anne of Green Gables, unbelievably boring! What about a decent story for a change?* He keeps a stack of Roald Dahls for Hannah. Mum and Dad say these books are vulgar. Hannah thinks they're hilarious. When Granda Pete reads *The BFG* he puts on a rumbly giant voice, like he's speaking through a mouthful of custard. It's absolutely hilarious, especially the bit where the BFG can't stop farting. They both make farting noises on the back of their hands.

When it's sleeping time, Granda tucks the duvet round her and says, 'There you go, Han, all tucked in like a sausage roll. Sleep tight.'

Hannah's not quite ready for sleeping.

'Granda,' she says, grabbing his arm. 'Can I ask you something?'

''Course you can, Pet. You can ask me anything.'

'What happens when you die?'

Granda Pete doesn't answer immediately. He crosses his arms and chews his lip. He makes this same gesture when he's stuck on a hard crossword clue. Eventually he says, 'Do you want me to be honest with you, Hannah? I don't want to scare you or tell you something different from your mum and dad.'

'They say you go to Heaven when you die. At least I will, cos I'm saved. People who aren't Christians go to Hell.'

'They may well be right, Hannah. I used to think that too. There's no real way of knowing for sure, though. It's not like anybody's died and come back to tell us . . .'

'Except Jesus.'

'You've got me there. I forgot about the big man himself. Listen, I'll be honest with you, sweetheart. I don't really know what happens when you die.'

'But what do you *think* happens, Granda?'

'Well, I think, maybe, we all go back to where we came from. That's my best take on it.'

Hannah thinks about this for a while. It has a ring of sense to it. She snuggles into her granda's side. 'Thank you,' she says.

'What for?'

'For being honest with me.'

'I'll always be honest with you, Hannah. Will you promise me you'll always be honest with me? If you're worried about anything, anything at all, you can tell me.'

He gives Hannah a long sideways look, as if he's waiting for her to tell him something. She's said enough for one night. It's helped talking to Granda. The fear's still there, and the muddle in her head. It just doesn't feel as tight as before. She knows she'll be able to get to sleep.

'I'm tired,' she says.

Granda kisses her on the forehead, leaning in so she gets a good whiff of his smoky smell.

'You're some pup, Hannah Adger. The best I know. Don't be telling your grandma I said that. She'll only get jealous.'

He slips out of the room, turning the light out as he leaves.

'Wait,' cries Hannah. 'You forgot to do my prayers.'

'So I did,' says Granda Pete, and goes on downstairs.

*

Hannah wakes in the middle of the night. She's not sure what has woken her. She's neither hungry nor thirsty. She doesn't feel sick. She lies very still with her eyes tightly shut. She's nervous these days, never knowing when some dead classmate is going to appear. She opens one eye, then the other, and scans the room slowly. Granny's spare room is less familiar than her own bedroom. When she's sure she's all alone, she sits up and swings her legs out of bed. The bedroom's dark, but there's a thin slice of pale light beneath the door. She can hear talking. They're all still up downstairs.

Hannah sits on the bed's edge, listening to the mumble of voices drifting up from the living room. She picks out Dad, then Granda, Granny and, finally, Mum, whose voice is so gentle it's often hard to hear in a crowd. She feels far away from them and separate, though there's only three foot between her feet and their heads, below. She'll go downstairs and join in. She'll claim to have a headache. Since the sickness started, they've been dancing attention, quick to respond to every wee twinge. They'll not say anything about her being out of bed, though it must be close to midnight now and it isn't even a weekend night.

Hannah puts on her dressing gown. She goes out on to the landing and pauses for a second at the top of the stairs. Something about the tone of Dad's voice – the sharpness, the loudness, the way it's pitched directly at Granda Pete – tells her this conversation isn't meant for wee girls. Hannah knows all about private conversations. Sometimes Pastor Bill and the elders come round to talk about *discipleship issues.* After Mum brings in their tea, she closes the living-room door behind her and ushers Hannah upstairs or out to play. She'll take herself into the kitchen and put one of her cassettes on the tape player so she can't hear what the men are talking about. *It's not like they're keeping secrets from us,* she's explained. *They're discussing pastoral issues in the church. We've no business knowing other people's concerns. We trust the men to sort things out.* Hannah's intrigued, but she's not bold enough to listen at the window or place a tumbler against the floor, pressing her ear against the cold glass like Nancy Drew in the detective books she sometimes reads in the library. Hannah's scared of what Dad would say if he caught her prying. She's way more scared of God. You can't get anything by him, especially sin. God sees everything you do.

Tonight feels different. Hannah's not sure if this is a private conversation. The grown-ups haven't bothered to close the door. She can hear her own name being spoken. First by Dad, then Granda, who says it like a sort of punch, then Mum, who is crying, *Hannah. Hannah. Poor wee Hannah*, like a record that's got stuck. She positions herself halfway down the stairs; close enough to hear everything, far enough up to be out of view if one of them happens to wander out.

Dad's filling his parents in on the evening's meeting. Granda Pete is full of questions.

'So, they've brought this fella up from the South to make sure we all stay calm?' he asks.

'That's about the gist of it,' Dad replies. 'He seems nice enough, though he kicks with the other foot.'

'Competent?'

'Aye, I'd say so. He's already managed to get us more information than we've had all week.'

'And tell me again, what does he think it is?'

'I wrote it down, Dad. Here, you can read it for yourself. Your man Seán Donnelly says they've found traces in all four weans of something called an organophosphate. It's the term for a group of chemicals. Apparently, they come in all sorts of forms.'

'And why in the name of God has it taken them a week to work this out?'

'Language, Peter,' Granny interjects.

Dad ignores her and motors on. 'Well, it seems the symptoms

are hard to pin down. If you're exposed to this stuff, it can look a lot like the flu at the start. And it progresses differently depending how much you've been around it and what particular version of the chemical it is.'

'Where on earth did the weans come into contact with something like that?'

'That's the strange thing. They haven't a clue. Obviously, they'll be looking at the school and the playground and other places children hang out. Your man says the obvious place would be a farm.'

The room falls silent for a moment. Hannah wonders if they're finished talking for the night. Then Granny speaks up and they're off again. There's a crack in her voice. Hannah can tell she's been crying and any second now will start again.

'I don't understand, John,' she says. 'If they know what it is now, why can't they do something about it? Surely there must be a treatment of some kind.'

'They're trying, Mum. They're doing their best. And Seán did say that some folks are able to fight off this kind of poison by themselves. Everybody's wired differently. Some weans are just naturally stronger than other ones.'

Mum takes over from Dad. Hannah can picture her on the sofa, curling an arm around Granny's shoulder, trying to reassure the older woman when she's going up the walls herself.

'The thing is,' says Mum, 'this is some strange version of the chemical. The doctors haven't come across it before. They need to run more tests before they can come up with an antidote. They're working round the clock to find one. They're doing everything they can.'

'What can we do?' asks Granda. 'I can't just sit here doing nothing while my Hannah gets sick and dies.'

'We can pray that God will guide the doctors,' says Dad. 'We can fast and pray. That's not nothing, Dad.'

There's a silence then. A heavy silence. Hannah pictures her dad shaking his head, Mum sobbing softly, Granny reaching for the box of Kleenex, helping herself before she hands it to Mum.

'What about Hannah?' Granda asks.

'They don't know,' says Dad. 'They just don't know. They're going to test all the children to see if the chemical's in their system. They've suggested we keep them isolated as far as we can. It's very unlikely this thing's contagious. But they're not ruling out anything yet.'

'Shit,' says Granda, and Hannah knows things are bad, because Dad doesn't even bother telling him off.

Mum's full-on weeping now. Hannah can hear her gulping the air in between sobs. Granny says she'll put the kettle on.

Dad says, 'Hold on, Mum. The first thing we need to do is bring this before the Lord in prayer.'

Five seconds later, Granda comes storming out into the hall. He heads off in the direction of the back door, where Hannah suspects he keeps his cigarettes tucked down the side of Granny's planters. The living-room door slams shut behind him. Now there are three separate groups in different corners of the house. This isn't good. They've always been strongest together; the five of them, like a kind of team.

Hannah pulls her knees to her chin. She makes a tent of her nightie and sits on the middle stair, rocking gently. She should be sad. She should be scared. If what Dad's said is right, then she might be dying. It just doesn't feel real. No, it's real enough. Hannah believes all the things she's heard. But they feel like they're happening to somebody else. She's sitting on the very edge of herself, watching the situation unfold. It's the same half-interested way she watches things happen to folks on TV.

Bearing Witness

THE TWINS DIE on Thursday morning. Mim goes first. Lizzy holds on for a few minutes longer. First to arrive and last to leave; Lizzy's always been the dominant one. She trumps her sister at both ends.

The Ballylack gossip circuit couldn't give a toss about accuracy. By the time the phone rings in Hannah's house – less than half an hour after the Twins have been trolleyed across to the hospital morgue – the facts have already morphed into myth. Mrs Nugent takes great pleasure in telling Mum that Miriam and Elizabeth died together, on the stroke of nine, holding hands in a hospital bed. Though Hannah's mum has no interest in such details, Mrs Nugent's also keen to point out that they were dressed in matching pyjamas. 'You'll not believe me when I tell you,' she continues, 'but just before they passed, the one looked straight at the other and gave a wee nod, as if to say, *Right now, it's time we were heading.* Then, they both smiled, and closed their eyes. Sure, you'd hardly have known they were dead. They went that quietly at the end.'

Mum resists the urge to ask exactly how Mrs Nugent knows this. It's clearly conjecture on the old woman's part. She often has to pray for extra patience when dealing with women of her ilk. She includes her mother-in-law in these prayers. Mum's learnt to take Meta Nugent with a pinch of salt. Most people in Ballylack are well aware of what she's like. The same woman once claimed she'd been for a fortnight in the Algarve when anybody with an eye in their head could see she'd been home the whole time, watching TV with the curtains drawn. When it was time to affect a return, she'd clarried herself in fake tan and come out claiming to have had a blast. *Why did she do it?* Dear only knows. Loneliness. Embarrassment. A misplaced attempt to keep up with the neighbours. Nobody asked her. It wasn't the sort of thing you could ask about.

Women like Meta Nugent don't even realize they're telling lies. They begin with the odd exaggeration – something to take the dull edge off their dreary existence – then very quickly lose the run of themselves, adding, embellishing and distorting until there isn't a word of truth in what they've said. There'd be no point calling Mrs Nugent out, no point quoting Bible verses about letting your *yes* be *yes* and your *no* an equally definite *no*. Meta Nugent actually believes her own claptrap.

Mum says, 'Thank you for letting me know about the Twins,' and puts the phone down quickly before Mrs Nugent can ask after Hannah's health. It takes her a few minutes to untangle herself from the phone cord. She's been twisting it nervously round her fingers. The circulation's nearly gone in her thumb.

Mum doesn't tell Hannah about the Twins. She phones Dad first, closing the kitchen door for privacy's sake. Dad works in a car showroom in town. He sells second-hand Fords and Vauxhalls to people who can't afford to buy a motor outright. He always wears a suit to work. He doesn't have to. His boss wants them to appear approachable; a smart pullover and slacks would be grand. Hannah's dad insists on a suit. He likes the way people look up to him when he's sporting a tie, as if he's the sort of man who drives a company car. He isn't. The Adgers have a three-year-old Cavalier, biscuit-coloured and bought with the same hire-purchase scheme Dad recommends to most of his customers. The electric windows don't work properly. They're stuck up, which is better than down, but hardly ideal in high summer when temperatures in Ballylack can reach as high as sixteen degrees.

Dad doesn't like Mum phoning him at work. It's unprofessional. She's only meant to call in an emergency. This morning feels like an emergency. Four children are dead and Hannah's mum's not sure how to manage her growing hysteria. She's tried praying. And crying in the bathroom, with the taps turned on to smother the sound. She's actually sworn, out loud, with her face pressed into a folded bath towel; not the worst sort of swearing, and certainly nothing involving the Lord's name, but she's still ashamed of such weakness. Nothing's helped. She feels like a finger pulled back upon itself.

For the first time in years she registers the lack of her own mother. She's not usually prone to self-pity. This morning she's too weary to resist. She wishes her mum was here to put the kettle on and listen and remind her that *all things work together for good to them that love God.* Hannah's mum has written these words in her journal. She's repeated them several times throughout the morning, but sometimes she just needs another person to speak the truth before it actually sticks. For the moment she's forgotten what a terrible old targe her mother was; how relieved she'd been when she finally died. There's a need in Mum to be held by a grown-up person. She considers phoning her husband's mother. Good sense wins out and she doesn't bother. Evelyn would turn the whole situation sideways. She'd make it all about herself. Her blood pressure will be going through the roof, her bowels playing up, her head thumping with the stress of it all. There's nobody in Ballylack who suffers as much as Hannah's granny does.

As a last-ditch option Hannah's mum phones her husband at

work. She gets no further than telling him the Twins are dead before she's sobbing softly down the line. She cries. He prays, cupping his hand over the receiver so his colleagues won't hear. He's not ashamed of his faith, but this morning he can't seem to muster up a bold, believing voice. Dad's colleagues call him Holy Joe. To his face. In the staffroom. On the shop floor. It's better this way; to be mocked openly like a classroom clown. At least Dad knows where he stands with the fellas in work. It's years since any of them asked him out for an after-work drink. Years since they shared one of their filthy jokes in his presence. He's on the outside now. Respectfully so. They accept his invites to Gospel Meetings and never pitch them back at him. They say, *Thanks, John. I'll think about it*, and take the invites home so he won't come across them languishing in the staffroom bin. Dad prides himself on the distance he's placed between himself and his colleagues; the Christian witness he's able to have.

They aren't bad fellas. They're also husbands and fathers. They're just not like him. They drink and profane and rarely darken the door of a church. Every living one of them's lost. This is motivation enough to keep Dad keen. He never stops inviting his colleagues to church or offering to pray when some small tragedy descends upon them: a sick wife or ailing parent, a relationship gone awry.

Dad knows his colleagues are watching him closely. They want to see how big his god is. If his faith will go the distance now the tribulations are knocking at his own front door. He sees it as a kind of test. In his stronger moments he feels like an Old Testament prophet. He's re-reading the book of Job for guidance. He's thinking about Abraham laying his own son on the altar. He's asked God for the strength to remain faithful, to be able to bear whatever comes his way. He can't be found wanting in the eyes of his colleagues. He cannot let them see him weak.

Dad holds the phone against his mouth as he prays and – for

his colleagues' benefit – smiles and smiles and smiles so hard there can't be a happier-looking man this side of Larne. He needs his face to be saying, *Here I am, walking through the valley of the shadow of death, and I could not be less fearful. I'm trusting God to see me through.* Inside he feels like somebody has his heart in a tightening vice. He hasn't slept more than one hour straight since Kathleen died. He can't bear to look at his daughter for fear of what it might be like to look and find her no longer there. There's nothing to him but fear these days. *But would Dad admit this to the fellas in work?* Not a bit of him. He'd sooner die than compromise his witness.

On the other end of the line Hannah's mum has finally stopped crying. It's taken some effort to reel her emotions in. She wipes her nose on her sweater sleeve, coughs to clear her throat and asks her husband what she should do.

'Don't panic, Sandra. Remember what your man said at the meeting.'

'I know, I know. We have to stay calm, so the weans won't get scared.'

'And Hannah's fine. I checked in on her before I left this morning. There's absolutely nothing wrong with her.'

'I know, John. I know she's fine. And I know there's no point panicking, but I can't help it. There's four dead now. All from her class. There's only the seven of them left. Surely it's only a matter of time.'

Dad takes a deep, steadying breath. He places the receiver close to his mouth and tucks his chin into his chest so Michael Maguire, whose desk faces his, won't hear him being sanctimonious. 'For God hath not given us the Spirit of Fear; but of Power, and of Love, and of a Sound Mind,' he whispers, and because he's learnt this verse off by rote, years ago in a Sunday-afternoon children's meeting, can't keep from adding, 'Second Timothy one verse seven.'

'I know I shouldn't be afraid. But I am. I can't help it. I'm her mum.'

'And I'm her father, Sandra. I'm just as worried as you. But getting yourself worked up into a state isn't going to help. You need to take your fears to the Lord. Trust Him.'

'I'm trying, John. I'm trying really hard. It isn't working. I can't stop crying since I heard about the Twins. Wee pets, I keep thinking about the last time I saw them, doing that poem about the bunnies at the Easter concert. Such lovely girls. I can't believe they're gone. I don't know what to tell Hannah.'

'Seán said we should be honest with the children; make sure they don't think we're keeping secrets from them. You should probably tell her. She'll find out anyway. People are talking about nothing else. At least if you tell her yourself you can do it the right way; reassure her that everything's going to be fine.'

'And exactly how do I do that, John? All her wee friends are dying. I can't promise her that everything's going to be all right.'

'Tell her she's in the Lord's hands, Sandra. Tell her He's still in control.'

Hannah's mum hangs up. In twenty-one years of marriage she's never done anything so bold before. She's never been drunk with her husband, never walked across the bedroom naked in his presence, never sworn in front of him or danced with him, privately or in public. She's never pitched an object, even a soft object like a scatter cushion, at him in rage. She has never made love to him anywhere but in a bed, under the covers, with the big light off. This morning she purposely puts the phone down, cutting him off mid-sentence.

In this moment, something significant shifts inside Mum. She now knows she could raise her voice to her husband. She could even raise her fists if the situation required it. This isn't something she's felt before. It sits in her belly like an iron weight. It will remain there, heavily present, throughout the rest of her marriage. For years and years. Later, she'll tell him she dropped the phone. She'll apologize for her clumsiness. She will realize this is a lie; the first she's ever told her husband. Mum won't feel one bit guilty about it. She'd do it again, in a heartbeat. She knows she's more than capable now.

Tests

WHEN MUM FINALLY tells Hannah about the Twins they're en route to Dr Simpson's. They're taking the scenic route. It's good to be out of the house for a while. The need to say something is like an itch. Mum can't ignore it, no matter how much she wishes she could. She does her best to avoid the subject, telling Hannah about the tests she's having: blood, urine, temperature and something involving a saliva sample. The tests won't hurt. At least not that much.

'It's nothing to worry about. Everybody's getting tested.'

'Will the results show if I've got the same thing as Ross and Kathleen?'

'Yes,' says Mum, and quickly adds, 'And if you do, Hannah, I don't want you to panic. It doesn't mean you'll get sick like them.'

'Is there medicine they can give me?'

'Yes,' lies Mum. 'There definitely is.'

Hannah has an image in her head of the pink antibiotic syrup Dr Simpson prescribes when she's poorly. She sees Mum spooning its thick strawberry-flavoured gloop into her mouth. This is what Hannah pictures when she imagines medicine. Mum knows different. She's seen the state of Ross McCormick, lying in his coffin; his beautiful wee face all pale and mottled. The treatment's not going to be pleasant, if a treatment even exists. There's no way she's for telling Hannah this.

'Yes, pet. Now they know what's making everybody sick, they'll be able to make you all better again.'

Mum's finding it easier and easier to lie.

All the schoolchildren are coming in for tests. The remaining P7s have been prioritized. Seán Donnelly's co-ordinating the appointments, liaising with the local GPs and the scientists who've come up from Belfast to collect samples for analysis. He's told the parents not to panic. The best doctors and scientists in Northern Ireland are working on the case. If necessary, experts will be flown in from Europe or America. Whatever it takes. No expense spared. The politicians have given Seán their assurances. Everybody's sympathetic. Nationalist and Unionist alike. Situations involving children tend to straddle the political divide. Now the scientists know they're dealing with an organophosphate, albeit a very complex one, they can start experimenting with treatments. They can put the word out internationally. There's bound to be somebody out there who's come across this stuff before. It's only a matter of time before they find an antidote.

It's vital that everyone cooperates with the doctors. They need to monitor the illness. The quicker they catch it, the more chance the kids have. The whole community has pulled together. Dr Simpson and Dr Mitchell are working around the clock. Regular patients have been diverted to a temporary clinic in the community centre. Until they're certain this thing's not infectious, they need to keep the children isolated. The last thing Ballylack needs is a wider outbreak. Not a single villager complains about taking their ingrown toenails and eczema over to the community centre. It makes them feel like they're doing something. It's horrible not knowing how to help. The ladies from the Presbyterian Women's Association have joined forces with the C of I women to provide meals for the families. Also prayer, if anybody wants it. You only have to ring up and ask. They've set up an information desk in the Presby's car park. Hot drinks, traybakes and the latest updates delivered with a friendly smile. The journalists are loving the free refreshments. There's nothing like a tragedy to rally the home-baking brigade.

'Isn't it nice to see everybody working together?' says Mum, rabbiting on, though she couldn't care less about the church ladies and their buns. She keeps her eyes on the road, her hands clamped to the steering wheel. She still hasn't mentioned that the Twins are dead. Hannah notices she's acting strange. Her mum's not all that difficult to read: the long pauses and flurries of chatter mean there's something lingering beneath the surface, wanting – and struggling – to be said.

She places her hand on Mum's hand, where it rests on the gearstick.

'What is it, Mum? Just tell me.'

Her mum keeps staring straight ahead. Her jaw clenches. Thin ropes of muscle appear in her neck.

'The Twins are gone,' she says.

'Both of them?'

'Yes.'

'Just now?'

'This morning.'

Hannah nods.

'Is anybody else sick?'

'No, I don't think so.'

'Well, maybe that's the end of it.'

'Hopefully,' says Mum, and swallows the lump that's formed in her throat.

She's grateful for her daughter's measured voice, the calmness with which she's taking this latest blow. It feels as if Hannah's the adult and she's the young one, seeking a bit of reassurance. She'd tell her daughter how proud she is, if she wasn't so certain that any kind of sentiment would come sliding out on a wave of tears. She changes the subject purposefully, pointing out an odd-looking tree. Hannah graciously takes her lead. For the next few minutes the two of them comment on every single thing they pass – the new build at the crossroads, the crows sagging along the telephone wires, the cows, the sheep, the cows again – until they arrive at the surgery and there are other people to stir the silence, to keep their fears from taking root. Mum reaches for Hannah's hand as they walk up to Dr Simpson's door. At eleven, she's far too old for babying, but they both need something to hold on to.

The Twins are in the waiting room. Lizzy's sat in one corner, flipping through a stack of *Women's Weekly*s. Mim's pacing round and round the coffee table, running her hands through the ends of her hair. It's much shorter than it used to be. Hannah thinks the style's called a bob. Last summer she'd wanted this haircut herself. Mum said no, it was too grown-up. Dad put the foot down immediately. Not while she was under his roof. A woman's hair was her crowning glory. Hannah hadn't understood what this meant. She'd filed short hair away alongside pierced ears, chewing gum and all the other small rebellions she might revisit, later, when she was older and better placed to fight.

The Twins still look identical, though they've aged years since school stopped. They've always had the exact same face. They've always dressed in the same trendy outfits, bought from the big shops up in Belfast: Miss Selfridge, Tammy Girl, C&A. They've always done their hair the same way. People say they're like two peas in a pod. They call Lizzy Mim and Mim Lizzy. It'd driven Lizzy mad. Hannah knows how to tell them apart. She can still tell who's who straight away. It's nothing to do with how the Twins look. It's the way they position themselves. Lizzy's always leading while Mim's doing her best to keep up.

There's no one else in the waiting room. Seán Donnelly's

arranged for each child to arrive separately and leave without encountering anyone else. He doesn't want them to get hysterical or infect each other accidentally. He's asked the local GPs to respect his rules and – as both are completely out of their depth, dealing with what appears to be an epidemic – they've followed his suggestions to a T. They are masked, gloved and gowned like hospital surgeons. They've gone overboard with the disinfectant. The surgery smells like a mortuary.

Hannah sits in the same chair she usually sits in at the doctor's, opposite the noticeboard. She likes to read the posters about impotency and contraception. She's hazy on the specifics but knows such subjects are a wee bit rude, something to do with S.E.X. and bare bodies. She gets a little rush just reading the posters while waiting for her name to be called. At first, she doesn't acknowledge the Twins. She waits till Mum reaches for a magazine then makes a little waving motion, subtly, so she won't see. She inclines her head towards her mum, as if to say, *I can't say anything while she's here.* Lizzy shrugs. Mim keeps pacing. Her eyes are hammy pink from crying.

Lizzy is the first to speak. This isn't surprising. In school it's always Lizzy who speaks and Mim who says, *I agree with what Elizabeth said.* Every teacher since P1 has tried and failed to get Mim to speak for herself.

'I'm guessing you know we're dead,' says Lizzy. 'Kathleen says you're used to it now.'

Hannah nods her head slightly, making out she's itching her eyebrow. Mum doesn't notice. She's reading the problem page. Dad doesn't let her have women's magazines in the house. When she has ten minutes at the doctor's she always takes full advantage of their stash.

'I know you can't speak in front of your mum, but I want to ask you something.'

Mim interrupts. 'What are you for asking her about?'

'None of your business, Miriam. Piss away off. Mum's not here any more. I don't have to hang out with you.'

'That's such a mean thing to say, Lizzy.'

'It's the truth.'

'I don't like you, now you're dead. You're not the same as you used to be.'

'I'm just the same as I've always been. Only difference is I'm not hiding it any more.'

Mim turns towards Hannah. 'She cut my hair off, so she did. She waited till I was asleep and chopped it off with some scissors she lifted from the community centre.'

Lizzy grins. 'I've been wanting to do it for years. I just never had the guts before.'

'We don't look like twins any more.'

'Exactly. Isn't it great? Nobody's going to mix us up now.'

'I liked it when people thought I was you.'

'Well, I didn't.'

Mim looks like she's going to cry again. She does another few laps of the coffee table to calm herself, then sits down and starts reading a leaflet about respite care. Hannah can see from the way her eyes are darting about that she's not taking anything in.

Lizzy rises and crosses the room to stand in front of her. Hannah's always admired Lizzy: her confidence, her bold talk, the way she doesn't seem to care what people think. If she could be anyone else in the class, she'd probably choose Lizzy, though she wouldn't want Mim following her around.

'Like I said,' Lizzy continues, 'I've something I need to talk to you about. Can you get rid of your mum?'

Hannah gives her a puzzled look.

'Tell her you're thirsty. Ask if you can have a glass of water.'

Hannah responds immediately. You don't mess around when Lizzy Ross gives you instructions. It's not that she's bossy. She just knows what she wants.

'Mum, I'm wild thirsty. Please can I have a glass of water?'

'I'll see what I can do, love. You stay there. I'll be back in two ticks.'

As soon as they're alone together, Lizzy drops down into the chair beside Hannah and begins talking at speed, leaning into her ear so her sister won't hear. Mim, noticing that she's been excluded, immediately takes the seat on the other side. Hannah's now bookended by Twins. She feels claustrophobic and a little dizzy. They keep talking simultaneously at a rate of knots until Mum returns with a beaker of water. Neither of them leaves her room to respond.

'I can't stand it here,' says Lizzy. 'It's like the walls are coming in. Kathleen's a bully. Ross is in a huff, and don't even get me started on Mim the leech. The thing that really drives me mad is the way they all act like it's brilliant craic. If you ask any of them, they'll tell you they love it down here. It's pure class. Even Ross'll dance and get on like he's up for it when Kathleen tells him it's party time. Kathleen has him wrapped round her wee finger. Do you see that stupid gang of hers? She uses it to boss folks around. She just has to says it's the rules and Ross'll do whatever she says. Mim too, if I don't watch her. They're doing my head in. All of them. Especially my sister. Every time I turn around, she's there. Like a flippin' shadow. It's worse since we died. She won't let me out of her sight.'

'We're fine,' says Mim. 'I mean, we'd rather not be dead, but we'll be grand as long as we're together. Can you tell Mum and Dad that we're fine? Are you allowed to tell people that you've seen us, Hannah? Can you say we're having loads of fun? We've got our own wee kingdom down here. That's what Kathleen says, anyway.'

'I keep trying to get out. I walk all the way to the edge of the village. Sometimes I even run. I get as far as Millar's Gap, but when I reach the Raggedy Tree the road just folds back on itself. I'm walking into Ballylack again. It's so weird. I don't think there's any way out. Not even if you crawl through a hedge or swim down the river. I've pretty much tried everything now. You just end up back where you started. It's driving me absolutely mad.'

'We've never been anywhere like this before. It's always quite exciting to be somewhere new, isn't it? This one time, Mum took us to London for the weekend, and it was class. Remember that, Lizzy, wasn't it class? Me and Lizzy are good with new experiences so long as we've got each other for company. And, I mean, it's not really even a new experience, is it? We've been in Ballylack a million times, although it doesn't feel the same any more. Anyway, we've never been dead before, have we, Lizzy? So that would actually count as a new experience, wouldn't it?'

'Seriously, Hannah, I kind of wish I was properly dead. Not just stuck here with her and those other two eejits, going round and round in endless loops.'

'I actually think it's better here. They'll never be able to split us up now. *Two peas in a pod*, like Mummy says. And we've turned out quite pretty. I'm not being up myself when I say that. I mean it as a compliment for Lizzy because Lizzy looks the same as me. Or at least she did till she chopped off my hair. I really wish she hadn't done that. Do you think we turned out pretty, Hannah? Kathleen keeps saying we're smoking hot *and* there's two of us. I think she's annoyed about that. The odds aren't great down here at the minute. One fella. Three girls. Somebody's going to be left out. That's probably why Kathleen's trying to take over. You've seen her, Hannah. She's still awful plain. If she wasn't bossing the rest of us about, nobody would notice her.'

'Do you see what I mean? The rubbish I have to listen to. It never stops. It goes on and on. I'm going to kill them, Hannah. I swear I am.'

'We don't mind Kathleen taking charge. Do we, Lizzy? She's always coming up with things to do. Like raking around other people's houses or trashing the community centre for a laugh. Last night we made a scarecrow of Principal Taylor. You should've seen it, Hannah. It was hilarious. We put ladies' knickers on him and gave him a turnip for a head. We spent the evening chucking stones at him until his head was in smithereens. Kathleen says it's good to get your anger out. That's the kind of thing you do in a gang.'

'What I want to know, Hannah, is can you help me get out of here?' asks Lizzy. 'You're the only one we can talk to. Maybe you know something we don't know. Do you know a shortcut into Heaven or something? They teach stuff like that in your church, don't they? My dad always said your lot were loonies, but right now I'm that desperate I'll take any advice you can give me.'

'We're fine, Hannah, basically fine, but I do miss the way it used to be,' says Mim. 'Lizzy's so mean now. And sad, too. She's always telling me to go away. Could you tell her to be a bit nicer? I don't mind being dead if we're still us, but it's starting to feel like we're coming apart.'

Hannah's trying to formulate a response. It's hard to hear herself think with the Twins going hammer and tongs. She's just about to open her mouth and ask them to stop for a second when Mum appears with a glass of water.

'OK?' she asks.

Hannah nods. She takes the glass from her mum's hand and downs it in one long gulp. Lizzy throws her arms up in exasperation. She stomps out of the waiting room.

'Thanks a lot, Hannah!' she shouts as she leaves. 'You're useless so you are; no help at all.'

Miriam looks a bit embarrassed by her sister's outburst. 'Sorry,' she mumbles. 'I told you she wasn't nice any more.' She hesitates on the edge of her chair but can't resist the pull of Lizzy. Thirty seconds after one Twin's left, the other's bolting after her. Hannah stays sat on her chair, nursing the empty glass, until Dr Simpson calls her name.

The tests don't bother her at all. She feels the needles go in and the lightness in her head as the blood drains out. It might as well be happening to somebody else. She pees into a cardboard dish. She lets Dr Simpson weigh her, measure her and cuff her arm in a tight balloon band to take her blood pressure. Under normal circumstances she'd probably complain about the discomfort. She'd be embarrassed about the peeing. This afternoon, she doesn't care. She has other things on her mind.

Five hours later, Dr Simpson phones the house. It's late, but he's sure the Adgers will want to know. Hannah's tests have come back completely clear. There's no trace of the organophosphate in her blood, saliva or pee.

'So, she's fine?' whispers Mum. She's listening in on the upstairs phone.

Dr Simpson confirms his diagnosis. 'A hundred per cent healthy as far as I can see.'

'Hallelujah,' says Dad. 'What an answer to prayer.'

'Hold on, Mr Adger. It's not so straightforward. I don't know how to tell you this. Your Hannah's the only child in the class whose tests came back clear.'

Mum makes a noise like a choking cat, somewhere between a screech and a sob.

'What?' says Dad. 'How can that be?'

'I don't know, John. I'm as baffled as you. We've double-checked all the tests. Your Hannah's a very lucky wee girl. Sorry,' he says, and as he's saying it realizes how many different kinds of sorry there are. This one's a hell of a lot lighter than the other six he's just passed on. 'Now, I'm not saying she's out of the woods. We know so little about this illness.'

'Do you mean she might still develop it?'

'It's unlikely, John. But we just don't know. I advise you to keep a close eye on her. Let me know straight away if anything changes. But it's good news, folks; really good news. I'd put money on her being fine.'

On the upstairs phone, Mum is struggling to find her voice.

'Should we tell Hannah?' she asks Dr Simpson.

'Well, Sandra,' he replies, 'that's entirely up to you.'

'But in your professional opinion, what would you suggest?'

'Like I said, Mrs Adger, I can't make that kind of decision. You're her parents; you need to decide.'

Mum and Dad are up all night, trying to work out what to do. By breakfast, they've decided not to tell Hannah anything unless she asks them directly. If she asks if she's got it, then obviously they'll tell her the truth. A lie would be a sinful thing. Evasion is entirely different. If Hannah doesn't ask, they'll let her assume she's in the same boat as the others. Mum wonders if it's cruel to let a child believe she's ill, possibly dying. Dad insists they don't really have a choice. The lesser of two evils is how he puts it. Hannah's always been emotionally fragile. Granny keeps saying she's far too soft. If she thinks she's the only one well, she'll drive herself clean mad with the guilt. It's best if they don't tell her. If they keep their heads down and ride it out.

Hannah makes it easy for them. She never asks. She just assumes she's ill like everyone else. There's no point in having the diagnosis confirmed. She feels like she's known it all along.

Intercession

THERE HASN'T BEEN a death in nearly three days. Sixty-two hours, if you want to be exact. Maganda Gardiner knows exactly how long it's been since the Twins passed. She's been counting the hours, marking them down on the back of an old gas bill, hope rising as she sees those wee blue lines stacking up. Once there are enough of them, it'll be over. She'll be able to breathe again. For the moment, she can't keep her eyes off her son. She follows Bayani round the house, constantly asking if he's feeling OK.

The boy's tested positive for the poison. All the children in his class have. They're still testing the younger and older children. Nobody else has it yet. The scientists still don't know where the kids have picked it up from. They're all over the village, taking samples. They've cordoned off the play area and the sports fields. They've taken swabs from Thompson's sweetie rack and the lolly freezer by the door. There's police tape looped all the way around the school. If they could just find the source, it might help with the antidote.

The volunteers manning the information desk are fed up repeating the same information. *No, there's no new developments to report. No, there isn't a treatment yet.* There's no point moving the infected children over to the hospital in town. They're better off at home, in their own wee houses, where their parents can keep a close eye on them. They've all been given a rake of tablets, generic drugs which boost the immune system. They're drinking lots of fluids and keeping warm. There's every chance the worst is over. Those who are left are likely stronger than the four who've died. The doctors hope their bodies will fight it off. Or perhaps the remaining children have picked up a smaller dose. With organophosphates the symptoms worsen the more you've been exposed. Seán Donnelly appears on the six o'clock news, emphasizing it's all just speculation until they track down the primary source.

Maganda's nothing but nerves since Bayani's results came back. Three or four times each night she'll wake and sneak into his room just to check he's still breathing and not running a temperature. He says he feels fine. He still insists on running every day, though she's told him to keep close to home. She doesn't stop him. Fresh air's supposed to be good for the ill. Somewhere at the back of her mind, she's holding to the flimsy belief that her Bayani is so fit, so fast, so perfectly healthy, he's bound to survive where others won't. It reassures her to see him lacing his running shoes on and disappearing through the back door, across the yard and over the fields. She watches him through the kitchen window. He looks the absolute picture of health. Maganda watches and counts the hours off one by one. She lets herself begin to hope.

You wouldn't know to look at him. But Alan Gardiner's also starting to hope. Maybe he's been given a second chance, an opportunity to atone. He hasn't loved like a father should love. He's let his wee lad down. He doesn't deserve a second chance. But Ben's not dead. The boy is thriving. In the eyes of the village, Alan is a lucky man. There are three families out there, possibly more, who'd give their left kidney to trade with him. He should call this moment his line in the sand. *He'll be a better father from now on.* Alan's going to make it up to Ben.

He tries. The problem is there's nothing to work with. There's nothing but silence between them now. They don't talk because they have nothing to say. Alan knows he's the adult. It's up to him to make amends. He wonders if it would help to take the boy out around the fields. If he were to speak freely – man to man – about the land, and what it means to him. Alan still remembers his elderly father weeping as he talked about the olden days, how good it was to be a farmer back then. He tries to picture the same scenario with his son. The two of them standing at the top of the back field, possibly leaning on a gate. Alan sweeping an arm across the vista. *This farm has been in your family for five generations, Ben. One day, all of it will be yours.* Even in these imaginary moments, the boy he's addressing isn't Ben. It's a better version of his son: stockier, with paler skin. A composite formed from one of his nephews and the young fella off *All Creatures Great and Small,* the one with the kind, approachable face. Every time he looks at the real Ben, Alan knows he doesn't belong. Ben has his name, but he's not a Gardiner. He isn't rooted, as Alan is rooted, to these fields and ancient trees. Without roots there's nothing binding him to the farm.

Still, Alan tries. He takes his second chance and runs with it. On Friday evening, after dinner, he asks Ben to help with the milking. *There's a fiver in it.* He makes his face smile and his voice sound warm. Ben looks up from the TV for barely a second. 'No, thanks, Dad,' he says, and turns straight back to the screen. Alan knows Ben understands exactly what he's turning down. It's nothing to do with chores or money. The boy's purposely denying him. All the old rage comes rushing up. It sticks in his guts and twists viciously. Alan stands in the doorway, watching the glow from the screen illuminate Ben's upturned face. The boy is transfigured in the flickering light. He is unfamiliar and grotesque. In the dark, with nobody watching, Alan admits that it's not just disinterest. He actively, furiously, hates his own son. He lets himself gorge on the thought of this. If the boy gets sick, it'll be his fault. Some small part of him has wished – is still wishing – to be shot of Ben. Alan steps out into the darkened hall. He closes the door between him and his son.

In the days that follow Alan Gardiner goes round in circles. Guilt's a powerful heavy thing to shoulder. He can't crawl out from under it. Awake, he's able to trick his thinking into line. He tells himself he's glad the outbreak's over. He is sorry for the grieving parents but glad – so glad – his son is safe. At night, his dreams are cruel and honest. He dreams Ben, dead and laid out in the coffin, all the colour drained out of his face. He dreams Megan crying and Lucy screeching. And he, himself, like a sort of monster, standing over the lidded coffin, grinning as he hammers the last nail in. It isn't right. It isn't natural. It should be easy to love your weans. You should struggle to imagine the world without them. Alan knows there's something desperately wrong with him.

Maganda's really worried now. She's started asking her husband what's wrong. She's noticed he's not sleeping. He barely makes a dent in his morning fry. He's pacing too; walking endless loops of the house, the ever-present mug of tea going lukewarm in his hands. The only thing which seems to calm him is Lucy. These days he's only got eyes for her. Every so often he'll dandle the child upon his knee, coo at her and get on like he's soft. Sometimes, when he's holding their daughter, Maganda notices a dampness in his eyes. She doesn't know what to do with this. Her husband's such a hard, unyielding man. She's never seen him cry before. She recalls an uncle back in the Philippines, a stern-faced brother of her mum's, who'd turned sappy at the end, when he knew his heart was packing in.

She wonders if Alan is sick. If he knows this in his body, like she

knew all four babies were present, long before the doctor confirmed it. The sickness hasn't touched an adult yet, but nobody – not
even the experts from Belfast – seems to have any notion what it
might do next. In her cruellest moments Maganda fantasizes
about losing Alan. Now she's sure he doesn't love Bayani, it's easy
to wish the worst on him. She'd be happier without him. What
they'd do for money, she doesn't know. The extended family would
turf her out. They've no love for her or her kids. Maganda is a
practical woman. Much as she'd like to stab her husband, she
knows it's best to put up with him. If he's sickening too, it'd be
best to let the doctor know. There's a rumour doing the rounds.
*This thing's contagious. The experts have already confirmed it. They're
just not telling the general public, for fear of causing hysteria.* It's
probably bollocks. Even if it's not, Maganda never considers the
possibility of catching it herself. It's the kids she's worried about.

When Alan comes up from the fields for his lunch, she makes
a point of sitting down with him. Usually she stands, hovering
around Lucy's highchair, trying to contain the hash the baby
makes of every meal. She's already fed her, cleaned her and tucked
her up for her nap. Bayani's out running. *Training*, he calls it,
though his dad says he's just trying to avoid his chores. He'll only
tolerate so much of it. For the moment they have the place to
themselves. Maganda places a bowl of hot stew in front of Alan.
There's a plate of fresh-baked wheaten, sliced and buttered, in
the middle of the table.

'Dig in,' she says, and lifts a sopping spoonful to her mouth.

Alan pushes the damp potatoes round his bowl. He reaches
for a piece of wheaten, then changes his mind. He takes a big
slurp of tea and makes as if to stand. Maganda reaches across the
table and places a hand over her husband's hand. It's rare for
them to touch outside the bedroom. The feel of her small hand
pressed against his causes Alan to pause. He hangs there awkwardly, already halfway out of his seat.

'Sit down. Please.'

Alan sits. He looks at his wife. He looks away. It's always been difficult for him to look people directly in the eye. These days, he finds it impossible.

'What is wrong, Alan? Are you sick?'

For a moment, he considers telling Megan everything. He suspects she already knows. Once he starts in with the honesty, he knows he won't be able to stop. He'll have to tell her how much he loves wee Lucy. How there's no such feeling in him for Ben. Or her, for that matter. How he's fond of her and grateful for the way she keeps the house. But really, she could be any woman with a reasonable figure and it wouldn't make much difference to him. How – and here he catches himself on, knowing he'd never go this far – he sometimes wishes she was a regular woman, with pale skin and a normal way of speaking. Somebody a bit more local. How this would've made things easier for him.

Alan Gardiner doesn't say any of this. Instead, he slides his hand out from under Megan's hand. He makes it into a fist and brings this fist down so hard both their bowls of stew go skittering up into the air.

'Jesus, woman!' he shouts. 'What's wrong with me? What do you think's wrong with me? There's four weans dead and all of them from his class. I can hardly think straight for worrying.'

It's not exactly a lie. It's hardly the whole truth either.

Maganda looks across the table at her husband. She can't quite believe what she's hearing. Alan's voice is ragged with emotion. She's waited years for him to profess any interest in their son. Now this. All at once. Like an avalanche. Perhaps he can be caring after all. Maybe she's read the whole thing wrong. The coldness. The silence. The lack of interest. Perhaps it's just the way men here are. Maganda chooses to give her husband the benefit of the doubt. She can't help thinking about what's best for the children. Everything she says and thinks is filtered through a motherly lens. She will try to meet Alan halfway. Maybe, she can even muster a little love. She could take or leave the man herself. But her children require a dad. She reaches for his hand again. To her surprise, he doesn't withdraw. It's uncomfortable to sit like this, arms extended across the width of the table. Maganda doesn't let go. She understands that this is a moment to be grasped and clung to. Such a moment may not present itself again.

'I am worried too,' she says.

Alan pats the back of her hand. Up and down his hand goes, feebly, gently, like an old man patting at a dog.

'What if Bayani gets sick?' she says, her voice cracking. 'What if . . .'

'Don't say it. It's not going to happen. It just can't.'

They sit in silence for a moment, thinking about the thing that is not going to happen. It's impossible to avoid the thought of it. When she raises her head, Maganda sees that her husband is crying. She slips out of her seat and walks around to his side of the table. She crouches down next to him and holds him like a baby, arms circling his waist as his shoulders heave. She lets his whole body sag against hers. She tells him that she's here. That she's not going anywhere. That everything will be all right. When his sobbing finally lets up, she puts him to bed with the curtains drawn, though it's only just gone midday and there are any number of things needing done around the farm.

'You're exhausted,' she says. 'You must rest now.'

As an afterthought she leans across the bed to kiss him on the forehead. She kisses her children in the same way most nights and tells them that they are loved. She does the same for Alan now and tucks the sheets tightly round his big shoulders. This is how Maganda will love her husband now. She will love him as she loves her children. She will be jealous for him, strong and protective, endless in her ability to forgive. They will never be bound together as a husband and wife should be, for there's no desire there on either side. But what they will cultivate is not without worth. It might well be fierce in its own quiet way.

When Alan wakes, Maganda brings him tea and toast. She perches on the edge of the mattress and asks if he's feeling better. He is. It's the first time he's slept longer than an hour all week.

'If I could just get a decent night's sleep, I'd be grand. But I'm plagued with nerves. I just can't get my head to switch off.'

Maganda suggests visiting the doctor. She's sure he'd be able to prescribe something for the insomnia. Alan can't imagine anything worse. The surgery's swarming with scientists and out-of-town doctors. No, he tells his wife, he wouldn't want to bother the doctor, though maybe he'll nip over to Tullybarret in the morning; there's a fella there who has a cure for almost everything.

'A cure?' asks Maganda.

'Aye, it's like something you have to take, or do, to get better?'

'Like a spell?'

'No, like a cure. Did youse not have cures in the Philippines?'

'We have doctors and we also have people who do spells.'

'Well, this is nothing like that. Cures are good things; there's no wickedness in them. Sure as anything, Mr O'Neill'll have a cure for nerves. My da used to swear by him. Any time one of us got sick, he'd send for the O'Neills and we'd be right as rain before the week was out. There used to be a rake of them – three or four brothers – all gifted the same. Tadhg's the last of them left. He must be eighty if he's a day. But he's still got the cure. Or so I hear. I'll go and see him first thing tomorrow.'

Maganda is unconvinced. She'd rather Alan saw a proper doctor, but she's not going to stand in his way. Not when things are better between them than they've ever been.

Alan Gardiner drives over to Tullybarret straight after breakfast. He has a chicken in the boot of the Land Rover and two jars of Megan's good freezer jam, for he knows Tadgh O'Neill won't take a penny. His sort never do. They prefer to have you beholden to them. He feels lighter in himself this morning. It could be the sleep, or talking to his wife, or the fact that there's been no word of further sickness. People are saying the Twins were the end of it. He turns the radio on, tunes it in to Radio Ulster and hums along to the country music they're always playing. It's only a ten-minute drive. Two tunes and a bit of patter from the DJ and he's arrived.

The two villages are practically neighbours. They couldn't be more different if they tried. As he pulls into the main street, Alan notes a certain through-otherness about the shops. There's a mural of Bobby Sands painted on the butcher's gable, grinning like he doesn't know what's ahead of him, and Herself, lit up in a wee glass box outside the chapel gate. Alan's not on home turf here. He turns the radio off. Glances up and down the street. It's best to be alert in places like Tullybarret. You've to keep your eyes peeled at all times.

Tadhg O'Neill still works part-time in the hardware shop. It's the sort of place that looks like the inside of a cupboard: shoelaces and superglue all thrown together on top of nails and shovels and devices for catching mice. It's a wonder anyone ever finds anything, though the shop seems popular enough. There's always a dose of locals browsing the cluttered aisles and somebody at the counter seeking advice about a broken toaster or a blocked drain. Alan approaches the counter. He takes his cap off and holds it in his hand like he's here for a Sunday-morning service.

'Would Tadhg be about?' he asks the young fella at the till.

He immediately turns around and gulders into the back room, 'Mr O'Neill, there's a man here to see you.'

'He'll be right out,' he tells Alan, and goes back to counting washers out of a wee footery-looking box, chasing them with his fingers as they go skiting across the countertop.

A few seconds later, Mr O'Neill appears from behind the beaded curtain. At first, he's just a shimmering shape of himself. The shop coat he always wears forms a royal-blue cloud behind the beads. Then, Alan sees him in slices. Finally, the curtains slip over his shoulders to reveal the whole of him: white-haired and heavily lined, the living spit of his da. He's nippy enough for an auld boy. He's out and round the side of the counter before Alan can even introduce himself. Alan extends his right hand. He shakes hard.

'Alan Gardiner,' he says, 'Jock Gardiner's oldest. You helped him out once with a poorly cow.'

'I did indeed. You're a Ballylack fella yourself?'

'I am.'

'Powerful business youse are having with them poor weans.'

'It is indeed, Mr O'Neill. Hopefully it's all over now.'

He finds himself incapable of looking the old man in the eye. His hands fall to his cap for something to do. He twists the fabric this way and that, for all the world looking like a guilty child. Tadhg keeps the eye on him. Alan's sure he knows more than he's letting on.

'You never know,' he says. 'It might well be over. On the other hand, it might only be getting started. You just never know with things like this.'

'I've a young fella in the class,' says Alan. 'Ben.' Just saying the boy's name makes his eyes swim. *What on Earth's happening to him? He's not a woman. He isn't usually weepy like this.*

'Dear, dear, youse must be going spare.'

'I'm grand, so I am. It's the wife. Megan. She's plagued with nerves, so she is. She's hardly sleeping. Would you have something for her, Mr O'Neill? Something to help her get over at night?'

Alan Gardiner isn't sure why he's lying. He could easily admit he's the anxious one. *Sure, isn't it completely normal to be worried about your children? Isn't it a laudable sort of complaint?* He can't bring himself to admit his own weakness. Not here in Tullybarret. With that young fella listening in behind the counter. And Mr O'Neill no doubt remembering the brick wall his father was. And the bloody Sacred Heart glaring down at him from the back wall. It's a different kind of Jesus they have here: a big-eyed, sappy saviour who's always wanting you down on your knees. Alan Gardiner'll be damned before he shows any weakness in front of this lot.

Mr O'Neill gives him a long, long look.

'It's her nerves, is it?' he says. He places a heavy emphasis on the word *her*. His tone's not quite sarcastic. It's definitely heading that direction, though.

'Yes, *Megan*'s plagued with nerves since the whole thing kicked off.'

'And you're grand yourself? No nerves, no bad thoughts, nothing troubling you at night?'

'Not at all. I sleep the sleep of the righteous myself; out for the count as soon as my head hits the pillow.' Alan forces himself to laugh.

Mr O'Neill makes a noise like a cushion being crushed. He disappears behind the beaded curtain, returning two minutes later with a wee brown envelope, slightly lumpy in the middle.

'Spoonful of that in a mug of hot water an hour before she goes to bed, and there's a wee thing in there for yourself, Mr Gardiner, should the nerves ever catch up with you.'

'Thank you, Mr O'Neill.'

'I'd say it's not over,' the auld boy says, mumbling quietly under his breath.

'What's that?' says Alan.

'There's worse to come,' he replies. 'Youse'll want to prepare yourselves.'

Then, suddenly his whole demeanour changes. He smiles broadly, shakes Alan's trembling hand, tells him to take his best wishes back to Megan and the wee fella. Alan wonders if he's imagined the last few seconds. He doesn't dare open the envelope here in the shop. He pockets the cure, shoving it deep inside the inner pocket of his bodywarmer. He offers money, knowing it'll be refused and, when it is, hands over a carrier bag containing Megan's jam, the chicken and two dozen eggs, still warmish from the coop. To pass himself he also buys a box of nails and a hammer off the young fella, though he has no more need of another hammer. There's dozens of them hanging in his shed. Then Alan scarpers back out to the Land Rover.

When he's sure there's no one but Bobby Sands watching, slightly cross-eyed, from across the road, he opens the package. It's full of dried leaves and what look to be wood shavings. There's a scrap of notepaper at the bottom. He fishes it out and unfolds it. There's nothing on it but the name of a priest – Father Kinsella – and the times when confession's available in the chapel across the street.

Alan Gardiner holds the wee scrap of paper in his hand for a minute or so. He knows the message is meant for him. For a brief, heady moment he's taken with the idea of dandering down to the chapel and telling the priest what a thoroughly awful man he is. It might help to get everything off his chest. But such avenues aren't open to Protestants and Alan's far too shaken by what Tadhg's said. He holds the steering wheel in both hands until his breathing returns to normal. Then, he folds the paper four times so it's no bigger than a postage stamp and tucks it into his wallet. He drives like the clappers all the way back to Ballylack. The radio's on. Yet more country. Garth Brooks. Patsy Cline. Charley Pride. Alan hums along without actually listening. He's thinking about his da. Big Jock used to warn him and his brothers about the O'Neills and their like.

' 'Tis a powerful good thing to have the cure. But the same ones that have it sometimes have other dark gifts too: spells and curses and the second sight. There's nobody but God has any business knowing the future or things they shouldn't know. Them lot aren't like us, boys. Mind and watch yourselves round them. Stay well clear if you can.'

The Leaving Ceremony

MEADOW ANDERSON HASN'T told anyone her son is sick. Not even the authorities. Meadow thinks she knows better than the doctors. She's made her own assessment of the situation. All four children were taken to hospital. All four children are now dead. Meadow doesn't fancy these odds. She's better placed to look after her boy. Meadow's done a course in alternative medicine. She has all manner of herbs and tinctures in her pantry. And a husband who doesn't know how to stand up to her.

The other parents have begun to hope they're home and dry. No more children have tested positive. Those who have aren't showing any symptoms yet. *Could the worst of it be over?* They discuss the possibility in hushed tones. *Maybe. Possibly. Dear God, let that be the end of it.* Seán Donnelly's noticeably more relaxed. Surely that's a good sign. Seán Donnelly knows everything there is to know. *Bollocks.* Seán Donnelly has no idea that up the road, on the outskirts of Ballylack, Lief Anderson has been desperately ill for three days now.

Lief dies at home with his mum, his dad and all five younger siblings gathered round him singing a cappella. The last sound he hears before slipping away is a reedy version of 'Where Have All the Flowers Gone?' He hears Meadow try, and fail, to harmonize with his father while the baby, Oben, howls manically. It's scorching hot and the poor child's sweltered. The whole fiasco takes place outside.

Singing is an integral part of Lief's 'Leaving Ceremony'. Meadow's invented this fiasco, lifting bits from Buddhism, parts from Celtic mythology and a chunk from a documentary about Haight-Ashbury in the sixties she once saw in the QFT. She's had Rob carry Lief outside. He lies on a mattress in full view of the trees, the birds and the bloody flies, which won't stop itching at his eyes. 'We're giving Lief back to nature,' Meadow announces. Behind the wailing baby and the insect hum, you can hear the wobble in her voice. She's doing her best to sound convincing. *This is a moment to celebrate.* She's not fooling anyone, least of all herself.

Lief isn't feeling celebratory. Poor Lief is in agony. It's not the symptoms that are killing him. It's all Meadow's natural remedies: the rubs and scrubs and weird-smelling potions she's been forcing into him. He's been coughing up blood for the last few hours; no idea whether it's the illness or her cure that's eating him alive. He's asked to see a doctor – literally begged for one – and been told the doctor can't help. Lief's dying now and it's best to end this way, at one with the spirit and natural world. Meadow cries when she says this and afterwards has to walk away. *But does she go and fetch a doctor?* Does she hell. Meadow Anderson's a determined woman. She won't compromise what she believes.

Lief suspects his dad's not overly enamoured with the 'Leaving Ceremony'. But Rob's always been the weaker parent. He consistently sides with Meadow. Though he's not without reservations. For the last two days he's been slipping his son Panadol Extras every time his wife turns her back. He's been telling Lief how sorry he is; how he wishes he'd done things differently. *But does he go and fetch a doctor?* Does he hell. Rob Anderson's spineless. There's no nice way of saying this. He knows it's too late to ask for help. People won't understand why they've left it so long.

Meadow's insisted that no one cries. This isn't to be a mournful moment. This is a celebration of life. Her eyes fill up as she's saying this. She mops her tears with the sleeve of her hand-sewn linen tunic. 'Good tears,' she says, her voice straining to convince itself. Lief wants to cry. He no longer has the strength. He wants to lift his head off the bogging mattress and scream and scream and scream. He'd hoped for something better than this. Lief might only be eleven. He might be small and babyish for his age. He still understands that he's been robbed. No TV. No sugar. No holidays. Nothing which might pass as normal. Lief's reasonably pragmatic when it comes to dying. The next life can't be half as bad as the crappy one he's leaving behind.

He takes one last look at his brothers and sisters. He lists their names inside his head: Clover, Sorrel, August, Rain and wee Oben, who's so red from gurning he looks as if he's about to burst. *Bunch of hippies, the lot of them.* They're standing around him listlessly, with their hand-me-down clothes and tatty hair. Their pale faces are smeared with what might be peanut butter or, just as easily, common muck. They've never been to the cinema, never owned a pair of trainers or even tasted Coke. Lief feels sorrier for them than for himself. He's getting out. They're all stuck. He wants to say, *Bolt the second you get the chance. Do all the things Ma doesn't approve of. Try, as hard as you can, to be normal, lads. The only thing that matters is fitting in.* He's not got the puff to say anything. He closes his eyes and drifts away. Meadow's singing, 'When will they ever learn?' The irony is wasted on her.

They're halfway through a wobbly version of 'Blowin' in the Wind' when Clover notices Lief is gone. Clover knows she's not supposed to cry, but Lief's her favourite brother and she's going to miss him. She throws back her head and begins to moan. Hysteria's contagious. It passes quickly from child to child. Even Meadow's powerless to resist. Lief was her first-born, her pixie boy. She can't imagine the absence of him. Abandoning her own

125

resolve, she drops down next to his body and cradles him gently in her arms. It's almost too much. She can feel herself coming apart. The grief's like a brick in the pit of her belly. It'd be easy enough to go under it, to abandon everything she believes and cry like a woman devoid of hope. No. Not Meadow. She's too determined. *For the sake of the children, she will press on.* Other people have religion. She looks to the earth for strength and comfort. The earth is always seeking to teach and here is today's painful lesson: nature gives, and nature takes. This is the proper way of things. Meadow understands. She must also accept it. Though losing a son – a precious boy – is an almost impossible weight to bear.

She looks to Rob. Rob is weeping. She'll have to be strong for him as well. Just once, she'd like her husband to carry her, but Rob has always been weak and watery. He doesn't understand, like Meadow. He's happy to follow. He'll never lead.

And so, Meadow leads, though her heart's in pieces. 'It's for the best,' she says, speaking slowly and with great determination. 'Nature gives and nature takes. Lief's complete now, wherever he is.'

'No,' Rob whispers, beginning to crumble. 'Not my wee boy.'

He turns his back on Meadow, then. He'll only hurt her if he stays. He doesn't consider his wife or children. He's beside himself with grief. He walks the two miles into Ballylack, stumbling and crying, cursing the stupid trees Meadow loves so much. He stops in Thompson's for twenty Benson and Hedges, a naggin of vodka and a sausage roll. The girl on the till won't meet his eye. He knows he looks a bit unhinged. He sits outside the community centre and consumes all three in quick succession. Each mouthful is a calculated blow: death to Meadow's stupid regime. He hasn't had meat in fifteen years. He gorges himself till the boke begins rising, then slouches down Main Street to the house where Seán Donnelly's staying. He doesn't want to be on his own. He hammers the door until Seán comes out. Half the neighbours come out too. They stand around, slack-jawed in their slippers, watching Rob weep and roar and vomit up mouthfuls of tofu and beansprouts, cut with flesh-pink sausagemeat.

Seán Donnelly's bleary-eyed with beer. He's been dozing in front of the telly. 'What the hell?' he mutters as he opens his door, then abruptly changes his tone when he sees the state Rob Anderson's in. 'What's wrong, mate? Are you all right?'

'It's Lief,' slurs Rob. 'He got sick and then he died.'

Seán can't think of anything to say. He wraps both arms around Rob and draws him into a smothering hug. He can hear the younger man howling into his shoulder. 'It's Meadow's fault. Meadow wouldn't let us get the doctor out.'

Thankfully, it's only Seán who hears this confession. The people who've come out to gawp are too far away. They feel sorry for Rob, these staring neighbours. They listen to him ranting, though it's the last thing they want to hear. *Dear love the man, he's lost a child.* They'd like to cross the road and put their arms around him. They would also like to weep. It's not that simple. There's judgement present: a hard knot standing in the way of their sympathy. *You brought this on yourself, Rob Anderson, acting like you were better than us.* The onlookers mumble their concerns from a pious distance, close their doors and return to their living rooms. They phone everyone they know, putting their own particular slant on the incident. *The wee Anderson lad's just died. The whole thing's starting up again.*

Seán Donnelly has no such reservations. He ushers Rob inside. He gives him brandy for the shock and lets him lie on his sofa while he makes all the necessary calls: ambulance, undertaker, police, scientists and – with his hand cupped over the receiver – Social Services. Rob hears nothing. He's hardly present. He doesn't sleep. He doesn't cry. He stares at the light switch for three hours. When the room darkens, he thinks about rising to turn it on. The grief's so heavy, he can't crawl out from under it.

No Good News

HANNAH'S WHOLE FAMILY are watching the news tonight. Her parents have made a point of it. There's a special feature on the outbreak. It's strange to see the TV reporter walking up and down Main Street, like it's a crime scene. Hannah recognizes some people she knows. They look different on screen: flatter and less colourful.

She's sandwiched between Mum and Dad on the sofa, absent-mindedly sucking an ice pop. It's hot out tonight, clammy and oppressive. Hannah's not in the mood for her usual warm milk. Her parents are on the tea. It could be one hundred degrees and they'd still drink tea. On the other side of the window, Lief is so still, so focused on the telly, Hannah doesn't notice him until he lifts a hand, shading his eyes against the glass. The shock of seeing him makes her flinch. Her elbow knocks against Mum's side, causing hot tea to slosh across her lap.

Hannah apologizes immediately.

Mum dabs at her damp dress with a tissue. 'Don't worry, pet. Accidents happen.'

Mum never gets angry over accidents or genuine mistakes. Deliberate disobedience is a different matter. Then, she comes down like a ton of bricks. Mum's just as strict as Dad when it comes to behaviour. She cannot abide a wayward child.

'Are you OK, Hannah?' asks Dad. 'You look a bit pale.'

'Maybe we shouldn't have let her watch the news,' says Mum, talking quietly over Hannah's head.

'Seán said it'd be good for the children to hear things were moving forward.'

'Aye, but it's a lot for them to get their heads around.'

Dad slips his arm around Hannah's shoulders. He puts his soft voice on. 'Did it upset you, Han? I'm sorry. We thought it might help to see nobody's sick. It looks like the whole thing's over. That's good news, isn't it?'

Hannah nods. A big, unswallowable lump has formed at the bottom of her throat. She glances over at the window. Lief's still there, peering in, his face older but somehow still the same. *He's dead*, she thinks. *And, if he's dead, then it isn't over.* Nobody knows what will happen next. Not her parents nor the scientists, not even Seán Donnelly, and he's the only one people listen to these days.

Only God has any clue what's happening and He's not for telling anyone. He never makes His ways known to ordinary folk. In the Bible God hardly ever speaks. When He does, it's usually to announce a plague or a flood; something dreadful and imminent. Hannah wonders if it's fair, the way God knows everything and chooses to keep it to Himself. He could reassure people if He wanted to. He could give them time to prepare. *It's a bit mean, isn't it?* All the kids in her class might die. Herself included. She might already be dying. Hannah doesn't want to die. A noise comes rushing up her throat: half scream, half choke. It sounds like she's been punched in the stomach. She starts to cry and, having started, can't seem to get herself to stop.

'I knew it,' says Mum. 'It was too much.'

'Sorry, love. We just didn't think.'

They both hug her at once, arms clashing, tea mugs slopping. Hannah feels like she's suffocating between the pair of them. She burrows her head out from under their arms and manages to catch her breath. She wipes the worst of her tears on her shirt-sleeve. Over Mum's shoulder she can see Lief rolling his eyes towards the back door. She doesn't feel like talking to him. But this might be her only chance, and it'd be good to get a few minutes away from her parents. She's smothering here, with Mum and Dad, and their never-ending, persistent concern. Given the choice, she'd take dead Lief over another earnest conversation, another round of serious prayer.

'I need some air,' she says, squirming free.

'OK, love,' says Mum. 'You're not really meant to go out, but we can take a wee walk down the lane and back.'

'No. I need to be by myself for a while.'

'I don't think so, Han,' says Dad. 'It's not a good idea, being alone when you're upset.'

'Please, Dad, I just want some space.'

'Let her go,' says Mum, placing a hand on Dad's arm. 'It's a lot for her to take in. She needs some room to think things through by herself.'

'And pray,' adds Hannah, because she knows Dad will be impressed by this. He often prayer walks round the forest when there's something weighing on his mind.

'OK. Just don't go too far. And not for too long. And don't be talking to anyone. Especially those journalists.'

Hannah's out the door and down the path before her parents can change their minds. Lief is waiting in the drive, leaning nonchalantly against Dad's car. The moment she sees him Hannah starts bawling again.

'You're dead,' she mumbles between sobs.

'No shit, Sherlock. I thought you'd be used to it by now.'

'I am. It's just, I thought that was the end of it. They said on the news. It's been a while since anybody died.'

'Not true. Sorry. I've been sick since the middle of the week. Meadow wouldn't take me to the doctor. She thought she could cure me. Crazy bitch!'

Hannah can tell Lief's quite angry. He's practically shouting. Mum and Dad can't hear him but it's still hard to relax while he's making such a racket.

'Come on away from the house,' she says.

Lief is reluctant to leave. He wants to watch television. He's always been a bit obsessed, grilling the other kids in school about their favourite programmes: *Gladiators*, *The Simpsons*, *The Fresh Prince of Bel Air*. He used to get on like he'd seen them all. Hannah could tell he was only fibbing. She saw something of herself in him. She wasn't allowed to watch those programmes either. When her class stood in huddles around the playground, talking about what they'd watched at the weekend, Lief would do his best to join in while Hannah migrated to the edge of the group. She knew she had nothing to contribute.

'You can't watch TV down here,' Lief says. 'Did the other ones tell you that?'

'No,' says Hannah. Lief's clearly got his own priorities.

'The rest of them miss their music more. They sit about singing pop songs all the time. *All that she wants is another baby*, and, *Young at heart*, and *Rhythm is a dancer*. Do you know that one? Nope, me neither. I don't know any of the words. Meadow wouldn't let us have a radio in the house. Or a TV, obviously. I can't remember if it was being Buddhist or vegan which stopped us getting one. Naw, hold on . . . it was because the radio waves would fry our brains. My ma had all these bat-shit theories about raising kids. No meat. No sugar. No shoes in the summer. And she didn't believe in cutting our hair. *Thanks for that, Meadow. Thanks a bunch.* I was always getting took for a girl.'

He pauses for breath. Hannah jumps in.

'Here, Lief, will we walk round to my granda's? He always has his telly on at night. You could watch through his window if you wanted to.'

'Class,' says Lief, his face breaking into a sudden grin. 'Let's do that.'

Any TV's better than nothing. Lief had hoped to spend the next life catching up on all the shows he's missed, especially the late-night programmes where people get murdered and you can see ladies' boobs. The lack of TV's been his main disappointment with the afterworld. On the other hand, it's also a plus. He's no different from the other kids now. He's dead. They're dead. None of them gets to watch *The Simpsons* any more. Hannah appreciates this logic. She has no desire to die, but if she has to – and this is looking increasingly likely – it's reassuring to know she might be less of a freak in new Ballylack.

It's only a ten-minute dander to Granda's, but they take it slowly, weaving backwards and forwards to avoid dog-walkers and the journalists who're wandering about like they own the place. Lief talks rapidly, barely giving Hannah time to reply.

The Dead Kids (this being the name they've chosen for their gang and – Lief stresses – it is an actual, proper gang) have been talking about Hannah a lot. They don't understand why she's their contact person. *No harm, Hannah, but you're not exactly the obvious choice.* They're not ungrateful. Lief wants her to know he's glad to see her. It's like going home for a holiday. He just doesn't understand why she's ended up their contact point.

Hannah has nothing meaningful to contribute here. She doesn't know why it's her they're lumbered with. Talking about it makes her feel awkward so she does her best to change the subject. She asks Lief what his new life's like.

'It's totally amazing. I mean, it isn't really. It's just Ballylack with less people. But we're making the most of it. Like I was saying, we have this gang. Me and Kathleen are the leaders. She's my girlfriend now.'

He pulls the neck of his shirt aside to reveal a pink, blistery circle on his neck. It looks a lot like eczema.

'Love bite,' he says, and lets his shirt collar settle back into place. 'Kat – she goes by Kat, now – gave me that. We're always facing round the back of the community centre. Tongues and all. I'm getting really good at it. I'm going to touch her boobs later on. It's OK. I think she wants me to. She keeps wearing these T-shirts that are really tight.'

Lief notices Hannah's blushing. In the excitement of telling her about Kathleen, he's forgotten how much younger she still is.

'So, yeah, Kat's in the gang, and maybe Ross. It's hard to tell with Ross. He does whatever you tell him to do but he never says anything himself. Kat says he's probably not all there.' Lief slaps his forehead with the back of his hand, rolls his eyes and lets his tongue flop out. 'Rossy Boy's a total head-the-ball, if you know what I mean.'

'The Twins. What about the Twins?' snaps Hannah. She doesn't like Lief making fun of Ross. It makes her wonder what they say about her, behind her back.

Lief shrugs. 'Lizzy's not into the DK. So – you know – Mim's not into it either. That one's not capable of thinking herself. And Lizzy's no craic down here. She's only interested in making rules and trying to work out how to escape. She says it's immature to be partying all the time. We should be trying to make things better. Like, if we can't get out, we should make Ballylack a nice place to live. Plant some flowers and decorate the place and stuff. I don't see the point myself.'

'Why not?' asks Hannah.

'I think we all know Ballylack's a bit of a shithole. No amount of hanging baskets'll change that. And it looks like we're stuck here, maybe for ever. We might as well have a bit of fun. The

DK's all about having fun. Did I tell you we drink all the time now? We get totally pissed, and I've started smoking. There's tons of good stuff in Thompson's store. You can just go in and help yourself. It'll take us ages to get through it all. When we have, we'll just start emptying people's kitchens; keep the party going for as long as we can. We have these mad dance parties down the community centre. We've no music to dance to, but we sort of sing and thump the wheelie bins for a beat. It's deadly, like. The three of us, off our heads in the dark, going absolutely buck mad.'

Lief raises both hands in the air, points his fingers to the night sky and starts punching in time with the rhythm in his head. *No, no, no, no, no, no,* he yells in a stilted, robot voice. Hannah assumes this must be a pop song, but she doesn't know who it's by. Dad doesn't allow her to listen to secular music, unless it's classical. There's no danger in classical music on account of the lack of words. Hannah quite likes music. She has a few cassettes of her own. They're all Christian songs: *Kids' Praise One, Kids' Praise Two* and a tape of carols for playing at Christmas. She doesn't recognize this *No, no* song. It sounds very defiant. Dad wouldn't approve.

'And I've changed my name,' Lief continues. 'I'm Lee now. I'm totally different from before. New name. New haircut. New threads. Nicked from Ross's big brother's wardrobe. Ross was too fat to fit into them.'

Lief executes a clumsy pirouette, spinning full circle in the street. He's right. He looks like a completely different kid. There's a swagger off him Hannah's never noticed before. He's talking the way she's heard big kids talking at the bus stop, swearing and acting like he's older than he actually is. She thinks he's putting on an American accent. She wonders where he's picked it up from if he didn't have TV in his house.

'Yeah,' she says after a second, 'you are really different, now you're dead.'

Lief takes this as a compliment. 'Well, thank you, Miss Adger. I appreciate that. Being here'll suit you too. You can finally shake off that stuffy Christian vibe.'

He runs ahead of her, punching the air, yelling, *No, no limits, we'll reach for the sky*. Hannah dashes after him. She puts a hand on his shoulder. It's cold and clammy. The deadness is leaking through his shirt. She spins him round to face her.

'Am I *definitely* going to die?' she pants. The shock and the running have knocked the wind out of her.

'We all die, Hannah. Do they not teach you that in your happy-clappy church?'

'You know what I mean, Lief . . .'

'. . . Lee.'

'You know what I mean. Am I going to die soon, like, with the rest of you?'

'It's looking very much like it. Five gone. Six left. You don't have to be a genius to work out them odds aren't great.'

They've reached Granda Pete's. Hannah feels as if she might fall over. She lowers herself on to the front wall. Lief sits beside her. He can tell he's been too blunt.

'Listen,' he says, draping a cool arm around her shoulders. 'I was only trying to tell you how great it is here since we got the DK up and running. You'll love it, Hannah. You won't have your folks bossing you around. You can actually have a bit of fun. You know, be a bit more normal for a change. *No, no limits*,' he hums softly into her ear. 'Focus on that. There's no fecking limits in this place. It's just one never-ending, crazeee party. Does that not sound awesome to you?'

Lief squeezes her shoulders a final time and slides off the wall. 'Is this your granda's place?'

Hannah nods.

'Do you mind if I hang about for a while? I'll be dead quiet. I'll just sit in the flowerbed and watch his telly through the window. I used to do that sometimes before I died. I'd sneak out at night and stand outside people's living rooms, watching whatever they had on.'

Hannah nods. She doesn't know how to refuse Lief. He's so grown-up now, so self-assured. Listening to him, she could almost believe there are some positives to being dead. She's jealous of his confidence, the way he's moved from the edge of their circle to the centre of everything. She's not too sure about the partying, though. It's wrong to drink. And wrong to swear. And definitely a sin to smoke. The S.E.X. stuff terrifies her.

Hannah tries to imagine what it'd be like to live without rules. The thought of this makes her so anxious her head feels light. She has to grip the edge of the wall until the wobbliness passes. *Do they even have God down there?* The Bible says there's no place in the universe where God can't go, except maybe Hell. *But did the people who wrote the Bible know about this other place?* Hannah wonders if the rules are different in new Ballylack.

She turns to ask Lief if God exists in the other place. Lief has already slipped away, taking up position in Granny's azalea bed. He's hoping for an episode of *The Simpsons*, but even *Dad's Army* would do in a pinch. He'll watch just about anything.

Hannah lets herself in with the key which is stashed beneath the milk-bottle stand. She can hear the hum of the TV drifting up the hall. She heels her outdoor shoes off and pads down to the living room. She's still thinking about whether God is actually everywhere. *How could you be sure? It's not as if you can actually see him.* Sometimes Hannah hears the Jesus talking in her head. That does feels like a kind of proof. But he's been quiet for ages now and when she presses into this silence, trying to make her prayers stick, it's as if there's nothing for them to catch on. It's like shouting into an empty room.

It's only half a dozen paces from the front door to the living room but, by the time Hannah arrives at the side of Granda's reclining chair, she's worked herself up into a state. She comes into the room sobbing and crawls up on his knee.

'Uch, Hannah Banana, where did you come from? What on earth's wrong?'

She burrows her face into Granda's neck and cries harder than she's cried in years. She's too scared to lift her head. She doesn't want to see Lief's white face peering through the double-glazing. She finally manages to tell Granda Pete that he's dead. It comes out in a big, mumbly rush. He doesn't ask how she knows this. Two streets over on Main Street, Rob Anderson is only this second breaking the news.

'Uch, pet, that's awful. You must be in bits. Do you want to talk about it?'

The old man fumbles along the side of his recliner, finds the remote and turns the TV off. He wants to give Hannah his full attention. A single bright line flashes across the screen then it goes black. On the other side of the glass Lief sighs and draws back from the window. Though his fingers have been pressed against the glass and his breath has fogged against it, he leaves no trace of himself behind.

He wonders if this will be his last opportunity to watch TV. He feels sad for the first time since dying. He quickly shrugs the feeling off. There's beer to be drunk and the possibility of doing dirty stuff with Kat. Lief picks his way out of the azalea bed. He stands on the edge of Granda Pete's lawn, right beside Granny's whirly-gig washing line. He raises both arms up in the air and, with curled fists, punches out the words. *No, no limits, we'll reach for the sky. No valley too deep. No mountain too high.* Lief decides that this will be the Dead Kids' anthem and, from this point on, it is.

The Raggedy Tree

THE VERY SECOND the news is over William's mum is on the phone to the Adgers.

'I'm sorry to bother you at this time of night, but could I have a wee word with your wife?'

Dad drags the cord down the hall so Mum doesn't have to get off the sofa. He hands her the phone and walks away, mouthing the words *Marlene Fowler* as he heads upstairs to run his bath. Mum can't be bothered talking to Marlene. No harm to her – *she's a lovely woman* – but she's the fourth mother to call today.

Hannah's mum's known for being a soft touch. If you're in need of a shoulder to cry on, or a friendly ear, or a wee handout, give Sandra Adger a shout. *Sandra never turns anybody away. She's not allowed to. She's a Born Again.* Usually, she sees this as a privilege. She tries to live her life by the principle of *Whatever you do for the least of these.* She's called to help. It's her vocation. Today she's not feeling particularly benevolent. She's started wondering if people see her as a doormat.

She's already had Caroline's mum on the phone, breaking her heart because her wee girl's never going to grow up, or get married, or have any wee girls of her own.

And she's prayed at some length for Liza Ross, though Liza

hasn't asked for prayer. She's not left her bed since the Twins died. It was Cliff who rang and asked if she'd pray with his wife. 'It'd be such a comfort,' he said. 'You're better placed than a minister, what with being a mum yourself.' He held the handset to his wife's ear and afterwards told Hannah's mum that she was a saint. She doesn't feel much like a saint today. She'd not actually meant the words she'd prayed.

In the afternoon, she'd spent two whole hours listening to Ross's mum gurn and moan and then gurn again. Part of her had felt like screaming, *What about me, Lorraine? Are you not going to ask me how I'm coping? I'm a mummy. I'm hurting as much as the rest of you.* The other part understood these calls as a kind of penance. Her child would be fine. She was certain of it. She was actively keeping this knowledge from the other parents. She feels sick to her stomach just thinking about this. It's a wonder they can't hear the guilt in her voice.

When you have a Christian witness like the Adgers have, other people assume you're above it all. They imagine you're taking all your worries to the Lord, leaving them there and walking away. *What a load of sanctimonious tripe.* Hannah's mum's no different from everybody else. Her faith is no great asset at the minute. It's just another thing to worry about. She's only going through the motions of faith these days. When she prays, God isn't listening and the cold side of faith is a lonely place. Yet everybody calls her a rock. They keep demanding things of her. Kind words. Reassurance. Comforting prayers. There's so little of Mum left. Yet everybody keeps asking for more.

She collects herself before answering the phone. 'Hello, Marlene,' she says, sliding into her pastoral voice. It's somewhere between Avon lady and hospital nurse: concerned, yet always the evangelist. 'How are you holding up over there? John and I have been praying for William and the rest of you.'

'Aye, grand, Sandra. William's not showing any symptoms

yet. The rest of us are muddling through. Here, I don't want to keep you away from Hannah. There's just something I wanted to ask you about.'

Mum realizes, with a degree of relief, that Marlene isn't looking for a pity party. She's a farmer's wife; not a big talker at the best of times. She's called with a specific purpose in mind. No chitchat or sympathy is required.

'I was wondering how youse told Hannah?'

Hannah's mum feels like she's been slapped in the face.

'It's just that we're going to tell our William in the morning, and we don't know how to go about it. Did youse just tell her she had it and she's probably going to die or did you soft-soap it a bit? Himself's all for sticking to the cold, hard facts. I keep thinking the lad's only eleven. It's an awful lot to take on board.'

Mum doesn't know what to say. Nobody's asked about Hannah's diagnosis. They've just assumed she's in the same boat as the others. The Adgers are sitting on an awful secret. They know it's best to keep it to themselves. They've told Granny and Granda. Only because Granny kept asking, every half-hour, till she wore Dad down. They've kept to their decision not to tell Hannah. Or, at least, Dad's decided and Mum's acquiesced. She's still not convinced that it's right to keep the child in fear for her life, but she understands her husband's reasoning. Emotionally, Hannah's all over the place. If she knew she was the only one not infected, it could tip her over the edge. They're hoping the others will make it through and Hannah will feel like she's on the winning team. If they don't – and they'll cross that bridge when they come to it – they'll do their best to convince her she's a very blessed wee girl.

In the meantime, if nobody asks, then they aren't going to go out of their way to reveal their daughter is fighting fit.

'So, what did youse tell her?' prompts Marlene.

Hannah's mum has to think on her feet. 'We haven't actually

told her yet.' This is technically not a lie, though she knows Marlene will read into it.

'Has she not been asking? Our William's never done asking if his tests are back. We've been fobbing him off for the last few days.'

'No,' says Mum and, in saying this, wonders why Hannah hasn't asked. She can be a very strange child at times. She's a worrier. A real Anxious Annie. She bites her nails and everything. Mum's noticed that she copes better when she doesn't know what's up ahead. Now she never tells her in advance when she has a dentist's appointment or if the school nurse is doing the rounds. Ten minutes before, in the car, on the way, is time enough to lean over and tell her what's about to happen. *Now don't panic, Hannah. Remember what Granda Pete says: This, too, shall pass.*

Hannah's anxiety came to a head last summer when Pastor Bill preached eight straight weeks on the Book of Revelation, explaining how the world was now entering the end times. Between the peace talks and the advent of the world wide web, barcodes and the EEC, all the Biblical prophecies had been fulfilled. The Lord would soon be coming again. Hannah had sat there every Sunday, drinking the Apocalypse in like a wee sponge. The four horsemen. The antichrist. The mark of the Beast. She'd worried so much she near drove herself mad. It was one thing knowing the world would end some day, another thing realizing it would be on her watch.

Hannah had cried herself to sleep every night for a month. When Mum finally worked out what was frightening her, she'd felt like wringing Pastor Bill's neck. It took her days to talk her daughter down. Hours and hours of explaining that the Lord's return wasn't a thing to be afraid of, but rather something to look forward to. Like a birthday. Or Christmas. Or both best days rolled into one. *Imagine, Hannah, being with the Lord for ever in a perfect place with no sin.* She seemed somewhat comforted by this but didn't properly relax until Mum – making sure Dad wasn't around – explained that Pastor Bill was talking rubbish. Only God knew when the world would end. Sure, didn't it say in the Bible, 'No man knoweth the hour nor the day'? After hearing this, Hannah was grand. She could put the Apocalypse to the back of her mind and get on with being ten.

Hannah's the sort of wee girl who prefers not to know. Mum imagines this is why she hasn't asked about her tests. If nobody confirms she's ill, she can keep on pretending that she's not. Mum's thinking about this as she finishes her conversation with Marlene.

'Every child's different,' she says. 'They're all going to react in different ways. You know your William better than anybody else. You already know what you need to say.'

Marlene agrees. She thanks Hannah's mum for her time and, before she hangs up, adds, 'If you ever need somebody to talk to, Sandra, just pick up the phone.'

Sometimes kindness hits harder than being ill used. Hannah's mum is still crying when the phone goes again. It's only Granda calling to say Hannah's round at his and would it be OK with the pair of them if she slept over tonight.

'She's a wee bit weepy,' he says.

'Aren't we all?' says Mum.

'I know, sweetheart. Listen, you're doing so well with all of this. I just thought it might be good for youse to have a bit of space. Have a good cry. Hannah's not there to see you falling apart. It'll do you the world of good. Let me look after her for a change.'

This sets Mum off all over again. She'll come round for Hannah in the morning. 'Thank you,' she mumbles. 'Thank you so much.'

*

Granny's gone to bed early with one of her complaints. Granda can't remember if it was arthritis-related or her bowels playing up this time. There's been a different issue every night since the outbreak started. It's either Granny's way of sympathizing or of ensuring she doesn't get overlooked. Hannah and Granda Pete have the house to themselves. He leaves her curled up on the sofa and makes her hot chocolate in Beatrix Potter. He hunts out Granny's visitor biscuits: the fancy ones she buys from Marksy's when she's up in Belfast.

By the time he returns to the living room Hannah's much calmer, though her face is still flushed. Granda lowers himself on to the sofa beside her. He draws her in to a big side hug.

'Right,' he says, 'you and me's going to make a dent in Granny's fancy biscuits. Tomorrow morning, we'll deny all knowledge. She'll probably think we have a mouse.'

Hannah hesitates for a moment then helps herself to a Viennese Whirl.

'Do you want to talk, pet? You don't have to if you don't want to, but I'm here to listen if it helps at all.'

Hannah takes a big slurp of hot chocolate. Granda can tell she wants to say something. She just doesn't know where to begin.

'I tell you what, Han. I'll tell you a secret, something the rest of them don't know about. Then, if you want to tell me something, we'd be even. How does that sound? I'm for telling you my secret anyway.'

Hannah considers this for a moment, then nods.

'OK, now promise you won't tell your granny. She'd have my guts for garters. Look at this.' He fishes around in his cardigan pocket and produces a half-empty carton of Benson and Hedges. 'I know they're bad for you and all. I'm going to give up soon . . . and you're never to touch them yourself. That's my secret, I go for a smoke behind the shed when I need ten minutes' peace from *you know who*.'

Hannah giggles. It's definitely a sin to smoke. But the way

Granda Pete puts it, it doesn't seem that bad. The Jesus in her head is laughing too. Hannah hasn't heard him in ages. It makes her feel a tiny bit better, knowing he's not annoyed with her.

'Now, Han. Do you have something you want to tell me? Are you a smoker yourself? Maybe it's whiskey you need to confess. Or have you gone and got yourself a tattoo?'

Hannah's laughing really hard now. Granda Pete has a knack for cheering her up. She feels like she could tell him anything. Even the awful ugly things Mum and Dad wouldn't want to hear.

'Do you pray, Granda?'

'Umm, I don't know is the honest answer. I mean I don't get down on my knees or talk to God out loud or anything like that. Sometimes I think good thoughts about other people or I kind of wish things for them inside my head. Would you call that praying? I'm not sure. What about you, Hannah? Do you pray yourself?'

'Yes. All the time. Especially at the minute. I keep asking God to help us, but I don't think He's listening. I'm praying as hard as I can, Granda, and everybody's dying anyway. It says in the Bible that God answers prayer. Am I doing it wrong?'

'No, Hannah. You're definitely not doing anything wrong.'

'Then maybe praying just doesn't work. Dad says it's the best thing we can do right now. I just don't know any more. I'm a bit mixed up. Everything used to be so simple. I just had to do what Pastor Bill said and it'd be OK. Now, I'm not sure about anything.'

Hannah considers telling Granda about the visits and the Dead Kids and the other Ballylack. She knows he wouldn't get cross or accuse her of telling lies. It'd be way easier to tell him than her dad. It's just that here, in Granny's living room, with her favourite mug cupped in her hands, everything feels so real and normal it's hard to believe the other stuff has actually happened. When Hannah thinks back to her conversation with Lief it feels a bit like remembering a dream. She's sure it happened. Still, it doesn't feel real. She wants to tell Granda Pete all about it. At the same time, she knows she can't.

'Do you think praying's the only way to change things?' she finally asks. 'It probably sounds a bit mad, but I feel like there might be other stuff out there, things that we don't talk about in church. You know . . . like magic. Uch, I don't even really know what I mean, Granda. It's just, I feel like I'm not doing anything sitting here, just thinking good thoughts. I want to help the others. I think maybe I'm meant to help them. I just don't know what more I can do. I'll keep praying. It's not really working but I know you have to persevere. I just wondered if there's anything else.'

Later Granda Pete will wish he'd kept his mouth shut. He'll question his motivations. He'll accuse himself of all sorts of things. Irresponsibility, in the extreme. Filling the child's head with fanciful nonsense. Taking his own hang-ups out on her. Hannah reminds him of himself so strongly. She's articulating his confusion. She's only eleven but, boys a dear, she's fairly hit the nail on the head. It's not that Granda Pete is anti-church. It's just the way they preach religion here. It's neither wide nor wonderful enough to accommodate his idea of the divine. He's always wondered why Ulster Prods are so intent upon putting God in a box. *What's that thing that Shakespeare said? There are more things in heaven and earth.*

Granda pauses for a minute, wondering how to convey all this to a frightened child. Hannah's already mixed up enough. He understands now why they haven't told her she's the only healthy child. The guilt of it would make her sick. She's breaking her wee heart wanting to help. She's trying to reconcile what she knows with this uncertain world everyone's suddenly been pitched into. He can't help but wonder what sort of reassurance he'd require if he were in his granddaughter's shoes. Granda Pete's a practical man. He's a doer, not a thinker. A fixer. A mender. An action man. Which is why he tells Hannah about the Raggedy Tree. He honestly thinks he's being helpful. The last thing Granda would ever do is harm his wee princess in any way.

'Let me tell you a story, Hannah,' he says. 'You'll not have heard this one before, and don't be telling your folks I told you. To be honest, it's really their story to tell, but they didn't want you getting up yourself, feeling like you were somebody special. Here's the thing, Hannah Adger. I do believe you're somebody special. You're a sort of miracle, and I think you deserve to know what happened when you came into the world. Am I right?'

'Uh huh,' says Hannah, her voice a bit wobbly.

'OK then,' says Granda Pete, putting on his book-reading voice. 'For your ears only, I give you the wondrous story of the greatest wee lassie Ballylack's ever seen. The day you were born was my best day ever. You were perfect, pet, like a tiny wee doll. I wasn't expecting to love you that much straight away. It came over me in such a rush. You were born early; nearly five weeks before you were due. You were that keen to meet us all. At first the doctors said you were grand. We were making plans to bring you home. Then you started struggling to breathe. Your lungs were so tiny you couldn't ever get enough air. They had to take you away from your mummy and put you in one of those special tanks. We couldn't touch you. It was awful, Han. We could only look at you through the glass. You were all pink and so little, like a just-hatched bird. The doctor said it was touch and go. You were doing your best, but you weren't really making anything of it.

'I couldn't imagine losing you. None of us could. You were the best thing we'd ever had. Your mummy and your granny cried that hard I honestly thought they'd never stop. Even me and your daddy cried. We didn't know what to do. We felt so helpless in the hospital. The ones from church said we should cover you in constant prayer. We didn't know what else to do. We prayed and prayed. We got other people to pray for you too. There were folks we didn't even know, praying for you all over the world. I prayed as hard as the rest of them. I was still going to church back then. I believed God was going to make you better, but after three days of praying the doctors told us you were on your way out. I felt just like you're feeling now, Hannah. I was praying and it wasn't working. It made me ask a lot of big questions; the sort of questions you're asking right now.

'I was fed up praying. I just wanted to do something. Something to help. I remembered a story my granny used to tell me about these places you could go if you were desperate. Fairy Trees, you called them. There was one on the outskirts of Ballylack, in the corner of Millar's Gap; people called it the Raggedy Tree. I'm guessing most people have forgotten about it. It used to be the go-to place for desperate folks when I was a lad, but nobody really goes there any more. Nobody believes in that kind of superstitious stuff nowadays.'

Hannah interrupts. 'I know about the Raggedy Tree, Granda. Miss McKeown was teaching us about it in school. The rest of them went on a trip to see it. Dad wouldn't let me go. He said it was evil. He didn't want me anywhere near it.'

'Aye,' says Granda, 'your dad would say that. I used to think the same thing too. But I was desperate, Hannah. I'd have tried anything to hold on to you. To cut a long story short, the rest of them kept praying. I left them at it in the hospital. I went down to Millar's Gap with a wee scrap of pink cloth cut from your baby blanket and I tied it to the Raggedy Tree. I said a prayer. Or made a wish. Whatever you want to call it. I asked for you to get better again. And you did, Hannah. You started breathing yourself that night. Your daddy said it was an answer to prayer. Maybe it was. I don't know. It might have been the Raggedy Tree. Or it might have been a miracle. Or maybe both. Or just the medicine starting to work. I couldn't say for sure. I just know I felt much better in myself after I'd been to the Raggedy Tree. I'd done something for you. I think I helped. I've never told anybody what I done.'

Hannah reaches for her granda's hand. She takes it in hers and doesn't let go. She hopes he can tell that she's grateful. For how he helped her as a baby. For how he's trying to help her now.

'Granda,' she says, looking straight at him. 'I want you to take me to the Raggedy Tree.' She isn't asking. She's telling him.

Millar's Gap

THEY TAKE GRANNY'S Astra. Granny's awful particular about her car. Granda's never allowed to drive it. At least not since the incident in the multistorey over in town. Granny's flat out, snoring away. They'll have her car back before she even notices it's gone. Granda reminds Hannah that she'll need a bit of material – something belonging to one of the children – to tie on to the Raggedy Tree. For a few minutes, they're both stumped. Then Hannah remembers she left her uniform at Granny's after the last day of school. Granda Pete checks the hot press. It's still there, washed and ironed, ready to go up into the roof space at home alongside all her other baby clothes. They take Hannah's school tie. It will be easy to knot around a branch. It'll represent all the kids in her class at once.

Granda keeps the low beams on till he's out of Ballylack. He's anxious not to attract attention. It's the Eleventh Night. Technically, it's already the Twelfth. People are out later than usual. They're wobbling home from Henderson's or standing around drinking in the street. There's a bonfire behind the community centre; a feeble wee pile of tyres and cardboard. It's hardly lit before it's out. Nobody's got much interest this year. There's a proper fire up the road in McAuley's field. The loyal contingent is making an attempt to be respectful. *Of course they'll shift their bonfire out of the village. They don't mind gathering somewhere a bit more discreet.* They don't, for a second, consider cancelling. It's the eleventh of July and burning Sinn Féin posters is their God-ordained right. Hannah and Granda pass the big bonfire on their way to Millar's Gap. Even from a distance of thirty-odd feet, the heat permeates the Astra's window. Granda turns the cold air on.

'I forgot it was the Eleventh Night,' he says. 'I suppose tomorrow'll be the Twelfth.'

He's not looking for a response from Hannah. It's just a thing he can feasibly say to fill the silence in the car. Granda Pete can't seem to stop talking. It's his way of keeping the nerves in check. He's used the drive between home and here to tell Hannah everything he knows about Millar's Gap.

It used to belong to Francie Millar, hence the name. Granda doesn't know who owns it now. Maybe nobody does. Hannah stops listening at this point. Her head's a muddle of anticipation and shrill fear. She counts the telegraph poles they pass. It's not easy to see them in the dark but it kind of helps her to calm down.

Granda Pete pulls the Astra up on the verge outside Millar's Gap. He fumbles in the glovebox for a torch. He tells Hannah to be careful and watch where she's walking for there's all sorts of rubbish dumped in there. 'Go on now, pet,' he says. 'Be as quick as you can, careful round the pond. I'll be right here when you get back.' He's not going with her. He's explained that he can't. If you're serious about the Raggedy Tree, you have to go by yourself. He watches his granddaughter climb out of the car. Her torch beam sweeps backwards and forwards as she opens the gate and walks away. He lights a cigarette. He's smoking inside the car, not one bit concerned about the smell it'll leave. He puts on one of Granny's Willy McCrea tapes. He thinks the man's an absolute headcase and – more to the point – can't hold a note, but he's doing everything he can to distract himself from the voice at the back of his head which is growing louder by the second, which is sounding more and more like his son's voice. *What are you doing, sending our Hannah off to talk to a magic tree? In the dark? All by herself? This is going to end in tears.*

Hannah picks her way around the pond. She keeps the torch trained on the grass. The ground is boggy. There's a putrid smell hanging in the air, like compost heaps and old, damp cloths. The wetness oozes up over her sandals. It soaks through her socks and begins to squelch between her toes. It's so quiet out here away from the village she can hear every one of her soggy steps. Her own breathing is loud in her ears. It's coming fast and shallow. There's a familiar tightness in her lungs. She does her best not to panic, to concentrate on why she's here. *It's just a field*, she tells herself. *It's just a pond. It's just a tree. And Granda's only a few feet away. I bet he's smoking in Granny's car.* The thought of this makes her smile. It's a bit like having him here beside her. It would be much less scary if she wasn't by herself. Hannah fishes around inside her head, wondering if Jesus might be in the mood for a chat. She could do with a bit of company. But Jesus isn't here in Millar's Gap. Hannah's not surprised. Jesus belongs to another world. He's church and home and Mum and Dad. This place is something entirely different. Hannah's not sure what it is.

She knows what she's doing is a sin. The Raggedy Tree is a witchy, pagan sort of thing. She can hear Dad's voice in her ear, reciting the verse he calls his Halloween text: 'Resist the Devil, and he will flee from you,' James 4:7. Hannah knows she isn't resisting. She's giving the Devil a great big foothold, dabbling in ungodly things. She should be running in the other direction, but she doesn't know what else to do.

Hannah finds the Raggedy Tree in the corner, between the pond's edge and a crumbling stone wall. It looks like no one's been here for years. All the little scraps of cloth have faded and shrivelled over time. She finds an almost empty branch and reaches for the school tie in her pocket. Her hands are shaking. She can't keep them still. There's no point telling herself to be brave. She's past the point of terrified. The dark feels so much darker out here. The air is heavy. It's like a blanket covering everything. She's so alone. So very alone. This is the most scared she's ever been. Her fumbling fingers drop the tie. It slithers into the edge of the pond. She grabs it quickly. It's dripping wet. The scummy pondwater runs over her hands and down her arms. She's about to pitch the tie at the tree, turn on her heels and run away when she hears someone whispering her name. *Hannah, we're here. Don't be scared. You can do this, Hannah. You're not on your own.* There are several different voices, all familiar. They're whispering right up close to her ear. It should be terrifying. It isn't. She's used to hearing the others now. It's actually less lonely when they're about.

She can do this. She knows she can. The rest of them are counting on her. She'll do whatever it takes to help her friends.

She grips the torch between her teeth to free her hands. The handle's covered in stinking pondwater. She tries not to think about the germs. She knots her school tie around the branch; double knots it so it won't slide off. She can hear the others whispering encouragement. *Well done, Hannah. You're so brave.*

She's not too sure what she should say. Granda's not given her any instructions about this part. Making a wish feels a lot like praying so Hannah puts on her best praying voice. 'Dear Raggedy Tree, please make us all get better soon. And can you help the ones who've already died? And also fix it so their mums and dads don't feel as sad. That's it. Thank you. And amen.' She waits to see if something dramatic is going to happen. A bolt of lightning or a ghostly voice. Like in the Bible when God spoke to Moses from the burning bush. Nothing happens. Her school tie just hangs there, slowly dripping on to the grass.

In case the others are still listening, Hannah says loudly, 'OK, well, I really hope that works.' She's not sure what she'd been expecting. She already feels a little daft. Standing in a boggy field. Talking to a stupid tree. She turns around and begins walking back towards the car. The car feels further away than it was before. All of a sudden, she's really tired. Her feet are freezing in their damp socks. She'll get Granda to put the heating on in the car. Granny might even have a rug in the boot. She tries to focus on the warm bed waiting at home.

Hannah's halfway round the pond when she hears it. At first, she assumes it is an owl. It's not an owl. It's a girl, laughing. A mean kind of laugh. The sort of laugh you'd aim at someone who'd accidentally rubbed pen ink into their face or tucked their skirt into their knickers. Hannah knows it's directed at her. She knows exactly who it belongs to. It's not the first time this voice has laughed at her. It's Kathleen laughing. And mocking her. She's getting everyone to laugh along. *Ha ha ha. Hannah's so weird. Hannah's mental. Hannah actually talks to trees. Hannah doesn't know who Take That are. Hannah wears Velcro trainers like a baby. Hannah doesn't know what French kissing is. Ha ha ha. Hannah's rare. Hannah's not like the rest of us.* Hannah picks up her heels. She sprints the last fifty yards back to the Astra.

'Did you get sorted?' asks Granda.

'Yes,' says Hannah. 'Can we go home now?'

She's done what she came to do. She's asked the Raggedy Tree for help. She's glad she did it. At least, she thinks she is. But she's never setting foot in Millar's Gap again.

The Glorious Twelfth

THE NEXT MORNING Hannah's barely in the door when Mrs Nugent calls. Amy Leung has died in the night. Mum didn't even know Amy was ill, though it doesn't surprise her. The Leungs like to keep themselves to themselves.

'She went quietly,' Mrs Nugent says. 'No fuss at all.'

'Poor wee mite,' says Mum. 'She must've been terrified. It's not like she didn't know what was coming.' Mum can't help but think of Hannah. Hannah still believes all this is ahead of her. Mum once again wonders if they should put her out of her misery.

Mrs Nugent is still whittling on. 'I'm sure the child was petrified. But there wasn't a peep out of her – not so much as a sniffle – even when they couldn't get the drip in at the end.'

Hannah is listening in on the upstairs phone, holding her hand over the receiver so Mum won't hear her breathing. Once more she wonders where Mrs Nugent is getting her information from. Perhaps she has some kind of second sight. There are people in church who seem to know things without being told. It's called having a prophetic gift. They receive messages from the Lord which they pass on to other members of the congregation. 'Like postmen?' Hannah once asked, and Mum said, 'Yes, sort of like a postman.' Dad said it wasn't like postmen at all.

154

Hannah's still not sure what it means to be a prophet but she's pretty sure they aren't meant to use their powers for spreading gossip. They're supposed to tell people God's noticed their faithfulness during difficult times, or God's calling them to the mission field, or to a life of singleness. Singleness messages are almost always given to plain-looking girls of a certain age.

Amy Leung's death sounds very similar to her life: quiet, cautious and a little bit sad. Hannah's already forgotten how she sounded. Amy rarely spoke and, when she did, her voice was so soft and feathery it seemed to evaporate on her lips. Sometimes, in school, Miss McKeown would pass right over Amy's raised hand to settle upon one of the louder children: Kathleen or Lizzy, who could never keep their answering arms down. Miss McKeown wasn't trying to ignore Amy. If anything, she went out of her way to include both her and Ben because other people looked straight through them. With Amy it wasn't easy. She didn't want to be noticed. She made a point of keeping herself small. Hannah can picture Amy in hospital; her mouth tightly shut, holding the hurt inside. She'd have hated being the centre of attention. She'd be so embarrassed by the way everybody's talking about her now.

Granda Pete once told Hannah that sick birds sometimes crawl under hedges to die in private, by themselves. She's come across a few of them – sparrows, starlings, once a tiny dapple-breasted thrush – their bird bodies unmarked by cats or cars or prowling foxes. They hadn't looked dead so much as sleeping. This is how it should've been for Amy Leung. A quiet end to a quiet life. There's been nothing quiet about Amy's death. It's happened on the loudest day of the year. In a few hours' time the whole village will go stomping past her front door. Everybody will be talking about the Leungs. Everybody will be staring like mad.

The window of the Chinese takeaway doesn't have curtains. Mr Leung has pinned towels across the glass to show the family is in mourning. In China they did not lower their blinds or close their curtains to denote a bereavement. In China they placed a white banner over the doorway. They sat with the body and let the funeral stretch out for seven days. The Leungs aren't in China any more and Mr Leung does not want to make a fuss. He lifts a stack of clean bath towels out of the hot press and uses drawing pins to fasten them up. He insists upon holding a proper Irish wake with tea and buns and trays of salad sandwiches, triangling limply on a tray.

Mrs Leung says there's no need. Mrs Leung says, 'Please do not be odd, Fai.' Mrs Leung says she'll lock herself in the bathroom if he invites people round at a time like this. Mr Leung says she can run naked round the backyard for all he cares. He will still be having the wake. It is, he explains to his wife, the proper way to mourn in this country, which is now their country too. He doesn't want to be different from his neighbours. The Leungs are already odd enough.

Mr Leung makes the sandwiches himself. He forgets to add the salad cream. Nobody mentions how dry they are. This would be unthinkably rude. They eat Mr Leung's sandwiches and his shop-bought cake, though they've only just risen from their breakfasts. They silently wonder what on earth he's doing. Doesn't he know there are different rules for tragic deaths: children and car accidents and people caught up in bombings? There's no need for a wake like this. No call for sandwiches and tea, or the stiff, stoic face he greets them with. *Cry and scream*, they want to say. *Turf the lot of us out of your house. Your wee girl's dead. You don't need to make us tea.* They don't want to make a scene or disrespect the Leungs. *Who knows*, they think, *maybe this is the way Chinese people mourn their children. Maybe they're more reserved than the rest of us.*

Granda Pete comes round to sit with Hannah so Mum and Dad can go and pay their respects. It's far too early for a wake but the bands will be starting to gather soon. They'd like to be home before the marching begins. Mum lifts a plastic tub of broth from the freezer. There's nothing fresh in the house; still, she can't arrive at the Leungs' empty-handed. It's just not done. She hugs Hannah on the doorstep. Dad hugs her too. He holds on so long Granda Pete has to slide his arm in between, prising the pair of them apart.

'We'll be grand,' he says. 'I'm going to do French toast for breakfast; special treat for the Twelfth.'

'You can't march on an empty stomach,' says Dad, trying and failing to sound upbeat.

It's a stupid joke. Hannah's family never march. They probably won't even watch the parade. They're not the normal sort of Protestants. They're the kind who don't believe in the Orange Order. They're in the minority around Ballylack. Almost everyone in Hannah's class has a dad in the local lodge. Before he passed away, William's granda was a Grandmaster. Everybody in the village knew who he was. Old men sometimes stop William to ask when he's for joining the junior boys. Hannah once asked him what a Grandmaster was. William wasn't sure, though he thought it probably meant leader because his granda always marched at the head of the parade and his sash was fancier than everybody else's.

Some of the children in Hannah's class are already in bands. Kick the Pope bands, they call them, though none of them could pick the Pope out of a line-up if he wasn't wearing his pointy hat. They practise during lunchbreak, holding imaginary pipes to their lips, funnelling air through the side of their mouths, marching in formation round the infants' playground. They sing 'The Sash', mumbling the bits they can't remember. They sing, 'We are, we are, we are the Billy Boys,' dropping their feet in time to the beat. They sing about following Rangers up the Falls and round Derry's walls. Hannah doesn't have a clue what they're talking about. She sits on the wall with Lief, who is just as clueless.

'Is your dad an Orangeman?' he asks.

'No,' says Hannah.

'Is he in a band?'

'No.'

'Are youse even Protestants?'

'I think so.' She isn't sure exactly what they are.

This morning, while she has Granda to herself, she will take the opportunity to find out what sort of Protestants her family are. He's told her she can ask him anything and this is what she wants to know. It'll distract her from thinking about Amy for a while. Not to mention last night's wee jaunt to Millar's Gap. Her head's been stuck in a loop since she woke up. Round and round the dark thoughts go, keeping their own unseemly beat. More than half the class are gone now and there's still no antidote in sight. The odds aren't great. Most likely she'll die.

Hannah has begun telling herself this, calmly and with some force. *You're going to die. There's nothing you can do about it. No point getting yourself into a tizz, Han. No point panicking.* She is trying to grow into the idea of dying to see it as something inevitable, like when she lost her baby teeth, which felt weird at first, then completely normal until, eventually, she'd grown used to the gaps. Unsurprisingly enough, it isn't as easy to get used to death. Every twitch and tingle has Hannah thinking the sickness has started. It's impossible not to wonder how long she has left. Maybe a distraction will help.

She pads into the kitchen, where Granda Pete is getting the big pan out for French toast. He's made eggy batter in a soup plate. There's a slice of white pan loaf already soaking in the mixture.

'Two slices or one, Han?' he asks, turning to smile across the kitchen.

'One. No, maybe two, please, Granda. I don't know how hungry I am.'

'Sure, I'll do you two and, if you can't finish, it'll not go to waste.' He pats his belly. It's a lot bigger than it used to be. 'Your old granda's a hoover when it comes to leftovers.'

Hannah pours herself a glass of juice and hops up at the kitchen table. She's back in her pyjamas and dressing gown, though it's almost ten thirty. There's no point putting real clothes on when she knows she won't be leaving the house. She lets the toes of her slippers drag against the lino, marking time until the moment's right.

'All good, pet?'

'Yeah. I'm fine.'

'No funny dreams or anything, after last night?'

Hannah shakes her head. She's not for telling her granda that she barely slept. She's not for telling him about the voices either, or just how scary the whole escapade actually was.

'We'll just keep last night to ourselves, won't we? And all the other stuff I told you. It's a wee secret between us two.'

Hannah nods. 'Granda, can I ask you something?'

'I told you, love. You can ask me anything.'

'Anything?'

'Absolutely anything. Is this about the Raggedy Tree?'

'No, I was just wondering why we don't do the Twelfth? Everybody else in Ballylack does. Are we not proper Protestants?'

Granda smiles. He seems relieved, as if he'd been bracing himself for a harder question. He pulls the pan off the hob and wipes his hands on a dishcloth. He sits down opposite.

'Do you even know what the Twelfth's about, Hannah?'

Hannah shakes her head. She's a bit hazy on the details. She thinks it's something to do with letting Catholics know they're wrong.

'At least you're honest. Half the eejits out there have no idea what they're marching for.'

'Why are they marching? What's the point of it all?'

'Well, they're remembering a big fight called the Battle of the Boyne that happened in 1690. A fella called William of Orange came over from Holland. Supposedly, he fought to save the Protestant faith from the Catholics.'

'Is that why they're called Orangemen?'

'It is indeed. They're named after your man from Holland.'

'That was ages ago. Why are they still marching? Do they want to fight the Catholics again?'

'Some of them would like nothing better. Some of them just like dressing up and having a day out. Some of them don't know why on earth they're marching but their daddies are Orangemen and their daddies before them. They've been at it so long they've forgotten what the point is.'

'It sounds a bit daft, Granda.'

'I think so. I never had any interest myself.'

'And my dad wasn't interested either?'

'No, pet. Thank goodness he never was into the Orange, and the folks in that church youse go to don't believe in mixing religion and politics. There's a lot of things I don't see eye to eye with them on, but I take my hat off to yon pastor of yours for his stand on that issue. The church is no place for political talk. This country's going to Hell in a handbasket because folks can't separate the two. Paisley and his lot have brought filthy talk into the pulpit. Damn them all. It shouldn't be allowed.'

Hannah stares at Granda Pete. He has that faraway look he gets sometimes when he's watching the news and something bad's happened up in Belfast: a pipe bomb, or some kind of shooting. It's as if he's not really there. He's watching some other scene playing out behind his eyes. He's not really thinking about her. He could be talking to anyone. When Granny catches him doing it she always tells him to wise the head. 'Earth to Peter James Adger' is what she says.

'And is that why we don't do the Twelfth?' asks Hannah, trying to reel Granda Pete back in.

He slides back into the moment, reaching across the table to take her hand. He looks her directly in the eye.

'These are powerful hard things for a wee head to take in, but you're a wise one, Hannah Adger, so I'm not for talking down to you. I can't speak for your dad or mum. Dear help me, I can't even speak for your gran, though the two of us are married these forty-odd years. I can only speak for myself and tell you I don't do the Twelfth and I'll never be an Orangeman. Sure, I hardly ever darken the door of a church. The truth is, I don't really believe we're all that different from the other lot.'

'You mean Catholics?'

'Aye, Hannah. I mean Catholics. It's not a popular view round here. Once I came to it, well, I wasn't able to find a church where they thought similarly, so I just stopped going altogether.'

'Does that mean you're not a Protestant any more? Are you even saved, Granda?'

'Protestant, Catholic, Christian, sure they're all just labels, aren't they? Who cares what people call you? I'd say the important thing is where you stand, in yourself, with the man upstairs. The rest of it's just labels we give other people so we feel better about ourselves.'

'What about my mum and dad? What do they think?'

'Well, you'd have to ask them that yourself, Hannah. Your dad's not out there marching with the Orangemen, I'll give him that. But he does spend a wild amount of time going round the estates, trying to convert the other sort to his version of God.'

'Protestant God?'

'You could call Him that.'

Hannah is confused. 'So, are there two kinds of God: a Protestant one and a different God for the Catholics?'

'Not in my opinion, though you'd think that sometimes, living here.'

The same faraway look has come over Granda. He curls his hands over the table edge and shakes his head.

'This bloody country. Always forcing you to pick a side.'

In the corner, the kettle comes to the boil and flicks itself off. The noise makes Granda snap back into himself.

'I've said too much, Hannah,' he says. 'Sorry. You should talk to your own folks about this.'

He rises from the table and returns to the hob. He continues to chat as he fries the French toast: light, nonsense talk about books they've been reading and the daft things Granny's done this week. He steers well clear of last night at Millar's Gap. When they sit down to eat, he says, 'There's no harm in watching the parade. After breakfast go on upstairs. You should be able to see them gathering from the spare-room window. Use your dad's binoculars. And, if Mum and Dad say it's OK, I'll take you down Main Street when it kicks off. It'd be good for you to see the Twelfth. I don't want you getting a fear of it.'

'OK,' says Hannah, tucking into her French toast. Any excuse to get out of the house.

A Bit of a Scene

WHILE GRANDA PETE washes the dishes, Hannah goes up to the spare room with Dad's binoculars. She stands on the lid of the laundry basket so she can see over the hedge. She peers through the big arch with its wonky paintings of the Queen, Princess Di and King Billy sitting on his pure white horse, to the C of I car park beyond. It's buzzing with bowler-hatted Orangemen and band members buttoning themselves into their royal-blue uniforms. She lets the binoculars swing across the horizon. She spots Caroline's dad, and William's, already lined up in their orange sashes. Ross's dad is in the band, back left with a deep drum strapped in front of his belly. Outbreak or not, there's a certain kind of Ballylack man who would never miss the Twelfth. Caroline should be marching with the band, and William too, but the parents have all been instructed to keep their weans at home.

This message hasn't made it as far as Matty. His mum's utterly clueless about things like this. When school sends notes home for the parents, Matty's always come back unread. Frequently he runs the roads from dusk to dawn. Gloria neither knows nor cares where her son is. Today Matty's up the front, where he always is, throwing his stick high into the air, twisting and squavering between catches, acting like everything's totally normal. It'll take more than an epidemic to faze Matty McKnight. When you're blessed with a mother like Gloria you get used to living through emergencies.

There are people missing: dads who would normally be stepping out with the Lodge, children who'll never play in the band again. Ross should be there, and Kathleen too. The other pipers have closed ranks to fill in the gaps. People still notice. They make a point of saying they're missed. Their names will be whispered by onlookers as the parade winds its way down Main Street. *Ross. Kathleen. Miriam. Elizabeth. Lief. And now Amy. Dear God, let that be the end of it.* The vicar appears on the church steps. He raises his hands like Moses on the mountaintop. All across the car park, men, women and children – though mostly men – bow their heads in the semblance of prayer. Hannah can't hear what the vicar's saying, but she can see his lips moving. She wonders if he's praying for the Leungs and the other families who aren't here today.

She slides her binoculars on down to the end of the car park, where there's a burger van waiting to feed the returning Orangemen. Her eyes meet the green grass field at the bottom of McAuley's lane and keep on sweeping. Disorientated by the magnified glass, she turns her head too far, hits wallpaper and a pale, peach blur which might or might not be her own hand. She lowers the binoculars and realizes it isn't her hand. It's Amy Leung standing in front of her, staring defiantly.

Amy is older in the face and slightly fuller in the chest, but no taller than she was two months ago. She's wearing what looks to be a traditional Chinese dress. It's made of red, shiny fabric, embroidered with gold flowers and fastened at the shoulder with a row of similarly coloured buttons. Hannah's seen this sort of get-up before in church, when missionaries show slides of their lives in faraway places. They'd have you thinking they always dress like this on the mission field. It's yet another sacrifice they've made for their calling. Hannah knows better. Mum sends old frocks and blouses out to the missionaries. The wives always write back saying how grateful they are.

'Hi, Hannah,' says Amy. 'I'm dead.'

Hannah looks down. The laundry basket has her towering over Amy.

'You probably already know. I've just come to tell you I'm grand.'

Amy's voice is clear and crisp; every word confident. She's not the shy, mumbly wee girl Hannah's already begun to forget. She perches on the edge of the bed and pats the space beside her. Hannah climbs off the laundry basket and sits down.

'What are you wearing, Amy?'

'It's my culture. Do you have a problem with it or something? I've a right to celebrate who I am. If your lot get to shout and stomp about all day, why shouldn't I get to dress up too?'

Hannah's shocked by how angry Amy sounds. Little bits of spit are flying out of her mouth. It's not what she'd expect from Amy. It's come from nowhere. People always said the Leung girls were far too quiet, that they needed bringing out of themselves.

'I'm not being a racist or anything, Amy. I'm just saying I've never seen you in an outfit like that before. I like it. It's really nice.'

'Cool. Thanks. Though, obviously, I don't need you to make me feel good about myself. I'll wear whatever I want to wear. I do whatever I feel like now. It's the best thing about being dead.'

'Don't you mind being dead?'

Even as she asks this Hannah's thinking Amy looks better than she's ever looked. Shoulders back, head held high. Amy's actually looking her in the eye.

'I love it. I mean, the dying part was no classic but, once it was over and I was down here with the rest of them, everything was so much better. I wish I'd done it years ago. I mean, I wouldn't've killed myself or anything . . . but then again, it's honestly so much better here.'

'Oh,' says Hannah, mouth gaping. She's so shocked by this revelation she can't think of anything to say.

'I can finally be myself. I've joined the DK and everything. I know you think you know me, Hannah, but you really don't. I'm totally into that sort of thing. You know, partying and going buck mad. Turns out, I just needed to let myself go a bit. You should try it sometime. I mean, there's no harm in enjoying yourself, is there? As long as you're not hurting anyone.'

'No, of course not,' says Hannah. She tries to smile encouragingly.

'Before, I didn't want to draw attention to myself. Dad was always telling us we needed to fit in. Now I don't give a toss. It's just so much easier to be real here.'

'What do you mean?'

'Well, we're all a bit odd to start with – because we're dead – and the more time I spend with them, the more I've realized I'm not the only different one. Everybody's weird in their own way. Like Mim won't do anything Lizzy's not doing, and Kat's obsessed with how she looks. Lief's gone crazy since he escaped from the hippies. And Ross. Well, you've heard about Ross?'

Hannah nods. She places a hand across her mouth, clumsily miming mute.

'None of us are what you'd call *normal*. But we get on like a house on fire.'

'You're all getting on?'

'Aye, well, not all of us. Did Lief tell you? There's a bit of tension between Lizzy and Kat. Lizzy didn't want to be in the gang. Then Kat said she was barred, even if she wanted to join. Lizzy said the DK was stupid. She'd rather die all over again than hang out with us. She's all *Stop messing about. We need to make plans.* Now she's pissed about the Orange Hall.'

'The Orange Hall?'

Amy smiles shyly. 'I might have burnt it down.'

'You did what?'

'Sure, we don't need one any more. It's not as if any of us are interested in marching. It was just sitting there, doing nothing. And it was the Twelfth.' She laughs. 'Sure, we had to do something to mark the Twelfth.'

Hannah stares at Amy, horrified. She can't imagine her doing anything so bold. Dying must have turned her head.

'You're joking, aren't you?'

'Nope, it was burning away when I came here.'

'Shit,' says Hannah. It's the first time she's ever sworn out loud. The word just slips out before she can stop it. 'What's wrong with you, Amy? Are you all right?'

'I've never felt better,' says Amy. She pauses and thinks for a moment. 'I'm finally letting myself be myself.'

'By burning things?'

'Yup. It turns out burning stuff's a lot of fun. Who'd have known? My dad never let us have any fun. He was always saying, *Don't cause a scene, Amy. Don't draw attention to yourself.* Do you know, when I was dying, he asked me to try and hold on till the thirteenth so I wouldn't ruin the Twelfth for everybody else. I don't think I realized how pissed off I was until I got down here and thought about it. Do you know how humiliating it is, pretending you don't hear when people call you Chinky, acting like you don't notice them pulling at their eyes, doing impressions of you? Or how small you feel when people talk at you all loud and slow because they think you don't understand English? I'm done being nice, quiet Amy. I'm actually raging, so I am. Kat says it's healthy to let your anger out. I've a lot of anger I need to get out.'

'I get that,' says Hannah. And she really does. 'But do you have to wreck things? I hate that you're all falling out. Could you not let your anger out in some other way?'

'And what would you suggest we do?'

Hannah glances out the window. She can't see anything past next-door's hedge, but she can picture the bands and the Orangemen lining up beneath their King Billy banner.

'I don't know. Maybe you could just talk about it.'

Amy looks pointedly at Hannah. She seems so much older now she's dead. 'Uch, Hannah,' she says in a weary voice, 'you've so much to learn. You'll understand when you get here. The older you get, the less you have in common. Everybody's different. And the difference just gets bigger and bigger till you've nothing left to talk about. Then, you either fall out or you find new ways to communicate.'

'What do you mean?' asks Hannah.

'You drink,' says Amy. 'You sing at the top of your lungs. You dance and dance till you can't stand up. And there's fighting and sex and raking about. Destroying stuff makes you feel like you're part of something bigger. It's like you belong.'

'That's sad,' says Hannah.

Amy Leung shrugs. 'It is what it is,' she says. 'No point stressing over things you can't change. I think it's like this for everyone. Take my parents, for example. They've nothing in common except the shop and us. They never really talk any more.'

'Don't you think that's sad?'

'My heart bleeds,' says Amy. 'Here, if you see the two of them about the place, tell them to try burning down an Orange Hall. It'd give them something to talk about.'

Amy grins then. An enormous, toothy grin. Hannah realizes she's never seen her smile before. She'd remember the way her eyes spark up and her dimples deepen and her whole face shines. Amy Leung's stunning when she smiles. *I wish we'd been friends*, thinks Hannah. *I wish I'd known what she was really like.*

Amy seems to read her mind. She places a hand on her shoulder. 'Don't worry, Hannah,' she says. 'I know you're a wee bit strange yourself. That won't matter when you get here. You'll be the same as the rest of us.' She points her fingers towards the bedroom roof and begins to sing, 'No, no limits, we'll reach for the sky.'

On the other side of the village the first dry *thunk* of the Lambeg rings out. The noise of it is like a series of muffled bombs. *Kadump. Kadump. Kadump.* Instinctively, Hannah looks towards the window. She feels something like a whisper pass down her side and disappear. The mattress rises a little beneath her backside. When she turns, Amy's gone.

Hannah never gets to the parade. Mum and Dad don't come back for ages. Over on the other side of Ballylack, Mrs Leung has locked herself in the bathroom. She's refusing to come out. Mr Leung says she is an impossible woman, that it would take a steamroller to shift her when she's in one of her moods. He shouts up the stairs in Cantonese. Then, accustomed to translating everything, repeats himself in English, 'You can starve in there, Shu. I do not care. You are embarrassing me in front of our guests.' Most of the mourners have already left. They've a parade to watch and, even if they didn't, the atmosphere in the little flat is making everyone uncomfortable.

Hannah's parents linger. Mum wants to make sure Amy's little sisters are OK. Once she has the pair of them settled in front of the TV, she turns her attention to Mrs Leung. Mum is good with sad people. She's had years of practice in church. She lies down outside the bathroom and whispers her sympathy under the door. Slowly, gently, in an almost prayerful tone, she reaches out to Mrs Leung until she quits cursing and thumping what sounds to be a toilet brush against the wall. She falls silent. Then she weeps. Furiously. Loudly. Without respite, for almost an hour. The toilet cistern drips in sympathy. In the hall outside, Hannah's mum prays wordless prayers. She clutches handfuls of carpet for something to hold on to. She tries to keep her own grief from leaking out.

Downstairs in the living room, Dad sits with Mr Leung. Everybody else has left. Dad offers to pray. Mr Leung says, 'Thank you. But, no.' They are not Christians. They do not want prayer in their house. Dad offers to make tea. Mr Leung accepts. The two men sit, holding their cooling mugs, neither drinking nor speaking. Dad doesn't know what to say if he can't bring God into the conversation and, muddled with grief, Mr Leung has reverted to his old ways of thinking. He can't remember the word for anything in English, except *thank you*, which he mumbles, every few minutes, looking at Dad with big, pooling eyes.

The parade is running almost twenty minutes late. There's been a disagreement at the car park. The older men think they shouldn't be marching. It's not respectful. Nobody's in the mood for it. There'll be another Twelfth next year. All this will be behind them then. The younger fellas, some of the fathers included, want to march and thump their drums and afterwards get shit-faced in the field. There's nothing like marching for forcing all thought out of a troubled head. The vicar weighs in. Eventually both sides see sense. A compromise is reached. They'll be marching today but the pipe band will only play hymns and they'll pause outside the Leungs' for a minute's silence. They'll take their hats off as a mark of respect for wee Amy and all the other youngsters they've lost.

'Is everybody in agreement?' asks the vicar. They all nod *yes, of course*, they'll abide by the rules. Then, with one loud thud of the Lambeg, the pipers raise their pipes to their pursed lips and launch into 'Onward, Christian Soldiers'. The Orangemen straighten their bowlers. The parade begins lumbering its way through Ballylack.

The people lining the road are quieter than usual. There are fewer flags to be seen, fewer old folks out with picnic rugs. Some people are too scared to leave their houses for fear of catching what the children have. They watch the parade from behind their curtains, from upstairs rooms with the windows wedged open so they'll still get the good of the music. There's a general feeling among the bystanders that the right decision has been made. The Twelfth should never be cancelled, even if it feels like the end of the world. In some strange way it helps to see everyone gathered and marching, to note how many are still strong and capable of striding. Sure, they're hardly depleted at all.

For the most part the parade passes off respectfully. In the flat above the Chinese takeaway, Mr Leung and Hannah's dad listen to the music grow louder as it approaches. *Tinka, tinka, tinka* go the pipes – sharp as toothache – then suddenly, they stop. Outside the Leungs' front door every single instrument falls silent. Dad goes to the window and peeks out.

'They've stopped,' he says. 'They've taken their hats off. Come and see. They're paying their respects.'

Mr Leung will not rise from his seat by the fish tank.

'We are causing a fuss,' he says. 'We are ruining their parade.' He holds his head in his hands as if it's too heavy for his neck.

'No, no,' says Dad. 'It's not a fuss at all. They want to show they're sorry for your loss. It's their loss too.'

Mr Leung looks up. There are lines of tears running down his face. For a moment he hesitates, gripping the arms of his chair as if intending to rise and join Hannah's dad at the window. He leaves it too long. The lead drum cracks at the back of the band. The first strangled notes of 'Abide with Me' float up and through the open window; one hundred pairs of polished shoes come down upon the asphalt. The parade moves on, up Main Street, past the community centre and Henderson's, where the usual suspects are already leaning, blootered against its gable wall. Past Thompson's and the doctor's surgery and up the hill towards the field, hesitating briefly outside Seán Donnelly's door, where, banned though it is, a renegade faction launches into 'The Sash'.

'Sure, it's old but it is beautiful,' they hum, and pause between verses to mutter, *Fuck the Pope and the IRA*, under their breath, before stumbling on. If Seán hears them caterwauling outside his window, he doesn't let on. He knows better. It's tense enough in Ballylack without adding a dose of sectarianism to the mix.

Later, at the field, when they're pissed on Bass and lukewarm Harp, Van McAuley's youngest starts into Seán. 'Why's he here anyway?' he mutters. 'Could they not have found a Protestant fella to sort this out? It's not as if he's sorted anything either. Them weans are still dropping like flies.' There's a want in Rick McAuley. He's always angling for a fight. Especially when there are Taigs around. The same raw thing's in the other young men, but they've not got mouths on them like Rick.

They want Seán to come over from Henderson's, where he's installed himself in the back bar. He's to come up to the field and defend himself or, God damn it, Rick and the lads will go down there and pummel him till he admits what's actually going on. A runner's dispatched: a wee lad from the pipe band who's quick on his feet and eager to please. Normally Seán Donnelly wouldn't let anyone get a rise out of him. He's trained to remain calm in the most stressful situations. But, by this stage, he's had a drink or two himself. And he's just off the phone with his own wife. She's taken the head with him on account of missing yet another weekend with his kids.

When the wee lad comes huffing into Henderson's, yelling, 'Mr Donnelly, Mr Donnelly, you've to go up to the field or they'll come down here and kick the living shite out of you!' the whole bar goes silent, waiting on Seán's response. Then Seán Donnelly loses the run of himself. He stands up, half-finished pint in hand, and makes a kind of proclamation.

'Tell them eejits,' he says, 'those children didn't poison themselves. Somebody's responsible and it isn't me. Youse should take a wee look closer to home.'

Straight away, Seán knows he's said too much. He's planted a doubt in their collective head. Granted, there's nothing to say a local's responsible. There's nothing to say it was a stranger either. They don't even know where the poison's come from. But Seán's almost certain there's a local source. As soon as he's said it, he could kick himself. He's gone and riled them up. On the Twelfth. With a load of drink taken. And half the day still to get through. Dear only knows what they'll do now.

Within ten minutes the rumours are doing the rounds. Seán Donnelly says one of their own's responsible. It doesn't matter one jot what the man actually said. There's much speculation. They have, until now, assumed the poisoning accidental and distant; nothing to do with any of them. The alternative doesn't bear thinking about. *Could one of their own be responsible? What sort of bastard would do a thing like this?* A farmer's the answer. There's nobody else round Ballylack who has access to these kinds of chemicals. They make a list of all the farmers. It's not a long list; there are far fewer farms than there used to be. The names on the list are all familiar names. Trusted names. Good Ballylack men, every one of them. Surely it can't be one of their own.

The End of All Time

THE WHOLE WORLD is watching the children now. Most decent folk wouldn't express it in such crude terms. In public they still talk of cures and miraculous interventions. In private they're all just waiting to see who goes next. There's only the four weans left: Hannah, Caroline, Matty and Ben. All look to be grand. But you never know, the poison could already be working on them. The smart money's on the wee foreign lad, Alan Gardiner's son. There's nothing to him. He's just skin and bones and big, sad eyes.

William Fowler's gone. And William was a great, strapping lad. He passed away early on Wednesday morning. That's three children in as many days. Mrs Nugent phones to break the bad news personally. She asks after Hannah. *And what about that wee lassie of yours? How's she bearing up herself?* Her voice puts Mum in mind of a mean old crow digging around for a juicy worm. She loses her temper. 'I've had enough, Meta. Don't be calling here again. You're nothing more than a vile auld gossip. You should be ashamed of yourself.' Afterwards she feels bad for snapping. Not bad enough to phone back and apologize.

William is the seventh Ballylack child to die. Seven dead weans is enough to instigate a press stampede. There are swathes of journalists camped out all over the village now. They're in Henderson's, demanding pub grub at all hours of the day. They're double-parked everywhere. They're complaining about the provincial accents, which don't come across well on TV. They joke about sticking the subtitles on. They're torturing the poor girls in Thompson's shop, wanting takeaway cappuccinos and herbal teas, when all they have's an electric kettle and a catering-sized jar of Nescafé.

The locals don't know what to make of these cosmopolitan strangers. They've clogged up Main Street with their special vans and big cameras. Their fuzzy mics, like skewered caterpillars, hang perpetually overhead. The behind-the-camera ones are normal enough, but the anchors don't look like real people. Up close you can see where their faces are painted on. The best are reasonably professional. They know not to block the locals' drives or stand in their flowerbeds for a better shot. The worst are vultures. They won't leave the bereaved families alone. They phone at all hours, wanting quotes and interviews, photographs of the children (*nice clear ones, that haven't been used yet*). They're not above going door-to-door. Seán Donnelly's repeatedly told them they need to wise up. He's threatened them with the press-standards people and, if that doesn't fear them, the RUC. They continue to knock on the families' doors, hunkering down to yell through letterboxes that they only want a quick word; that really, they're just here to help.

Hannah's mum and dad won't have anything to do with the press. They've drawn the curtains in every room, even upstairs. 'You never know,' Dad says, 'they could get ladders. I wouldn't put it past them.' Every time Hannah peeks through the curtains, she can see eight or ten fellas lolling against their front wall. The idea of strangers watching her makes her skin feel like it's on too tight. She hasn't left the house since Millar's Gap.

Dad still insists on going to work. He could probably take

some annual leave. His boss would definitely understand. But Dad keeps turning up each morning at nine o'clock. He is proving something to his colleagues. *I'm not panicking. I'm trusting the Lord.* He's doing his level best to convince himself he is OK. *I am not for going under this. I am stronger than everyone else.* And he is OK, though no one in work can possibly know this. There's nothing wrong with his wee girl. Dad should feel grand, but he doesn't. Every day he feels closer to falling apart.

Mum and Hannah stay inside. With the curtains drawn and the lights on, it's stifling. They don't dare open any windows in case the journalists hear them talking and put it on the evening news. It's the strangest feeling, being trapped inside your own house, hearing the click and stutter of camera flashes every time somebody arrives or leaves. The folks from church have been very faithful. There's always two or three in the living room, praying. They've drawn up a rota, so they can cover Hannah in prayer. Pastor Bill never leaves. Dad joins them as soon as he's home from work. Mum's always in the kitchen, making tea and setting out wee plates of buns. It's not unlike a wake. The curtains drawn. The constant tea. The house full of solemn, low-voiced visitors. It is exactly like a wake. *In fairness, how could it be anything else?* There's been seven deaths already. The smell of death is in the air.

Hannah tries to keep out of the believers' way. She stays in her room. Every couple of hours she's summoned downstairs so they can pray for her in person. She stands in the centre of the circle, flushed and swaying slightly, while they all lay hands on her. The weight of their words bears down on her head. She almost always starts to wilt. The guilt feels sharpest with their eyes on her. *What if God reveals where she's been?* It's not unheard of for believers to pick up on guilty thoughts and Hannah can't get the Raggedy Tree out of her head. Mum would be mortified if she knew. Dad would be absolutely furious and she knows fine rightly what Pastor Bill would say. *Dear oh dear, you've gone and given the Devil a foothold, young Hannah. The Lord Jesus is so disappointed in you.*

Hannah half wishes Granda hadn't mentioned the Raggedy Tree. It doesn't seem to have made any difference. Despite her efforts, Amy still died. Now William's gone, and she's pretty sure God is mad at her. He doesn't look kindly on those who dabble with wicked things. If God's cross, he probably won't stop Hannah from getting sick. He might even bring the sickness on her, as a kind of punishment. And if it's God's will for her to get sick, it won't matter how many believers pray, she's definitely heading to the other Ballylack. It's pre-ordained, as Dad would say. Hannah's head gets dizzy if she spends too long thinking about predestination. It starts to feel like she's stuck in a loop. *If God's already decided what's going to happen, then what's the point of doing anything?* She asked Dad to explain it once. He said predestination was both very complicated and very simple and not something she needed to worry about. Not at her age. Which only served to make Hannah feel helpless. Everything was beyond her control, and she couldn't even question it. It felt a lot like careering down a hill in a car with brakes that didn't work.

If God's decided she's going to die, there's nothing anybody can do about it. He's got His plan and His purpose; He'll stick to it. Still, Hannah doesn't want to appear rude. It's kind of the believers to keep appearing in the living room, bringing casseroles and traybakes, offering to pray for her. She wishes they weren't wasting their time. They're yet another thing to feel guilty about. Hannah accepts their prayers and leaves as soon as they say *Amen*, bolting back up to the safety of her bedroom. She sits in the dark with the curtains drawn, eating Fifteens and caramel squares, waiting for the sickness to start.

William appears about three o'clock. Hannah's expected him a good bit sooner. It's six whole hours since she heard he'd died.

She returns to her room after a particularly vigorous session with the senior elders and finds him sitting on the windowsill, peeking through a gap in the curtains.

'Wow,' he says, 'I thought it was bad outside the hospital. But there's millions of journalists out there. Leeches, my da calls them. He said he'd take his shotgun to them if it wouldn't just give them more crap to write about.'

'There's only the four of us left,' says Hannah. 'They want to make sure they don't miss anything.'

'Bloody leeches.'

William lets the curtain drop. The room falls back into darkness. Hannah automatically reaches for the light switch.

'No,' says William, 'leave it off. I like it better in the dark, so you can't see how much I've changed. I'm not used to it yet myself.'

Hannah takes a seat on the end of her bed facing William. Once her eyes are accustomed to the half-light, she's shocked to see how different he is. The new William looks like he's been taken by the wrists and stretched. There's not enough flesh to fill all of his tallness out. Hannah's reminded of the pumpkin-head scarecrow which stands at the top of McAuley's field. Only his face remains familiar, still topped with a shock of bright red curls. His head looks out of proportion now, overly large and unbalanced, bobbling about on the end of his neck.

'You look *really* different, William. I don't know if I'd recognize you in the street. Your hair's the same, though,' she adds, as a kind of consolation.

William runs his fingers through his fringe. 'Once a ginger, always a ginger,' he says, and smiles broadly. His eyes smile too. His nose crinkles up across the bridge.

There you are, thinks Hannah, *your smile's not changed one bit*. Of all the boys in the class, she's always liked William best. He's not particularly funny or good-looking. He is kind, though. Powerful kind. Hannah's always appreciated this.

'You smile the same,' she says.

'You too.'

'I am the same.'

'Oh yeah, I forgot. I'm the dead kid with the different body. I'm the one haunting you.'

They both laugh. Spoken aloud, it sounds totally daft.

'You're in good form for a dead kid.'

William shrugs. 'What's the point in freaking out? I'd rather be dead than sick like that again.'

'Was it awful?'

'Not at the start. At the start it was just like having the flu. Then there were lumps everywhere. Then all my organs started switching off. I'll be honest, that bit was pretty shite. At the end I just fell asleep.' He pauses, then, noticing Hannah's face, adds, 'I mean, that was my experience. It's different for everyone.'

'Right,' says Hannah. She's keen to move the chat away from dying. The less she knows, the less there is to panic about. 'And what's it like being dead?'

'Uch, it's not that bad. It's basically the same as before only minus the adults. I have to say, I'm not really missing the old way that much. All I did when I wasn't at school was help my da around the farm. It's nice in a way, not having Big William breathing down my neck. Then again, it's not perfect either. It's tense at the minute, so it is. Everybody's angry. Have you heard the DK are taking sides?'

'Aye,' nods Hannah, 'Dead Kids versus the Twins.'

'It drives me mad. They're ruining something that could be good. I think they've forgotten we're all in the same boat. One side's dead. So's the other. You'd think they'd be able to get on.'

'It makes me sad, hearing about it.'

'Try being around them. It's not much craic. I don't really fit into either camp. I'm not interested in fighting. I try to keep myself to myself. I'm definitely not DK material. All the partying they do; it feels put on. All big talk, if you know what I mean. Underneath it, I think they're hurting. We probably all are in different ways. Doesn't mean you get to take out your frustrations on everybody else.'

'What do you mean?'

'Well, Kathleen and Lief – *sorry, Lee* – took over the flat above Thompson's. They've trashed the place. They've drunk everything they can lay their hands on and now they've started picking fights. Like, actual fights.'

'How bad is it?'

'I think it started as a bit of a laugh. When you have a gang, you need another gang to be up against. Like, there's always two sides to every war. Not that I'm saying it's a war or anything. But they're all taking it so seriously. Especially the DK. They've got really mean. They've been writing stuff about Lizzy all over the village.'

'What sort of stuff?'

'Uch, you know, silly crap – *Lizzy Ross is a bitch, the Twins are Freaks* – daft stuff like that. You can tell Kathleen's behind it. It's not exactly imaginative.'

Hannah lets herself smile. 'They're not actually fighting, though, are they?'

'Not yet,' says William. 'I wouldn't put it past them, though. Kathleen keeps threatening to trash the house where the Twins are living. Lizzy's not helping matters much. If you ask me, she's doing her best to stir things up. Her and Mim go round tidying up after all the DK's parties, making a holy show of themselves. Lecturing the others. Saying they're really immature. Lizzy's, like, all the worst bits of your mum rolled into one. If she doesn't stop winding Kathleen up, it could get nasty. Kathleen said she'll burn them out.'

'Do you think she's serious?'

'Naw. Yeah. Well, maybe. They done the Orange Hall a wee

while back. I wasn't dead then, but they told me that was Amy Leung's doing. *Amy Leung? What the flip?* I can't get my head round that one. You can never tell what somebody's capable of when they're pissed off and they've had a few drinks.'

Hannah has nothing to say to this. She's never seen anyone drunk in real life. Now he's admitted he's a smoker, she's pretty sure Granda Pete drinks as well. She's smelt a funny smell off him – like vinegar and sour apples – when he comes in from the bowling club. But Granda Pete's a very nice man. He'd never get drunk and fight like people on *EastEnders*. He might go to the pub, but he probably just wants to see his friends. And he'd only have one beer while he's there. A wee small beer, in a wee small glass. Strictly speaking, drinking's not a sin in itself. It's only getting drunk the Bible's against.

Hannah changes the subject back to William. She doesn't want to hear about the DK or the problems in the other Bally-lack. At the rate they're wrecking, half the village will be in rubble by the time she arrives.

'What are you going to do?' she asks.

'Uch, I'm trying not to get drawn into it, Hannah. I really don't want to start taking sides. If there's a chance to sit down and talk sense to either of them, I'll do my best. I don't see any point in the way they're getting on.'

William's different from the others who've come before. He doesn't sound like a kid trying to be an adult. He actually sounds like a man. Or, if not a man, then a much older fella. There's sense to what he says. And how he says it. It's easy to believe in him. For the first time since Millar's Gap, Hannah feels a little easier in herself. She doesn't want William to rush away.

'I could help,' she says, 'when I arrive. I could help you try to talk to them. Nobody wanted to talk to me before. It's different now. They might actually listen to me.'

William pats her gently on the knee. It's not the sort of touch

181

you'd give a girlfriend or even a girl you fancied a bit. He touches her lightly on the knee of her pyjamas in the way you'd touch a child. His voice, when he speaks, is even older. Hannah knows he's talking down to her.

'That's so kind, Hannah. I appreciate it. But you do know you're not coming to join us? Has nobody told you you're going to be fine?'

'What?' says Hannah. It comes out like a squeak, so she takes a deep breath and repeats herself. 'What?'

'You're not for dying. At least not for a good while anyway.'

'I don't understand.' She starts to cry. Just a bit. It's possible William's not noticed in the dark. She wipes her eyes and nose on the cuff of her pyjama top.

'Smile, Hannah. It's good news. Anybody else would be over the moon.'

'I don't understand,' she repeats. 'How can you be sure?'

'Did you not wonder why everybody was coming to see you? Did you not think, why me and not somebody else? You're not like the rest of us.'

'Set apart,' mumbles Hannah. When Dad says, as Christians, they're set apart, he makes it sound like a brilliant thing. Now *set apart*'s lost all its positive associations. Hannah's odd. She's weird. She's not the same as everyone else. She thinks about the time Granny's cat Mo had all the kittens and nobody wanted the runty one with the misshaped leg. In the end they kept it, though Granny never had any love for it. Hannah doesn't want to be set apart.

'Am I going to be left behind by myself?' Hannah's properly bawling now. Snail trails of snot leak out of her nose.

'Sorry. Yes. It's looking that way. But seriously, it's good news. Do you really want to die if it means being stuck for ever in Ballylack? You've your whole life ahead of you. Years and years. Think of all the things you're going to do.'

'I know that. And I am glad, William. But I don't want to be the only one left. I'm always the one who misses out.'

'Thank your lucky stars you are. If your dad wasn't so uptight, you'd be in the same boat as the rest of us.'

'What do you mean?'

'We've worked out where this whole thing started. It took a wee while to compare notes but in the end it was pretty obvious. The only thing we all did together was that school trip to see the Raggedy Tree. You know, over in Millar's Gap. Lizzy says there was a funny smell coming off the pond; a sort of chemically smell. I remember noticing the grass had died all around the edge. We're ninety-nine per cent sure we caught whatever this is in Millar's Gap. Has your man Seán Donnelly not worked it out yet?'

Hannah shakes her head. No. Words aren't coming easily. She's still processing his first revelation. Now, William's turned her world upside down again.

'So, like I said, Hannah, you're going to be grand. Your super-strict dad has saved you this time. You're not for dying. You won't get sick because you never set foot in Millar's Gap.'

Later, she'll wish she'd managed to control herself for long enough to explain everything. She feels sure William would've known how to comfort her. In the moment, she is a child. A tiny, terrified, overwrought child. She turns her back on him, buries her face in her pink gingham pillow and cries until her eyes dry up and her throat is raw.

William doesn't rush away. He stays for half an hour or so. It's kind of him. Hannah's grateful for it. She can feel his hand, unmoving, on the small of her back; the cold, damp press of it through her pyjamas. Dad used to sit like this on the edge of her bed when she'd had a bad dream and couldn't get back to sleep. He never spoke. He didn't need to. The weight of his hand was an anchor, reminding her that he was there, and he had her. Safe and sound. The dark was never just as dark when Dad was sharing it with her.

When she seems a little more settled, William finally removes his hand.

'Goodbye, Hannah,' he whispers. 'I promise, it's going to be all right.'

He leaves quietly, pulling the door behind him. Hannah listens for the stair creaking. The third stair from the top always creaks. She hears nothing but the adults' voices below. When she opens her bedroom door, he's gone. Mum is standing at the bottom of the stairs asking if she'd like a sandwich brought up. Some believers are leaving. Another handful have just appeared with a Tupperware of stew. Mum says she should eat something now because it'll soon be time for bed.

'Is Granda Pete here?' Hannah asks. 'Can you send him up? I have to tell him an important thing.'

The Bad Books

SEÁN DONNELLY'S IN the bad books again. He's not done anything specific this time. It's what he hasn't done that's riled up his wife. He's been away that much this year, his daughter seems to think he's left them. The infants' teacher is only after calling Seán's wife, to see if everything is all right at home, because Cliona's most recent piece of art featured Mammy, Cliona and wee Ruairi and a space where Dada used to be. Apparently, Cliona was fit to say that Dada was gone, far, far away. The teacher had rung to find out if Seán was dead or they'd just got divorced. His wife is raging now, understandably so, and Cliona's refusing to speak to him. Seán's wife holds the phone up so he can hear the child shouting, 'I hate you, Dada. I never want to see you again.' If he could just tell her that children are dying; children not much older than her. That he's spent the afternoon up in Belfast at Forster Green, where they're carrying out autopsies on the last three kids. How he had to blink back tears at the sight of Lief and Amy and William, pale and splayed out on their gurneys. He'd never felt more like a father: simultaneously grateful and terrified. If Seán could just explain this to his daughter, he's pretty sure she'd understand. Cliona might even be proud of him.

But you can't tell a five-year-old children are dying. She'd have nightmares for weeks. Instead, he mumbles something about having to help some people who are sad and poorly. Dear knows what Cliona thinks his job is. She used to draw pictures of him with big blue wings, like a superhero. She doesn't draw him at all any more. Seán promises to make it up to her: whatever she wants from the big toyshop and McDonald's for tea two nights in a row. 'Dada promises, sweetheart. He'll be home soon.' 'You better be,' snaps his wife. 'I've every sympathy for those poor folk, but your priority should be us, Seán. Now, you get that situation sorted out quick sharp. I want you back down here by next weekend.'

Seán Donnelly's only just put the phone down. He's made it into the kitchen and extricated a bottle of vodka from the ice box. He's planning to get righteously pissed. It'd do him good to forget everything for one night. He's rooting through the cupboard for a clean drinking glass when somebody gives his front door a clatter, pauses for a second, then thumps it again. There are two young officers on his doorstep. One has a moustache. The other doesn't. Seán's noticed that there's a disproportionate number of men with moustaches in the RUC. *Do they think facial hair lends gravitas?* The pair of boyos have their hats tucked under their armpits, as is customary when delivering bad news. For a moment Seán panics. *Something's happened to his wife. Or worse still, Cliona, or wee Ruairi.* Then he remembers where he is.

'Jesus, lads,' he mutters. 'Tell me there's not another one gone.'

'No, sir,' says the lad who doesn't have a moustache. 'All's grand on that front, as far as we know. That wee girl Caroline's been moved to the hospital, but she's not too bad. They're hopeful she'll respond to the drugs.'

'It's not the children this time, Mr Donnelly. There's been a bit of an incident over at the Adgers',' explains his moustachioed friend. 'The grandmother called us. She said her son was going to kill her husband and we'd to come immediately.'

'We have to take those sorts of calls seriously,' his colleague replies, 'even when we know there's nothing in it. Just women being hysterical.'

'Women!' says Moustache, rolling his eyes. 'By the time we got there, it'd all blown over. The pair of them were just sitting glaring at each other. They weren't for talking to us – *no, siree* – we get that a lot, though usually from the other sort. The mother said you might fare better. Apparently, they think very highly of you.'

'Right,' said Seán. Secretly, he's a wee bit flattered, though his face doesn't register it. 'I'll pop round tomorrow and have a word with them.'

'She said it couldn't wait till the morning,' says Moustache.

'It's a matter of life and death,' adds his mate.

Seán thanks the officers. He puts the vodka back in the ice box and locates his outdoor shoes. The last thing he needs is a bloody domestic. He'd been hoping for a night in front of the telly. Maybe a big bar of Fruit and Nut. But he's the family liaison. And if there's something bothering the Adgers, then it's his job to see it's sorted out. He turns down a lift in the squad car. It's only a five-minute walk. The fresh air will settle his head.

When Seán Donnelly walks into the Adgers' he can tell something serious has just gone down. The atmosphere's so heavy he tastes it at the back of his throat. It's yeasty sour, like the taste of just-chewed bread. It's also quiet. So deathly quiet he can hear the electrics humming overhead. Nobody's talking. Nobody except Hannah's mum, who says, 'Thank God,' when she finds him on her doorstep. She ushers him quickly down the hall, all the time repeating, 'I'm so glad you're here. What about a cup of tea?' Seán turns the tea down. He soon regrets this. Tea would've been a conversation starter. *Do you take sugar? How many spoonfuls? What about a Custard Cream?* Now it's just him and four silent, blank-faced Holy Joes. They stare at each other and stare at him. For once, Seán feels that he isn't the sore thumb. They look like they want to stab each other. Violently. In the eyes.

'Nice evening, folks,' he tries as a starter. Nobody bites. 'Is there something you wanted to talk about?' The mother leaps out of the chair and suggests more tea. Nobody responds. She sits back down. The father's glaring at his father. The old man looks like he's been crying. Nobody's saying anything.

Bloody Protestants, thinks Seán. He immediately corrects himself, for he's had personal experience of Protestants who wouldn't think twice about screaming or heckling or pitching dog shit at the other side. *Bloody tight-lipped Born-again Prods. That's more like it*, he tells himself. He can see they're thinking murderous thoughts, but will they ever spit them out? 'Course they won't. This lot hold themselves so tightly. They never shout or fight. Sure, most of them won't even dance for fear of losing control. They'll sit there silently, cradling their anger, turning sour on the stink of it. A proper session's what they need. Seán would prescribe one if he could. *Drink until youse run your mouths off. Get all your crap out in the open. Curse each other. Throw a few punches. Then, drink a bit more. In the morning, you'll not remember any of it. But I tell you what, youse'll feel all the better for having whatever's bothering you off your chest.*

Seán knows the Adgers aren't the sort – the religion's gone too deep with them – though he's spied the tattoos on Granda Pete's arms. The old boy may be good-living now; clearly he hasn't always been. If it comes down to actual fists, Seán'd put his money on Granda Pete. He's encountered men like this pair before. Stubborn. Belligerent. *Thran*'s the word for it in these parts. The stand-off could last for hours and hours. Seán thinks fondly of his bed. He'd like to see it at some stage tonight. He rolls up his sleeves. He's instigating full peacekeeper mode, channelling all he's learnt in the Middle East, in South Africa and West Belfast. There are two separate factions in the room. It's up to him to get them talking. There's nobody in Ballylack more qualified.

Seán's eye lands on the granny. She's his in. He can tell just from looking that she's a talker. It's in the twitchetty way she's folding and unfolding her hands. It won't take much to get her going. Seán locks eyes across the coffee table. He addresses his question directly to her. 'Fill me in, Mrs Adger. What exactly's happened here?'

It's as if he's flicked the detonator. Granny draws breath and out it all comes in one incessant, angry blast. The family have information about the source of the outbreak. They thought they should tell him immediately. Their Hannah's been thinking – *she's a clever wee thing, you find the shy ones often are* – and she got to wondering if anybody had checked on Millar's Gap. The whole class was up there for a nature trip at the end of term. Everybody went except her. And now everybody's getting sick except Hannah. Well, it wouldn't be the biggest leap to suggest they picked up whatever's sickening them on the school trip to Millar's Gap.

Granny's just repeating what Hannah's told Granda. He's repeated what Hannah told him. Hannah hasn't said anything about William or the others. She was afraid they wouldn't take her seriously.

Seán Donnelly's up off the chair before Granny's stopped talking. He asks Hannah's mum if he can use their phone. This is the first he's heard of a school trip. Nobody's thought to mention it. A school trip would make a lot of sense. None of the scientists can understand why the whole class has tested positive but this one wee girl is completely grand. Seán needs to phone his boss immediately. This is the breakthrough they've been waiting for. An antidote's a lot more likely if they can trace the source of the chemicals. And it's good news for the Adgers too. If Hannah's had no contact with the source, then there's no chance of her developing the sickness. It's not infectious. They've ruled that out. So, it's good news. Great news. Positive news. Seán says as much to the Adgers. The Adgers still look like someone's died.

'Sit down a minute, son,' says the granda. 'There's something else we have to tell you.' Out it comes in fits and starts. How he only had the best intentions. How he'd never do anything to hurt his Hannah. How he wishes he'd never heard tell of the Raggedy Tree. Three days ago, Hannah Adger was a lucky wee girl. Now, she's in the same boat as the rest of the weans. It's almost worse for her, thinks Seán Donnelly, knowing how close she came to escaping it all. Now, he understands why the room feels like rubber stretched to breaking point.

'I'm sorry,' mumbles Granda Pete, cradling his face in his hands. 'I'd give anything to go back and change things. But I can't.'

Granny comes down on him like a ton of bricks. 'I can't believe you could be so stupid. What were you thinking, Peter? Were you even thinking at all?'

'Hannah,' mumbles Mum. 'My poor wee Hannah.' She's crying again. She's been crying off and on since Granda told them. She's wondering if this is some kind of punishment. These last few days, she's been proud of Hannah's wellness. Just a little proud, but it's still a sin. She let herself believe the Lord was looking after his own. He'd noted their faithfulness and rewarded them. When she thinks about the other mothers – Marlene Fowler, Liza Ross and poor Mrs Leung, whose name she doesn't know how to pronounce – she feels thoroughly ashamed of herself. She'd imagined their family more worthy than the others: home and dry because they believed. *Will the Lord take Hannah to teach her a lesson? Possibly. Maybe. Does God work like that?* She should've known better; putting Hannah on a pedestal when she knows fine rightly that all children are equally precious in his eyes. 'Poor Hannah,' she wails. 'She's going to die.'

'And if she does,' hisses her husband, 'it'll be on your head, Dad. You know it will. If it was up to me, I'd never have anything to do with you again, but Hannah's begged me not to throw you out and I'm not going to hurt her any more than she's already been hurt.'

Granda Pete deflates in his chair. He's ten years older than he was yesterday. 'I'm sorry,' he says. He's apologized a hundred times already. What else is there left to say?

Seán Donnelly crosses the room to stand beside him. 'You didn't mean any harm, Pete,' he says. He does his best to sound comforting. He rests a hand, gently, on his shoulder. The old man is trembling. 'Look, let's not panic,' says Seán. 'There's no point leaping to conclusions. Hannah might well be OK. I'm going to make some phone calls, let the lads know about Millar's Gap. And we'll get Dr Simpson out tonight to test Hannah and her granda. It's best to know what we're dealing with.'

'You don't need to test me, Seán,' mumbles Granda.

'Best to be on the safe side, Mr Adger.'

'I don't have it.'

'We can't be sure of that until the tests come back. If the source is Millar's Gap, you're just as likely to be infected as Hannah and the other kids.'

'I'm not, son. I let her go into that place by herself.'

'Jesus,' mutters Seán under his breath. He'll have to get a counsellor round to talk to the old boy. His head must be in a shocking state. Maybe the counsellor can have a word with the father too. John Adger's looking murderous. It'll be a miracle if the family make it through this in one piece.

'Right,' says Seán, adopting a confident tone. 'We've a long night ahead of us. Mrs Adger, and uh . . . Mrs Adger, I think we could do with that cup of tea after all.' He goes out to the hall to use the phone. The ladies migrate towards the kitchen. The men remain behind in the living room. Granda Pete cries quietly into a big cotton hankie and every so often blows his nose. Dad says nothing. Absolutely nothing, for the duration. He's fighting a battle in his head. *How are you meant to forgive your own father when he's possibly, probably, killed your wee girl?*

Last Orders

D R SIMPSON RUSHES Hannah's blood sample through the lab. By 2 a.m. Mum and Dad know she has it. She's in the same boat as the others now. There's no need to make an announcement. Everyone else thinks she's had it all along.

Millar's Gap is a different matter. It necessitates a public announcement. As soon as the source has been confirmed, Seán Donnelly books a press conference in for the morning. The Ballylack grapevine gets there before him. By breakfast time, everybody knows. Millar's Gap's been cordoned off from the roadside to the moss. They're having to restrain the journalists and the nosy locals who've gathered around the entrance gate. A tent's been erected: a pitched white affair like the ones which cover dead bodies on *Inspector Morse*. Investigators have descended with Geiger counters; actual, ticking Geiger counters. They're wearing white boilersuits, double gloves and strange, hooded hats. They look more like beekeepers than scientists.

When they dredge the pond they find all manner of suspect things. No bodies (thank the Lord), though a body wasn't beyond the realms of possibility. It's the four rusty barrels that grab their attention. Two of them are intact (thank the Lord a second time. There's no telling how bad things might have been).

The barrels contain the same organophosphate they've found traces of in the children's blood. As people keep saying, it's the sort of thing you might find on a farm. Though this kind's not listed – it's clearly black market – and is far more complex than anything the scientists have seen before. Two of the barrels are empty, their contents long since dispersed into the pond. The scientists have been expecting this. The speed with which the poison's progressed suggested direct contact of some kind.

They photograph the edge of the pond. The grass. The weeds. The bugs and insects. Everything living is now dead. They rope off an area next to the weird-looking hawthorn tree. This, they've been told by the children's parents, is where they sat to eat their packed lunches. Where they rolled around in the soggy grass. Where they stood in the puddly edges of the pond, flicking stones and floating sticks. This is where the outbreak started. Knowing where and when brings them one step closer to the bigger questions of who and how.

They're in two minds about telling the teacher. She's sick already. Seriously so. Though as the only infected adult, she's much more likely to recover. They wonder if she'd want to know she's responsible. Not culpable, like whoever dumped those barrels, but she's definitely played an active part in the deaths of all those kids. A thing like that could drive you silly. You could torture yourself with alternative endings. *What if you'd kept the weans in class? What if you'd taken them someplace else? What if this? What if that?* You could drive yourself completely mad. They never get the chance to tell the teacher. Miss McKeown is already unconscious when they find the barrels. A day or so later she'll just sleep away, dying before she has a chance to blame herself.

The barrels prove that someone is definitely responsible. The outbreak can no longer be called a coincidence. It's not even accidental in the truest sense of an accident, though you'd have to be one callous bastard to have set out to poison little kids.

Ultimately, somebody's to blame. The people of Ballylack want to know who. If nothing else, the parents deserve an explanation; somebody to pin their anger to.

The RUC visit the families one at a time. They begin with the McCormicks, for their lad went first, then Kathleen's grandparents and the Twins' folks. They bring along the lady police officer. The poor woman has her work cut out offering tissues to sobbing mothers and rising to put the kettle on. She's not a particularly maternal type. Hugging doesn't come natural to her. Nor does offering platitudes. But the extra money's not to be sniffed at. These last few weeks she's clocked enough overtime to pay for a holiday at the end of the summer. She fancies Ibiza. Apparently, the nightlife's great. There are some benefits to being the only female officer in town.

The mothers cry and, after some crying, blow their noses and ask if there's more hope now of an antidote.

The fathers thunder. They get up and pace around their living rooms. Their hands make fists at the end of their arms. They want to beat the living shit out of the fella who dumped those barrels. They want him to suffer like they're suffering.

The remaining children stand quietly in halls and by windows. They tuck themselves behind closed doors. They peer through keyholes and peek over ledges. They press their ears up against the walls, listening to what the adults say. It's their story, but it is being kept from them.

In Henderson's front bar, where the regulars drink, the bad news is all they're talking about. The children are no longer other people's children. They belong to the village as a whole. It is *their* weans who've been poisoned. *Their* weans are sickening. Seven of *their* weans have already died. Ballylack shakes its head and sighs. The village is no stranger to tragedy. This is Northern Ireland, after all. Every village has lost someone. Dead children are different, though. The whole place reels when a wee one dies.

Everybody has a theory. Everybody's quick to share. *I bet ones from Tullybarret dumped them barrels. Naw, it'll have been Travellers. Travellers are always dumping shite. Or provos, I'd put good money on the provos. I tell you it was boys come up from the South.* By the time Mal Henderson's calling last orders, Wullie McClean is in full flow. Nobody's quite sure how old Wullie is. He could be anything between eighty and a hundred and three. He's sharp as tacks, though, and great on the old days of Ballylack. He remembers every family who's ever lived here; everything that's happened too. People know to listen when Wullie McClean has the floor. 'Sure, it's Francie Millar's curse come back,' he says, addressing what's left of the regulars. 'I knew we'd not heard the last of the Raggedy Tree.' It's almost gone midnight. Almost everybody's plastered, yet not a single soul laughs at Wullie.

Mal Henderson pulls the shutters down. He produces a half-decent bottle of Bushmills from behind the bar. 'On the house, lads,' he says as he doles out the measures. 'Desperate times and all that.' Wullie's absolutely loving this. Aye, he's a face on him like a Lurgan spade, it's a sober occasion, weans have died. But, boys a dear, his heart's fairly thumping as he starts to speak. He's not had such a captive audience in years. Wullie McClean takes his time. He milks the moment. He recounts the sad story of Millar's Gap.

Back in the day – fifty years ago – the land belonged to Francie Millar. The Millars were big dairy farmers hailing from the far side of Ballylack. Francie himself was quite the catch, a bachelor farmer of some standing, high up in both Orange and Young Farmer circles. When he finally decided to settle down, the farming families of Ballylack lined up to let him know their daughters were free and as close to willing as made no difference. In the end he went for Elsie Watson. She came complete with all her own teeth and a lovely figure, half a dozen of her daddy's heifers and a wee straggly bit of moss. This strip of land was hardly worth cutting. No more than two acres total. It was boggy and liable to flood. Still, it provided Francie and his new bride with enough turf to keep their home fire burning. And that wasn't nothing in Francie's eyes.

It soon became known as Millar's Moss. Ballylack farmers were far from creative when it came to the naming of things. This included weans. It was common enough to find a William or Davy present in every generation. The old ones would claim it a family name. There was truth in this. It was not a lie. If you pushed a bit, they might also admit they only knew a handful of decent, Protestant names. They were lesser-travelled, homely men. They had little knowledge of the wider world.

Sandwiched between Millar's Moss and the main road was a small patch of stony field which came to be known as Millar's Gap. It wasn't fit for growing anything. Potatoes failed on account of the soil, which, like a hormonal teenager's skin, was simultaneously damp and dry. It was too small and shingly to contemplate wheat and could not be used for serious grazing on account of the stagnant pond which spread like an open sore across its centre. A goat might have managed on the Gap. Francie Millar didn't have a goat, nor had he any interest in acquiring one.

Francie was buggered if he knew what to do with the Gap. The problem wasn't the field itself, which could be left to rot at little expense. It was the single tree which sprouted unbidden in the corner, next to the pond. This tree was older than his father's father. A gnarly-looking bitch of a hawthorn which hadn't blossomed in a dozen years. It was known locally as the Raggedy Tree. Any eejit could see where it got its name. The tree was fairly blooming with hundreds of coloured scraps of cloth. These wee snippets of shirts and dresses were tied at intervals along its branches. They fluttered and fumbled in the breeze. Each scrap represented a particular ailment, peculiar to a particular soul.

Each knot spoke of an earnest prayer – *or* wish *might've been a more accurate term* – for the wellness of a much-loved one.

The tree was thought to have healing properties linked to the fairies or the little folk. Nobody was very clear on specifics, though they knew enough to leave the tree be. Bad things happened if you were daft enough to harm a Fairy Tree. It'd been in the Watson family for generations. The Watsons had considered it a privilege to be the Raggedy Tree's protectors. They had, on several occasions – Flossie's gout and Wee John's issues with his waterworks – availed themselves of its properties.

The problems had started with the new minister: Reverend James P. Abernathy, a third-generation seminary man. He'd recently completed a stint in Korea as chaplain for the Royal Ulster Rifles and arrived home full of pious rage. He preached Christ alone and nothing before him. No flaffing about with the old superstitions, which he claimed tantamount to idolatry. There were even rumours that Abernathy would question a man's devotion to the Orange Order. *Dare you put the Sash before our Lord?* Abernathy cooled in time but remained righteously adamant on the supernatural front. There'd be no elders welcome in his session, no Sunday-school teachers or committee men who dabbled with cures or what he called Satan's business. Mr Watson, who was Clerk of Session at the time, saw a conundrum coming his way and swiftly passed the buck to his new son-in-law. The Raggedy Tree was now Francie's problem. Would he cut it down and risk spiting the fairies to curry favour with the cloth?

Francie Millar was not a superstitious man. His folks were Scotch originally. They'd their own fool notions about the spirit realms; still they kept no truck with magic trees. Francie was only a junior session man but he'd his eye on making Clerk. He was keen to impress the new minister, to set himself above the rest. Eighteen months after his wedding he started telling anyone wont to listen he was for chopping down the Raggedy Tree. It took less than ten minutes with a hatchet. The trunk was no thicker than a table leg. Afterwards he cut it into smaller sections and burnt it in a corner of the Gap. Nothing happened. The tree went up like a normal tree. Nothing happened for six more months.

Francie began to believe it had been nothing more than an ordinary tree. He dug his turf. His wife fell pregnant and bore him a son. He got good and tight with Reverend Abernathy. He let the smugness settle in his bones. He went so far as to brand the Gap with a Gospel sign. It was three-inch plywood, blackboard-sized, raised up to be visible over the hedge. On the side which faced the road he painted, *For the wages of sin are death*, in foot-high letters with black gloss paint. He'd fully intended to add, *but the gift of God is eternal life*. However, having arrived at the end of *death*, there was no room left for *eternal life*.

Six months after removing the Raggedy Tree, things began to go wrong for Francie Millar. First his mother slipped on a just-washed floor, impaling herself on a sharp bread knife. Then he'd a rake of calves born with deformities: two heads, no mouths, missing limbs, intestines outside when they should have been in. Then his wee fella, who was just toddling, tripped on the hearth rug and fell into the fire. Elsie, seeing the state of Francie Junior's face, passed out in shock and lost the fourteen-week baby in her belly. She never quite recovered from this. Though she gave Francie three more healthy boys, there was no light left behind her eyes. When the fourth of the fellas was up and weaned she took to her bed with a bottle of whiskey and drowned herself slowly over five long years.

Francie himself was never afflicted. He continued to be in the best of health, though his herds caught every disease going, and the back fields flooded while the front ones dried up, and the fancy new John Deere he'd dropped a fortune on got totalled by an uninsured driver the first time he took it out on the road. Francie couldn't help but see it as the ultimate insult when the Raggedy Tree managed to resurrect itself. Up from its severed trunk sprang brand-new branches and glossy leaves. Soon the tree was bigger and stronger than ever before. A few folks noted this and steered well clear. There was no debating the tree's potential, but every time they saw Francie Junior dragging his melty face around the village, they were reminded that it was safer to avoid the Raggedy Tree.

In 1965, ten years after acquiring the Gap, Francie Millar finally admitted, first to himself and then to others, that there might be something in this talk of a curse. He quit cutting the Moss and stopped repainting his wayside pulpit. He took a half-page ad in the *Chronicle* stating clearly that he no longer held any interest in the piece of land known as Millar's Gap. It continued to go by Millar's Gap. The tree itself was largely forgotten and the Gap became a dumping ground. Anything you wanted rid of could be driven out there in the dead of night, tipped into the pond and never heard tell of again. Folks said the pond was like Mary Poppins's handbag: bottomless and infinite. The men who used it to hide their secrets – *and it was almost always men* – never stopped to question its depths. It swallowed everything it was offered. Dead cows riddled with BSE. Magazines and videos you didn't want the wife coming across. Guns and stuff for making bombs. Fridges. Freezers. Nasty and unwanted things.

It's gone three by the time Wullie McClean's done saying his piece about Millar's Gap. Every man in Henderson's is sober as a circuit judge.

The Fathers

CAROLINE'S DAD APPEARS on the doorstep at ten to eight. 'Hello!' he yells through the Adgers' letterbox. 'Are youse up yet?' He rings the doorbell – six, seven times in quick succession – rattles their letterbox and finally resorts to pounding on the door. 'Are youse up? Let me in.'

Mum and Hannah are having a lie-in. They're exhausted. Mum's let Hannah sleep with her. She hasn't let her in their bed since she started school but last night raised no objections when Hannah claimed *bad dreams* and crawled in next to her. They pull their duvets over their heads, trying to muffle the racket outside. Neither has any intention of getting up. Dad will have to deal with this.

Dad's already up and about. He has been since six thirty. It's his custom, on weekdays, to rise before seven and have his quiet time before work. He's in the kitchen when Tommy starts knocking, making a round of sandwiches for his packed lunch. Work's been understanding enough, but they won't let him take time off, especially when it's not his kid who's sick. Yet. *Best to hold on to your annual leave*, the boss keeps saying. *Sure, you never know when you're going to need a few weeks off.* The boss is not a cruel man. He has grown-up children himself. Like the rest of Dad's colleagues, he's hoping for the best. John Adger's a decent man, if somewhat irritating. The boss wouldn't wish this shit on his worst enemy.

Dad doesn't need it spelt out. The fellas in work are expecting the worst. At some stage soon he'll need a whack of time off. For the sickness. And the funeral. And the bit that comes after, which might last months. He understands. He wants to prove them wrong, to say quite boldly, *My wee girl's going to make it. Just you wait and see.* He has to maintain his witness, though everything's changed since Hannah tested positive. She's positive, yes. But no symptoms yet. Dad has every faith that she'll be OK. What else can he do but hope and pray, and continue brave-facing around his colleagues? Note the choice of term. They are colleagues, not real friends. Dad is different with believers. He can be honest in their company.

He keeps heading into work at the usual time, bringing his sandwiches in a Tupperware. It's Thursday today, which means ham and cheese. Friday's egg. Dad keeps selling cars and answering phones, processing all the necessary paperwork. He talks about the weather when talk is required and otherwise keeps himself to himself. He clocks off at five thirty. Not a minute earlier, though there's no part of him wishes to be anywhere but home. He drives carefully back to Ballylack, keeping well within the speed limit. The next day, he does the very same. This is how he's been keeping his panic under control. Though today feels different – the stakes are higher after last night – Dad's going to work anyway.

Caroline's dad isn't trying to manage his rage. Caroline took a turn for the worse and left them around about midnight. Just after four, a young RUC officer – assigned to stay with the family – broke the news about Millar's Gap. *Some bastard's dumped barrels of chemicals in the pond.* Tommy's been in a blind rage ever since. Drinking and weeping. Punching walls. He's rung everybody he can think of, working his way through the *Yellow Pages*, becoming increasingly nonsensical as the drink takes hold. *What the hell are you doing about the outbreak in Ballylack?* He's phoned the RUC headquarters up in Belfast. The BBC and UTV. Downtown Radio. The *Belfast Telegraph*. Three different ministers, high up in three different denominations. The army barracks. The casualty department of the Royal Victoria. And Big Ian himself, though he'd had to leave a message there. The constituency offices don't open till nine.

Tommy Fletcher's an angry man. His daughter's dead. *Poisoned*, he says, fairly spitting the bad word out. Somebody's to blame. *Somebody local*, Tommy thinks. And if the authorities won't intervene, then he'll find the scummy bastard himself. He can't rightly say what he'll do then.

By the time he arrives at Hannah's front door, he's already knocked up four of the fathers. He's been banging away since just after six. He's very persuasive once he gets started. There's something threatening about the bulk of him. Ross's dad is in, Mr Leung, Ricky Ross and William's father, who's offered to round up a wheen of his brothers. 'Much appreciated, mate,' says Tommy, 'but us fathers have to do this by ourselves.' Kathleen's dad's already back in Scotland so there's no point trying to get him involved. Matty doesn't seem to have a father and, to be very honest, Tommy would rather not involve Rob Anderson. *Feckless hippy.* Him and the wife haven't the sense they were born with. Nobody'll notice the lack of him.

It's breakfast time now. The drink is starting to leave Tommy's system and the auld head has him in a vice. He's eaten nothing but a Lion bar since Caroline passed. He could do with something to sop up the booze. The Adgers' door swims as he approaches. He has a wee bit of paper with the eleven names on it. He takes it out of his pocket and squints at it, reads *Hannah Adger* and checks it off against the hand-painted sign. He rings the doorbell. The folk inside aren't moving quickly enough. He keeps banging and shouting till somebody appears. The journalists haven't appeared yet this morning but Tommy still knows he's making a scene. He sees curtains twitching across the road. He doesn't care. The sooner they get started, the sooner they can get this over with.

Tommy's never killed a man before. He's come close a few times, with his fists and his feet. Of course, he's slaughtered plenty of beasts: pigs, cows, sheep, once a horse that needed putting out of its misery. Sure, there's not much difference between a horse and a man. If anything, the horse would be bigger. Tommy knows he could kill a man. He's already limbering up for it, in his muscles and his blood. He won't hesitate when they find the bastard. He's already picturing the shape of the moment. The gun, tucked inside his waterproof jacket, coming swiftly out. The dull *thwack* of the barrel emptying. The blood spattering. All those wee bits of brain and skull, whiting through the red. The smell; the burnt-metal stink of it. The feeling of release which always comes with a spent bullet. The relief of having the thing finally done.

Tommy Fletcher's been chewing on this image for hours now, ever since his daughter choked her last and left. He won't let himself think about Caroline. At least not at the end. Her beautiful face all swollen and raw like somebody had taken their fists to her. He can't bear to dwell upon his wee girl in such a state, or even the thought of her afterwards, so very still on the hospital bed. There are some thoughts so vile they can't be let in. *Blowing this bastard's brain out?* Well, that's another matter entirely. Tommy's fairly loving the thought of that.

As soon as Hannah's dad opens the door, he steps inside.

'Sorry to barge in. I came to tell you our Caroline's died.'

'I heard,' says Dad. 'I'm so, so sorry, Tommy. Is there anything we can do to help?'

'Yes, John. There's something I need you to do.'

He elbows his way past Dad. He heads down the hall towards the kitchen. Hearing the noise of him stomping about, Mum comes downstairs in her dressing gown. She makes a quick assessment of the situation and takes control.

'Go on, into the sitting room,' she says. 'I'll put the kettle on.'

She puts her arm round Caroline's dad and steers him through the connecting doors to the bigger room beyond.

'You look famished, Tommy. Would you take a round or two of toast?'

'Yes,' says Caroline's dad. All of a sudden, he's desperately hungry for toast dripping with butter and maybe a wee slice of bacon. 'Would you have a bit of bacon too?'

'I'll get the pan out.'

Normally Mum would take exception to a drunk man coming into her house and giving orders. But Tommy's out of his head with grief. A bacon sandwich is the least she can do. She retreats to the kitchen, pulling the door behind her. She doesn't want Hannah hearing their chat. There's no knowing what a man like Tommy might say. While she's waiting on the kettle, she makes two phone calls.

She rings her husband's work and tells the boss's secretary he's come down with a dreadful migraine. The strain he's under has obviously started working on him. She's quite firm with the woman; John won't be coming in today. Then, she phones Tommy's wife. It isn't Susan who answers the phone. Susan's in bed. The doctor's given her something to knock her out. It's a sister-in-law who answers: Fiona somebody or other with a Belfasty accent. This makes it easier for Hannah's mum. She expresses her sympathy in vaguer terms. She says she's praying for them and is there anything else she can do. She says, 'Listen, this is a bit awkward. I just wanted to let you know, Tommy's here. Judging by the state of him, he's been out all night. He's grand. My husband's sitting with him. He'll run him home later. I'm only telling you in case youse were worrying.' The sister-in-law sighs. It is clear that she would quite like to give Mum a mouthful on the subject of her no-good brother-in-law.

Hannah's mum arranges a tray and takes it into the men. As she passes her husband his tea, she leans across the coffee table and whispers, 'I phoned work. They're not expecting you this morning.' A look of pure rage passes across his face. It's so rare for Dad to let himself go, Mum's never seen this face before. It doesn't suit him. He composes himself quickly. There's company watching. 'I told them you were stressed,' she says, and slips out before he can tell her off for lying. Hannah's dad doesn't believe in stress. There's trusting God and there's not trusting God. He has no concept of anything in between. She closes the door behind her. It's better to leave them alone. There are things a man won't say in the presence of a woman, even if that woman is his wife.

'Well, Tommy,' says Dad as soon as she's gone, 'should you not be getting back to your wife? I'm sure she could do with you home today.'

'Susan'll be fine. Her lot are up from Belfast. They're more than capable of holding the fort. Naw, I'm not for heading home yet. There's business to take care of first.'

'Business?'

'Aye,' says Tommy. 'We've to go out and find whatever bastard – *pardon my French* – is responsible for what happened to Caroline . . . and the rest of them. Justice is what I'm after, mate. Somebody needs to pay for this.'

'Justice?'

'Aye, proper justice. Eye for an eye and tooth for a tooth; all that stuff it says in the Bible. His life, for all the innocent wee lives he's taken.'

Tommy Fletcher sits back on the sofa. He opens the flap of

his jacket to reveal a gun handle poking out of an inner pocket. It's not the first gun Dad's ever seen. Once, during the early eighties, he was held up by three fellas in balaclavas. They were after a Ford Cortina for a bank job over in Magherafelt. They'd waved their guns in his face. When he didn't move fast enough one of them hit him a bit, around the head. He's seen guns before, though he wouldn't call himself an expert by any means. He has no idea what sort of weapon Tommy's packing: a pistol maybe, or a revolver. He can say with certainty it's not a shotgun. That's as far as his knowledge goes.

'Put that thing away. Sandra'll throw us both out if she sees it.'

Tommy closes his jacket, zippers it to the chin. He edges forward so he's in Dad's face.

'Listen, John, I know you lot are Born Agains. Youse aren't into violence or anything like that. But is it not driving you mad, knowing your wee girl's upstairs, *maybe* – no, let's be honest about this – *probably* dying and there's some cock-of-the-walk eejit out there, some fella we probably both know, responsible?'

'Hannah's fine.'

'Catch yourself on, John. Sure, it's only a matter of time . . .'

Tommy pauses for a moment. He takes a long look at Hannah's dad. The man's gone white as a clean sheet. Revenge might not be the best angle for a Holy Roller like John Adger. He changes tack. 'Look, John, maybe you're right. Maybe it's not too late for the ones that aren't sick yet. Still, you'd want them to catch whoever done this. You'd want this fella punished for what he's done.'

'Seán Donnelly says the police will get him.'

'Forget Seán Donnelly. Has he made any headway? Has he hell. Donnelly has no real interest in getting to the bottom of this. He's a Taig, John. First and foremost, he is a bloody Taig. He doesn't care about our weans. He couldn't give a rat's ass whether they live or die. He's only here to keep us from taking matters into our own hands. Soon as it's all over, he'll be in that big jeep of his, heading back over the border, to his Fenian wife and his own Fenian kids. Not so much as a backward glance will he give Ballylack and the mess he's left behind. Let me tell you, John, your man Donnelly is only in it for the money. I heard he's getting paid a clean fortune to keep the peace.'

'Really?'

'As God's my witness.'

'He seems like a decent enough fella to me.'

'Uch, John. Never trust a Taig. They're a sleekit breed of folk; always saying one thing, meaning something else entirely. Do not be fooled by your man's big talk. He doesn't give a toss about your wee girl.'

A short silence descends upon the living room. Tommy Fletcher watches the mantelpiece clock as the hands inch closer to eight. Hannah's dad sits back in his armchair mulling over what's been said. The sweat's begun to pool at the base of his spine; he can feel his trousers starting to stick to the leather upholstery. He's not good with confrontation. Not good with awkward silences either. He speaks first.

'I wouldn't want to be involved in any vigilante stuff,' he says slowly, hesitating over each word. 'I don't believe in violence. You know it's not our place to deliver justice.'

'*Vengeance is mine, saith the Lord.*'

'Exactly.'

'Listen, forget all that nonsense about killing the bastard. That was just big talk on my part. Let's pretend there's nothing in my jacket pocket but a pack of smokes.' Tommy pats his breast pocket and winks suggestively at Dad. 'I only want to get a wheen of lads together to go over the fields. We'll see if we can't find any trace of this stuff around the farms. They say it came from one of us. I don't trust the Peelers, John. Sure, they're not getting anywhere. The likes of us know this bit of the world better than anyone. One good day of looking and I bet we can find the bastard responsible.'

'And we'd go to the police if we found anything.'

'Straight to the police, John. You have my word.' Tommy catches Dad's eye and holds it for a good ten seconds. He's finally figured out how to play a man like John Adger. 'Now, you wouldn't want to be the only dad in Ballylack who's not out there searching? The only one who's not prepared to defend his child? You wouldn't want this boyo getting away scot-free, would you, John?'

'No,' says Hannah's dad. *No, he wouldn't want any of that.*

He doesn't know whether it's Tommy's strong talk, or the smell of whiskey rising off him, maybe it's the gun, sitting silently between them, like a tiny ticking bomb, but Dad feels more like a man than he has in years. He looks down at his hands. He has one of Sandra's scatter cushions all twisted up between his fingers, fabric straining at the seams. He's not been aware of his hands, the way they've needed something to destroy. *Could I punch another man?* he wonders. The situation's never come up before. But he thinks, *Yes, maybe I could. Could I kill somebody? Definitely not.* There's no coming back once you've taken a life. Besides, he doesn't think he has it in him. Though, then again, could he be absolutely certain in the moment, if somebody was hurting his wee girl?

Hannah's dad is about to open his mouth and say, *Count me in,* when the door opens and Mum elbows her way in with a trayful of bacon sandwiches.

She shuffles the furniture around, unfolding a card table for the tray. She avoids looking either man in the eye. She places the food in front of them.

'Get that knocked into you, Tommy,' she says. 'It's nothing fancy, but it'll line your stomach at least.' As she slips out of the room, she turns to call over her shoulder, 'Eat up, lads. Tommy's brother-in-law's on his way over. He's offered to pick him up.' She's only just decided on saying this, but she's pleased enough with the way it sounds. There's a kind of swagger which comes with making statements in retreat.

Once the door's closed Mum goes straight to the hall phone and calls the Fletchers' farm again. The same sister-in-law answers. They're probably taking shifts to mind the phone. 'Would you be able to send your husband over to pick up Tommy?' she asks. 'Normally, my husband wouldn't mind running him out, but he's got a terrible migraine this morning and, well, I don't think it'd be appropriate for me to drive Tommy, myself. Not in the state he's in.' The sister-in-law sighs again. She'll send one of the men over straight away.

Hannah's mum hangs up the phone. She leans against the wall, waiting for her nerves to steady. She should be repenting for all the lies she's told. She should be on her knees asking the Lord to forgive her for not trusting her own husband, for listening at doors and hearing things he wouldn't want her to hear. Weak moments. Sinful moments. The flesh rising to lord it over the spirit. She's witnessed her husband sorely tempted; on the verge of giving in. It's not her place to interfere. He's the head of the house. The head of her too.

When Mum peels her emotions back, she finds not one jot of sorrow present. There's nothing in her heart but relief. She's caught her husband just in time. She's seen his weakness and acted quickly. She knows it's not right for a wife to lie. Neither is it Biblical for a woman to rise up and control her husband. The Bible's crystal clear on that. But her man's blind this morning: overcome with pride and rage. Surely, the Lord will make an exception. Maybe, he'd even be on her side. And if not, sure she can always beg forgiveness later. Isn't that the great thing about grace? There's no sin so dreadful the Lord won't deem to forgive.

The Bones of It

ALAN GARDINER HAS a problem. He knows the walls are closing in.

After the third wean died, he'd put two and two together himself. He'd known in his guts there'd been more than diesel in those barrels. He'd known the sickness was his fault. He was afraid then. Much afraid. First for himself. Then for his boy. Realizing Ben was an afterthought had only added to Alan's guilt.

He's gone over and over that night in his head, especially these last few days since the police started draining the pond. He knows he was careful with the dumping. Nobody saw him going or coming. He disinfected the horsebox afterwards and put his boilersuit through a hot wash. He's pretty certain he left no fingerprints. He'd worn a pair of Megan's washing-up gloves. No, there's nothing linking him to Millar's Gap.

Still, he should've called the police first thing, the very second those barrels were found. He should've admitted everything. He should have. But he hasn't yet. He knows the fathers are out for blood. He can't blame them. If the circumstances were different, he'd feel exactly the same himself. If he tells them now, they'll crucify him. He deserves to be crucified. Seven wee ones are dead. Seven other people's children, and Alan knows it's his fault.

If it was only him, he might do it – phone Seán Donnelly and take the blame – but he knows the reprisals wouldn't stop with him. They'd take it out on his family too. Ben. Megan. Wee Lucy. He can't bear the thought of anybody being cruel to her. He imagines folks saying horrible things, shouting and getting on, maybe even spitting at her in the street. It's not her fault. It's not Megan's fault either. He can't even bring himself to think about Ben. If the boy gets sick, he'll be to blame. Maybe he's wanted this all along.

The problem begins and ends with Ben. If the boy had been a bit more normal, which is to say, more like him, then Alan would never have gotten into this mess. And Ben would be safe. And the other weans too. *God Almighty*, thinks Alan Gardiner for the hundredth time, *how did I end up with that for a son?* The farm has required a son of him, yet Ben's made it abundantly clear that he does not require a farm.

Alan has considered leaving the land to his daughter. Lucy could turn out to be a hardy one, the kind of woman who can work with beasts. But Ballylack's the sort of place where farms still pass to sons or grandsons; a nephew if there's nobody else. You wouldn't leave your farm to a woman. Women were grand for keeping house and children, occasionally ploughtering about with hens. It would take a man to run his farm and Alan knew Megan hadn't another baby in her. If Ben didn't take his farm on it would be lost.

Damned if Alan was for sitting back while it passed down to his brothers' boys. Hadn't they land enough already – a hundred-odd acres in the next townland – and weren't they both gobshites, big, florid-faced lads who call his weans darkies behind his back? He'd made his mind up years ago. It didn't matter whether Ben wanted to farm or not. Alan would make the decision for him, as his father had decided for him. To hell with the boy's fool ambitions. Book learning. Teaching. Running. Alan couldn't give a toss.

In a year or two Alan intended to sit Ben down and tell him

how it was going to be. *When I'm gone, the farm'll be yours. You need to learn the tricks of the trade.*

Bollocks to that. Alan knew exactly what he'd say. Ben didn't do scenes. He'd just shake his head and say, *No, thank you,* as if he was turning down a second helping of spuds rather than his own birthright. Ben was thran, like his father. If Alan wanted to convince him, he'd have to get Megan on side. She was the only one Ben listened to. Yes, Megan would have to remind the boy that she came from nothing. And he came from her. Which is to say, he was nothing too. Ben could be the first in her family to own his own land and a house with two storeys, to have a car – two cars, actually, if you counted the Land Rover – and the possibility of education beyond high school.

Alan wouldn't have any problem convincing his wife that Ben should go to Agricultural College. Though buried in layer upon layer of other names, Maganda was still the same wee girl who once devoured paperback novels on the front porch. She'd want her Bayani to have what she'd never had. An education. The minute she heard Alan was keen on college, she'd be in like Flynn with all the reasons why Ben should go. *You will love it, son. It is a great opportunity for you. Think of all the doors it will open.*

She wouldn't care that college could give Bayani a love of farming and the basics of his trade. That he'd be around other young ones, some of them from far-flung places more open-minded than Ballylack. That there'd be girls present – just a few, and mostly of the homely type – but all the same, girls. And there'd be drinking, too, and gadding about in souped-up motors; the sort of thing young fellas should be up to at his age. No, all she'd hear was her wee boy, with actual letters after his name. She'd picture a certificate framed on the wall. Photographs of Bayani on his graduation day. Photos she'd send back to Marikina so all the naysayers would have to admit that Maganda Rosamie Mendoza had come up in the world.

With Megan on side, Alan was reasonably confident he could talk his son into the farm. Still, a bribe would help: a wad of cash to make the compromise more appealing. *Buy yourself a fancy car*, he'd say. *Do the house up whatever way you like.* The young ones were mad keen for the mod cons. Ben could install a hot tub in the backyard for all he cared.

Alan had opened a bank account in Ben's name. This last year, he'd been putting money aside. He'd started taking a tenner out of the housekeeping every week and putting it away for Ben instead of his mum. Last spring, he'd sold an extra calf at auction. Then, he'd laid off the young lad who helped with the morning milking. Though he'd been wiped out doing the whole thing himself, Alan had been pleased to see his savings mounting up. By the time Ben finished his GCSEs he aimed to have twenty grand to offer his son, maybe even twenty-five. Surely that kind of money would turn a young lad's head.

Alan Gardiner's not a bad man. He's not even particularly greedy. He never meant to hurt the children. He's innocent of everything but stupidity.

It's the two fellas from Donegal Town who're actually to blame. 'Unknown One' and 'Unknown Two', whose name, Alan thinks, might be Paddy. Not that this'd been any help when it came to tracking the bastard down. Every other eejit in the South goes by Paddy. *Paddy the Irishman and all that.* The pair of them are the guilty ones. Not Alan Gardiner. He had the very best of intentions. He was only trying to set his boy up. He was doing his best to hold on to his farm. He should've had more sense. He can see that now. Even the most wet-eared fool knows not to take shit off fellas you meet in pub car parks. Doesn't matter how plastered you are or how much cash they're offering. You're supposed to say, *Do you think I was born yesterday?* You're supposed to up and walk away.

But Alan was desperate the day he met the pair of boyos from

Donegal Town. Ben had just that morning refused to sign up for the Young Farmers. He could feel his daddy's farm slipping away. Desperate times. Desperate measures. Alan was only thinking about the money. The way it'd help to pin the boy down. He'd never stopped to consider the right or wrong of loading those four big barrels into his horsebox. He'd only said, 'You're sure there's nothing dangerous in there?' and chose to believe them when they said, ''Course not, mate. It's only a bit of dodgy diesel. We were planning to shift it in Letterkenny, but apparently the Guards are stopping everybody on the border tonight. Some fecker must've tipped them off. We can't take the risk of getting caught. Your man over there's already got form.' Alan was barely listening to the pair of them. He'd been thinking about the five hundred pounds sterling they were pressing upon him; the way it would bolster Ben's funds. *Easy money*, he was thinking. *I'll just dump the barrels in Millar's Gap.*

Alan Gardiner's a stupid man.

When the second kid died, he'd phoned the fella from Donegal Town. Surprise, surprise, the number didn't work. The fellas had taken him for a fool. He'd tried various combinations of the digits – dragging the telephone into the downstairs toilet so Megan wouldn't hear – and, after a dozen or so attempts, given up. He'd cursed his own stupidity. *What sort of halfwit takes unmarked barrels off a pair of lads he's only just met?*

Alan Gardiner's not a bad man. Still, children are dead, and they keep on dying. Ballylack's ruined, and he's to blame. For years to come, grief will catch like a rag nail on everything the villagers touch. Every baby born will be more precious in light of *their* loss. Every small occasion rendered significant simply because *they* are not present. Time will stick and take on a new beat. It will be slower and stiffer from now on. People will refer to the following years as *After*. While everything preceding will be known as *Before*. There'll be no need to clarify these terms. No need to mark or date them. Something seismic has taken place this summer. Nothing in Ballylack will ever be the same.

Alan would be the first to admit it's all his fault. But he has yet to open his mouth. One day's folded into the next. The guilt's grown heavier every day. Megan's noticed him dragging it around the house, though he's done his best to avoid her gaze. He's held his secret for so long, what would be the point in speaking up now? The damage is done. He can't undo it. Those who are sick are already sickening. He isn't God. He can't turn back time. If Alan keeps his head down and doesn't panic, maybe he'll get away with it.

It's no longer a question of doing the right thing. Alan Gardiner's just trying to survive.

Convictions

Hannah is upstairs not praying when Caroline appears. She's avoiding the believers in the living room. They seem to have doubled since yesterday. Dad must've told them about her wee visit to the Raggedy Tree. They'll think she's brought the sickness on herself. Pastor Bill says there's no such thing as sinning without consequence.

Hannah's lying in bed with the sheets pulled up, hands clasped tightly in front of her. She looks like she's been laid out for the coffin. She's emptied her head of everything but Jesus. Or rather, she's trying. It isn't easy to empty her head. It's like a cattle market in there. One minute she's driving herself mad with guilt. Two seconds later, she's crippled with fear. Guilt and fear and fear and guilt. It's never quiet in Hannah's head.

She's finding it impossible to pray. Mum says this is understandable, given the circumstances. Mum's struggling herself. Hannah doesn't stop trying, but her prayers feel like they're bouncing back. They're fasting again. Mum and Dad, and Granny too. Even Granny's taking it seriously now, consuming nothing but dry toast and water. They don't listen to Granda Pete when he insists they need to keep their strength up. Granda Pete's lost the right to have an opinion on anything related to his family. Thankfully, Hannah's exempt. Dr Simpson's prescribed a high-protein diet and plenty of fluids to give her body a fighting chance. No fasting for Hannah. Just ordinary praying. And she's making a total hash of that.

Mum says when you find it hard to pray, you can meditate on a scripture instead. 'God knows what you're trying to say,' she explains. 'He sees the intentions of your heart.' Hannah's a bit wary of meditation. *Is that not something Muslims do?* They've done Muslims in RE class. It's all right to learn about other religions, in the same way that it's OK to learn about wars and other bad things which happened in history. *Forewarned is forearmed,* Pastor Bill says. Hannah has no notion what this means. It is not OK to dabble in other religions. Most Protestants would agree on this. It's why Lief's mum wasn't allowed to do her yoga demonstration at the last school fair. It's why Granny stopped watching *Songs of Praise* after they had an ecumenical carol service, broadcast from a Roman Catholic chapel with a priest saying the prayers.

'Hmmm,' says Mum, when she asks, 'I think it's actually Buddhists who meditate, Hannah. The kind of meditation I'm talking about is different. It's of God, not the Devil. You just think really hard about a Bible verse.'

Hannah has been practising ever since. Taking a verse or two and bouncing it round inside her brain: whispering it, humming it, sucking on every syllable in the hope that the Jesus in her head will be pleased and maybe talk to her. He hasn't said a single word since she visited the Raggedy Tree. Hannah suspects he's huffing with her. Today, to show him she's really serious, she is saying her prayers out loud. Hannah's always felt self-conscious about this. Speaking out loud sounds weird when there's nobody there. It's better with an audience. 'Dear Heavenly Father, I'm scared,' she says. 'I'm scared,' she repeats. 'I'm really scared.' Something in Hannah's thinking is stuck. She can't seem to squeeze any other words out. 'I'm scared. I'm scared. I'm scared.' *Is this praying?* She isn't sure, though she's lighter the second it's out of her mouth.

When she opens her eyes, Caroline is staring at her. Her head is next to Hannah's on the pillow. Her face is so close, she's little more than a pale blur of skin and dark brown hair. Her lips move. 'I'm scared too,' she says. 'We all are.' Hannah shuts her eyes and screws them up tightly, forcing them to focus. When she opens them, Caroline's sitting on the bed's edge. She still has the same farmy smell: sheep feed, Dettol and warm dung. It's quite a nice smell if you don't think about what it is.

'Move over,' she says. 'I'm coming in.'

She crawls under the duvet and snuggles up next to Hannah. Hannah can feel her bony elbows angled into the hollow of her back. Her forehead presses bluntly between Hannah's shoulder blades. She tucks her bent knees into the back of Hannah's and snakes a single cold arm around her waist. She shuffles a little, finds a comfortable position and settles. 'Warm me up, Hannah. I'm absolutely freezing down here.'

Hannah's not sure what to do. She's never snuggled with any-one except Mum and, when she was younger, Dad. Even before the sickness, he'd stopped touching her like he used to. Now, he only ever kisses her on the cheek. *It's because you're growing up*, Mum's told her. *You're becoming a woman.* Hearing this, Hannah knows they've talked about the training bra she's just started wearing. They might even have discussed what they'll say when her periods start. She goes red in the face just thinking about this.

Caroline has a sister. Hannah doesn't. Caroline's well used to snuggling up with wee Emily, especially on winter nights, when their old farmhouse struggles to keep the heat in. Hannah doesn't know how to hold another girl. She is stiff with Caroline. She rubs her hands roughly, up and down her arm, both wanting and not wanting to have her this close. Caroline feels like a plucked chicken: cold and slightly damp, puckered with lumpy goosebumps. It's not a pleasant sensation but Hannah keeps rubbing, all the time telling herself this is absolutely normal, not at all weird. *Sure, aren't the girls in Enid Blyton books always bunking up together in their posh boarding schools?* She checks her body. No part is tingling or excited. This is a relief. It would be wrong to feel romantic touching a girl.

Caroline talks. Hannah feels the shape of her mouth moving against her back, the dry heave of her shoulders when she starts to cry. A damp spot spreads across the neck of her nightie where Caroline's tears are soaking in. One of Hannah's ears is pressed into the pillow so it's hard to hear exactly what she's saying. She strains to catch the shape of it.

Caroline doesn't like being dead. It's lonely, even with all the others there. She hates the way they're fighting, taking sides and being mean. It makes her angry. It makes her sad. She misses ordinary things: watching *Corrie* with her mum, playing the computer with her sister. Her friends. Her cousins up the road. She doesn't know what to do with her body. The hips. The tits. The hair in places you shouldn't have hair. It's far too sudden. It doesn't feel like her actual self.

'It's like being an adult while you're still a kid,' she explains. 'We look like grown-ups, we're pretending to be grown-ups, but nobody really knows what they're doing. Oh God, Hannah, I'd do anything to go back. I hate it here.'

Caroline hauls herself up into a sitting position, giving herself room to rant.

'If you listen to Lief and his lot, they'll tell you dying's the best thing that ever happened to them. Maybe it is. If my ma sent me to school in my dad's hand-me-downs and everybody constantly took the piss, I might think being dead was better too. It's just, I can't decide if they're actually happy or only talking themselves into it. You should see them, Hannah, they take the whole gang thing so seriously. They have jackets now: old school blazers with the badges ripped off and DK wrote on the back in permanent marker. They're rare as got out, but you wouldn't dare tell them that.

'I mostly hang around with the Twins. I like Lizzy. Lizzy tells it like it is. She doesn't pretend she's anything but sad. The others are only acting up so they don't have to admit how much they miss the way it used to be. I've heard that sort of talk before. Big talk. Bragging. Acting the eejit. My dad's like that, so he is. He never takes anything seriously. Even when I was dying he wasn't able to deal with it. He just talked rubbish and left Mum with me when it got too much. Dear only knows what he's like now. Any money he's blocked and shooting his mouth off, blaming everybody but himself. Have you seen him, Hannah? What's he like?'

'Drunk and shouting,' says Hannah. 'He was round this morning trying to recruit my dad. They're away off to find whoever dumped those barrels. I think your dad might beat them up.'

'Yup, that sounds familiar. Big talk and brute force, that's Tommy all over. He never thinks about what he says or the way he hurts everybody around him. Kathleen reminds me of him a lot. These last few days she's been working on Mim, telling her she belongs with the DK, that Lizzy doesn't care about her. Mim's not cracked yet, but I've seen her looking funny at her sister. She's still upset about what Lizzy's done to her hair. She's started dressing more like Kathleen; tarty, like. That's probably not a good sign.

'William says we need to make up before it's too late. William's awful sensible. I'm glad he's here. It's almost like having a grown-up around. He keeps saying we've only got one shot at this. There's nobody else to hang out with. We have to do our best to get on. William's brave. He'll stand up to Kathleen, even if she's in one of her shouty moods. He doesn't care what the rest of them think. I wish I was a bit more like him. Being a dead kid's not that different from not being dead. You still feel sort of small in yourself. You want people to like you. You don't want to be the odd one out. And there's stuff you aren't able to fix or change. Do you think it's different for grown-ups, Hannah? Do they feel more in control of things?'

'I don't know,' says Hannah. She thinks about her family, and the way they looked at her when they found out about Millar's Gap.

'I used to think that when you got older, you'd have all the answers,' says Caroline. 'You'd know what to say. You'd know how to make everything all right. Maybe adults don't know what to do either. Maybe they're just as confused as us.'

'I think you might be right,' says Hannah. She's specifically thinking about her dad.

'Anyway, the DK want me to tell you it's brilliant here. Lief and Kathleen will kill me, but I can't lie to you. It's awful, Hannah. I wish I could leave. Whatever you do, try not to die.'

'I'll try,' says Hannah. She gives Caroline's arm a reassuring pat. They both know she won't have any choice.

Eventually Caroline falls asleep, arms belted around Hannah's waist. Hannah lets her sleep. She lies in bed, feeling the weight of the other girl pinning her down. Caroline is so easy with her body. She doesn't seem to know it's there. Hannah's never done thinking of hers. She's constantly tugging her shirt down over her belly and hunching her shoulders to make her little breasts disappear. When Mum's not coerced her into a ponytail, she'll wear her hair in a mousy brown curtain, drooped over one eye and cheek. She prefers it like this, with half her face hidden. She'd be happier if nobody could see she had a face at all. Hannah would never crawl into anyone else's bed and assume they wanted her there. She couldn't relax enough to fall asleep with another person. Except maybe Mum. When she thinks about being married, in bed, with a man, the thought is absolutely ludicrous, like imagining herself on TV.

Part of Hannah wishes Caroline would wake. She could be honest with Caroline. She could ask her things she wants to know. She could admit how scared she feels. The other part of her is content to lie here, held and safe, for a little while. She blurs out the adults' voices downstairs and the sunlight shivering through the curtains. It's actually quite nice to feel someone close, nice to listen to Caroline's breath rising and falling in time with her own. So nice and comfortable, Hannah eventually falls asleep. She dreams about sleeping. *Does this even count as a dream?*

When she wakes, it's lunchtime. Her bed is empty. Caroline's gone. Hannah yawns and stretches her arms and as she loosens back into her body realizes it doesn't feel right. There's a tiny lump beneath the skin at the base of her neck. She feels around it with her fingers. There's one on the left side and another at exactly the same point on the right. When she presses against them the lumps are tight and muscly like the topmost part of her ear. It feels like a bruise when she pushes hard, though there's nothing to see in the bathroom mirror. Nothing but the normal shape of her neck. She pulls her hair down so it hides her neck. She should tell Mum. She knows she should. But she isn't ready for what will happen after that.

On the other side of Ballylack the fathers have gathered in the C of I car park. There are seven of them in total. Three of the seven are farming men: Alan Gardiner, Tommy Fletcher and William's dad. Tommy Fletcher hasn't the sense to be fearful – sure, he gathered this posse up himself – but the other two would rather be anywhere else this morning. In their heads they're pacing around their farms, opening cupboards, peeking into outhouses, wondering what might look bad if stumbled upon. There's not a farmer this side of Belfast that hasn't got some small skeleton to hide. The suits from the Department have no notion what it's like managing an actual, working farm. If they kept to the letter of their law, they'd all be bankrupt in a bloody year. They're not doing anything out-and-out illegal. It's not even bad practice, in the truest sense. To be honest, it's more what you'd call common sense. Which is not to say the farmers round here look forward to inspections, especially impromptu witch hunts like this. They'd prefer a bit of warning; some time to get the dirty washing in.

If Tommy Fletcher had stopped to think, he might have remembered the unregistered sheep currently grazing in his back field. There's a couple of items in Jimmy Fowler's shed he'd rather the lads didn't come across. Alan Gardiner's worried about his horsebox. He thinks he's been thorough with the clean-up, but there's no telling how rigorous this lot will be. He glances round the gathered circle. They're grim of mouth and determined-looking. Maybe, hopefully, best-case scenario, they won't even make it to his farm. He's hoping they find something suspicious at somebody else's place. He's praying for a sudden downpour. He catches Jimmy Fowler's eye. Jimmy's looking a bit sheepish too.

Every child is represented this morning, everybody except Kathleen, Matty and Hannah. In the absence of Hannah's dad, Tommy's decided to include Rob Anderson. He can't stand the fella himself, but they could do with another pair of eyes.

When the other fathers ask about John Adger, Tommy says, 'The wife wouldn't let him out.' This isn't exactly true. In the end, it was John himself who'd refused to come. The rest of the fellas make jokes about Sandra wearing the trousers. They wouldn't let their wives tell them what to do. Tommy lets their laughter run its course. He's not sure why he's out to mock the fella. Maybe he doesn't know how to say, *John's sticking to his convictions*, when he's long since lost his own faith. Maybe, this morning, with his wee girl dead, he wishes he had some religion left. If he's honest – and God knows Tommy Fletcher's not ready for honesty – he needs to laugh John out of town. It's the only way of softening his own shame, dispelling the image of his own wife, clinging to him at their front door. The poor woman beside herself with grief, begging him to stay, and he, like a cold beast, turning from her and shouting, 'Catch yourself on, Susan. I'm away to sort this out.'

It's the easiest thing in the world to ridicule John Adger. The daft bugger's set himself up for it, with his softly talk and his gentle faith. *He's hardly even a man, is he?* The truth is, Tommy would love a bit of whatever John's got. Since Caroline died, he can't look himself in the eye. Can't look at his wife or his other wean either. He's ashamed of what he's put them through. All that shouting and getting on, just because he can't find the words to tell them that his heart's broke too.

The Search

THE FATHERS FIND nothing.

They spend all day searching local farms. At lunchtime they hear that the teacher has died. She'd gone home to her folks in Augher at the end of term. They've heard very little from her since. Seán Donnelly's fit to tell them they'd put Miss McKeown into an induced coma to take some pressure off her heart. It'd been peaceful enough at the end. 'She just slept away,' he tells them. He can't help but wish the weans had gone so easily. The news about Miss McKeown is disheartening. As an adult, folks hoped she'd be better placed to fight off the poison. They can't help but consider the three kids who are left. Ben. Matty. Hannah. None of them are particularly strong. It's a miracle they've lasted this long.

The news doesn't slow the fathers down. If anything, it makes them more determined. *Poor wee lassie. Due to get married this coming August. That bastard's got a lot to answer for.* They only stop searching when Caroline's mum turns up about dinnertime. Susan is hysterical. She threatens to kick her husband out if he doesn't come home and help with the funeral. She's got a nightdress on and wellington boots. The light filters through the thin fabric of her nightie as she comes stomping across the fields.

She's wearing nothing under it; not so much as a pair of knickers. All the fathers turn away. Susan Fletcher's a fine-looking woman. She goes in and out in all the right places. Under normal circumstances, most of them would have an eyeful. Not today. It wouldn't be right.

'Lads,' says Tommy as soon as he has Susan settled in the car, 'will we call it a day? Away on home to your wives and children.'

The fathers say it's probably for the best. They disperse in twos and threes, sharing lifts to different parts of the village. Rob Anderson leaves on the same beat-up bicycle he arrived on this morning. He must've borrowed it off one of his kids. His knees are banging up against his chin. Nobody offers him a lift, though most of them drive the sort of motors you could easily fling a bike into.

The search has been a waste of time. The fathers do not see it as such. They feel better in themselves – more competent and responsible – for having done something. *At least we tried*, they mutter to each other. When they get home, they'll say the very same thing to their wives and take no shit on the subject of wasting time. Though they've no means of expressing such a sappy sentiment, it has been good to be with other broken men. Not talking. Just standing next to each other. Knowing this isn't the time for talk. *Comforting*, is how Rob Anderson puts it, but then Rob's always been a bit of a fruit.

The fathers have covered roughly three square miles. They've poked the ground with sticks and swept their gloved hands carefully through patches of thicket. They've gone hoking through various outhouses and sheds. None of them has had a clear idea what they're looking for. *Dead animals, foul smells, empty canisters with skulls printed on the side?* Consequently, they've not found anything suspicious. They've felt serious, though, and organized, like people in a TV drama sweeping the moors for dead bodies or guns.

Alan Gardiner is glad the operation's over. He's been walking on knives all day. A handful of the fathers have searched his fields and sheds: three of them, with sticks and spades.

'Just a formality,' Tommy said. 'Sure, we know it's not you, Alan. But we've to be thorough about the process. Make sure we don't miss anything.'

Alan understood completely. He said he wasn't offended at all. Then, he took himself off to the back shed with a shotgun and spent the hour it took to scour his property wondering what he'd do when the shout went up. If he'd have it in him to pull the trigger. If such a move would be hard on Megan or, in the long run, easier.

They'd found nothing on Alan's farm. Not so much as a shrivelled leaf. If they'd come with the proper gear, they might've found traces on his horsebox floor. But the same lads didn't know what they were looking for. Alan put his shotgun away and emerged, smiling, from the back shed. 'Youse'll stay for a cup of tea, lads?' he announced in a big, broad voice. 'Megan already has the kettle on.' He made them all sit at his kitchen table and eat freshly baked scones, though he'd hardly any appetite himself. When they finally moved on to the next farm over, he felt like he'd dodged a bullet. *Literally. Metaphorically. In every possible sense.*

Hannah's dad's been thinking constantly about the other fathers. He prays for them – naming each one in turn – every time they come to mind. 'Heavenly Father, look upon thy dear son Tommy with grace. May he turn towards thee for strength and purpose in the days to come. Protect his marriage. Protect his children. Give him an extra measure of thy peace which passeth all understanding.'

Dad's still fasting; skipping breakfast, lunch and dinner. The hunger's driving him to his knees, but he won't ask the Lord publicly, or even in his private prayers, for an answer. It's not his place to question. *Trust and obey. Trust and obey.* This has always been Dad's mantra. He sees no reason to abandon it now. He'll pray safety for the fathers, comfort and healing; repentance, where he deems repentance necessary. He won't ask God who's responsible. Such a revelation could only lead to hate, and Dad's been called to love everyone, even the kind of people who poison weans. He won't enter into the witch hunt. But tonight, when he's lying in bed not sleeping, he'll think of nothing else. He'll dream of pummelling a faceless man, of smashing his skull in with a brick.

When Mrs Nugent calls to let them know the search is off, Dad says, 'That's great news. What a relief.' Secretly, he's disappointed. Part of him's been hoping for a lynching. Though he'd never admit it, he'd like to see the culprit hurt. He wouldn't condone a killing or anything, but a decent hiding would seem proportionate. Officially, he'd condemn any kind of punishment beating. Still, he can picture himself on the sidelines, watching. No blood on his hands. No reason for anyone to say, *Shame on you, John Adger. I thought you were a Christian man.* He'd be sure to distance himself from the mob, yet still get the good meat of their anger. He'd enjoy seeing justice served and, afterwards, play the good Samaritan, tending the man's wounds, driving him over to Casualty. Maybe he'd even say, *I forgive you,* in a strained and hesitant voice. He'd feel clean doing this. Other people would find it commendable. *Look at John Adger,* they'd say. *He's been through so much, but he can still forgive.*

Hannah's dad wants other people to think well of him. It's a kind of weakness. Not pride exactly, but something similar. Other men covet their neighbours' wives. They strip them naked in their minds and do things to them – *dirty things* – they'd not dare attempt on their own wives. Hannah's dad's not greatly into that kind of stuff. Most women scare him a little. He's never been with anyone except Hannah's mum. When he lets his mind drift during a sermon, or while he's brushing his teeth in the morning, he's only ever thinking about himself. He's picturing John Adger as an entirely different fella: a leader, a bold speaker, the sort of man others listen to. He's seeing himself easy in company, wearing fashionable clothes and marching confidently around the village, maybe even smoking a pipe. He'd be Tommy Fletcher if he could: strong and charismatic, minus the temper. It's nothing more than a fantasy. Dad's never been comfortable around other men. He's not even comfortable with himself.

Hannah's the same. She's never been good with other people. Adults. Children. Strangers. Folks she's known her entire life. Close family excepted, Hannah's awkward with everyone. It's not that she's shy. When Miss McKeown asks her to read in class, it takes nothing out of her. She doesn't stumble or mix up her words. She'll always answer when spoken to. She's very competent. It says so on all her school reports. *Hannah can follow rules. Hannah does what she's told.* Hannah hasn't a clue how to navigate those moments when there are no rules or adults telling her what to do. Like last February, when the Twins had their birthday disco. Everybody from class got an invite. Even her. It didn't say *disco* on the invitation. If it had, she wouldn't have been allowed to go. It said *birthday party* and birthday parties were deemed just about acceptable in her parents' eyes.

Hannah had been to parties before. Her church held an annual Christmas shindig for the Sunday-school kids. Santa came and presented them all with gift-wrapped selection boxes. They ate cocktail sausages on sticks and ice cream with jelly in disposable bowls. There were party games such as musical chairs and passing a balloon around the circle in a kind of race. Mr Adair provided musical accompaniment on the Minor Hall piano. The only Christmas songs he knew were 'Jingle Bells' and 'Away in a Manger', which he played at a sped-up, jaunty pace.

Other birthday parties Hannah's attended had all been

variations on this theme. Sometimes there was pizza instead of cocktail sausages. Sometimes, if it was nice outside and the child's garden big enough, a bouncy castle had been hired for the day. Once, at Caroline's birthday, they'd watched a video of *Three Men and a Baby*. Hannah didn't tell her mum, for she knew Mum wouldn't approve of a film about three men living together, with a baby, and none of them married. Kathleen had said they were clearly gay. These parties came easily to Hannah because there was a structure present. They rarely deviated from the same set pattern: nice dress, gift for the birthday child, games with rules, special food, and, when you left, a slice of birthday cake wrapped in kitchen roll.

The Twins' birthday was different. The ones in school talked of nothing else. Nobody had had a disco before, though sometimes a couple of the girls got together in their bedrooms, drew the curtains and flicked the light switch on and off, simulating a disco-like atmosphere as they bounced around to pop music. Bananarama. Cyndi Lauper. The Pet Shop Boys. The music they loved was already a little outdated, borrowed as it was from big sisters and brothers, who were barely adults themselves.

As soon as she heard the word *disco*, Hannah became terrified. She'd seen a disco once, on an episode of *Grange Hill*. She'd watched it with the sound turned off, because it was a forbidden programme on account of the smoking and the language, and that one girl having a baby at fifteen. Hannah didn't think there'd be drinking or smoking at their disco. They were only ten, after all. It was the idea of dancing that frightened her. Also, the girls in trendy outfits. Their hair crimped, gelled and sprayed into outlandish shapes. The way they'd stand round the edge of the dance floor talking easily in groups, laughing and making eyes at the boys. There were no rules to a disco, yet, from the talk in the playground, it sounded like everybody knew what to do. Hannah didn't and she could hardly ask her mum for advice.

In the days running up to the Twins' party Hannah practised in her bedroom, humming made-up songs and moving her arms and legs around. She wasn't sure if she was doing it right. *Did you do disco dancing on your own? Or would you have to do it with a boy? Were there movements to learn, like the actions which accompanied Sunday-school choruses? Did you just make it up as you went along?* Every few seconds she'd catch a slice of herself in the wardrobe mirror. She looked like she was having a seizure. She knew she wasn't doing it right.

She'd spent hours putting outfits together. Pairing dour Sunday dresses with different-coloured tights and cardigans and the trainers she wore for PE. Adding jewellery. Removing jewellery. Dragging her hair up into a high side ponytail. Wishing she had crimping irons like Kathleen and the Twins. There was little point in experimenting with outfits. Mum wouldn't let her out of the house in anything trendy. She'd insist upon a nice frock and everything matching. She'd do her hair in a plait. Not a French plait like Caroline's; the same ordinary braid Hannah wore to church, her hair hanging limply between her shoulders like a heavy horse's tail.

In the week leading up to the party Hannah hardly slept. Every time she thought about the disco, she'd picture herself standing stiffly in the Twins' double garage, dancing stupid or not being able to dance at all. She'd imagine people – specifically, Kathleen – pointing and laughing, saying, *Look at the sketch of Hannah Adger. She looks like she's having a fit.* In the end, she'd faked an upset tummy and stayed home. Mum phoned the Twins' mum to apologize. She'd told Mrs Ross that Hannah had *diarrhoea*. Hannah couldn't believe she'd used the word *diarrhoea*. A less specific term would've done the job. The shame of it was almost worse than making an eejit of herself on the dance floor. Mum said the Twins were really disappointed she wouldn't be there. Hannah knew this was a lie. Lizzy and Mim wouldn't even notice her missing. Lizzy and Mim were popular.

Everyone's noticing Hannah now. She's something of a celebrity. There are so few children left. With every death, attention falls heavier on those left behind. They say a fella over in Tullybarret's opened a book on which child will go next. He's giving fifteen to one on the wee foreign lad because he's a sickly-looking child. It's a filthy rumour. There's not a man in Henderson's who doesn't register his disgust, though none of them are that surprised. It's the sort of thing you'd expect from Tullybarret folk. Cold-hearted bastards, the lot of them.

Hannah's paying close attention to her body. The lumps are no bigger. That's a good sign. She's tired. But surely that's to be expected. It's been a traumatic week or two. And she's warm. But not what you'd call feverish. It's close in the house with the curtains drawn and all the extra believers downstairs.

She might be fine.

Or she might be getting a summer cold.

Or she might be dying.

It's a possibility she's trying to ignore.

Hannah knows she'll have to talk to Mum soon. Later tonight, or in the morning. She doesn't want to be deliberately deceitful. But every hour she holds out feels precious. It's another hour of being OK. The second she opens her mouth, everything will change. She'll be the centre of Ballylack. Everyone staring. Everyone talking. Everyone thinking about her constantly. She'll no longer belong to herself.

Hannah knows it's coming. It can't be avoided. She'll put it off for as long as she can.

All Is Lost

H ANNAH CAN'T KEEP her fingers away from her neck. It's like
the time her tooth came out in an Opal Fruit during church.
All the way through the sermon she couldn't stop tonguing the
salty space it'd left behind, pushing the loose flesh this way and
that till the bloody drool started dribbling out of her mouth.
Eventually Mum had leant over and told her to stop squavering
about. Once you know a bit of you's broken, it's the only thing
you can think about. Hannah's taken to hooking her hair behind
her ears every few seconds so she has an excuse to run her fingers
over the lumps. It's reassuring to feel they're no bigger or sorer
than the last time she investigated.

When the believers lay hands on her, Hannah bows her head
demurely, angling her neck away from them. She wouldn't be
surprised if they already knew. The Lord's particularly keen on
giving people messages about illness. Pastor Bill leaves time at
the end of every service for people to share these prophetic
words. There'll be healing prayer available for a sister with a
wonky left leg or a child who has allergies associated with lac-
tose. He'll lower his voice if the healing's for someone with
woman's problems. Hannah has only recently come to realize
this means something wrong with your lady parts. She's always

afraid he'll call out something specific to her body, some embarrassing ailment like constipation or wetting the bed. She'd be scunnered, but it'd be sinful to ignore the Lord if he was speaking directly to her. Though she knows it's wrong, it hasn't stopped Hannah asking the Jesus in her head not to tell the elders about her lumps. So far, he hasn't said a word.

In a way, it's a relief to finally be getting sick. For weeks now, she's been bracing herself. It's felt like waiting for a bomb to go off. Now she's actually dying it's not quite as scary as she'd anticipated. Maybe, it's the knowing that helps. She's already mapped the next stages out in her mind. She knows from the ones who've gone before. First the lumps will get bigger. She might develop other lumps around her glands. Exhaustion. Headaches. Nausea. Like a flu, but ten times worse. Eventually her organs will shut down. That's the part that hurts a lot. And then, someday, quite soon, she will be dead. She's taken to rolling this thought around her head, meditating on it. *I am going to die. I am going to die. I am going to die*; she hums the words to the tune of 'What a Friend We Have in Jesus'. She's settled on an upbeat melody. It helps to distract her from the fear. There is much to be thankful for. Dying won't be the end of her story. The others are already waiting for her.

Hannah keeps the lumps to herself for as long as she can. It's hard enough dealing with her own sadness. She couldn't cope with Mum and Dad's too. She knows Granda Pete will blame himself. She pictures herself telling her parents. Their faces crumpling up like wet paper bags. Mum crying first. Then Dad. The pair of them trying to keep it together for her sake and not quite managing it. She might be able to bear Mum crying. Sure, there's hardly a day goes past at the minute when she's not bawling her eyes out behind a closed door. Dad's different. He's made of sterner stuff. He never ever lets himself doubt. All will be lost when he wells up. Hannah fears this almost as much as she fears the dying. Every time she tries to imagine it, it feels like the walls are coming in.

So, she holds her secret tightly. For an hour. Three hours. A day or so. She lets herself grow accustomed to the idea of it until the lumps are as much a part of her as the hair they're hidden behind. The thought of being dead no longer scares her. *At least, this is what she tells herself.* In a way, it's kind of exciting. She'll be part of one of the gangs; a Dead Kid like Lief and Kathleen or, more likely, one of the other lot. Hannah's never been in a gang before. She can't really count the Girl Guides. Kathleen once told her she looked like a Custard Cream in her brown shirt and yellow scarf. Kathleen said the Guides were for Fenian-lovers. The Girls' Brigade was the only uniformed organization Protestant girls were allowed to be in. The GB marched around with a Union Jack.

Being dead will be a new start for Hannah. She's not sure just how far she'll go. She's toying with the idea of trying beer, maybe even cigarettes. She can't wait to sing the sort of songs that normal young people sing. Like Lief said, it might actually be the making of her. Of course, she'll miss most parts of being alive: Mum and Dad, Granda Pete. Granny's cooking, especially her apple tart. But she's almost convinced herself that she's looking forward to the next place. It's the bit before that terrifies her. Hannah's never been good with pain and she's heard the part where you die is excruciating. At least Mrs Nugent claims it is.

Granny's always said that Hannah is feeble. *It's not uncommon with an only child. Her mother has her mollycoddled. She dances to her every whim.* Granny refuses to dole out the Nurofen every time Hannah has a wee twinge. Granny says when Hannah gets to her age, she'll know what real pain's like. Granda Pete says Hannah's just sensitive; all creative people are. He doles out painkillers and plasters every time she asks for one, even if it's just a dry bruise he's sticking a Band-Aid on.

By the next morning Hannah's wondering if she's overreacted. The lumps are the same size as yesterday. They only hurt when she pushes her finger hard against them, and even this pain is the dull ache of yesterday's sprain. And the headache's gone and the achy joints. Though she still feels warmer than she usually feels. Maybe she's worked herself up into a state over nothing. She examines her neck in the bathroom mirror and is pretty certain the lumps are already starting to shrink.

Hannah stops humming, *I am going to die*. Instead, she tells herself, *This, too, shall pass*, and does her best to meditate on this. She takes a short nap – Mum's started insisting – and lets the words infiltrate her dreams. Her dreams are full of happy, smiling Hannahs and her happy, smiling parents. They're running through fields of grass and picnicking by the river. She's not sure what river. It's way less mucky than the one which runs through Ballylack. God must be giving her a vision of the future, because she's older in this dream, and so are her parents and they're having such a lovely time, eating sandwiches and being together. Maybe Hannah will have a future after all.

When she wakes she's all of a sudden hungrier than she's been in weeks. She has a second bowl of stew for dinner and afterwards is still famished, so Mum makes her a round of toast. Everyone's so pleased to see her appetite back Hannah thinks about forcing down a second slice. It's good to see them all smiling again. Even Granda Pete has perked up a bit. She asks if, next summer, they might be able to go on holiday somewhere foreign, like France or Cornwall. Mum turns away from the sink, where she's drying the dishes. She scrunches the damp tea towel against her chest and tries to smile.

'I hope so, pet,' she says. 'We'll have to wait and see.'

'OK,' says Hannah, 'but I really do think it's going to be all right.'

'God willing,' says Mum. She glances across the kitchen to

the closed door of the living room. The believers are all inside, praying. The noise of them permeates the walls, like a kind of insect hum. 'God willing,' Mum repeats.

God willing is a thing her parents always say when Hannah's looking forward to something nice. They don't want her being too disappointed if the nice thing doesn't happen after all. Hannah wishes they'd stop saying, *God willing*. Half the fun in looking forward is letting yourself get excited. Every time they say, *God willing*, Hannah imagines God, up in Heaven, watching her get more and more excited until, eventually, He loses His temper and says to Jesus and the angels, *Will you look at that? Hannah Adger's all worked up over a school trip to the Folk and Transport Museum. That trip's in danger of becoming an idol. She's going to lose the run of herself and forget about me altogether. I will intervene with bad weather or a tummy bug. I'm only doing what's best for her soul.*

'God would want me to be OK,' says Hannah. 'I'm going to be fine.'

'God willing,' says Mum firmly.

Hannah feels as if the ground beneath her is not as solid as she thought it was.

Before bedtime, Mum makes her take a shower. Hannah's washing her armpits with a facecloth when she finds a new lump nestled into the fold of her arm. She doesn't need a mirror to see this one. It's bigger and firmer to the touch. She's sure it wasn't there this afternoon. Since the first lumps, she's been carrying out hourly checks, feeling herself all over – even round her private bits, which she's not supposed to fiddle with – just to make sure everything's OK. This lump's new. It feels sore when she touches it. It throbs like a toothache when she moves her arm. She checks herself all over. Yes, she is feeling really warm. And a little dizzy. And her head is thumping. It feels like her forehead is on too tight.

Hannah turns the shower off. She hasn't even had a chance to shampoo her hair. She towels herself dry and sits on the edge of the bath in the same spot where Ross sat a few weeks ago. It seems like months – years, even – since the Dead Kids started appearing. In another sense, everything feels like it's only just happened; all the visits have blurred together in her head. She struggles to put the deaths in order, though she knows Ross came first and Caroline was the last to visit. Time's run differently this summer. It's gone too fast. It's also dragged. *Will her last living days fly in, like the way holidays go faster than ordinary days?* Time's a stretchy kind of thing. It isn't reliable. It shifts with your mood. Hannah's only just started to notice this.

She rubs the wetness out of her hair. It's a relief to let her body run through its usual ablutions. She doesn't have to think about what her hands are doing. She brushes her teeth. Turns the immersion heater off at the wall. *Mum gets cross if somebody leaves the immersion on.* She washes her face with warm water and the special scrub Mum's bought for keeping her spots at bay. She puts last night's pyjamas back on and sits on the toilet seat, staring at the soap dish on the sink. The whole room's swimming. It helps to keep her eyes focused on one spot.

She knows exactly what she has to do. She won't be able to keep the sickness from them now. Just saying it out loud will make it real. All thoughts of gangs and flaffing about with the DK leave her. Hannah's not ready for the real of it. She needs a little longer to steady herself. A week. A day. An hour to hold the fear quietly inside her head until the right words rise up and she can open her mouth without screaming. Hysterics won't help anyone.

She wonders where Jesus has got to. He doesn't feel very close right now.

Granny has this bookmark tucked inside her Bible. There's a story on it about a man walking along a beach with either Jesus or God. Hannah can't remember which one it is. Probably Jesus, because he walked around a lot in the Bible. She's not sure if God has actual feet. In the story there are two sets of footprints in the sand. Then, when things start going badly for the man, there is only one set of footprints. The man says, *Hey, Jesus, why did you abandon me when life was hard?* And Jesus replies, *You are a silly man. There's only one set of footprints because I was carrying you during the difficult times.* Granny loves this story. She's forever pulling the bookmark out of her Bible and reading it to people who are having troubles. She wasn't best pleased when Hannah asked if the story really happened, like to a missionary or somebody from long ago, or if it was just made up, like a poem. 'That's beside the point,' said Granny. 'It's meant to remind you that God's always looking after his children, even when they don't feel him there.'

Hannah thinks again of Corrie ten Boom hiding all those Jews behind her wardrobe and the missionary fella from *Chariots of Fire* who wouldn't run on Sundays but won all his medals anyway. God looked out for them, even the behind-the-wardrobe Jews who were kind of His children, but kind of not, on account of them saying Jesus wasn't His son. Granny is right. God will carry her through this hard situation just as He did with the footprint man. It doesn't really matter whether Hannah feels He's close or not. It would be nice to feel Him, though. It would remind her He was on her side.

She draws her shoulders back and takes a deep breath. She says the verse that starts, *I will never leave thee nor forsake thee*, out loud into the silence of the bathroom. Mum says this verse is just the ticket for times when you're feeling a wee bit fearful. It works best if you say it out loud. She's right. Hannah feels stronger for bringing the Lord's word into her moment of despair. She can do this. She just needs a little more time, an extra dose of heavenly strength, and then she'll be able to tell her parents.

Once it's out there, nothing will be the same again. Hannah will no longer belong to herself. Everyone will want to carry her. Not just God. Her parents and the believers from church. Granny and Granda. Everybody in Ballylack. They'll all mean well. Hannah knows they'll only want to help. But it won't be her sickness any more. It will belong to everyone. You'd think this would spread the weight of it out. Hannah's pretty sure it won't. It will actually feel so much heavier once everybody knows what's happening to her.

Confession

THERE'S A GAGGLE of journalists camped out at the end of Alan Gardiner's lane. He notices them standing around, smoking and chatting, when he's out seeing to the beasts. They've come no further than the cow gate. They wouldn't dare. There's an RUC officer stationed in the yard, a young fella by the name of Clive. He's made it quite clear he doesn't think much of the assignment. *They're blowing each other up in Belfast and I'm stuck out here in the sticks, babysitting weans.*

Maganda sympathizes. She thinks it's a bit much herself. Surely there's no need for round-the-clock surveillance. It's not as if the journalists are going to attack. Every hour or so she brings the young fella a fresh cup of tea and a wee bit of something home-baked. She tries to coerce him into the house, to eat a more substantial meal. But Seán Donnelly's put the fear of God into Clive. Under no circumstances should he leave his position. Seán has an officer stationed outside each of the three houses. They report back to him every couple of hours. *What are they taking note of?* Comings and goings, overheard talk, anything which strikes them as odd. The families think they're being looked after. They moan and mumble – they're Northern Protestants – it's in their nature to gripe. Secretly, they're glad the authorities are looking out for them. Seán lets them think this. He doesn't want them realizing the officers are his eyes and ears.

Seán needs to know what people aren't telling him. The locals don't trust him. He could spend the rest of his life in Ballylack and still be a blow-in. It's his name, and the Southern plates on his car, the way his accent pulls the sharpness out of softer words. The people here only trust their own. Nobody told him about the fathers' search until it was over. He's heard on the Henderson's grapevine that Tommy Fletcher had been thundering about, flinging accusations like loose fists. There's no shortage of men propping up Henderson's bar who'd not be responsible for their actions if they got their hands on the fella responsible. Seán has no idea if there's any weight in such talk. Drinking men talk all manner of shite.

Then, there's the source itself. They're still no closer to knowing where the poison's come from. There's no hard evidence for an insider, but Seán's guts are telling him somebody in Ballylack knows more than they're letting on. Maybe the guilt'll get to them. Eventually, the bastard will talk to somebody and that fella'll talk to somebody else and it will get back to him. Seán Donnelly's a patient man. He can wait weeks, months if necessary. He doesn't have weeks. There are only three children left. And what if there are more barrels dumped elsewhere? They can't be sure till they find the source.

The tension's building. Seán can feel it every time he steps outside. The very air is thick with it. The people of Ballylack want answers and somebody to blame. They've not been given any answers. They've nobody to blame but themselves. If something doesn't shift soon, they're going to start turning on each other. It only takes one eejit with a loose tongue, one pint too many, one punch thrown and, just like that, he'll have a riot on his hands. It's not Seán's first situation of this kind. He knows he needs to watch them all closely. The key to this is vigilance.

Alan Gardiner doesn't like being watched. Every time he crosses the yard Clive's there, pacing up and down in his bottle-green get-up. He's like an overgrown fruit fly. Alan's polite enough. He doesn't want to get on the officer's wrong side. The last thing he needs is some nosy bugger with a warrant poking round his farm. The fathers might not have known what they were looking for. He's certain sure the RUC would be more on the ball. Them lads are trained to nose out suspicious substances. Sure, don't they have special dogs for it? So, Alan keeps up the banter and the weather talk. *Morning, Clive, how's yourself today? Is there anything I can get for you? A wee sandwich? A cup of tea? A chair?* He encourages Megan to feed the young lad every time they're eating. He tells Ben to be polite to Officer Marcus, to smile and pretend he isn't holding a gun. He wishes Clive would piss away off and leave them all alone.

Alan's glad enough of Clive when Ben takes his turn. He'd have been lost without the lad. He's useless himself. Frozen to the spot. He comes through the gate and there's Ben, passed out by the sheep trough, a thin trickle of blood running down his forehead from where he's fallen against a rock. He can hear himself thinking, *This is not good, not good at all.* But he can't seem to move his arms or legs. Can't get the old mouth open to scream. The bucket drops out of his hand, spilling sheep feed across the grass. Startled by the noise, the sheep scatter. A whole flock of starlings rises from the hedge and goes stuttering across the field. Alan Gardiner doesn't even flinch. He just stands there, gawping at his son, who might well be dead or in the process of dying. Everything slows to glacial pace. Time doesn't run straight during moments like this.

It's only fifteen minutes since Ben excused himself from the lunch table.

A quarter of an hour since Megan said, as she's said every day for the last few weeks, 'I don't think you should be running, son.'

Since Ben replied with the same set phrase as yesterday and the day before, 'I'm grand, Mum. I'm going to go mad, though, being cooped up inside.'

Megan had not explicitly forbidden it, yet still sighed heavily as she said, 'Don't go down the lane, Bayani. I don't want that lot taking photos of you.'

It's just fifteen short minutes since Ben rose from the table a little too quickly and thus dismissed the dizziness in his head in the same way he'd been ignoring his temperature all morning. It was stifling inside the farmhouse. The fresh air would do him the world of good.

Alan should've said something at this point. Something simple, like *Enjoy your run, Ben.* Something stronger, like *I'm proud of you, son.* Even if it hadn't been true, there'd have been comfort in knowing these were the last words to pass between them. It would've given him something to hold on to. But Alan was reading the paper at the time, flicking through the farming section, noting the current price of beef cattle. He hadn't even raised his head.

Now, as he stands over his son's limp body, watching a couple of old ewes creep back to nuzzle his side, he pictures Ben preparing for his run. He sees him stretching his calf muscles out: one trainered foot braced against the back-door step, the other leg scissored out behind him, making a wide, wide arch. His shins taut. His skin smooth and glowing slightly in the afternoon sun. Black eyes beaming, as they always did when he was anticipating a run. Alan's watched his son go through the same palaver every day for years and mostly rolled his eyes or muttered something under his breath. It's an old image he's sucking on now. Because today, he was too preoccupied to go to the window and watch his son take off across the yard, legs and arms blurring like a little god. Shame on him. He'll never get the chance again.

Alan's never thought his son beautiful before. Fragile, yes, and somehow lacking. A tad girlish at times. But never – *not even as a tiny baby* – beautiful. Now, as he stands over Ben's broken body, not knowing how to get his own limbs moving, this is how he sees his son: young and perfect and incredibly fast.

My beautiful boy, he thinks. He knows Ben will never run again.

And just like that, Alan Gardiner is nothing but a godless howl. Once it has been loosed, he cannot rein his shrieking in. His voice goes scrambling over the hedge and down the lane, where all the journalists hear and, rising from the car bonnets and verges they're perched upon, turn to one another and mumble, *What the hell is that? It sounds like some kind of animal's dying!* Up the lane goes Alan's voice, past Maganda, who is in the chicken coop lifting eggs. Maganda is no stranger to grief. She's heard people howl like that before, in the nursing home, when a corpse was still warm to the touch. She drops her egg basket and runs, welly boots flapping like wet fish round her shins.

My boy, she's thinking. *My beautiful boy.*

Into the yard goes Alan's voice, reverberating off the sheds and outhouses. It finds its way into the ears of young Officer Marcus, who's been waiting his whole working life for just such a call to arms. *Hey ho*, he thinks, *action at last*. He drops the Stephen King he's been flicking through and runs like a man possessed, across the yards and through the fields, passing Maganda at the gate.

Up, up, goes Alan's voice. Somewhat diminished by distance, it finds its way through the open window of baby Liezel's room. It wakes her from her afternoon nap. She's not old enough to differentiate between sounds and, being a farm-raised child, most likely associates it with a beast of some kind. The sound doesn't scare her as it scares the adults. She snuffles a little, bunches the hot blankets to the bottom of her cot and drifts back to sleep. She dreams of Bayani tickling her, swinging her, holding her against his chest as they run together through the uncut hay. She sleeps with a smile on her face and cries out only when a strange woman comes rushing into the room to lift her out of her sleep and whisper, 'Now, now, wee Lucy. Mummy's had to nip out for a while.'

Clive is the first to arrive at the scene. The boy's not dead. Even from a distance, he can see his chest rising and falling. If anything, he's more concerned about the father. Alan's lying on the ground. There's no colour in him. He has his arm and half his body flung across Ben so it's impossible to get near the child. He's crying and talking nonsense, repeating the words *Ben* and *sorry*, over and over. Clive's only a year out of training. He's never dealt with shock before. He can't rightly remember what to do. Hot tea with sugar comes to mind, and tinfoil blankets. That's hardly relevant in a field, especially when there's a child requiring medical attention. He calls the incident in on his walkie-talkie. He asks for an ambulance and another unit of police. With all those journalists hanging about he doesn't want to take any risks. It'll take five minutes for back-up to arrive. Until then, he's on his own. 'You'll have done your first-aid training, won't you, son?' says the operator. Of course he has, but under pressure Clive can't remember anything except how to fit an arm sling. He clips the walkie-talkie back on to his belt and approaches Alan.

'Mr Gardiner,' he says, doing his best to imitate the calm, reassuring voice Seán Donnelly uses when talking to the families, 'can you move back and let me have a look at your son?'

Alan clutches the boy closer. Ben's skin has begun to turn grey. Up close, he doesn't look well at all.

'It's my fault,' mutters Alan. 'I did this.'

''Course you didn't,' says Clive. 'You're in shock. You're not thinking straight. Let me have a look at him. I can help.'

'What's the point? He's going to die anyway.'

'He's only going to die if we don't get him to hospital.'

'You're not taking him anywhere.'

'Alan!' yells Clive. 'Move away!'

He's beginning to wonder if he should draw his gun, or at least mention its presence. Could he get in between the two of them, try to prise the older man off the boy? Training doesn't prepare you for this kind of shit.

'You're not making any sense, Alan. I need to help Ben.'

'No, you're not listening. I made this happen. I deserve to lose my son.'

The penny's not dropping for Officer Marcus, but the whole situation's immediately clear to Maganda. She arrives huffing at the top of the field, hears the two men yelling and, in one brief, clarifying flash, understands exactly what her husband's done. A hundred tiny moments from the last few weeks slide through her brain like a quickly shuffled deck of cards. Alan's moods. His loss of appetite. The long silences. The time he went over to Tullybarret for the cure. All the sympathy she's offered. All the kind, kind words. *What a fool she's been. What a stupid bitch.* She looks at Alan and no longer sees her husband. She can only see the man who's taken her son away. She lifts her foot and kicks him sharply in the ribs. If it weren't for the two pairs of socks she wears stuffed in the toes of her wellies, she'd be doing real damage. She'd be breaking bones. Killing Alan, if she could.

'You bastard!' she screams, and lays into his face with her tiny fists.

'I'm sorry,' Alan says, repeating these words till they lose their shape and slop into each other, becoming one long, stretched-out syllable. Maganda doesn't let up. She keeps right on pummelling her husband: hair and spit flying, tears streaming down her cheeks. Alan looks up. Her face is contorted with grief. She's like a beast, tearing at him with her hands. She is ferocious, his Megan. Very brave and very strong. He wonders why he's never noticed this before. They've wasted so many years just tolerating each other. Circling round the edges of their marriage. Now that everything's lost, Alan can see what he has with Megan. *Love*, he thinks, *this has been a kind of love. I won't know anything like it again.*

Clive has no idea what's happening; still, he knows the adults aren't his priority. Let them tear each other limb from limb. They'll be standing tomorrow morning. It's the boy who needs his help.

'Stop it!' he screams, trying to pull the two of them apart.

Maganda keeps kicking and punching. Half the blows miss their mark and fall on Clive. She's not that bothered who she's hurting, so long as there's something solid to rage against.

'Stop right now, Mrs Gardiner.'

'Go away, son,' she says, spitting the words out between punches.

Clive has her by the shoulders. He's trying to trail her off Alan. She's too strong for him; too quick and fierce. He glances down at his wristwatch. It's only been two minutes. It'll be at least another four before back-up arrives. *Jesus*, he thinks, *at least you know where you stand with a punishment beating. This kind of carry-on's something else.*

'I'm not leaving you here with him!' he shouts. 'Youse'll kill each other.'

'It's no more than he deserves. He's killed my son.'

'Your son's not dead.'

'What?' says Maganda, pausing to look up.

'I said, your son's not dead. But he will be if he doesn't get help.'

This revelation is like a bucket of cold water. Maganda's up and off Alan in an instant. She shoves him aside so she can get to Bayani. She takes his head in her hands and thumbs the blood off his forehead.

'Ambulance?' she snaps at Clive.

'It's on its way.'

'How long?'

'A few minutes.'

The English leaves her then. She can't remember the word for anything but *No*, and this is not the sort of word she wants Bayani carrying into the next world. Maganda's no fool. She knows the boy hasn't long left. Later – much, much later – she will be thankful for this. *At least he went quickly*, she'll tell her family on the telephone, knowing they can't possibly understand what the other children went through. She'll explain how it was actually a head injury that took him. The dizziness tripped him. He hit a rock on the way down. Maganda sees this as a kind of mercy. The other parents would probably agree, though whether the Gardiners deserve such mercy is another matter entirely.

Maganda's not prepared to lose her son. Then again, she'd not been prepared for his coming either: two weeks early, in a bloody rush. *Wasn't she more than able then? Didn't she rise to the occasion rightly?* On her knees now, ploughtering around in the sheep dung and muck, Maganda makes a split-second decision. She'll be strong in this moment. She must be everything her son needs. Bayani will leave this world as he came into it: known and wanted, swimming in love. She bends her face over his face and begins to keen soft butterfly words. His eyelids flicker. She knows he's listening. She blinks back her tears and presses on.

It could be a prayer she's whispering. It could be a song. It could simply be the boy's name spoken over and over with the correct inflection. Clive doesn't understand a word she's saying. He knows enough to keep his distance. This is a private sort of moment. He can't leave. There'd be hell to pay if he wasn't here when the ambulance arrives. Still, he can do his best to absent himself. They teach you this in training college. When you're calling at doors to break bad news you need to be able to disappear. You need to give folks room to nurse their grief.

Clive kneels at the boy's feet. He slows his breathing down to silence and, every so often, checks his watch. Three minutes. Two minutes. One minute. And another. Seven full minutes after his call he hears the sound of sirens shrieking up the lane. He gets up from his knees, slowly, reverently, like a postulant leaving the place of prayer. He takes two careful backward steps and then belts towards the lights.

Where is Alan Gardiner while his son lies dying? He's stood fifteen feet away. He makes no move to join his wife, though he's turning the thought of it round and round in his head. It would be good, he thinks, to hunker down next to Ben and take the boy's hand in his own. He could tell his son he loves him, though he's not sure whether this would ring true. He could hold him at the end, so Ben knows he's not alone. That's what a father should be doing. But it's much too late for closeness now. Alan's once more on the outside, looking in.

When the ambulance arrives, Alan sees his son into it before handing himself over to the police. He tells them he is responsible. 'For everything,' he says, and begins to cry. The female paramedic asks him if he's the father, and Alan says *yes*, like it is something he has to apologize for.

'What's his name?' asks the other paramedic.

Alan says, 'Ben. Ben Gardiner.' Then corrects himself and tries to say Bayani. It comes out wrong. He puts in vowels where there shouldn't be vowels. It's years since he tried to pronounce his son's real name. The misshapen word leaves a bitter taste in Alan's mouth. He weeps with the shame of it, all the way down the lane, and through the village to the RUC station in town.

When they arrive at the front door, the press are already gathered: snapping, flashing, shouting at Alan as soon as he's out of the car. This is how he learns Ben's dead. He hears it off a big English bastard who's shoving a microphone under his nose. He can't even lash out at the fella for they've cuffed his hands together at the wrist. He bows his head and lets them lead him through the crowd. Something damp rolls down his cheek. It could be tears. It could be spit. Alan Gardiner's beyond caring. He knows he's brought this on himself.

Running Fast

HANNAH CAN'T BEAR another second in the house. She finds her trainers and a tracksuit top, which she pulls on over her pyjamas. She sneaks quietly downstairs and out the back door. None of the grown-ups notice she's left. Once she's climbed over the back fence, she runs as fast as she can towards the forest park. She sticks to the backstreets and keeps her hood up. The place is crawling with journalists. Hannah knows shortcuts only locals know. It's about half a mile to the forest's edge. She's run much further in PE, but by the time she arrives the sweat's dripping off her. She can hardly catch her breath. It's probably the sickness. It could be the fact she's hardly left the house in two weeks.

Hannah pauses for a moment, resting a hand against the rough trunk of a pine tree while she coughs and splutters her breathing back into rhythm. When she unbends, Ben is standing there in his running gear. He's jogging on the spot, black hair flopping about as his whole body jiggles from side to side. He's the least changed of them all; hardly any bigger or older than the last time they met. Every part of him is glistening with sweat, as if he has just finished a run.

'You're not really dressed for it,' he says. 'Running, I mean.'

He lets his eyes drop to take in Hannah's rabbit-print pyjama bottoms.

Hannah says nothing. She's finding it hard to draw breath.

'You don't look too good either,' he continues.

'I'm dying here,' she wheezes.

'I had a sneaky suspicion you might be next.'

'No. I mean I *feel like I'm dying*. I'm that unfit . . . I'm probably actually dying too.'

Ben smiles – just a brief smile – it's on his lips and passed before it's had time to impact the rest of his face. Hannah smiles back through gritted teeth.

'Best thing is to keep moving. Otherwise, you'll stiffen up. Here, walk with me. I'll not go too fast.'

Ben quits running on the spot and turns towards the forest. He strides off down the path, looking over his shoulder to check Hannah's following.

'Come on. We've a lot to catch up on.'

Hannah takes a deep breath. The air in her nose tastes like pine air-freshener. She concentrates on easing each breath into her lungs. In through her nose. Out through her mouth. Her head's pounding. She'd been hoping for a little thinking time, but Ben's here now. She can hardly tell him to go away. She shoves her hands into the pocket of her tracksuit top and follows him into the foresty dark.

'So,' he says, as soon as she's caught up, 'where should we start? You dying? Me being dead? My dad poisoning us all? I'm taking it you've heard old Alan's responsible. I've suspected as much for a while now.'

Hannah shrugs. This is news to her. She's taken aback by Ben's confidence. He's like a tiny steamroller, telling her what to do, taking the lead, walking briskly off the path and into the shadowy gaps between the trees. He's said more in the last two minutes than Hannah's heard him say all year. He's kind of funny, too. She didn't think Ben knew how to be funny. He notices her staring.

'You thought I was quiet, didn't you?'

'I suppose so. You didn't say much in school. I thought you were just shy.'

'Kat said the same thing. She says she's sorry she never got to know me before. Apparently, I'm actually dead on. It wasn't racism that made her keep her distance. She just thought there'd be no banter with me. Apparently, foreigners don't usually get the sense of humour here. There's no point in putting her straight. I'm so used to people saying ignorant things, I hardly notice any more. Anyway, I want to make sure I'm in their good books before I tell them about Dad.'

'Are you going to tell them?'

'I don't have much choice, Hannah. They'll find out eventually. I just want to make sure they're all mates with me before it comes out. So I've joined their stupid gang. Kathleen says it's like a Benetton ad now me and Amy are in it. God, you wouldn't believe the crap she says. And does. I let her shove poor Amy at me. It looks like I'm her boyfriend now. I feel a bit bad about that. They think the two of us make sense together. Different belongs with different. At least Amy's fit, and she's way more craic than she used to be. The pair of us can party as hard as the rest of them.'

'You do seem a lot more confident now,' says Hannah.

'I was never shy. I just wasn't that bothered about getting to know any of youse. I listened, though. You can learn a lot when you listen to people. It's one of the good things about being on the outside. You're always watching.'

'Like God?'

'Aye, that's me, Hannah. Just like God. I know exactly what makes you lot tick.'

'What do you mean, my lot?'

'Uch, you know, the Ballylack-born-and-bred contingent.'

'Sure, that's you, Ben. Your folks have had that farm for ever.'

'It's half of me, Hannah,' he snaps. He stops walking so he can square up to her. He gets so close – angling his face into her face – she can smell the last thing he ate souring on his breath. 'One half of me is Ballylack. The other half's not.' Each word he says is a kind of jab.

'Oh, you mean your mum's side. We all know she's not from Ballylack originally. But you were born here. You're the same as the rest of us.'

'Do you know, when I was smaller people used to ask my mum, *Who does the wee lad take after?* They probably thought they were being funny. Nobody could see beyond the foreigner in me. Even my dad didn't think I belonged. He never once tried to claim me. He called me *the boy*, or sometimes *Ben*. Never my real name. Never *son*, though everybody knew I was his. You're meant to be half your dad and half your mum. And I am, Hannah. Look at me. I've got her eyes. His frown. His mouth. Her hands. Nobody ever noticed any of that. They'd just see the colour and call me foreign. *Half-caste. Darkie. That wee foreign lad.* I heard it all. I just never let them get a rise out of me.'

Hannah doesn't know what Ben wants her to say. She can tell this moment's been brewing for years and years. She wouldn't be surprised if he's practised, going over what he'll say when the opportunity presents itself. His words sound rehearsed. Like somebody giving a speech on TV. She feels too young to be of any use.

What would her parents do if they were here? Hannah tries to imagine herself into their shoes. They'd probably just be present with Ben. They do this a lot, sitting silently with other believers when somebody's died or received bad news. Mum says people don't really expect answers. They just want to know they're not alone. Job's friends do this in the Bible. They sit for ages in sackcloth and ashes just being miserable with him. This is why they're called Job's comforters. Hannah can't do sackcloth or ashes. To be honest, she's not that sure what they actually are. She can still keep Ben company for a while. She lengthens her stride to meet his. For a few minutes they walk in silence through the trees.

'Is it better now?' she asks.

'You mean, now I'm dead?'

'Yes. Do you not feel more included?'

Ben shrugs.

'I suppose so. There's less of them here. They can't afford to be so picky about their friends.'

'And you're in the DK?'

'Aye, it's crap, but it's a way of letting off steam, burning shit and breaking stuff. Yelling mean things at the other lot. It's good not to be on the receiving end for a change. When it all gets too much, I put on these trainers I nicked from somebody's wardrobe and I run laps round the village till I'm totally knackered. The other Dead Kids think I'm running because I want to keep fit. I'm not. I know I'll never race again. I run for the same reason I've always run. It helps me get away from myself. The faster I go, the less there is of me. Sometimes, I completely forget I exist. I'm nothing then, Hannah. Nothing at all. It's so much better than being what I actually am.'

'What are you, Ben?'

'In-between. Neither one thing nor the other. I've never fitted in. I've seen the way people look at me.'

'Come on now. You're being paranoid.'

'I'm not. I've had years and years to get used to it. I can see the way they're afraid of me.'

'Afraid of you? Don't be daft. Sure, you're only a kid. Even now. Why would anybody be afraid of you?'

Ben shrugs. 'It's not just me. You lot are afraid of everything. Ballylack's pure stinking of fear.'

'What exactly are we afraid of, Ben?'

'Where do I start? You're afraid of anything that's different. You're afraid of things changing. You're afraid of everything staying the same. You're afraid of upsetting the folks around you or drawing attention to yourself. You're afraid of being honest about what you're really like. Basically, you're all afraid of yourselves. None of you are half as nice and normal as you pretend to be.'

This last one hits Hannah like a punch in the guts.

'I don't think that's fair, Ben. You're making us sound like monsters.'

'If the shoe fits, Hannah.'

There's no point arguing with Ben when he's in this state. Instead, Hannah tries to reassure him. 'You belong here, Ben. In Ballylack, with the rest of us. It doesn't matter who your dad is or what he's done. It doesn't matter where your mum came from. You're one of us.'

It's kind of a lie. In school Hannah hardly gave Ben a moment's thought. She wouldn't go as far as saying she hadn't liked him but, when it came to pairing off for group projects, she was always a bit relieved not to end up with him. It was nothing to do with Ben having a foreign mum. He was just so quiet and starey. He's doing the starey thing again now. Hannah clears her throat and says, 'I'm glad you're here,' in a warm and kindly voice. She chances a reassuring pat on his shoulder, removing her hand quickly so the coldness doesn't seep through. She's trying to convince herself as much as Ben.

Ben swings his whole body round. He looks Hannah straight in the eye and holds her gaze. He doesn't blink. His eyes are like pokers burrowing into her brain. She knows he'll hold his silence for as long as it takes.

'What's my name?' he asks, still staring straight at her.

'Ben,' says Hannah.

'What's my real name?'

'Benjamin?'

A kind of cramp passes across Ben's face. For a moment all his muscles seem to spasm at once. His eyes disappear into his head. His teeth curl briefly over his lips. He looks a lot like a snarling dog.

'Jesus,' he says, 'you people can't see anything but yourselves.'

Then, he turns on his heels and runs. He runs so fast he's a blur of marl grey and blue. The shape of him shifts between the trees. Then he's gone. Hannah stands where she is, watching Ben run. She often watches the runners on TV. Sport is one of the few things her parents approve of watching. Dad's big into football himself. He's been a Liverpool supporter since he was a lad, although last year, when Carlsberg started sponsoring them, he couldn't wear the kit any more. Mum bought him an Aston Villa shirt for Christmas. She liked the colour and Villa weren't sponsored by an alcohol brand. Dad thanked her for it, then asked politely if she'd kept the receipt. For months and months after, Granda Pete wound him up about being a Villa fan. Hannah's parents let her watch all the sports except darts and snooker, which aren't really proper sports anyway. Athletics are her absolute favourite. She likes the way the runners are like fish swimming through the air, arms and legs more fluid than limbs should be.

She's seen Ben run before. People in the village are always saying he's like a bullet when he gets going. *That wee foreign lad'll end up running for Ulster someday*, they say. It's hard to tell whether they see this as something to be celebrated or lamented. This morning Ben is ugly to watch. His arms and legs pump in the normal fashion. His feet fly. But there's no ease in his limbs. Nothing but stilted, pounding rage. It looks as if he's trying to outrun himself.

Half an hour later, Hannah's back home. Everybody's praying so hard they haven't noticed her gone. She keeks her head round the living-room door and, with carefully measured politeness, says, 'Sorry to interrupt. Can I talk to my mum and dad for a second, please?' 'Of course,' say the praying believers, all at once in unison. They don't leave, though. They've assumed ownership of the living room. They pause for a moment, while Hannah's parents slip out. As soon as the door closes, they begin praying again. She can hear the loudest of their voices, thundering all the way down the hall. The others add the occasional *Amen*, or *Yes, Lord*, like punctuation pressing the strongest points home.

In the kitchen, Hannah does not speak. She removes her tracksuit top and shoves the sleeve of her pyjamas all the way up to the armpit. If it was just Mum, she'd take her shirt off, but she'd feel self-conscious now, standing semi-naked in front of her dad. She raises her hand to point out the lump. They notice it straight away. It's pinker than the rest of her skin.

'I think I've got a temperature too,' she says. 'And my head's been thumping for a while.'

'No,' says Mum. She clasps her hand across her mouth as if she's trying to stop herself vomiting.

'How long?' asks Dad.

'Just this morning,' says Hannah. This is both a lie and not a lie. *What purpose would it serve telling them about the earlier lumps now?*

At first, they don't cry. All three of them are entirely silent. They're like people on TV when the sound's on mute. They are not still in their silence. They grasp their own shoulders and wrap their arms around their middles, contorting their bodies into outlandish shapes as if they're suffering from terrible cramps. Dad hunkers down on the floor and, grabbing his ankles, rocks slowly backwards and forwards like a traumatized child. Mum snakes her arms around her head and twists on the spot. Hannah stands, bolt upright, not moving, just staring. Then, slowly, like a train approaching, the noise begins to leak out of them. Shapeless, animal noises. Not words. Groans and mumblings and pitiful strangled sounds. There is a kind of music to the racket they make. *Bass and elemental. They harmonize. They improvise. They make room for each other's lament.*

Only then, when their separate howls begin to ricochet off the fitted cabinets, do they become aware that they aren't alone in this moment. They move, like dumb magnets, to meet in the middle of the kitchen, holding whatever parts of each other they can reach, clawing at each other's bodies.

They'll stand like this, just the three of them, with the kitchen door shut, for almost forty minutes. Almost nothing will be said. *For what could be said that is not insinuated with lowered heads, with clasping hands and so many tears?* Afterwards, when her parents break the news to the believers – still faithfully praying in the living room – Dad will say, 'At least we have each other.' All the believers will nod then, knowing the Adgers have so many people holding them up: their family and the whole of their church community and the Lord, of course. He is ever present in times of need.

Mum will think, in her quiet head, of Megan Gardiner, who has no one now to hold her up. Nobody praying for her. Nobody bringing casserole dishes of hot food to the door. Nobody will show up with buckets of warm, soapy water to scrub the painted white letters off her barn wall. *S.H.A.M.E.* Daubed on the road-facing side of their barn in six-foot-high capitals for everyone passing to see. *That poor woman's got nobody,* Mum will think, *and she's lost more than anyone else.* She will hold this thought at a cold distance, knowing it's something which should bother her. Normally, she'd be the first to offer support. She'd be straight round with a pot of broth. She has no room for sympathy tonight. No wish for it either. Hannah's mum will be selfish in her grief, oh so selfish and terribly stern.

Sickening

BY THE TIME Hannah and her parents make it to the hospital, Pastor Bill and the elders are already there. There are five of them today: four men and a wife, sitting on a row of chairs in the reception area. They are stern and suited – even the woman's wearing a sort of blazer – like candidates waiting for an interview. They've been talking among themselves while they wait for the ambulance to arrive.

News of Ben has yet to leak out. The gossip circuit's still unpacking Miss McKeown's death. 'The poor wee lassie wasn't much more than a child herself,' Pastor Bill says as he whispers his concern down the line. He keeps his voice low and his eyes downcast. He wouldn't want to be seen to be gossiping.

'Dear, dear,' mutters the next elder down. 'I heard she was only twenty-three; the same age as our Stephanie.' He turns to the elder next to him and passes it on, adding a little colour to the telling. 'The parents took her home to Augher,' he says. 'It was only right. You'd want to be with your own folks at the end.'

This elder says, 'It'll be another closed coffin, I should think. They say her face is an absolute sight,' and the wife adds something about Susie being a powerful nice girl, a regular attender at the ladies' Bible study. By the time the information's arrived at the end of the row, the last elder's getting chapter and verse on poor Susie McKeown. Tomorrow's obituary in the *Belfast Telegraph* won't be half so comprehensive. *I'm only telling you this so you can pray for the family*, each one begins. If you're planning to pray, you can say whatever you like about somebody else.

Pastor Bill's sat himself at the head of the row. One look at him and you'd know he's the head honcho here. His shoes are blacker and shinier than the other men's. He polishes them every morning with actual spit and a clean J cloth. He's holding an enormous leather-bound Bible clasped against his chest like a sort of breastplate. In fact, he often refers to this particular Bible – a family heirloom – as his *Breastplate of Righteousness*. He thinks this sounds like something a pastor should say: old-fashioned and a little verbose. Bill's first to rise when the paramedics wheel Hannah in through the doors.

'We're here for you,' he says, patting her lightly on the hand that isn't sporting a drip.

'We appreciate it,' says Dad. He shakes Pastor Bill's hand firmly, though it's less than half an hour since they parted in the drive. Dad rushing to help Hannah into the ambulance. Pastor Bill hanging back to shoo the journalists away, swatting at them with the King James.

Mum isn't saying anything. She's holding the trolley's railings so tightly you can see the white nuts of her knuckles gloaming through her skin. Her eyes are scuttling all over the show, trying not to light upon the big, swinging doors which open into the main hospital. On the other side of this door are wards and operating theatres, scanners, surgeons and the morgue, where all the others have ended up.

'We're not staying,' Mum announces to everyone and no one in particular. 'Hannah can have the tests. Then she's coming home. We're not for leaving her here.'

They all nod. Dad. Pastor Bill. The elders. And the wife. They understand. None of the other children have made it out of hospital alive. They'll do whatever it takes to get Hannah home.

Mum was all for keeping her in her own wee bed. 'Let the doctor come to us,' she'd said, and tore strips out of Seán Donnelly when he insisted she'd need assessing first.

'They won't be able to treat her if they don't know what they're dealing with.' When Mum looked unconvinced, he'd added, 'You never know, Sandra, there might be something they can do to help.' Dad had backed him up. And Granny. And Granda Pete too, though he's still in the doghouse and nobody really listened to him. *Everything that could be done should be done. Hospital didn't necessarily mean the end.*

Mum could see in their eyes they didn't believe this. But there were four of them and one of her and people kept saying the scientists were only days from a cure. Eventually they'd worn Mum down. *Yes, they could take Hannah up to the hospital. Only for tests and then straight home.* There was no way she was staying overnight. There wasn't any need for it. 'Look at her,' Mum said, pointing to Hannah sprawled on the sofa, wolfing down several rounds of cheese on toast. 'It's probably just a summer flu. She doesn't even look that sick.'

Hannah is sick. There's no point pretending she hasn't got the same thing the others had. Hannah isn't *that* sick yet. *Yet* is an awful little word. It's a kind of hinge. Her future could swing in either direction. Only time will tell which way the *yet* goes.

Pastor Bill remains very hopeful. As do the elders. They have faith that God will intervene. In the car between Ballylack and the hospital they've been singing hymns. *Battle songs*, Pastor Bill calls them. He's very comfortable with the rhetoric of war. They are fighting the good fight this afternoon. They are standing firm; obeying the Lord's command, no matter how bleak the situation looks. It's easier for them. It's not their child. Mum would like to point this out. There's a need in her to scream at

264

them. She'd like to see how they'd respond. They'd probably just pray that bit louder. They're used to being heckled at open-air meetings. Mum wishes they'd piss off and leave her family alone. She needs to be hysterical. There won't be any room for hysterics while they're helping her hold it together. Mum's at the point where she needs to let go.

As soon as Hannah's settled on a side-ward the five believers – plus Dad – gather round her bed and begin praying. Mum pulls the curtains for a bit of privacy. The other five patients on the ward can't see what's going on. They would have to be deaf not to hear. Pastor Bill has the Bible open. He's reading that bit from Revelation about the Lord drying every tear. Reading isn't the most accurate description; *bellowing* would be more like the thing; *guldering*, if you prefer the local term.

Pastor Bill's never one to pass up a chance to preach. He's noticed the other patients on the ward. He doesn't see five women waiting for minor surgery. He sees five souls who'll one day meet their maker; possibly sooner rather than later, for aren't they all about to go under the knife? He is particularly drawn – *called* is the word he prefers to use – to the lady lying next to Hannah. *Sinéad McConville – Nil by Mouth*. With a name like that he's certain sure her soul is lost. It'd be remiss of him not to share the Gospel with Mrs McConville and her four roommates. He opens his mouth and lets his street-preacher voice come roaring out. It's the same voice he keeps for the open-air at the Saturday market, for door-to-door evangelism and beach missions down on Portstewart Prom. He slips seamlessly from Bible reading to prayer, barely drawing breath between words, never once lowering the volume. 'Almighty God,' he booms, 'we bring our dear sister Hannah before Thee today.' Sinéad McConville Nil by Mouth gives him the finger and then, adding insult to injury, swiftly crosses herself.

In the bed, hunched beneath her hospital sheets, Hannah

feels every eye on the ward pressing into her. The pale green curtains offer no protection. She can actually feel their glares. She tries to make herself as small as possible, drawing her knees up to her chin, pulling the sheets over her nose so it's only her eyes peeking madly out. She digs her fingernails into her palms, hoping the pain will lift her out of the moment, to a place where she doesn't care what people think, or how they'll talk about her later, when their husbands and children come to visit. She imagines what they're going to say: *That wee Adger girl was on the ward for a while. Dear love her. You'd think dying would be bad enough. The poor girl's surrounded by lunatics.*

Hannah wishes Pastor Bill and the elders would go away.

The instant this thought finds a solid shape inside her head, the guilt kicks in. The Bible says you shouldn't be ashamed of the Gospel. You must always be ready to give a word in season. Pastor Bill's only being obedient to the Lord. Hannah should try to be more like him; a better witness to her faith. Still, she can't help wishing they'd all bear witness in quieter voices. She's not sore at all, but she starts to get on like she is: moaning a little and rubbing her belly, looking up at Mum with big, pleading eyes. She hopes the elders will take the hint and leave her to get on with being sick. The more she moans, the louder they pray.

Mum looks down at Hannah. She can tell her daughter is mortified. She's far from comfortable herself. She desperately wants to say, *Why don't youse call it a day?* But this would be considered disrespectful, not to mention insubordinate. She knows her place. Dad's the only one who can speak up to Pastor Bill. He's in the thick of it, praying away with the rest of them. Mum looks down at Hannah again. Only the top third of her face is visible above the sheet. She can see the child's about to cry.

'Excuse me,' she says, pressing her voice insistently through the circle of prayers. 'I think Hannah needs the bathroom.'

'Yes,' says Hannah, immediately understanding that Mum's offering her an emergency exit. 'I'm sorry. Can I be excused?'

They don't stop praying immediately. Like cars losing speed at a junction, they let their prayers come to a gradual halt. Mum and Hannah hang there, open-mouthed, waiting for the final *amen*.

'In your precious name, amen,' says Pastor Bill.

All the elders open their eyes and shuffle a little, easing the stiffness out of their limbs.

'On you go, Hannah,' says Dad. 'We'll be here when you get back.'

The elders part so she can swing her legs over the bed's side. She toes her way into her slippers and shuffles off across the ward; Mum comes trailing after her, trundling the drip stand. Pastor Bill and the elders regroup. They continue praying over the ruffled sheets. They don't really need Hannah to be present. Healing can happen at any time. *Anywhere. At any time. Even when the subject's wandered off.*

Hannah stands outside the toilet door with her mum.

'I don't really need the toilet,' she says.

'I know,' says Mum.

'I was just getting a bit . . .'

'. . . uncomfortable,' suggests Mum, reaching to squeeze her shoulder.

'They're so loud.'

'They mean well.'

'I know, and I'm glad they want to pray for me.'

'Me too, Han. But it might be easier if they did their praying somewhere else.'

'Yes, Mum. Sorry.'

'There's nothing to be sorry about, pet.'

'I'm not ashamed of the Gospel,' Hannah says, the words swimming out of her in a big, urgent gush.

'I know you're not. You're just a bit shy. I am too. Don't be saying anything to your dad, but I wish they'd leave us alone for a while.'

Hannah smiles. She can't believe Mum's actually saying this. It gives her a warm, tickly feeling inside, the same feeling she sometimes gets when she looks in the mirror and recognizes a tiny slice of Mum or Dad's face staring back at her. It's reassuring to know there's a part of her that's the same as her mum. It makes her feel a bit braver. She wraps her arms around Mum and breathes in the familiar smell of washing powder and flowery perfume. Mum kisses her three times quickly on the top of her head. *Peck, peck, peck*. These are called chicken kisses in their house.

'I tell you what, Han,' Mum mumbles into her hair. 'Why don't you hide in the toilet for a few minutes and I'll get the sister to shift that lot on. Maybe she could tell them they can't come back till visiting hours or something.'

'Is that not a lie?'

'Maybe it is. Maybe it isn't. I'm past caring.'

She gives Hannah a parting squeeze and wanders over to the nurses' station. When Hannah returns to her bed five minutes later, Pastor Bill and the elders have been replaced by Granny and Granda Pete. He's brought her Ribena, a quarter of Midget Gems and a stack of Roald Dahl books, hidden inside a carrier bag. She stashes them quickly in her locker. Dad's still raging about the Raggedy Tree. She doesn't want to give him any more reason to be angry with Granda Pete.

All afternoon the doctors poke Hannah with needles. They take her blood, her spit, her pee. They excise a tiny tube-shaped sliver of flesh from her armpit. They keep saying, 'Don't worry, this won't hurt.' It always does. They measure her height, her weight, her temperature and blood pressure. Mum is adamant. Hannah is coming home tonight. She's not sleeping here, in this vile place, which swallows up children and leaves them dead.

Seán Donnelly is summoned to the hospital. His negotiating skills are required. He's more used to brokering deals with terrorists; this should be wee buns in comparison. He takes the consultant radiologist to the side so the Adgers won't hear. He talks to her in a hushed, urgent voice, his eyes darting backwards and forwards between her face and Hannah's. The radiologist nods. She argues back. She understands the outbreak is an emergency but the place is absolutely chockers today: there's been a bus crash out at Sandy Knowles and a bomb underneath a prison officer's car. Technically speaking, these patients are much iller than Hannah. They should be taking precedent.

Seán's voice rises a notch or two. On the other side of the ward, Hannah's mum hears the phrase *last chance* and tries to convince herself she's heard no such thing. Seán raises his hand to the woman as if to say, *Enough of this nonsense, we're wasting time here.* He brings his fist down sharply against the cup of his hand. He shrugs and shakes his head. The consultant radiologist looks at her clipboard. She makes a *maybe I could squeeze her in* kind of face. Twenty minutes later Hannah's lying back flat in a plastic tube. Around her lights flash while the scanner stutters its way through a series of clicks and frantic, metallic shudders.

Nobody tells her how bad it is. She doesn't need to be told. She can see it in the way they look at her. The sag of Mum's shoulders. The overly chipper way Seán Donnelly calls her *champ* when he says she can head home now. The sister gives Mum a big paper bag of painkillers. 'Let her have as many as she needs,' she says. 'At this stage, they'll not do her any harm. Your own GP'll call in every few hours to make sure you're managing. If needs be, he'll set up a morphine drip. Fingers crossed it won't come to that.'

'Thank you,' says Mum. 'We appreciate everything you've done for us.' She looks over her shoulder for Dad, but he's down in reception giving Pastor Bill the latest update. For a moment she considers crying. Granda Pete places a gentle hand on the pit of her back. The moment passes. She takes a deep breath, steadies herself and ploughs on.

'If it gets too much, you can bring her back in at any time,' says the sister.

'We won't be coming back.' Mum's using her *absolutely no nonsense* voice.

The evening passes in a blur of contentment. It's like Christmas in the Adgers' house. They are determined to make the most of every moment they have left. Dad's even called a temporary truce with Granda. For Hannah's sake, they'll pretend to get on. They'd never admit this, but all four adults understand tonight must be as perfect as they can make it. Hannah understands this too.

Dad puts a fire on. Technically, it's still summer, but there's a nip in the air tonight, excuse enough to light a fire. There's a comfort in gathering around the flames. Granda Pete makes pancakes for a treat and, even though it's a kind of pudding already, Mum allows Hannah three scoops of chocolate ice cream for dessert. Hannah knows she could ask for almost anything this evening and they'd probably give it to her. She tries not to dip too deeply into this thought. It's so good to have everyone she loves together in one room she doesn't want to ruin it. She lies on the sofa, curled up like a kitten in a nest of blankets. She is lumpy and tired and a bit achy but not yet what she'd call sore. If she lets her mind stay loose and sleepy, she can almost forget what's brought them here. It could be a birthday or Christmas Day evening. It could be a happy kind of night.

The elders are notably absent. Hannah wonders if Mum's said something to them. She thinks not. It's one thing to have the nurses shoo them away, another thing to speak out herself. More likely Granda Pete's given them an earful. He has no time for Pastor Bill. Hannah's heard him giving off to Granny. *Interfering*

old goat is how he refers to him. This seems like the wrong animal entirely. Goats are bony creatures. Pastor Bill's swimming in
flab. He actually slobbers when he eats. Hannah thinks he's more
like a slug than any other creature. She'd never say this out loud.
Though maybe she might chance it now, just with Mum, because
she's dying and because Mum seems fed up with the elders too.

It's nice to have a night to themselves. Her mum's said this
half a dozen times already and looked pointedly at Dad, every
time. It's nice, but there's very little to talk about, and they're
loath to turn the TV on. There's no point making future plans.
Hannah won't see the end of the week. It would be morose to
talk about the past – all the precious moments they've had
together – the implication being there won't be any moments to
come. They smile at each other and drink lots of tea. Somebody
opens a box of Roses and passes them around. Hannah gets first
dibs on the caramel barrels. Even Granny doesn't object. They
make small, fluttery comments about the weather and recent
happenings round the village: who's having a baby, who's bought
a new car. They're careful to avoid any talk of the sickness. It's
present, though. Ever present. It's crouching by the standard
lamp, hanging off the mantelpiece, colouring every part of this
last, perfect evening a particular shade of bleak.

They find a way to link themselves together. A leg draped
over another's leg. A hand laid on an arm. A head resting against
the warm slope of a shoulder. All five of them are joined up like
a chain. They move, without intention, closer together as the
evening progresses. They cannot bear any distance tonight.

The heat and the strain of the day begin to work on Hannah.
She drifts off in Mum's lap, and wakes, and sleeps fitfully, and
wakes again. Every time she wakes, she finds herself held by
Mum or Dad, who are held on either side by Granny and
Granda, like bookends leaning towards each other. She knows in
these moments how fortunate she is. She thinks about Matty.

Poor wee Matty. Matty's the only other kid left. Everybody knows Matty's mum can't even manage to look after herself. When she isn't drunk, she's taken to bed. When she's not in bed, she's off on the tare with her mates from town. Hannah's got all these people to look after her. Matty'll have to make do by himself.

When Hannah wakes in the morning she's in her own wee bed. Dad's carried her upstairs and tucked her in. She's still wearing her dressing gown, but somebody's pulled her slippers off. One minute she's asleep. The next she is entirely awake, every inch of her loud and alert. There's a pain like daggers, stabbing her belly. It's the start of the end. Hannah knows it. The pain's occupying every part of her. She calls out for Mum. Mum comes immediately, with Nurofen, juice and a hot-water bottle tucked underneath her arm. She calls out for Dad. Dad doesn't come.

'Sorry,' says Mum. 'He's gone to Ben's funeral. Nobody's going to be there for Ben's mum.'

'But I'm sick!' howls Hannah.

She knows she's being selfish. She knows her dad is doing a very good thing; a brave thing too, when there's so many folks in Ballylack who'd like to see Alan Gardiner shot for what he's done. On any other day Hannah would be proud of him. Not this morning, with the pain twisting her insides into knots.

'Daddy should be here with me.'

His absence hurts in a different way.

'I know,' says Mum. 'He'll be back soon. I'll make sure he doesn't leave again.'

Hannah looks up. It's only a few hours since she last saw her mum. She seems like another woman now. Her face has lost its softness. She's all lines and angles. It's in her voice too; a sharpness Hannah's never heard before. She has the sleeves of her jumper shoved up to the elbows, her hair scraped back in a tight ponytail. And her eyes, Hannah's never seen anything like Mum's eyes: they're laser sharp, determined, unflinching. She looks formidable. Like a woman who's about to go into battle.

'You're not on your own, Han,' she says. 'We're doing this together, as a team.' For one, tiny half-blip of a second, all the pain goes sliding out of Hannah's body. She is clean and fearless and very, very strong. She is ready to do battle too.

The End Times

I T IS A sin to wish yourself dead.

Hannah knows this now. She won't be saying such a bold thing again.

She doesn't want Dad to get angry. She doesn't want to make Mum cry.

Mid-morning, the headache got so loud she couldn't see round the side of it. Every part of her was shrieking. Head. Bones. Skin. Teeth. All she wanted was an end to it. Mum kept coming at her with Calpol and cold facecloths, neither of which made a blind bit of difference. Dad paced up and down, because there was nothing he could do. Granda kept saying, 'Are you sure we shouldn't take her back to hospital?' But nobody seemed to be hearing him. Finally, the pain grew so loud it loosed Hannah's tongue. She opened her mouth and let out a howl: 'I wish I was dead.' She bellowed. She screamed. She was positively shrieking. They could hear her downstairs and, no doubt, next door. They could probably hear her in Tullybarret and all the way up the M2 in Belfast.

'I really, really wish I was dead.'

Hannah hadn't thought the whole thing through. The thick black line death would draw between now and the days to come.

The actual overness of dying. She hadn't really meant the dead bit. Only the part where the soreness stopped. Afterwards she attempted to take her words back.

'I didn't mean it,' she said. 'It just slipped out.'

Dad took a deep, gulpy breath. He sucked all the anger back inside him and smiled, though it was a watery sort of smile, as if his mouth was beginning to melt.

'Right,' he said. 'We'll forget all about it. But I don't want to hear that kind of talk again. Life's a gift from God. It's sinful to say you don't want it any more.'

Hannah knows she's fearfully and wonderfully made. There's a cross stitch of this verse above her bed. Granny sewed it for her before she was born. Fearfully and wonderfully made means she must be happy with herself, even the parts that are broken and sore. And she's so sore today. There's pain in her bones and behind her eyes and even tiny, biting pains in the hard parts of her teeth. The pain screams so loud she can't get to sleep. She begs Mum to ask Dr Simpson for something to stop the pain. She's so exhausted from being sore and worn out from trying to be brave. Hannah's not just keeping her own hopes up. She has to be hopeful for everyone. Her parents. Her grandparents. All the believers. Everybody in Ballylack. Everybody in Northern Ireland. Half the world's got its fingers crossed for her. It's an awful lot to carry when you're only eleven. Hannah wishes she could just let go.

Every so often she does her best to cheer everyone up. 'I'm feeling a wee tiny bit better,' she says. 'I'm not as sore as I was this morning.' Little white lies. Not quite truths. Hannah doesn't feel guilty about them any more. Not when they make Mum's eyes turn bluer blue, as if there's a light inside her and she's all of a sudden switched it on. Dad's just as keen. He'll latch on to any good news he can get.

Everybody wants to believe. They want it more than anything

else. Of course, they all know they're pretending. They're smiling so hard they don't look real. Any minute now, they'll start to unravel and everything will fall apart. For now, they smile and say only the things they can bear to hear. *She's looking better. She's not so pale. There's a bit more spark in her eyes.* Lie, lie, lie and smile, smile, smile. When their cheeks grow tired from too much smiling, somebody's always ready to pray.

Hannah's just as bad as the rest of them. She's been playing down the sickness for twenty-four hours. She tiptoes round the edge of it, never admitting how sore she is. Otherwise, Mum will get sad and Dad'll go quiet and all the believers praying below will feel discouraged. Everyone's happiness is resting on her. She can sense their sadness. It's like an unstoppable flood, spreading out to fill the entire house. Hannah can't carry everybody else's sadness any more. She takes her mum's hand. She squeezes it hard and doesn't let go. 'Please, Mum,' she cries, with actual tears and actual sobs, 'it's getting really bad. Can you phone Dr Simpson? I need something stronger than Calpol.'

Dr Simpson gives Hannah an injection in her hip. Within seconds, Hannah's thoughts have gone swimming out of her head. She can't feel her body. The pain's still there, but it's far away and so much softer, as if it's happening to someone else. The room sways and bobbles. She tries to speak. 'Thith ith del-ithyuss,' she mumbles through her furry mouth. She wants to thank Dr Simpson for the medicine, but she can't put her finger on the word for thanks. Her eyes are so heavy. And the room sounds as if it's underwater. All she wants to do is sleep. Sleep and sleep, till the pain leaves her be.

Hannah closes her eyes and drifts away. When she opens her eyes, she's standing outside Thompson's shop. It looks exactly like it's always looked. The Coca-Cola awning scallops over the window. The *Belfast Telegraph* sign's sitting up front, next to the bin and the lolly freezer. It's the same. It's also different. It's so much quieter than it usually is. There isn't a solitary person in sight. Hannah wonders where everybody's got to. It doesn't feel like Ballylack.

She walks down Main Street, past Dr Simpson's surgery, Henderson's pub and the funeral parlour. There are no people to be seen. No cars or tractors. Not even a dog. Nothing's moving except Hannah. Even the trees are strangely still. There's graffiti scrawled across the community centre. *Up the DK. Lizzy Sucks. No, no Limits. Fuck the Pope and the IRA.* She thinks the last one was always there. The Orange Hall's in a bit of a state. The roof's come in. The windows are shattered and covered in soot. And it's not the only building the DK have wrecked. There are smashed windows and burnt wheelie bins, piles of rubbish and old furniture spread across the entire village. It looks like a tornado's moved up Main Street, destroying everything in its path. There's no mistaking where Hannah is.

This isn't Ballylack as she knows it. This is the other, after place. She can taste the tension in the air. It doesn't feel like a happy place. She glances down at her legs. She knows what she'll see but she looks anyway. Her legs are longer. Her feet are bigger. She's wearing shoes she doesn't recognize: trainers with laces, not the rare-looking Velcro ones Mum always buys. She runs her hands over the rest of her body. She has hips and breasts and shorter hair. Her legs are a completely different shape. Hannah doesn't recognize any of it. Only her hands look slightly familiar. It seems she's not been able to quit biting her nails.

So, this is what happens next, she thinks. It's a muted sort of feeling. She tries to find some words for it. She's excited, yes. But also scared. And confused. It'll be much easier when she finds the others. They've all been through this part before. They'll know how to help her settle in. They must be hiding. Maybe even watching her. Kathleen probably put them up to it. *Here, lads, let's all hide when Hannah gets here. Just for a while, to wind her up*. It isn't funny. But it's the sort of thing Kathleen would find hilarious.

Hannah doesn't dwell on this thought. Kathleen making fun of her. Everybody else playing along. Things have to be different for her down here. She remembers what Lief and Amy said. She can be a different person now. She doesn't have to be Hannah Adger. Boring. Sensible. Fuddy-duddy. She can reinvent herself. Pick a new name if she wants one. *Tiffany's a name she's always liked.* Learn how to act like a normal kid. Drink. Smoke. Dance. Join the DK. She can trash the village and have a laugh. She needs to start as she means to go on. She has to show the others she isn't on the outside any more.

She walks out into the middle of Main Street. She stands up straight with her shoulders back and her belly sucked in. She raises one arm in the air, doing her best to remember what the others did. She takes a big deep breath and opens her mouth. *No, no, no, no, No, no, no, No, there's no limits*, she sings, punching the beat out with her fist. She's hoping they're watching and she's getting it right. She waits for them to emerge from wherever they're hiding. Nobody appears and nothing moves.

She tries again. Louder this time and a little less tuneful. *No, no, no, no, No, no, no, No, there's no limits.* She feels a bit daft but keeps persevering, belting out a third and fourth verse. She can hear her own voice echoing off Thompson's window. It sounds pathetic. All wobbly and unsure of itself, like a little kid who's lost its mum. *Where are the others? How come they're not here? Why is she all on her own again?* She calls out their names. One by one. Cupping her mouth to make a megaphone as she walks up and down Main Street, shouting. *Ross. Kathleen. Lizzy. Mim. Lief. Amy. William. Caroline. Ben.*

Nobody answers. Nobody comes. Hannah knows that nobody's here. She realizes this long before she admits it to herself. She can feel the loneliness in her bones.

After what feels like hours and hours she sits down on the kerb outside Henderson's. It's still painted red, white and blue from the Twelfth. She tents her T-shirt over her knees. It's a bit of a stretch now that she has boobs and longer legs. She perseveres. There's something comforting about being tucked tightly into herself. She ducks her chin down into her chest and closes her eyes and tries to pray. After a few minutes she gives up. *What's the point in praying?* Jesus isn't here in this in-between place.

Hannah doesn't hear Caroline at first. Her voice is so small and faraway it sounds like it's floating on the breeze. On the third or fourth repetition, she hears and looks up instantly. She peers up and down Main Street. Glances at the windows on either side. There's no sign of Caroline or anyone else. But there's no mistaking what she's heard. A calm little voice. Like a tiny bird whistling in her ear. 'Go home, Hannah. You don't belong here.'

Hannah stands up. She's not exactly sure where she's going, but the need to leave is suddenly urgent. She turns to walk away from the pub and as she turns feels someone grab at her arm. She glances down. There's a pale white hand circling her wrist, fingers digging in viciously. There's bright pink varnish on every nail and a sugary, nauseous smell in the air like vanilla ice cream mixed with chemicals. Hannah picks up her heels and runs and runs.

She's still running when she comes round from the morphine. Her arms and legs are thrashing through the bedsheets. The duvet's slipped right off the bed. Mum's sitting beside her with yet another cold facecloth, wiping the sweat off her forehead. 'You're all right, love,' she says. 'You're back with us again. You just took a wee reaction to the morphine. Dr Simpson says you'll be grand now.'

Hannah doesn't feel grand at all.

She feels like she's being split in two.

The Laying-on of Hands

DAD CARRIES HANNAH downstairs to die.

She can't remember the in-between of it: the stairs, the landing, the way he must have turned sideways to manoeuvre her through the door. She only remembers leaving her bedroom. Knowing she'll probably never see it again.

She remembers Mum leaning over her, pushing the sweat-damp hair from her forehead. Mum whispering, 'It's time to go down, my love. Everyone's waiting.' Mum following them out the door with Best Ted tucked underneath her arm. Hannah's far too old for cuddlies, but Best Ted's different. Mum knows she'll want him close.

She remembers Dad snaking his arms beneath her bottom. Dad carrying her like you'd carry a baby, curled up into his beardy neck. The smell of him, which was dish soap on his hands, sweat and wool around the neck. 'I've got you, pet,' he'd whispered over and over, as if he was trying to convince himself.

Hannah remembers hearing the words of this, though the see-ing was already slipping away. Seconds later, she was gone again. Swimming through the dark. Then, she was downstairs in the living room, lying under Granny's patchwork quilt. Then absent again. Then, on her side with a hot-water bottle tucked close to her tummy. Now, she looks up and sees eight pallid faces peering down at her. From this position they're like turnip lanterns: all eyes and grinning teeth. She can smell Mum's vanilla-scented candle burning on the mantelpiece, waging war on the sickness smell. It's a blanket of sugary sweetness, too strong for her head, what with the bile so high up in her throat. Everything is too much now. The smells. The noise. The press of their hands. The slightest movement is a siren going off inside her skull.

'Is it nearly over?' she asks.

Granda Pete says, 'Yes, pet. Just close your wee eyes and let go.'

And Pastor Bill says, 'I don't think the Lord's done with her yet. Press into Him, Hannah. There's further blessing to be had.'

And Dad says, 'Hannah, my Hannah,' in a gulpy sort of voice. Like a fish. Like a big, gloopy fish.

And Mum says silence. Perfect silence. Hannah can hear everything she wants to say in the way she's holding her hand.

All of them hang over her like a roof that's coming in.

Then, she's melting. Then, she's gone. Not dead yet. Not far off.

Hannah's dipping in and out of herself. When conscious, she is nothing but pain. She begs for morphine, for more morphine, for an end to the whole ugly mess.

Granda Pete can't bear it. It's all his fault. The shame has driven him out of the room. He sits on the landing stairs, high up, where they won't see him. He wonders why he's left it so late – far too late – to say something about the charismatics in the living room. *Fanatics*, he'd call them, if anyone would listen. He'd tell his son they're not helping at all. But he's lost his right to have any input. John looks straight through him now. Granda has to eggshell around him for fear of being told to leave. He can't risk that. He'll hold his tongue if it means he gets to stay with Hannah. He can hardly ask for more. She wouldn't be in this state if it wasn't for him.

When unconscious, Hannah's lost to them all. She's lost to herself. She doesn't even dream. She wakes from these slipped moments and can't remember where she's been. Every so often she's briefly lucid. She gets tiny two-minute windows while the morphine kicks in. Then, the pain, though present, is a little blunter. And her head, though fogged, has not yet folded. And almost all her senses are sort of working, though each is duller and slower than normal. The feeling's comparable to drunkenness. Hannah's too young to know this yet.

The others come to her during these moments. They sit crosslegged on the end of the camp bed and talk softly or maybe pray. Sometimes it's Caroline or William. Sometimes it's her old teacher, Miss McKeown. Sometimes she couldn't say exactly who it is. People are all the same to her now. There's no distinction between flesh and spirit. Hannah's starving for comfort in any form. At times it's hard to hear them speaking over the believers' incessant drone. But there are moments during the papery-thin pauses between one prayer and the next when a voice will bubble to the surface. It soothes her, to hear them speaking to her. 'Come on now, Hannah. There's life in you yet,' whispers William. 'Don't be afraid. I'm right here with you.' That's Miss McKeown, and she's using her *I'm proud of you* voice. 'Fight hard, Hannah. Keep on fighting.' Hannah knows, without looking, this is Caroline. And it helps. It almost carries her. To know she isn't alone in this moment. It's like having Jesus back in her head. Even when her eyes aren't seeing and her ears can't hear, Hannah knows there's somebody watching over her. There's a drag at the far end of the camp bed, a slim elevation at the end where they've laid her head. It's easier to sleep when the bed's slightly tilted. When she knows they haven't abandoned her.

The living room's full of dark-suited men. She doesn't recognize most of them. She sees their faces mooning above her, smells their stale breakfast breath. She feels their hands clamp on to her head. They say her name strangely in prayer. *Hannah, Hunnah, Hunnar,* stretching the syllables round their various accents. They call out to her fifty times an hour. She wonders how many of them actually know her. *If they'd take any interest in her if she wasn't dying right now?*

Dad's taken out the second sofa to make space for her camp bed. Pastor Bill says it'll be more comfortable and handier for her parents. Everyone can gather round. Mum. Dad. Granny. Granda Pete. They can surround Hannah with their love. What Pastor Bill really means is it'll be easier for the elders to get at her. He wouldn't take them upstairs, to lay hands on a child in a bedroom. He has to be careful around children, especially wee girls. People can easily get the wrong idea. It's different in a front room, with the door open, and the parents looking on.

When he looks at Hannah, passed out on her camp bed, Pastor Bill gets a picture of the paralysed fella from the Bible, the lad who's lowered through the roof to land at Jesus's feet. There's a painting of this he's seen in a book and it wasn't much different from the Adgers' front room. A bed in the middle. A great crowd of folk gathered round it. Jesus – or in this case, Bill himself – laying hands on the sick one, praying and praying till the healing comes. The trick with healing is to keep at it. You could be looking at hours, or even days. There's no theological case for wearing the Almighty down but, in Pastor Bill's experience, the longer you keep going, the more likely you are to get a result.

He's taken the liberty of drawing up a rota. He wouldn't normally put such emphasis on a death, but a dying child's a priority. He's drafted in every available elder. Nights are busiest for most of them are working men, unable to nip round during the day. Still, they've managed to pray without ceasing. Round the clock. Twenty-four seven. Call it what you like, they haven't given up yet. It's been thirty-six hours now and they've seen no improvement. *Are they discouraged?* They certainly are not. Perseverance is the name of this game. *Sure, didn't the Lord Himself go forty days in the wilderness? Didn't the same fella sweat blood and stay up all night, petitioning the Father in Gethsemane's Garden?* They only stop praying when the doctor appears. Even then, they stand quietly in the hall, silently mouthing their prayers till they can get back in. Physical presence is not a prerequisite. Healing can happen at any time. Still, there's something about the laying-on of hands which seems to give a prayer a bit more clout.

Dr Simpson's been this morning. He's said it's hours they're looking at. This evening most likely; tomorrow morning if Hannah continues to fight. Far from deflating Pastor Bill, this news gives him a second wind. He phones up to Belfast, explaining the situation in the direst terms. He asks for a team to be dispatched immediately. 'We'll take anybody who has a gift for healing,' he whispers into the kitchen phone. 'Unless the Lord intervenes, this wee lassie won't see the morning.'

By lunchtime the Belfast pastor's en route to Ballylack. He has two young fellas and a woman from Whitewell in the car with him. They're well known in charismatic circles: healers, the lot of them, even the woman. Individually, and occasionally as a team, they've seen lame folk walk and blind folk see, a rake of ones with cancer cured, and more common miracles besides: relief from asthma, psoriasis and diabetes, which is the dickens to prove once the healing's occurred. All the way up the motorway they pray earnestly, dipping in and out of tongues. They keep their eyes closed and their palms turned upwards, hoping to receive the Lord's favour. The Belfast pastor would normally posture himself likewise, but he's on driving duty. He has to keep his eyes on the road.

Hannah's still hanging on when the healers arrive. They stand for a moment, lingering at the living-room door. It's good to get the lie of the land. They're working out who's family and who's nothing more than a hanger-on. It will help them pray more specifically. Mum's hunkered down beside the bed, pressing a cold cloth against Hannah's head. She's burning up. Every time they take her temperature the mercury's risen another notch. Dad's pacing. Granda Pete's headed outside for a smoke. He's through a whole pack already today. He's not even trying to hide the smell. Granny hovers with a tray of teacups, already milked for handiness' sake. Some of the elders have taken a cup in their hand. Nobody's lifted a biscuit. It would be disrespectful to think of biscuits at a time like this.

Outside, in the street, word has reached the press: the last but one child won't see the morning. The journalists try to imagine what's going on behind the curtains. They can't, or won't, because placing themselves in the Adgers' shoes would make a shame of what they're doing, standing out here with their microphones and cameras, hoping for a juicy scoop. They're not bothered enough to disperse. But they're quieter today. When somebody leaves or enters the house they don't shout or follow them down the street. They simply ask, 'Any change?' or 'How's wee Hannah?' They say her name like she's somebody they know. They understand that a lowered head means nothing new to report.

When the Belfast pastor arrives, one of the lads from the *Belfast Telegraph* recognizes him immediately. 'It's Pastor Davison!' he shouts. The local crew pick up on this. The flash bulbs start firing. The questions are flying. *Are you here to pray for Hannah? Have her parents called you in? Have you anything to say about Stephen McFetridge?* It's only the Ulster contingent who know to ask. The McFetridge case never broke across the water. People over there don't understand the nuances of Northern Irish religion. Still, the out-of-towners can sense a story in the way their colleagues have focused in on the thin man in the double-breasted suit. They aim their cameras at Davison. *Why are you here, Pastor Davison? What are you doing in Ballylack?* They're so fixated on Davison they don't notice Seán Donnelly sneaking down the side of the house to let himself in through the back door.

285

Seán's wired to be suspicious. It comes with the job. When you're constantly straddling two sides of an awkward situation you always see the worst in folk. You do this automatically, without wanting to. Maybe it's knowing what people are capable of. The lies. The betrayals. The self-serving shit. *Shower of shites, the lot of them. Even the harmless-looking ones.* As Seán's passing the journalists, he hears Stephen McFetridge and Pastor Davison mentioned in the same breath. It's a good eighteen months since he last heard those names, but the whole sick story comes straight to mind. *Jesus*, he thinks, *Davison's the very last person we need around here.*

He opens the back door as Granda's slipping out. They meet for a moment in the utility room, eyeballing each other next to the tumble drier. Granda Pete already has a cigarette drooping between his lips. Seán knows an ally when he sees one. He grasps the older man by the shoulder.

'Here,' he says. 'Clifford Davison's just appeared.'

'You're joking,' says Granda Pete.

'What's he doing here?'

'That halfwit of a pastor'll have called him. Their lot have Davison on a pedestal, just one rung lower than Christ himself.'

'You know he's not to be trusted.'

''Course I know. I'm not stupid. I've read the papers.'

'The press have already spied him. It'll not look good for the family.'

'Do you think I give a toss what the family looks like right now? Your man can run laps round the lawn for all I care. The only thing I'm concerned about is keeping him away from our Hannah.'

'You're dead right, Pete. Listen, if there's anything I can do. Anything at all. Do you want me to have a word with John? I know you're not the flavour of the month.'

'Thanks, son. But no. I'm her granda. If her da's too spineless to stand up to that chancer, then I'll have to. I don't care if John never speaks to me again. Davison's not for getting anywhere near her.'

Cigarette forgotten, Granda Pete turns on his heels and heads back into the house. He looks like he's about to wade into a bar-room brawl. His cardigan sleeves are already shoved up to the bicep. Seán can see the rounded edge of a UVF tattoo, peeking out beneath his cuff. Granda Pete wasn't always a meditative man. He'd a past to confess back in '73, when he met the Lord Jesus Christ in Tullygarley Mission Hall. He's channelling that past now, picturing himself throwing Clifford Davison out on his beak, maybe delivering a few timely toe pokes to his ribs. Twenty-odd years of letting the Lord lead in the justice depart-ment hasn't purged his system entirely. Pete's blood is up. He'll do whatever it takes to keep Hannah safe.

He's too late. Davison's already laying into her. He's brushed aside Granny's offer of a cuppa, saying there's no time for nice-ties. The wee girl'll be dead if they don't get started straight away. He's cleared the room of everyone but the healers. Pastor Bill's allowed to stay. He has a touch of the gift himself. Every-body else has been relegated to the hall. Davison's insisted upon a closed door. It's common practice, he explains. The Spirit requires privacy.

Mum says, *No*, she's not leaving. She'll sit quietly in the cor-ner, but there's no way she's leaving Hannah on her own with – and she mutters this under her breath – *that man*. Mum knows exactly who Pastor Davison is. Everybody in Ulster does. Dad draws her aside. He grasps both her arms tightly just above the elbow. The next morning she'll find bluey-grey bruises in the shape of his grip. By then, she'll be past caring. She won't even bother trying to cover them up.

'Sandra,' Dad hisses, 'Hannah's going to die. We've been praying for days and nothing's worked. I know you don't like Pastor Davison. I'm not a big fan myself. But he has a gift and sometimes it works. Maybe this'll be one of those times. We might be able to hold on to our wee girl.'

'Yes,' says Mum. 'No. Yes.' Her thinking's all over the place. 'Ten minutes,' she says. 'He can have ten minutes. Not a second more.'

'Thank you,' says Dad. He kisses his wife on the forehead. His lips are dry. They grate against her skin. In this moment Mum doesn't know who he is. He could be any man leaning heavily upon her, asking for something he's going to take anyway.

When Granda and Seán Donnelly appear in the hallway they find almost a dozen people perched against the radiators and sitting at intervals up the stairs. The door to the living room is firmly shut. There are noises coming from within. Shouts and screams and strange voices talking loudly in a language Seán's never heard before.

'What's going on?' asks Granda Pete.

'Pastor Bill's brought a friend up from Belfast. He has the gift for healing,' says Dad.

'Are we talking about Clifford Davison?'

'Yes,' says Dad. 'He's in there now.'

'Are you completely mad, John? You've left your wee girl in there with that man. Do you know who he is? What he's done?'

All the other believers try not to look like they're listening. They have their eyes closed and their hands clasped as if they're praying. Beneath their eyelids their eyes are darting about furiously, thrilled to be party to such vicious talk. Granny's put the tea tray down. It's the first time she's had her hands free all day. She crosses the hall to stand beside Granda. She places a hand on his shoulder. In another couple such a gesture might be an act of solidarity. But Granny rarely wishes to be associated with her backslidden husband. Right now, her hand is an authoritative one. It's saying, *Give over, Pete. Stop causing a scene.*

Dad squares up to his father. This moment requires strong words and stiffness, but when he looks at his dad's soft shoulders, sloping beneath the grey cardigan they gave him for Christmas last year, all he wants to do is lay his head on that familiar shoulder, to weep like a baby and let Pete take the lead. Still, the elders are listening. And Sandra's visibly wilting, looking like she'll slide if he doesn't stay firm. So, Dad angles himself up, straightens his spine and looks his father in the eye.

'You don't get to have a say here,' he says. 'You lost that right when you took my wee girl into Satan's lair. I don't care what you think about Pastor Davison. I'll do whatever it takes to save Hannah's life.'

'Not that,' says Granda. 'Don't put her through that.'

'It's Biblical.'

'It's barbaric.'

'It can work!' screams Dad. 'Sometimes it works.'

'You try telling that to Stephen McFetridge's mummy. You tell her how well it works.'

All the believers are open-eyed now. They're not even making a pretence of praying. They're turning their heads to stare as Granda Pete makes a lunge for the door. They're periscoping over the banister as Dad wrestles the older man away from the living room.

Seán Donnelly attempts to slide between them, shouting, 'Come on now, lads. Calm yourselves down.' All his mediation skills go out the window. He falls back on brute force: fists, feet, and elbows where he can get an arm squeezed in. Eventually he manages to separate the two men. They stand at either end of the hall, glaring and panting like cornered flyweights. Dad fixes his tie. Refastens his top button. He takes a long, steadying breath then looks straight at his father. He points a single accusing finger in his direction.

'This is my house,' he says, 'and that's my wee girl in there. I will decide what's best for her. If you don't like it, then you can leave.'

A Kind of Miracle

A T THE KITCHEN end of the hall, Mum lets herself slip down the wall until she's sitting on the carpet, legs flopped out in front of her. She's not listening to the two men screaming. She's thinking about Stephen McFetridge. She has a picture in her head of his poor mammy. It's the same picture everyone associates with the case. A mousy wee woman from the Antrim Road. Standing on the steps of the Crown Court. Fishing up the sleeve of her Dunnes anorak for a usable tissue. Sobbing into the camera. Saying she hadn't understood what Pastor Cliff was doing. She'd only wanted her Stephen better again.

In the end the judge had been lenient with Deirdre McFetridge. Her solicitor played all the right cards. The husband, who'd buggered off the moment Stephen received his diagnosis. The impoverished background. The lack of education. Stephen, the only good thing in Deirdre's life. The poor woman, caring round the clock for her bedridden son; rising five, six, seven times a night when the seizures got worse. 'Look at her,' the solicitor pointed out to the jury. 'She's exhausted. She's not a bad mother. She was just at the end of her tether when Davison turned up.'

Clifford Davison's solicitor had been well prepped too. The

church had rallied round their disgraced leader. It wasn't just Davison on trial. It was everything they stood for as a congregation. They'd put their hands in their pockets and dug deep, providing the best legal representation money could buy. In Davison's defence, his barrister listed all the reasons he wasn't culpable for the boy's death. Firstly, this was not a boy they were discussing, rather an adult of nineteen years, diminished perhaps by months of pain, but nonetheless capable of autonomous thought. Then, there was the history between the two. Deirdre McFetridge had been part of Davison's fellowship for years and Stephen, though incapable of leaving the house, was visited often. In the weeks leading up to his death the congregation had been very faithful, providing meals and respite care, praying constantly, both *for* Stephen and *with* him, till he'd made a profession of faith and asked to be baptized into the church. Stephen, the barrister pointed out, had taken his beliefs very seriously.

And was this not still a free country; legally part of the United Kingdom, regardless of where your political beliefs lay? Didn't the law state all citizens were entitled to freedom of religious practice? Yes, the jury had silently agreed, this was a free country, though it sometimes didn't feel much like one. They weren't idiots. They could see from the start of his argument where this sharp-suited man was heading. They knew he had them in a corner. They'd all be voting Davison innocent. The law was the law, though it went against everything they knew to be true. Most of the twelve, excepting the Born-again contingent, would've liked to see Davison do serious time. There was something unsettling about the way he sat through the court case, smiling over at Mrs Mc-Fetridge like they were old friends, all the time knowing he'd killed her son.

Then, the details, which were difficult for those of an unbelieving background to comprehend. Somebody in the congregation had had a prophetic word for Stephen. The Lord was going to heal him and make his poorly brain whole. Two other believers had confirmed the word. Davison himself went round to the Mc-Fetridges' to share the good news. He'd quoted that verse from the Book of Matthew: have faith, and even if it's as small as a mustard seed, you'll be able to move mountains. Mrs McFetridge had been very specific about this in court. She'd quoted the whole passage, chapter and verse. Davison had explained that healing could only happen if Stephen and his mother believed enough. This would require total reliance on the Lord, which, in human terms, meant coming off all his medication, straight away.

Mrs McFetridge had been hesitant at first. It didn't sound safe. *It wasn't safe. Anybody with an ounce of sense could've told her that.* She'd been worn down, talked round, reassured, when Pastor Davison said, 'Listen, Deirdre, the Lord wants to give your boy his health back. You wouldn't stand in his way, would you?' She didn't have anybody to consult with, what with the husband gone and her only sister living in Canada and hard to get on the telephone. Stephen had had no such hesitations. He'd said anything would be better than lying in bed all day, with hammers thumping in his head. He had faith enough for both of them. This was all it had taken to convince his mother.

Half an hour later there were five of them gathered round Stephen's bed: praying, laying on hands, speaking in tongues and casting out demons. Calling these demons by their specific names: *anger, lust, self-pity, depression.* They'd bound him to the bed with belts to stop him thrashing about when the demons left. 'And could these so-called demonic episodes have been mistaken for seizures?' the prosecution asked. Pastor Davison replied, 'I've been in this business long enough to know the difference between a seizure and a demon.' They'd persevered for three whole days, starving the boy so his body would be keener for the Spirit until, on the evening of the third day, a massive seizure shook Stephen so hard he tipped the bed over and fell face first on to the floor. He was dead before the paramedics could even get to him.

He'd weighed less than six stone at the time of his death. The prosecution made much of this. The cruelty of subjecting such a desperately ill boy to a barbaric ritual. The defence made a point of calling Stephen a man. The defence said the practice was Biblical and common in many developing countries. The defence reminded the jury that Stephen McFetridge was a consenting adult. And he was. There were six separate individuals willing to testify that he'd asked for this; that he'd never once resisted or implored the healers to stop. There'd been no way for the jury to vote Davison anything but innocent.

Hannah's mum is remembering the whole thing now. Deirdre McFetridge, sniffling outside the court, bowed down beneath a guilt she shouldn't have been carrying. Clifford Davison, striding across the forecourt, raising a hand to the press, smiling, calling out, 'The Lord's will has been done today. Take note, folks. He will not be mocked.'

Mum lets her mind settle on that face. She pins all her anger, all her fear and pent-up fury, to Pastor Davison, until he isn't human in her head. His is a devil's face, louche and leering, and he's in the next room with her wee girl. She picks herself up off the carpet. She steps round the feet of the three elders perched on her radiator, squeezes round her in-laws and skirts the abandoned tea tray until she's standing at the living-room door. There is nothing but two plywood panels and a husband keeping Mum from Hannah now. She knows herself capable of kicking the door in should such a show of strength be required. Her husband will be harder to navigate.

'Where do you think you're going?' he asks.

'I need to be with Hannah,' she says.

'We're letting Pastor Davison pray with her.'

'No,' says Mum, '*we* are not.' She reaches under his arm for the door handle.

'Yes, we are.' He elbows her hand away.

'Let me past, John.'

'No, Sandra. Trust me. It's for the best.'

He's blocking the door with his whole body now. All the believers are staring. Dad can feel the heat creeping up his neck. He gets a terrible rash on his neck and face when he knows people are looking at him.

'Do you need a hand, John?' calls one of the elders from the top of the stairs.

'No, I do not need a hand. I can control my own wife. Go back into the kitchen, Sandra, and make yourself a cup of tea. You're causing a scene.'

'No,' says Mum.

She places both hands on her husband's chest and pushes him hard. She has not intended to do this. Her hands only understand what they're doing when she makes contact with his shirt. Dad isn't expecting it either. He isn't quick enough to control his response. He lifts a hand and slaps his wife across the face. It isn't a hard slap, but the noise of flesh meeting flesh is thunderous in this quiet space. Every single person in the hall draws breath at the same time, creating a soft, gushing sound like water drawn across a pebbly beach. Just as the room falls still with the shock, Hannah screams. The noise of her is hardly human. It's like an animal, frantic with the pain. It is, as one of the believers later explains, *the kind of sound that would lift paint.*

Everyone turns to look at the door. Everyone also looks at Mum. Her hair is coming down in strips. Her face is pink as sausagemeat. Both of her hands are clawing at the door, trying to get a grip on the handle. When Dad goes to stop her, Granda's there, pulling him back. Even Granny is saying, 'Let her be, John.' And Mum is yelling at him, her voice louder than it's ever been, 'Get the Hell out of my way!' Dad can actually feel her spit flecking against his cheek. In this moment he doesn't know her. She could be any woman railing against the natural order of things. Any brazen, unhinged bitch. It'd take a bulldozer to stop her. Or the hand of God Himself. He steps aside. He lets her past. He wonders how they'll ever recover from this.

Hannah's stretched out on the living-room rug. She's wearing her good pyjamas, the button-up ones with the matching dressing gown. Her hair is plastered across her face. One of her slippers has come off in the struggle. Her little white foot flares against the dark carpet. She's so pale. So pale and still. Mum can't tell if she's alive or not. She strides across the room, shoving Pastor Bill and the lady healer out of the way. She actually, physically, shoves them, so they topple over like shocked skittles and come to rest at comic angles. She hunkers down at Hannah's side and lifts her daughter. Hannah's head lies heavily in Mum's lap.

'What have they done to you, Han?' she whispers. 'I'm so, so sorry.'

Hannah isn't clear on what they've done to her.

She's been slipping in and out of herself with increasing speed. At first, she was present. She could see the dark suits hovering. She was very afraid. They were holding her down, screaming at her. Their voices went *click, click*, quick, like knitting needles. They were spitting out normal words and also tongues. *Yes, yes, yes, Spirit come.* The *s* of their yessing like snake tongues slithering into her ears.

Then she was gone.

The blackness was no longer still. It was hectic down there. Full of hands that hauled her in every direction at once. Lief shouting out, *Get a shift on, Hannah. We're all waiting for you.* Ugly pink nails scrabbling at her throat. Somebody humming the *No, no, no* song. Somebody else laughing cruelly. While a kinder voice whispered, *Hold on, Hannah. Just a wee bit longer.*

And repeated this sentiment over and over. In other voices. In other ways. There was such a choir inside her head. Caroline urging her to *just hold on*. And William. And Lizzy. And also Mim. And Ross. Poor Ross. Who'd found his lost voice just to say, *Hold on, Hannah, you're almost there.*

Then she was back in the living room. Possibly screaming. She could hear someone screaming. *Was this scream coming out of her?* The various parts of her body were beginning to separate. And the black suits were calling out demons which didn't exist – *stubbornness, pride, disobedience* – and spitting their names into her face. Shaking her roughly to prove these demons were actually real. *Keep praying, brothers, this one's not going without a fight.* Someone in the corner was reading the Scriptures at speed with a megaphone voice. She did not recognize the speaker. She did not recognize anyone. She only wanted her mum and dad.

Then she was under the black again, and the hands were dragging, and she thought, for sure, they'd rip her in two. They pushed. They pulled. They pushed some more. She was too far gone to say which side she was leaning towards. *Life or death. Here or there.* She couldn't tell. They all felt the same in the hungry dark.

Then she was back in the living room. And they were leaning heavily on her arms and legs. Pressing on the top of her head, where the pain was worst. The one with the thin face, who was clearly in charge, had his hand on her belly. She could feel the swish of something happening inside, parts of her knotting and rumbling like a washing machine. She felt like her body was not her own, and this scared her more than the idea of death. Every part of her wanted – no, needed – the healing to stop, but her mouth could not word this and her beat-up body wouldn't move at all.

All Hannah could do was place a wall between herself and

their words. She pitched her last ounce of self against the healing. It would not take if she did not allow it in.

She closed her eyes and left them to it, knowing this would be the end of it all.

When she opens her eyes, Mum is there. She's shouting at all the dark-suited men. 'Get out of my house. All of you. Now.' And they are doing as they're told. They're muttering angrily as they go. *Crazy woman. Out of control.* Now, Mum is cradling Hannah in her arms. She's telling the others, 'Gather around. She hasn't long left.' Granda Pete's holding one of her hands. Dad's holding the other. Hannah's drawn the pair of them together again. Granny's knelt down on the floor. Her skirt's caught up in a most undignified manner. She hasn't even noticed it. Every one of them's crying, snuffling into sleeves and balled-up hankies. Someone else is also there. Hannah can't see him, but she feels him standing over her. Smiling, just a little bit. Possibly glowing. Like in pictures she's seen of him. She wonders how long he's been with her. *Just now? Always?* She can't be sure. She lets herself picture all the kind faces. One by one. One after the other. She names them silently. She calls them her friends. She knows they're here. She knows they're gone. So many people have gathered round her. It doesn't matter that she's too tired to lift her head and look at them. Hannah's spent enough time on the edge of things to understand this is how belonging feels.

Now the black suits have left the room is quiet as water in a glass. Time is running extremely slow. Mum bends her head down over Hannah's head. She presses her lips against Hannah's cheek. She whispers, 'Oh, Hannah, we love you so much. We only want what's best for you.' Granny says, 'Amen.' And Granda says, 'Don't be scared.' Dad can't manage words, so he squeezes her hand to show he's still there. Somewhere up above her head, somebody with a thick Ballylack accent says, 'Well done, Hannah. That's you now.'

And this is when the healing happens.

In the silence.

When no one's actually asking for it.

Hannah feels it instantly. Wave upon wave of warm water comes coursing through her body, head to toe and all down her arms. Every bit of her is light and floating. She knows straight away what this means. She's heard enough brothers and sisters testify. And yes, it is the most glorious feeling. It's like swimming in pure white sunlight. She can feel the pain just washing away.

Hannah closes her eyes.

She allows it in.

She chooses living.

She is not afraid.

The Remnant

THERE IS SOME confusion over the timings.

Hannah is healed. Then, Matty dies.

There is a matter of hours between the two incidents. One hour and thirty-two minutes, to be exact. It would be wrong to give credence to those individuals – meddlesome gossips and conspiracy freaks – who try to claim concurrence.

First, Hannah is healed.

Then, Matty dies.

By the time the paramedics are dashing up Gloria McKnight's stairs to place their paddles on Matty's pigeon chest, cranking up the defibrillator and shocking him once, twice, three times in a row, each shock more vicious than the previous blast; by the time the female paramedic is laying her hand – gently but firmly – on her colleague's shoulder, whispering, 'Leave it, Gary, the wee lad's gone,' Hannah Adger's already healed. She's sitting up on the living-room sofa, bold as brass and starving hungry. She's ordering fish fingers and chips for dinner, with a fried egg on the side. Oh, she's all lip this evening: demanding an extra pillow, wanting the telly on, asking to stay up late. She thinks she's got something to celebrate.

Dr Simpson's been and gone. It's four hours since he last saw

Hannah. She was at death's door then, the rattle already rising in her chest. There's not one thing wrong with her now. Her temperature's down. The colour's back in her cheeks. She's a wee stroke skinnier, but that's no bad thing. The sickness has taken the hefty look off her. Dr Simpson's never seen the like of it. 'Make her rest,' he says, 'and get some flat Coke in her to settle her tummy before she eats anything. As far as I can see, that wee lassie's fighting fit.' He consults with Seán Donnelly before he leaves. Neither says the word *miracle* out loud. They circle around it but can't bring themselves to say it straight.

'Jesus,' says Seán as the doctor's leaving, 'what on Earth will I say to the press? They'll think I'm mental if I tell them what's happened. Especially the ones from across the water. The English don't go in for this kind of palaver.'

'Just say she got better,' says Dr Simpson. 'Since when were that lot concerned with the truth?'

Forty-five minutes later the doctor's standing over Matty's bed. The mother's going ballistic in the living room. He might have to give her something for her nerves. It's hard to be sympathetic. The child's been deathly ill for the last few days. Gloria hadn't even realized. She's been in her pit, watching telly and eating chocolate digestives, feeling sorry for herself. The thing with the weans upset her, but not enough to look out for her son. Not so much as a sideways glance or a dose of Calpol has she given him. She hadn't heard a peep out of Matty, so she'd just assumed he was grand. It was not uncommon for Gloria to go for days without clapping eyes on any of her weans.

It's too late for Matty now. Dr Simpson's only there to sign the death certificate. He places his hand on the boy's eyes and draws his eyelids gently closed. He's already started to lose his heat.

Hannah is healed. Then, Matty dies. The doctor's very clear on this.

The papers have it the other way round. The journalists know exactly what they're doing. A story's nothing without some spin. *Here*, says one hack to another, *would it not sound better if it ended with the girl?* The other one's sharp enough to see the potential. *You're dead right. Readers like a bit of closure.* Round here most stories don't end well. The disappeared stay disappeared. Talks continue in endless rounds. Everybody dies and the Conflict drags on.

Wouldn't it be something if the last child survived? Who cares if it's not strictly true? Nobody used the word *healed*. *Cured* is a much less contentious term. The journalists stress the influence of science. It's semantics really, but the implication's clear. It is human effort, not divine intervention, which has ended the outbreak in Ballylack. In the old days, people – especially the Catholic contingent – were powerful keen on miracles. They were forever seeing Herself in trees and walls. They took tremendous comfort from such things. Since the Troubles, there's less interest in apparitions and the like. God's all very well for Sundays and Christmas. People want something you can actually hold on to when there's bombs going off all over the place.

The papers print Hannah's story on every front page. They are keen to point out that *she's a fighter*, as if the other children weren't. *Last Child Lives*, runs the *Tele*'s headline. While the *Mirror* tugs at the nation's heartstrings: *Loneliest Girl in Ballylack*. They've found an old picture from Kathleen's funeral: Hannah wearing her school uniform. She's captured alone with her back to the camera, walking towards the cemetery gates. There are other photos they could have used. The editor takes one look at the cemetery picture and cries, 'Bingo, lads! That's the money shot.'

Poor Matty slips to the fifth page back. He becomes a footnote in a story that's already over. Nobody's interested in the last-but-one victim. In a way, it's fitting. Matty's well used to being ignored. He doesn't have parents raising Hell. Gloria's useless. She hasn't left the house since the day he died. She's permanently tanked on Bacardi Breezers. She would've missed the funeral if it weren't for Seán Donnelly dragging her out, forcing her to act like a mother should. Matty gets a two-line obituary and a cut-price funeral, a headstone purchased by the benevolent fund. The inscription reads *Matthew McKnight. 1983–93.* Funds won't stretch to anything more.

Elsewhere, Meta Nugent's at it again. Some halfwit's interviewed her in the street. Most of the villagers have the sense to ignore him. It's not their place to speak of other people's children. They're polite, of course, but also firm. Not Meta Nugent. She has no sense. She'll give her ten cents to anyone.

'I know Hannah well,' she says. 'She's a nice wee girl. Not what you'd call a looker. You often find the chubby ones have great personalities. Compensating, if you know what I mean.'

Mrs Nugent has the two events occurring simultaneously. In her version Hannah is healed just as the McKnight boy slips away. The reporter doesn't ask how she knows this. He's already regretting approaching this one. On Meta goes, with her wild conjecture. She's quick to point the parallel out. 'Just like that, in the blink of an eye: one child taken, the other one healed.'

'Healed?'

'Oh yes,' she says, and looks straight down the camera. 'God healed that wee lassie, but not the others. Makes you wonder what the Adgers did to deserve His favour? It might not seem fair to the likes of us. I suppose His ways are higher than ours.'

The reporter turns to face the camera. He raises an eyebrow questioningly. 'There you have it,' he says. 'This local woman says a miracle's happened here in Ballylack.' The camera slides away from Mrs Nugent. It cuts to a shot of the C of I graveyard and the new headstones lining either side of the children's plot. It swoops low enough to read the names. Kathleen. Ross. William. Elizabeth and Miriam engraved in long form. The reporter reads from his scribbled notes. 'I'm not sure the families would call it a miracle. One child has survived, ten are dead, and a young teacher too. The Ballylack Outbreak may be over, but this small community will be feeling the repercussions for many years to come.'

Hannah's mum and dad watch the report when it airs at lunchtime and, once again, mid-afternoon. Mum is sure Mrs Nugent's talking directly to them.

'Do you think people hate us?' she asks. The last few days have made Mum bolder. She's started talking differently to Dad. Directly. Honestly. With some gumption.

Dad chews on the question for a second or two. He's never been anything but painfully honest with Mum. But he can't be cruel at a time like this.

'Well, they might, a bit, at the minute. It's understandable. They're bound to be raw. They'll come round eventually. I don't think they'd begrudge us Hannah.'

'Are you sure?'

Mum's thinking about the writing on the side of Alan Gardiner's barn. She's recalling Tommy Fletcher's face, the morning he showed up at their door. It doesn't take much to turn folks against you in Ballylack.

'I'm sure they'll be grand,' says Dad.

Really, he's not sure at all.

He's never been in a situation like this before. He's been praying about it continuously, asking for patience, wisdom and strength. Normally, he'd consult Pastor Bill. But that friendship's cooled since his wife threw Davison's lot out of their house. Dad's hardly heard anything from his fellow elders. You'd think Bill would be pleased about Hannah's healing, yet on the phone he's been noticeably curt.

The Adgers have barely left the house since the healing. Eventually they'll have to venture out. They can sidestep the journalists. Most of them have already gone. It won't be as easy to avoid their neighbours. God bless them; they will try to be kind. They'll stop the Adgers to say, *We're so glad to see wee Hannah up and about.* The men will shake hands. The women, hug. They're nice enough people. They'll say the things you're meant to say. Still, Dad knows there'll be distance between them now. They probably wish the Adgers would move away and make it easier on everyone. He'll accept their hugs and their firm handshakes. Hannah's dad's a nice man too. He knows what is expected of him. He'll say, *We're very thankful. Hannah's doing really well.* He'll do his best to make this sound like an apology. *What on Earth is he meant to say?*

By the third or fourth of these encounters the edge will wear off Dad's meek and mild. He'll want to push their hands away, to cross the street and hide from his neighbours, or roll his window down and yell, *It's not our fault. I won't apologize for my daughter.* He'll take to shopping in the next village over, just to avoid encountering them in Thompson's. He will start to hate them – actually hate them – for making his joy a guilty thing.

The final press conference hasn't helped matters. Seán Donnelly's fallen into the same trap as the journalists. People need to know the outbreak's definitely over and, though an antidote is yet to be found, Seán's encouraged to skirt round the topic. *Tell them the last wee girl's been cured. Make it sound like the scientists have come up with something. It'll reassure the parents. Even if it isn't strictly true.* Seán does what he's told. Twenty-four hours after the final death, he makes his last statement in the C of I Hall. The set-up's familiar. It's his seventh press conference of the month. Tonight, there's a sense of finality to the procedure. He puts more thought than usual into his words. He feels like Poirot addressing the suspects in the billiards room.

He starts strong, reading from his notes. 'Friends, I'm so glad to tell you the outbreak's over.' This is all that most of them hear. Most are parents of younger or older children. They've not lost anyone specific this summer. They couldn't care less how the end has come. They're just relieved to hear their own kids are safe. Seán stands behind the makeshift lectern, watching couples reach for each other's hands. He listens to the soft ripple of relief run around the room. It shuffles and sighs like central heating. People smile and try not to smile. They can't rein their own daft faces in. Seán is struck by how selfish human beings are. They can't see beyond their own front doors.

He tells them the sad news: Matty is dead. Most of them have already heard but he feels the need to make it official. They drop their heads and make soft clucking sounds. There's no weight to their grief today. They're far too high on their own relief. Seán feels bad about this. He should've started with Matty, given him his moment to be sorely missed. *These people are heartless*, he thinks, though he knows he'd be exactly the same if the situation involved his kids.

He tells them, then, that Hannah's recovered. He keeps the details loose and thin. He's been told to stick to medical terms – *full recovery, cured, prognosis* – and avoid all mention of holy shenanigans. He tells them Alan Gardiner's likely to go down for manslaughter. The sentence for this will be at least twenty years. Millar's Gap is being treated by a specialist decontamination team. There'll be counselling provided for anyone who wants to avail of the service. An information evening will take place next week. A benevolent fund has been set up to support the families and there's talk of erecting a memorial of some kind. Each point is met with a murmur of acceptance. Heads nod. Feet shuffle. Everyone's keen to see the matter closed.

Seán glances down at his notes. He's ticked almost every item off his list. All that's left is thanks and goodbye. He doesn't feel like he's ready for this. Three hours from now, he'll be home with his wife, his wee ones asleep upstairs in bed. It's hard to believe they still exist. They're no longer real to him as the people of Bally-lack are present and real. It will be a wrench to leave this place; a shock to the system to be, suddenly, home. He wonders if he shouldn't book himself into a hotel in Newry or Drogheda and take a wee day to readjust.

He asks for questions. All the questions are variations on a theme. *Are you sure the outbreak's really over?* Seán reassures them over and over and, when it gets to seven, says, 'If there are no other questions, I'll call it a night. It has been an honour to be with you this summer. I can't begin to imagine how you'll go on, but I know you will. This is a strong community. Look after each other in the days ahead.' For this section Seán consults no notes. He speaks slowly. He thinks his way around each word before it leaves his mouth. The people can see he's earnest. They rise from their chairs to clap him out. They throw their arms around him and say, *Thank you so much, son. Thank you for everything.*

Seán Donnelly feels like he's let them all down. There's so much more he could have done.

After the Rapture

HANNAH'S DAD ISN'T happy about the press conference. He can see how Seán's spun the story to his own advantage. This is lying, in Dad's book. He's quick to call it a form of sin. Pastor Bill is on the phone as soon as the statement airs. 'You've missed an opportunity there, brother,' he says. 'The Lord healed your wee girl, yet His name wasn't mentioned once tonight.' Dad's too raw to ask where the pastor's been these last few days. He's just glad to have somebody confirm his suspicions. Things haven't been handled correctly.

'You need to share your version of what happened.'

'You're right,' says Dad. 'I'm worried about how people will react to Hannah. I don't want them resenting her.'

'Exactly. If you had an opportunity to tell your story, people would be more sympathetic.'

'Do you think so?'

'Absolutely, John. And you could talk about what the Lord's done here. It's such a great opportunity to share the Kingdom with so many people.'

'I suppose it is, Bill. I don't like the way the press have removed all mention of God. I mean, I'm not surprised. But it's still a shame.'

'Leave it with me. I'll have a few words with some people I know, see if we can't get something set up.'

Dad never finds out who Pastor Bill's talked to. It's probably best he doesn't know. Twenty-four hours later, everything's arranged. A small TV crew will come to the Adgers'. They'll keep it relaxed, more like a conversation than an interview. The family will have a chance to tell the story in their own words. Mum's reluctant. She resents the intrusion. She doesn't want Hannah getting upset. Dad says they have to. It's a chance to bear witness. It'd be remiss to let the opportunity pass.

'Not everyone's going to find it easy, seeing Hannah about the village. This is our chance to tell them what it's been like for us. You want them to be sympathetic, don't you?'

'Yes,' says Mum. She doesn't sound sure.

Neither is Granda Pete. He wants nothing to do with the interview; more so when Pastor Bill shows up in his black Sunday suit.

'What's that chancer doing here?'

'He's offered to be on hand if they want to talk to someone from the church about the healing or anything.'

'He wasn't here for the healing.'

'Yes, well, maybe he wasn't present the moment it occurred, but he's been very faithful these last weeks, praying and visiting.'

'He's a leech, John. He's only appeared because he likes the idea of getting on TV.'

'If you don't like it, you can leave,' says Dad.

A voice in his head is telling him to listen to his father. The same voice is saying he should throw Bill out. Dad's reasonably sure it's his own fear talking. It can't be the Lord, for the last few weeks have proved his father has no interest in the things of God. He peeks into the living room. Pastor Bill's sat on the sofa making small talk with the crew. He smiles and says, 'Is there anything I can do to help, John?' Dad's reassured. There's no harm in Bill. He steps back into the hall, pulling the door closed.

'I think it might be best if you leave, Dad,' he says.

The words hang heavily in the air.

'I'm sorry you feel that way, son,' says Granda Pete. 'I'll not make a fuss. You know where I am if you want me.' Hannah's granda lets himself out. He makes it no further than the front wall. He sits there for the duration. Smoking. Praying, though he wouldn't call it praying. He's just waiting for his family to need him again.

Hannah's in the bath when Matty appears. She's getting cleaned up for her interview. There's a symmetry to this. It's about a month since Ross showed up in the very same room. She's had eight visitors since. She's still not sure why they chose her. *Did they know, all along, she'd be left behind?* Maybe they only wanted to rub it in. She's thinking about this as she lathers her hair. *Why her? Why not somebody who could actually help?* She pinches her nose, ducks her head back beneath the water and rumbles her hair around till the shampoo slides off. Then she tips forward suddenly, soap and water streaming over her forehead, nose and chin. Matty is sitting on the bathmat, staring at her. His eyes are on a level with the side of the bath so he's looking straight at her barely-there boobs. He has a towel in his hand. He passes it to her.

'For your eyes,' he says. 'The shampoo always gets in them.'

Hannah scrambles madly at the shower curtain. She tries to close it one-handed and, with the other hand, cover all her private parts.

'It's OK. I have wee sisters. I've seen it all before.'

'You've not seen me before. Turn around!'

Matty sighs dramatically. He throws his arms up in a wide arch as if to say, *Women! What are youse not like?* He still swivels around so he's facing the sink. Hannah stands up in the milky bathwater. She wraps the towel round her like a bandage, toes the plug out of the plughole and steps out of the bath. She sits on the edge, careful to arrange her legs so nothing's showing which shouldn't be.

She tells Matty he can turn around.

'Sorry I'm only getting to you now,' he says. 'I heard you were run off your feet. You're Ballylack's big celebrity these days.'

Hannah shrugs. She's not sure whether Matty's making fun of her.

'So,' he says, sucking on the word till it's several syllables longer than it should be.

'So,' repeats Hannah. Holding his eye.

'You made it. I didn't.'

'Sorry.'

'Nothing to be sorry about.'

'I know. But I feel bad, being the only one. I'm sure you're all raging with me.'

'Well, Kathleen is. It doesn't take much to get on her bad side.'

Hannah smiles sheepishly. 'Forget about Kathleen. I'm talking about the rest of you. I'd understand if youse hated me.'

'They're too busy raging at Ben. The eejit went and told them it was his dad that killed us. I swear, I thought Lief was going to kill him all over again. Even the nice kids were really pissed off. You'll hardly believe this, Hannah, but Caroline actually decked him one. I didn't think she had it in her. Turns out she was really missing home.'

'Poor Ben.'

'Actually, sorry, I forgot, he's going by Bayani now. That's his real name. He told me once, years ago. I just forgot. I should have remembered. It's wee things like people not remembering your name that make you feel really shit.'

'Bayani,' repeats Hannah, 'I'd forgotten too. And is he all

right down there? Did the DK kill him? It's not his fault. None of this is.'

'Exactly. That's what I tried to tell them. There's none of us responsible for the shit our parents do. Or, in my case, don't bother doing. Auld Gloria's useless, so she is. It was me that cooked all the dinners in our house. Me that made sure my sisters brushed their teeth and had clean socks and stuff to put on. I mean, most kids are terrified of the Social, but we were always hoping they'd rock up and take us away. It's not my fault my ma's rubbish and it's not Bayani's fault his da poisoned us all.'

Hannah nods in agreement. 'Did they listen to you?'

'Who?'

'The ones that wanted to beat up Ben . . . I mean Bayani.'

'Aye,' Matty smiles. 'It took a wee while to talk them round but I think I got them to see that we're all in the same boat. Sure, none of us would've chosen this. We're all here because somebody else ruined things. It's not ideal. It's not the worst set-up either. I'll tell you what, Hannah – and don't be spreading this around – I don't really mind being dead. It's a lot less hassle than being alive.'

Hannah gives Matty a good long look. He's filled out a bit. He must be eating better in the other place. He used to wolf his school dinners down like he hadn't seen food in weeks. Now, the beginnings of a belly is pouching beneath his T-shirt, his eyes are clear and his skin looks clean. Death suits him. He seems so much healthier than before.

'Here now,' he says. 'A wee bird told me that somebody done a miracle on you.'

'Yes, I think so. I still don't know exactly what happened. Some people prayed. And I made a wish at the Raggedy Tree. And this man cast the demons out of me. And, well, something in there must've worked. I'm not sure which part, but Dr Simpson says I'm fine now.'

311

'Flip sake, Hannah. Why do you not look happier about it? You got a miracle done on you. You should be bouncing off the walls.'

'It doesn't feel right celebrating when you're all dead. I keep thinking about your mums and dads, how much they're missing you. It isn't fair.'

'Do you honestly think my ma's missing me? Gloria'll only notice I'm gone when nobody's there to make her tea.'

'What about your wee sisters?'

Matty goes quiet. He lets his head drop. He starts picking bits of fluff out of the bathmat, rolling the lint between his finger and thumb.

'Matty?'

'Aye, Hannah, I'm going up the walls about my sisters. They'll not be able to manage without me. Like I said, I done everything for them.'

'Sorry, I didn't know. I knew things weren't great at home. I didn't realize it was that bad.'

'It was about as rough as it could get. And Gloria'll be worse after this. She always spirals when bad things happen. She always makes it about herself.'

They fall into silence. Matty continues to pick at the bathmat. Hannah runs her fingers through her damp hair, combing out the worst of the tangles. She doesn't have anything to say. She's well used to this feeling now.

'Look, I know it's a big ask, but I'd like to get back to my wee sisters. It's nice enough down here. It's not all that different from the old Ballylack. It's just, I'm going spare worrying about them. They'll be terrified with me not there. I was wondering, could you maybe pray for me?'

Hannah's horrified. She can't think of anything more awkward. Maybe kissing. Even kissing Matty has more appeal than praying for him. Still, a genuine prayer request, from an unbeliever, isn't something she can refuse. This is the kind of opportunity Mum and Dad are always asking the Lord to give them. Maybe Matty wants someone to lead him to the Lord.

'I suppose so,' she says. 'We prayed for all of you while you were sick; me and Mum and Dad and the ones from church.'

'No. I don't mean that sort of praying, Hannah. I mean, the special praying you do when you make a miracle happen. You know, where you talk funny and put your hands on me and then I get healed. William says they do it all the time in your church. Is that not what they did on you?'

'Yes, sort of. Look, I don't know how to do that kind of praying. You have to have a gift for it.'

'Just try, Hannah. Go on. Maybe there's a wee bit of the miracle still left in you.'

'I don't know how to say this in a nice way. You're dead, Matty. Nobody – not even the elders – can heal people after they've died.'

'What about Jesus and that other lad we done in RE? The pair of them came back, didn't they?'

'I can't raise the dead. Only God can do those kinds of big miracles.'

'Well, ask Him to do it, then? Ask Him to bring me back for my sisters. Do you not believe He can?'

'God can do anything He wants,' snaps Hannah.

Even as she's saying this, she wonders if it's actually true. Her heart is pure thumping. She shivers as the cold water drips off her hair. She shouldn't be here, alive in her own skin. Yet she is. She's proof that God can do whatever He fancies. It should be easy for her to believe. But when she places her hand on Matty's cold forehead, all she feels, humming beneath her fingertips, is doubt. God isn't going to bring Matty back from the dead. It's not that He can't. She just knows He won't.

The problem isn't Matty. She glances down at his old, young

face. His pale eyelids drawn shut. His lips sealed tightly. His palms turned upwards in the posture of prayer. He's mimicking some holy thing he's seen on TV. Hannah feels jealous, watching him. His faith is pure. Hers is muddy. It's a barely-there pulse. All talk, no conviction. *What's wrong with her?* She has been given so much proof.

She mumbles a few words about healing, parroting what she's heard the elders say. *Yes, Lord Jesus. Spirit, come.* She lets her hand flutter in front of Matty's face. She's seen Pastor Bill do this before, in church. She keeps it up for five minutes, repeating herself when the words run out. Nothing happens. Of course nothing happens. The problem's with Hannah. Her faith is too weak.

'I'm sorry,' she says, when it's finally over.

She wraps her damp arms round Matty and hugs him while he cries.

He thanks her for trying. She can tell he's not angry. He asks her to keep an eye on his sisters. He'd appreciate it if she could get a message to them. Just so they know he's OK.

He says, 'Nobody blames you. We know it's not your fault.'

'Even Kathleen?' Hannah asks.

Matty grins. 'Kathleen's a headcase. She blames everybody but herself.'

Hannah thanks him for coming. She asks him to stay. She cries a little. She can't help herself. There won't be anyone coming after. It's only her now. For the duration. The loneliest girl in Ballylack. She mops up her tears with a wad of toilet roll.

'Don't be scared, Hannah,' he says as he rises to leave. 'You've your whole life ahead of you. Make sure you enjoy it. And don't be worrying about us lot. We're figuring out how to get along with each other. Once we do, we'll be grand.' Saying this, he doesn't sound like a child, or even a lad on the cusp of sixteen. Hannah can see in this second the man Matty will never get to be. He doesn't say goodbye. He smiles instead and opens the bathroom door gently. He has one foot out the door when she remembers what she's wanted to ask.

'Why me?'

'Why not?' he says, and that's all the answer she's going to get.

Dad says she's been blessed. He thinks she's been chosen for something special. He only says this when Mum's not around. 'There must be a reason why the others were taken. God's chosen you, Hannah. There's a plan and purpose for your life. There's lots of stories like yours in the Bible. Remember, Baby Moses in the Bullrushes and Daniel in the Lion's Den, Joseph getting rescued from Egypt.'

'And Jesus,' adds Hannah. 'Sure, they tried to kill him when he was wee.'

Dad says it's a bit prideful, comparing herself to Jesus, though she's certainly on the right track.

All this and Matty are fresh in her head as she brushes her hair and zips herself into her Sunday dress. She walks downstairs slowly, placing both feet on each individual step. She's hoping her mind will settle before the interview begins. It doesn't. Neither does it help to find Pastor Bill back and stationed on the corner sofa. She sits down between Mum and Dad. She listens to them answer the questions. It's mostly Dad speaking. Mum just nods and sort of smiles and shreds the tissue in her hands.

After a few minutes the journalist lady with the very white teeth turns the microphone towards Hannah. She asks, 'Well, young lady, how does it feel to have survived the outbreak?' She hangs there, arm outstretched across the coffee table, waiting for Hannah to speak. Hannah's mouth refuses to work. Her brain starts picking the question apart, until she's not sure how she feels or if she's feeling anything at all. She looks at the lady journalist's tight, smiling face. She's nodding at Hannah with her head and her arm. 'How are you feeling?' she repeats.

The only word which comes to mind is *lonely*. Hannah parts her lips and lets it out. It isn't the scoop they've been angling for. It's not what the viewers want to hear. It's hardly the testimony Pastor Bill expects. It won't be mistaken for closure or anything like a hopeful new beginning. It will not sit easy with her dad. But it is honest. And the people of Ballylack deserve her honesty.

As the journalist begins to wrap up the segment, Hannah remembers Matty's sisters. 'Hold on,' she says, 'can I say one more thing?'

The journalist nods to the soundman. He passes a second mic to Hannah. Hannah takes a deep breath and looks straight down the camera. She pictures all the people watching at home. All the sisters and brothers and mummies and daddies and grannies and grandas like her own. They deserve to know the truth. Maybe this is why she's been left behind.

'I've been talking to the others,' she begins.

'The others?' asks the lady journalist.

'The other children. My friends from school. They're OK, so they are. They're in a good place. It's a lot like this. They're safe there and I think, soon, they'll start to be happy too. They have each other so they're not alone. And they want me to tell you that they really miss you. But they're grand. They honestly are. You're not to worry about them any more.'

'Right,' says the lady journalist, 'I was not expecting that.' She brings the segment to a brusque close. She clearly thinks Hannah's talking rubbish. Pastor Bill obviously thinks similarly. He's giving her daggers from the far side of the living room. Dad's hand on her shoulder is starting to pinch. His fingers are speaking up for him. Mum says nothing. She just takes Hannah's hand and gives it a reassuring squeeze. 'That was kind,' she whispers into her ear, so quietly only Hannah hears.

Tonight, when they're sat in front of their TVs, watching the Adgers say their piece, all the other mums and dads will see

Hannah's face crumple and all animosity will be set aside. They'll see how young and scared she is. This child could be any one of their children. *Dear love her*, they'll say, *it's not easy being the only one left*. When she speaks on behalf of the children they've lost, the fathers will roll their eyes, dismissing her mumblings as fanciful. Some mothers – most mothers – and grandmothers too, will listen and hear exactly what they need to hear. And they'll silently think her a brave little girl. *I hope she's all right*, they will say and let themselves cry. Though their grief isn't ready for anything showy, and healing is months and years away, these people already mean what they say. They don't blame Hannah. They wish only good things for her. Bearing in mind what they've been through this summer, such grace is a kind of miracle.

14 September – Hannah

IT'S A SIN to wish yourself dead.

I know this now. I won't be saying such a bold thing again.

So many people are depending on me.

I watch them watching me round the village. I'm still here. The others aren't. I know what they're thinking when they look at me. I see them pretending not to look. I'm not just Hannah to these people. I'm all their children and something more. I'm not allowed to let them down.

So many people are depending on me.

Mrs Nugent. Principal Taylor. All the old ones lined up and leaning against the front wall of Henderson's pub, sucking the smoke from their cigarettes. The Fletchers. The Fowlers. Lief's poor dad. Ross's brother. Matty's useless mum. She's back selling papers in Thompson's shop, necking drink from a Seven-Up bottle hidden beneath the sweetie counter. Social Services have taken his sisters. They're with a foster family in town. Ben's – I mean Bayani's – mum. She doesn't get her messages in Ballylack any more. I feel sorry for her. She knows what it's like to be stared at. I think it's probably worse for her. Sometimes I catch her looking at me through the mucky window of her Land Rover as she rattles down Main Street off to Crazy Prices in town. I want to lift my hand and wave. I never do. It might make her feel even worse.

It's Mr Leung who makes me the saddest. I try not to walk past the takeaway. These days he's always standing outside, scanning the road. It's like he expects to see Amy coming over the hill on her way back from school. Three times now he's taken me for her. He looks so disappointed when I get closer and he sees I'm not her. I'm still just me. I can't bear the way he tries to smile when he says, *Hannah, so nice to see you.* His voice sounds like it's beginning to peel.

So many people are depending on me.

What would they say if I told them the truth? If I didn't smile and nod like a puppet. If I looked them straight in the eye when they asked, *How's you, Hannah?* and said, *Most days, I manage. I'm always lonely. Every so often, I wish I was dead.*

It would not help. It's not what they need. I have to be happy. My happiness has cost them so much. I have to live enough life to make up for ten. I understand this. Though it's an awful heavy thing to be lugging around. There's only one of me. There's so many of them. All they want is for me to be happy. Which isn't all that much to ask. So, I do my best to be happy for them. I say I'm looking forward to my birthday, to big school and Christmas. I don't say it in actual words, but I'm careful to let them know I am looking forward to years and years of being alive. I have to be happy for all of us.

It's almost autumn now. The leaves are loosening on the trees. In October I'll start big school in town. Mum already has my uniform bought. It's green with a stripe; the colour of custard and Christmas trees. Everyone else has gone back to school. Dr Simpson's decided that I should wait. He says my body needs time to recover. 'Sure, you'll not miss much the first few weeks,' he says, and takes Dad out into the hall, to whisper about me, like I'm not there. It's not my body he's worried about. Bodies heal quickly. Minds take longer. He thinks I might have this condition called PTSD. That's when you've been through something so awful it's messed up your head. I learnt this from listening at the door.

Dad says, 'Seriously, Roy, PTSD? Is that not something soldiers get?'

Dr Simpson says, 'You don't have to go to war to develop PTSD. Jesus, John, half of Ulster's probably got it, just from living through this shit. Your wee girl's been through a lot this summer. She could do with talking to a professional.'

Dad wants to run the decision by Pastor Bill. Real Christians don't go in for therapy. You're meant to take your problems to Jesus instead. Granda Pete and him argue about it over Sunday dinner and Granda Pete swears and all. 'For God's sake, John, get the wee lassie a counsellor and, while you're there, get one for yourself.' Dad's about to shout back at him when Mum places her hand on his hand and says quite calmly in her new bold voice, 'There's no need to take the Lord's name in vain, Pete. I've already made the appointment. She has her first session on Wednesday.'

Dr Simpson found me a nice lady counsellor in town. Mum takes me on the bus three times a week. She waits in the reception area, flicking through ladies' magazines, while the woman asks how I'm feeling and if I'm finding it hard to sleep.

I don't enjoy these sessions. It makes me feel sadder to sit in that room. There's a bus stop right outside the building. Sometimes, in the afternoon, the sound of schoolchildren comes creeping through the open window and I wonder what I'm doing here, talking myself sadder and sadder when life is going on without me. It feels like a waste of being young. The whole world's out there, and it's already moving on without me. Things are changing here. There's talk of peace talks on the radio. Young ones, not much older than I am, are saying they want a better future. They're determined to be part of the change. I'm not part of anything right now. I'm stuck inside, crying to a stranger, wishing I could be somewhere else.

I tell the lady that I am sad. I tell her the same thing at every session. I feel guilty being the only one left. After two weeks, I admit that sometimes I wish I was dead. I cry a lot when I'm saying this. She doesn't snap or lose her temper. She doesn't say it's a sin to talk like this. She says, 'Oh, Hannah, that's perfectly natural,' and nudges a box of Kleenex across the table.

I say, 'So many people are depending on me.'

I say, 'They all look at me funny in the street.'

I say, 'I'm going to let them all down.'

I am really crying by this stage. It isn't pretty when I cry. Not like women crying on TV. A lot of snot comes out of my nose. My breath comes in gulps and gasps. I shake a bit. My whole face goes splotchy, like I have a rash. When I get to the end of myself and try to say, 'Why am I the only one left?', it comes choking out in fits and bursts.

The lady counsellor rises from her seat. She steps round the coffee table and sits next to me on the sofa. She asks if it's OK to give me a hug and I nod, *yes*, though normally I don't like to be hugged by anyone except Granda Pete and Mum and Dad. She holds me with one hand and with the other pats my shoulder until I stop sobbing.

'Hannah,' she says, 'I'm going to tell you something. I want you to listen. This is very important. You need to remember it, OK?'

I am listening. I am listening with my ears. I am listening inside my head. There's a stillness in there I've not had all summer. Every part of me is leaning in.

'I'm sorry this happened to you,' the lady says. 'But it isn't your fault. Do you hear me? It's not your fault. You're just a child. You don't have to carry any of these hard feelings by yourself. You don't have to make things OK for everyone else.'

I nod with my body. I nod with my head. I know this lady is talking sense. I will ruin myself if I don't let go. If I spend the rest of my life blaming myself.

It is one of those days when the window is open. The sounds from the bus stop are filling the room. A beam of sunlight slices through the gloom. I watch it dancing around on the coffee table and I do not want to be in this sad place, crying, any more. Later, when I am older, I will tell this moment to close friends and lovers. I will say, *Honestly, it was that quick. I could hear the world happening outside the window and I wanted to be part of it.*

I'm glad the counsellor's told me it isn't my fault. She is the first to lift the guilt off me. Lots of others will come after. They'll put me back together with their words and their gentleness. They will teach me what it means to move away from this lonely place. But I am the one who decides to get better. I do it myself. I make a split-second decision. This summer isn't going to be the end of me.

I thank the lady counsellor. I give her a final hug. I say, 'I think I'm going to be all right now,' and she says, 'I have every faith in you, Hannah. You're stronger than you think you are.'

Mum is waiting for me. She sets down her *Woman's Weekly* and we go to leave. When the receptionist tries to book my next appointment, I say, 'I don't want to come back.' The lady counsellor says, 'Well, I wouldn't advise it. I think we should keep meeting for another few months,' and I say, 'No,' and look at Mum with a look I've lately learnt from her, the same look she's started giving Dad when he suggests Bible study on a Saturday night, or tries to pray out loud when we're out for dinner in a restaurant. 'If Hannah says she's done, then she's done,' says Mum. 'She's more than capable of deciding for herself.' Even though this makes me feel like an adult, I still reach for her hand as we walk downstairs, out through the door and into the sun.

There's a group of children gathered on the other side of the road, waiting on the bus to Ballylack: ten or so, dressed in the various uniforms of local schools. Some are smoking. Some are leaning against the bus shelter, flirting awkwardly in pairs. Others are standing alone, hands shoved into blazer pockets. For a moment the sun falls on their heads, blurring their features, baptizing them in a halo of bright, white light. They could be my schoolmates, the Dead Kids resurrected and casually waiting on a bus. A pulse runs through my body. I feel myself being tugged towards them. I should be there, standing with them. We should be bumbling through the future together. Angsty teenagers. Students. Adults. Maybe someday, parents ourselves. It's a sore sort of feeling to know I'll never be with the others again. I'd like to think they're happy, wherever it is they've ended up. I hope they're learning how to muddle through. I hope they've finally worked out that they are not responsible.

I smile from the other side of the road. I hum the *No, no, no* song under my breath. I always do this when I think of them.

When the light shifts, I can see the faces belong to strangers. They're kids I've never met before. They aren't my people. I don't belong with them. Yet. Mum squeezes my hand and bends down to whisper, 'Some of those girls go to your new school. You're going to make so many friends, Han. I think you're going to love it there.' I test the idea of this in my belly. I think I could be OK with it. I am still fearful and a little angry. I'm sad and lonely. But, behind all the heavy feelings there's a flicker of something bright and strong. I'm going to believe that I will be grand. It doesn't just happen. It is a choice.

My name is Hannah Adger. I've just turned twelve.

Ten went before me. I'm the only one left.

Most days I'm glad I made it.

Sometimes I wish I wasn't here.

Eventually, things are going to get better. I have to believe it will not always be like this.

Acknowledgements

This novel begins with a promise borrowed from Lyra McKee, whose wisdom, generosity and vision left a shining trail for the rest of us to follow. Thank you to Sara Canning for graciously allowing me to echo Lyra's words.

Thanks also to the wonderful team at Doubleday, who've once again shepherded me along the path from mad idea to actual book with patience, humour and a great deal of sense. It is a very fortunate thing to have so many stellar women on your team. Thanks especially to Fiona Murphy, Alice Youell, Sophie Wilson, Sorcha Judge, Tabitha Pelly and Irene Martinez Costa. Endless gratitude to the world's best agent, Kate Johnson, whose enthusiasm and encouragement never falters, and also to the amazing Rach Crawford and the rest of the team at Wolf Lit.

Writing and publishing a book during a global pandemic was never going to be a walk in the park and I have been daft enough to publish three. I am grateful for amazing support from Damian Smyth and the good folks at Arts Council NI, Sinéad MacAodha and the Literature Ireland team, Jasmina Kanuric and all at EUPL, Rebecca DeWald at Cove Park, Marjorie Lotfi and Claire Urquhart from Open Book Scotland, and Valerie

Bistany and her team at the Irish Writers Centre. The friendship, financial support and opportunities offered by these organizations and others have kept me writing and hoping during this difficult period.

This novel was mostly written and edited on the second floor of Jack's coffee shop in East Belfast. Thank you to the incredibly patient staff who've let me linger for hours over their coffee (which is very good). Thanks also to David, Claudia and the folks at No Alibis Books, and Joan and her team at the QFT, who keep me constantly storied and inspired.

As the world's laziest researcher, it would be remiss of me not to thank the hundreds of Twitter friends who've provided me with endless answers to odd questions about the geography of Ulster, cutting turf and regional variations on the spelling of 'boke'. Special thanks go to Alan Meban, James Kerr and the Michael Hughes and Anton Thompson-McCormick family WhatsApp groups for services above and beyond the call of duty.

Most books begin with conversations and *The Raptures* sprang from hundreds of ongoing conversations over many years, many cups of coffee and even more glasses of wine. I'm especially grateful to Kristen Kernaghan, Andrew Cunning, Lucy Caldwell, Hannah McPhillimy, Mícheál McCann, Olwyn Dowling, Hilary Copeland, Peggy Hughes, Emma Must, Caoilinn Hughes, Emma Dai'an Wright, Sinéad Morrissey, John Bittles, Bernie McGill, Malachi O'Doherty, Odd Henning and Hild Reidunn Johannessen, Myra Zepf, Conor Garrett, Kelly McCaughrain, Caroline Magennis, Claire and Nate Grubbs, Nicky Bull, Paul and Jean Bleakney, Carl Henrik Frederiksson, Emily DeDakis, Paddy and Darlene Meskell, Moyra Donaldson, Philip Orr, Michael Shannon, Heather Dornan Wilson and Maggie Cronin. Time, friendship and conversations with you have helped me write the book I've been trying to write for twenty years.

Final and most heartfelt thanks go to the rest of the Carson clan. Mum, Alan, Laurie, Caleb and Izzy. Thanks for putting up with me. Dad, I'm so sorry, you'll never get to read this one, but I feel your blessing all the same.

JAN CARSON is a writer and community arts facilitator based in Belfast. Her first novel, *Malcolm Orange Disappears,* was published in 2014 to critical acclaim, followed by a short-story collection, *Children's Children* (2016), and two flash fiction anthologies, *Postcard Stories* (2017) and *Postcard Stories 2* (2020). Her second novel, *The Fire Starters* (2019), won the EU Prize for Literature and was shortlisted for the Dalkey Novel of the Year Award. Her second short-story collection, *The Last Resort*, was published in 2021 and read on BBC Radio 4. She specializes in running arts projects and events with older people, especially those living with dementia. *The Raptures* is her third novel.